I0688006

Charles A Phelps

Life and Public Services of General Ulysses S. Grant, From His Boyhood to the Present Time

And a biographical sketch of Hon. Schuyler Colfax

Charles A Phelps

Life and Public Services of General Ulysses S. Grant, From His Boyhood to the Present Time
And a biographical sketch of Hon. Schuyler Colfax

ISBN/EAN: 9783337011024

Printed in Europe, USA, Canada, Australia, Japan

Cover: Foto ©Raphael Reischuk / pixelio.de

More available books at **www.hansebooks.com**

PEOPLE'S EDITION.

LIFE AND PUBLIC SERVICES

OF

GENERAL ULYSSES S. GRANT,

FROM HIS BOYHOOD TO THE PRESENT TIME.

AND

A BIOGRAPHICAL SKETCH OF

HON. SCHUYLER COLFAX.

BY

CHARLES A. PHELPS,

Late Speaker of the Mass. House of Representatives, and President of the Mass. Senate.

Embellished with Two Steel Portraits, and Four Illustrations from Designs by Hammatt Billings.

BOSTON:

LEE AND SHEPARD.

1868.

Entered according to Act of Congress, in the year 1868, by

CHARLES A. PHELPS,

In the Clerk's Office of the District Court of the District of Massachusetts.

BOSTON:

Electrotyped and Printed by Geo. C. Rand & Avery.

PREFACE.

IN answer to the question which may be asked, " Why
write another Life of Grant?" the author would say, that
he has endeavored to prepare a biography of the MAN,
Ulysses S. Grant, from his boyhood to the present time,
differing in some respects from others which have fallen under his observation ; showing how, from a Western boy with
no special advantages, he has come to be the foremost man
of his time. He has not attempted to give a history of the
late civil war, nor a military criticism upon its campaigns,
nor a passive narration of battle-scenes, but to portray the
character of Gen. Grant as boy, cadet, lieutenant in the
army, business-man, general, secretary of war, and his
actions in each period of his career. While the author has
no desire to conceal his deep sympathy with the principles
of freedom which warred with the Rebellion, and whose
final triumph is involved in the approaching presidential
election, yet he has sought to avoid a partisan harangue.

He has availed himself of all reliable sources of information ; and special care has been taken to verify statements
of fact from official sources. He has consulted freely, and
acknowledges his indebtedness to, the elaborate and candid

work of Horace Greeley on "The American Conflict," and the admirable and most interesting Military History of Gen. Badeau. Wherever anecdotes were authentic they have been inserted, as anecdotes often reveal character more clearly than great achievements.

In a word, the book has been written for the masses of the *people*, and from a desire to furnish an accurate and complete Life of Grant and Colfax in a compact form for general circulation. It is but justice to add, that the author has been encouraged in the work by the offer of the publishers to prepare an edition at about the cost of manufacture; thus placing it within the reach of all those brave men whom Gen. Grant led to victory in war, and the millions of his countrymen whom he is to lead to more glorious victories in peace.

CHARLES A. PHELPS.

Boston, July 9, 1868.

CONTENTS.

CHAPTER I.

BIRTH AND EARLY LIFE.

CHAPTER II.

ATTACK ON FORT SUMTER. — BATTLE OF BELMONT.

CHAPTER III.

FORT HENRY.

CHAPTER IV.

CAPTURE OF FORT DONELSON.

CHAPTER V.

BATTLE OF SHILOH.

CHAPTER VI.

BATTLE AT PITTSBURG LANDING.

CHAPTER VII.

SIEGE OF CORINTH.

CHAPTER VIII.

BATTLE OF IUKA. — BATTLE OF CORINTH.

CHAPTER IX.

VICKSBURG CAMPAIGN.

CHAPTER X.

RUNNING THE BATTERIES.

CHAPTER XI.

CROSSING THE MISSISSIPPI. — BATTLE OF PORT GIBSON.

CHAPTER XII.

GRAND GULF CAPTURED.

CHAPTER XIII.

BATTLE AT JACKSON.

CHAPTER XIV.

BATTLE AT BIG BLACK RIVER.

CHAPTER XV.

THE SIEGE OF VICKSBURG.

CHAPTER XVI.

PORT HUDSON TAKEN.

CHAPTER XVII.

THEORIES OF TRADE. — ENGLAND'S NEUTRALITY.

CHAPTER XVIII.

BATTLE AT WAUHATCHIE.

CHAPTER XIX.

PREPARATIONS AT CHATTANOOGA.

CHAPTER XX.

BATTLE OF MISSIONARY RIDGE.

CHAPTER XXI.

THE BATTLE OF RINGGOLD.

CHAPTER XXII.

SIEGE OF KNOXVILLE.

CHAPTER XXIII.

RESULTS OF THE CAMPAIGN.

CHAPTER XXIV.

APPOINTED LIEUTENANT-GENERAL.

CHAPTER XXV.

RE-ORGANIZATION OF THE ARMY. — THE ADVANCE.

CHAPTER XXVI.

CAMPAIGN IN THE WILDERNESS.

CHAPTER XXVII.

BATTLE OF COLD HARBOR.

CHAPTER XXVIII.

SIEGE OF PETERSBURG.

CHAPTER XXIX.

SHERMAN'S MARCH.

CHAPTER XXX.

LEE'S RETREAT.

CHAPTER XXXI.

CAPTURE OF RICHMOND.

CHAPTER XXXII.

THE SURRENDER OF GEN. LEE.

CHAPTER XXXIII.

GEN. GRANT SINCE THE WAR.

CHAPTER XXXIV.

CONCLUSION.

CONTENTS TO SKETCH OF COLFAX.

CHAPTER I.

CHAPTER II.

APPENDIX.

Grant's Birthplace.

LIFE OF GENERAL GRANT.

CHAPTER I.

BIRTH AND EARLY LIFE.

ULYSSES SIMPSON GRANT was born, April 27, 1822, at Point Pleasant, Clermont County, Ohio, a small town on the Ohio River, twenty-five miles above Cincinnati. The Grants are of Scotch descent; and the motto of their clan in Aberdeenshire was, "Stand fast, stand firm, stand sure." Grant inherits from many of his ancestors a love for freedom, and a determination to fight for its cause. In 1799, his grandfather, a Pennsylvania farmer, joined the great tide of emigration moving to the North-west Territory.

This fertile and attractive region had recently been consecrated to freedom forever by the great Ordinance of 1787. There, there would be neither slaves nor slavery; there, labor would be honorable in all.

His great-grandfather, Capt. Noah Grant of Windsor, Conn., and his brother, Lieut. Solomon Grant, were soldiers in the old French War, and were both killed in battle in 1756; and it is not to be forgotten that grandfather giving the name of Hiram ; his grandmother, who was a great student of history, giving the name of Ulysses, whose character had strongly attracted her admiration. The member of Congress who appointed Grant to his cadetship at West Point when a boy of seventeen, by accident changed his name, in filling his appointment, to U. S. Grant. Grant repeatedly endeavored to have the mistake corrected at West Point, and at the War Department at Washington ; but this was one of the few things in which he failed: his applications were 'never complied with. As if fate foresaw the patriotic duty, the filial love, the transcendent services, he was one day to render his country, the government seemed to insist, when adopting him among her military children, on renaming him, and giving to him her own initials, — " U. S.," which he has ever since borne.

It has been thought remarkable that the mother of Napoleon should have happened to give birth to her warrior-son beneath tapestried hangings on which were wrought battle-pictures from the Iliad. Is it not a little singular that the maternal relative of Grant should have chosen for her admiration, from all history, the character of the hero of the siege of Troy ; have given his name to the infant Grant ; and that forty years after, when leading the Union armies of the Republic, he should have exhibited the same invincible fortitude, untiring patience, and unconquerable perseverance, so celebrated in the immortal song of Homer ? Ulysses of old was himself the *very* man who " fought it out on the line he had chosen, if it took all summer."

Grant was neither a precocious nor a. stupid child:

he was a well-behaved, dutiful boy.   He attended the public school in the village ; he learned well, but was no prodigy. The first book he read was " The Life of Washington," which made on his mind and imagination a profound and lasting impression.   A Canadian relative of about his own age visiting him soon after, Washington was very naturally spoken of by the two boys. His Canadian cousin said " he was nothing but a rebel, after all."   Both boys were excited ; and Grant said, " If you say that again, I'll thrash you."   It was repeated with defiance.   Off went their jackets, and the Canadian soon had the worst of it.   Years after, Grant was reminded of the incident by his cousin ; and he assured him pleasantly that he should do the same thing again with like provocation.

His special fondness was for a horse, and he attended the circus whenever it passed through the village.   One came along in which there was an innocent-looking pony, which was brought out during the performances ; and then the question would be mildly asked with a smile, " Is there any little boy here who would like a ride ? "

The pony was trained to go furiously round, and, at a given signal from his master, throw the boy head first on to the tan in the ring ; when the surprised and mortified boy would pick himself up, and retreat amid the laughter of the crowd.   When the question was asked, Ulysses stepped into the ring, mounted ; and the pony started.   On he went ; crack, crack, went the whip ; faster and faster went the pony. At the signal, he kicked up his heels, reared, plunged, shook his back. The people shouted ; but the boy sat still.   Out came a large monkey, and jumped up behind him, tore off his cap, and clutched his hair. Ulysses looked neither to the right nor the left; he spoke not a word, but clung like grim death to the saddle, until the ring-master gave it up, and stopped the pony.

This anecdote is of no consequence, except as exhibiting a native and early-developed trait in Grant's character, — of always doing what he attempted to do. He had undertaken to ride the pony, crowd or no crowd, monkey or no monkey; and *he rode him.* "The difference in boys," said Dr. Arnold, "is not so much in talent as in energy."

Another anecdote illustrates the same trait, but exhibits more strategy and ingenuity. When twelve years old, Mr. Grant's men were hauling heavy logs from the woods. Ulysses drove the horse. One day, when he reached the woods, he found the logs, but not the men. He waited; but the men did not come. He determined not to go home without the logs. So, after contriving some time, he hitched the chain to one end of a log, and drew it up on to a tree which had fallen, so that one end was higher than the other. When he had three logs in position, he backed the hind end of the wagon under them, and then, with the chain, hauled the logs on to the wagon, and drove home in triumph. Quite a little feat for a boy of twelve years of age.

He never liked his father's business of tanning. It was disagreeable; and he early determined not to follow it. He wanted an education. He said he would be a farmer, or trade down the river; but a tanner he would not be.

His father, with limited means, did not feel, that, in

justice to himself and his other children, he could afford the money to send him to college.

He applied, with the boy's assent, for a vacant cadetship at West Point. The appointment was to be made by Hon. T. L. Hamer, the member of Congress from the district. His term of office expired at noon, March 4, 1839. Mr. Grant's letter, asking for the appointment of his son, reached him on the night of the 3d. On the morning of the 4th, the appointment was made.

It is remarkable, that, without any special preparatory study, he passed the rigid examination which all cadets are obliged to undergo, and was at once admitted to the academy.

The story which has been told, that Grant was "hazed" at West Point, and had a fight with some of the cadets, is an error. Grant had no difficulty, either with the officers or his fellow-cadets. He never struck nor was struck while there by any person whatever.

It was in the years passed at the academy that Grant laid the foundation of his greatness. Wellington, once looking at the playground at Eton with a friend, said, " 'Twas there Waterloo was won." It was at West Point that Donelson and Vicksburg and Chattanooga were made possible to Grant. Gibbon says every man has two educations, — one acquired from others ; one more important, which he gives to himself. Grinding gerunds may be study, but is not necessarily education. Education and wisdom are different things. A man may be very learned, and very unwise ; he may know a great deal, and be very ignorant ; be highly educated, and be very foolish. A man, like a gun, may be overloaded to his own injury and that of others ; may possess every sense but common sense; understand words, and be ignorant of affairs. Such men are "wells that hold no water;" or rather they hold it so closely, no one's thirst is quenched. Like Shakspeare's purblind Argus, they are "all eyes, and no sight." Such are the medical scholars who lose all their patients; legal scholars who lose all their clients; and, last of all, military scholars who lose all their battles. They are educated, but to the death of all usefulness.

But Grant received at West Point the best education a man can receive; namely, that which fits him for his work in life. He was not compelled, as most men are under our college systems, to waste years in studying the rules of Greek accents and scanning Latin verse; making them, often, alive to the "dead languages," while dead to most living things. He was subjected to a course of physical training which invigorated his body. He was taught fencing, drawing, riding, dancing; he was taught science, mathematics, the modern languages, constitutional and international law, and engineering.

Men are not educated by books alone. "The gods forbid," said Plato, "that to philosophize should be only to read a great many books." "I know neither art nor science," said Pythagoras; "but I am a philosopher."

Young Grant appreciated and improved all the opportunities which were offered to him. He gave those years diligently to self-improvement in the widest sense. He graduated with a good rank in his class; and, what was better, without vices which enfeebled his body, or mental habits which depraved his mind.

On leaving the academy, he could recall his life there

with a satisfaction similar to that with which Curran
so touchingly recalled to Lord Avonmore their early
days and nights of study together :—

> " We spent them not in toys or lust or wine,
> But search of deep philosophy."

In July, 1843, he entered the United-States army
as a brevet second lieutenant in the fourth regiment of
infantry. He was ordered to the frontiers of Missouri,
among the Indians, then on the outer borders of civilization. Here Lieut. Grant remained nearly two years;
when, in 1845, he was ordered to Corpus Christi, Tex.,
where United-States troops were gathering under command of Gen. Zachary Taylor. War ensued, not long
after, between the United States and Mexico, on the
question of boundary-lines. From the first attack on
Fort Brown, opposite Matamoras, Lieut. Grant was in
every battle in the Mexican War except Buena Vista,
—fourteen in all. At Palo Alto, Resaca de la Palma,
Monterey, Chapultepec, in every engagement, he conducted himself with distinguished bravery, which elicited
special mention from his superiors in command. In
1847, he was appointed brevet captain ; his commission
dating from the day on which the battle of Chapultepec
was fought. In 1853, he was promoted to a full cap-
taincy.

In 1864, Gen. Scott said to Col. Badeau of Gen.
Grant's staff, the accomplished historian of his military
life, that he remembered a young officer named Grant,
who distinguished himself in the Mexican War ; and at
Appomattox Court House, at the surrender of Gen. Lee,
the latter remarked to Grant, that he remembered having seen him in Mexico during the war.

But Grant's service in Mexico gave him an opportunity of showing that he had a warm and grateful heart, and could do something manly beside fighting. Hon. Mr. Hamer, who, as member of Congress, had appointed Grant to his cadetship, and to whom he felt greatly indebted for his education at West Point, went out to Mexico as a general of volunteers, and, while there in camp, was taken sick. Lieut. Grant nursed him with the love of a son and the tenderness of a woman, performed for him the last offices of affection, and closed his eyes in death.

CHAPTER II.

ATTACK ON FORT SUMTER. — BATTLE OF BELMONT.

AT the close of the Mexican War, Capt. Grant returned to the United States, and was subsequently stationed on the Canadian frontier, in California, and in Oregon. But garrison life in that lonely region offered no opportunities of usefulness to himself or others. His years were wasting away in the small duties of an outpost; and as the country was at peace, and had no special need of military service from him, he determined to resign his commission, which he did in July, 1854.

He moved to St. Louis, and there married Miss Julia Dent, a sister of his classmate, Major Frederic T. Dent, of the United-States army, and a daughter of Frederic Dent, Esq., a merchant of that city. He soon took a farm in the suburbs of St. Louis, and labored in the life of a farmer. He would cut wood, and haul it to Carondelet: and citizens there tell of buying wood of Capt. Grant; adding, that he dressed according to his work, wearing a slouched hat, a blouse, and his pantaloons tucked in at the top of his boots.

But the wood-lot and the small farm did not yield an adequate income for the support and education of his family; and in 1859 he moved to Galena, Ill., entered into business, and was residing there on the morning of the memorable 12th of April, 1861, when the telegraph flashed the news over the country that the rebels had fired on the old flag at Fort Sumter.

"The obligations of the intellect," it has been said, "are among the most sacred of the claims of gratitude." Macaulay, in his history of the attack of James the II. on the Universities of Oxford and Cambridge, has given us a beautiful picture of the attachment which all men feel for the place of their education, and the gratitude which accompanies it. There are exceptions; but Grant was not one of these. The country had adopted him and educated him. It had a claim of honor on his services in the day of peril; and he joyously recognized the bond, — all the more cheerfully, because it could not be enforced. There are some things which it is impossible for a noble, manly nature to do.

It would have been impossible for Grant to do as did Robert E. Lee, — be educated, supported, and honored through life by the munificence of the government; to remain in personal and official intimacy with Gen. Scott, studying his plans, and the numbers of the Union army, until the last day or two before the first battle at Bull Run; then steal into Virginia under pretence of visiting his family, join the rebels, and fight against the government which had made him all he was. For the honor of human nature, such instances are few. Grant could not have done this, any more than he could have struck the mother who bore him.

None of this generation who witnessed it will ever

forget the majestic uprising of the people at the attack on Fort Sumter. The old flag, which had been regarded chiefly as an ornament for festal occasions, became at once the dear symbol of our undying love for our native land.

The human soul is so organized that it always requires a visible sign of its emotions: such was the eagle to the Roman, the cross to the Christian, the crescent to the Mahometan. The same sentiment in the heart of man was recognized and invoked in that most heartbreaking and mournful scene in human history, — the institution of the Last Supper, and the visible emblems of the body broken and the blood shed. The national ensign, representing all that was precious in national life or sacred in patriotic duty, was at once flung out from spire and balcony and mast-head, on land and sea. The occasion moved Grant to the utmost depths of his being. He said to a friend, " The government has educated me for the army. What I am, I owe to my country. I have served her through one war, and, live or die, will serve her through this." Noble words, and nobly have they been redeemed.

Immediately he began recruiting and drilling a company in the streets of Galena ; and, four days after, he went with it to Springfield, the capital of the State of Illinois, the home of Abraham Lincoln, and offered it to Gov. Yates. So modest was he, that he only applied to be their captain, thinking his military education would be of use to them : but another member desired the place, and informed Grant of his wish ; and the future lieutenant-general gave way. So little was the North prepared for war, that many of the States had no war department or adjutant-general's office. In many instances, the office of adjutant-general was not filled by officers experienced in the routine of military organization. After a few days, Gov. Yates said to Grant one morning, "Do you know about these military details? — how many men it takes to make a company, and how many to make a regiment, and what officers each must have?"

Grant replied, "Oh, yes, sir! I was educated at West Point, and served eleven years in the regular army."

"Then," said the governor, "sit right down in this arm-chair, and act as Adjutant-General of the State." He did so, and was of special service at Springfield in organizing and forwarding regiments. Gov. Yates has since spoken of his first impressions of Gen. Grant in the following terms : —

"In presenting himself to me, he made no reference to any merits, but simply said he had been the recipient of a military education at West Point; and, now that the country was assailed, he thought it his duty to offer his services, and that he would esteem it a privilege to be assigned to any position where he could be useful. I cannot now claim to myself the credit of having discerned in him the promise of great achievements, or the qualities 'which minister to the making of great names,' more than in many others who proposed to enter the military service. His appearance, at first sight, is not striking. He had no grand airs, no imposing appearance; and I confess it could not be said he was a form

'Where every god did seem to set his seal
To give the world assurance of a man.'

He was plain, very plain; but still, sir, something — perhaps his plain, straightforward modesty and earnestness — induced me to assign him a desk in the executive office. In a short time, I found him to be an invaluable assistant in my office and in that of the adjutant-general. He was soon after assigned to the command of the six camps of organization and instruction which I had established in the State."

He had previously written to the Adjutant-General of the United States, at Washington, offering his services, during the war, in any capacity in which he might be wanted; but it was merely from some unknown officer out West, by the name of Grant; and this letter, which would have been read with interest by thousands for years to come, was not even preserved.

He remained five weeks at Springfield, with the exception of a flying visit to Cincinnati, which he made to see Gen. McClellan, whom he had known in the army, and with the secret thought that possibly McClellan would offer him a place on his staff; but McClellan was absent, and he returned.

On the 15th of June, 1861, Gov. Yates gave him his commission as colonel of the Twenty-first Regiment of Illinois Volunteers. The regiment at once felt the hand of a master. Its reduced numbers were raised to a thousand men: order, discipline, exactness, were everywhere seen. He reported to Brig.-Gen. John Pope, by whom he was stationed at Mexico, in the State of Missouri. He at once showed such skill and efficiency as a trained military man, that in August following, unknown to himself, upon the nomination of Hon. E. B. Washburne, member of Congress from Illinois, who early discerned his abilities, he was appointed brigadier-general of volunteers, his rank dating from the 17th of May.

Gen. Pope had been succeeded in the Western

Department by Gen. Fremont; and, on the 1st of September, Grant was ordered by the latter to Cairo.

Cairo is situated at the southern extremity of Illinois, on a tongue of land which thrusts itself out exactly where the Ohio and Mississippi Rivers meet, a hundred and seventy-five miles below St. Louis. It is within striking distance of the five States of Illinois, Kentucky, Tennessee, Arkansas, and Mississippi. It is said, that, in the first consultation that Gen. Scott had with the cabinet at the opening of the war, he placed his finger on the map at Cairo, and spoke of it as in every way one of the most important places in the country to the military power of the United States.

Paducah was on the Kentucky side of the Ohio, at the mouth of the Tennessee River. Kentucky at this time had a rebel for governor, by the name of Beriah Magoffin. It was evident from the first that the border States, Maryland, Kentucky, and Tennessee, would be the first battle-ground for the Union. The rebels in the two latter did not dare attempt to carry them at once over to secession; but their policy was to talk "armed neutrality." The "sacred soil of old Kentucky must not be invaded by the troops of either party." These fine words were to be used until they could be carried boldly into the Rebellion. But, in the war for the Union, there could be no "neutrality" for any State, least of all for States which held the ashes of Andrew Jackson and Henry Clay. Every State and every man was either for the Union or against it.

The Legislature of Kentucky was for the Union by a large majority. On his arrival at Cairo, Grant had telegraphed to them that a rebel force had entered Kentucky. Gov. Harris of Tennessee telegraphed, " it had been done without his consent;" "President Davis would order their withdrawal;" "Gen. Polk would withdraw them." But Grant preferred to trust his soldiers rather than Jeff. Davis, Beriah Magoffin, or Gen. Bishop Leonidas Polk; and accordingly took possession of Paducah the next morning with two regiments and a battery. He found the rebel flag flying in all directions, rations and army supplies in great quantities (among the latter a large amount of *leather*, of which Grant considered himself an excellent judge); and he appropriated all for the use of the United-States troops. He issued the following proclamation to the inhabitants : —

PADUCAH, KY., Sept. 6, 1861.

TO THE CITIZENS OF PADUCAH, —

I have come among you, not as an enemy, but as your fellow-citizen; not to maltreat or annoy you, but to respect and enforce the rights of all loyal citizens. An enemy in rebellion against our common government has taken possession of, and planted its guns on the soil of Kentucky, and fired upon you. Columbus and Hickman are in his hands. He is moving upon your city. I am here to defend you against this enemy, *to assist the authority and sovereignty of your government. I have nothing to do with opinions. I shall deal only with armed rebellion and its aiders and abetters.* You can pursue your usual avocations without fear. The strong arm of the government is here to protect its friends, and punish its enemies. Whenever it is manifest that you are able to defend yourselves, and maintain the authority of the government, and protect the rights of loyal citizens, I shall withdraw the forces under my command.

U. S. GRANT, *Brig.-Gen. commanding.*

The tone of this proclamation was admirable, and represented the spirit of the Union people : " I have come among you, not as an enemy;" "I am here to assist the authority and sovereignty of your government."

In the camp at Cairo, it was noticed that Grant made no display of bright buttons and shoulder-straps, plumes and gold-lace. Instead of the regulation-hat with the gold cord and acorns, he generally wore a citizen's common felt hat and a blue blouse. He put on none of the airs, and made none of the pretensions, of little greatness. A few of the soldiers, who had been in Mexico, were reminded of Gen. Taylor, "Old Rough and Ready," who, when a Mexican officer of high rank was suddenly announced at his headquarters, found himself in an old brown linen coat and straw hat, and had to dive down to the bottom of his trunk, and search some time, before he could find the elegant coat, sash, and chapeau of a major-general, which the army regulations required him to wear.

Rev. J. L. Crane, the chaplain of the regiment of which Grant was colonel, thus writes of camp-life at this time : —

"Grant is about five feet ten inches in height, and will weigh a hundred and forty or forty-five pounds. He has a countenance indicative of reserve, and an indomitable will and persistent purpose.

"In dress he is indifferent and careless, making no pretensions to *style* or fashionable military display. Had he continued colonel till now, I think his uniform would have lasted till this day ; for he never used it except on dress-parade, and then seemed to regard it a good deal as David did Saul's armor.

"'His body is a vial of intense existence;' and yet, when a stranger would see him in a crowd, he would never think of asking his name. He is no dissembler. He is a sincere, thinking, real man. He is always cheerful. No toil, cold, heat, hunger, fatigue,

or want of money, depresses him. He does his work at the time,
and he requires all under his command to be equally prompt.
This promptness is one of Grant's charateristics, and it is one of
the secrets of his success.

" On one of our marches, when passing through one of those
small towns where the grocery is the principal establishment, some
of the lovers of intoxication had broken away from our lines, and
filled their canteens with whiskey, and were soon reeling and un-
governable under its influence. While apparently stopping the
regiment for rest, Grant passed quietly along, and took each canteen,
and, wherever he detected the fatal odor, emptied the liquor on the
ground with as much *nonchalance* as he would empty his pipe.
On this point, his orders were imperative : no whiskey nor intoxicating beverages were allowed in his camp.

" Grant belongs to no church ; yet he entertains and expresses
the highest esteem for all the enterprises that tend to promote
religion. When at home, he generally attended the Methodist-
Episcopal Church. While he was colonel of the Twenty-first Regiment, he gave every encouragement and facility for securing a
prompt and uniform observance of religious services ; and was
generally found in the audience listening to the preaching.

" Shortly after I came into the regiment, our mess were one
day taking their usual seats around the dinner-table, when he
remarked, —

" ' Chaplain, when I was at home, and ministers were stopping
at my house, I always invited them to ask a blessing at the table.
I suppose a blessing is as much needed here as at home ; and, if
it is agreeable with your views, I should be glad to have you ask
a blessing every time we sit down to eat.' "

Reconnoissances and skirmishes took place occasionally ; and prisoners were taken, concerning the exchange
of whom the following correspondence took place with
Major-Gen. Polk : —

TO THE COMMANDING OFFICER AT CAIRO AND BIRD'S POINT, —

I have in my camp a number of prisoners of the Federal army,
and am informed there are prisoners belonging to the Missouri

State troops in yours. I propose an exchange of these prisoners, and for that purpose send Capt. Polk of the artillery, and Lieut. Smith of the infantry, both of the Confederate-States army, with a flag of truce, to deliver to you this communication, and to know your pleasure in regard to my proposition. The principles recognized in the exchange of prisoners effected on the 3d of September, between Brig.-Gen. Pillow of the Confederate army, and Col. Wallace of the United-States army, are those I propose as the basis of that now contemplated.

Respectfully your obedient servant,
L. POLK, Major-Gen. commanding.

This is an innocent-sounding letter: but Gen. Grant was not to be entrapped into recognizing any Southern Confederacy, or conceding the rights of belligerents, by an exchange of prisoners; and returned the following answer, showing himself thoroughly acquainted with the legal bearings of the points in discussion: —

GENERAL, — Yours of this date is just received. *In regard to an exchange of prisoners, as proposed, I can, of my own accordance, make none.. I recognize no Southern Confederacy* myself, but will communicate with higher authorities for their views. Should I not be sustained, I will find means of communicating with you.

Respectfully your obedient servant,
U. S. GRANT, Brig.-Gen. commanding.

To Major-Gen. POLK, Columbus, Ky.

The rebels were gathering troops and supplies in great force at Columbus, on the Kentucky shore of the Mississippi, below Cairo, and sending them across the river, through Belmont, to the rebel Gen. Price in Missouri.

Grant had several times suggested an attack on Columbus. Finally, on the evening of the 6th of

November, Grant embarked for a reconnoissance with 2,850 men upon four transports, convoyed by the gunboats "Tyler" and "Lexington," and dropped down to Island No. 1, eleven miles above Columbus. Early the next morning, the troops were landed at Hunter's Point, on the Missouri shore, and marched about three miles to Belmont. Grant had no purpose to hold Belmont, which is on low ground, and every inch of it commanded by the rebel guns on the right bluff at Columbus opposite. His design was to stir up the rebels, scatter their camp, and capture the munitions. The rebel camp was in an open space, protected by fallen trees.

The line of battle was formed with Col. Fouke in the centre, Col. Buford on the right, and Col. Logan on the left. These divisions advanced together, each contending for the honor of first planting the stars and stripes in the rebel camp. The fight was very severe for about four hours. Grant was in advance with the skirmish-line, and had his horse shot under him. But the Union troops drove the enemy foot by foot, and from tree to tree, back to their encampment.

There were about 6,000 rebels. At last, Grant ordered a charge ; and his whole force, now less than half the number of rebels, with loud cheers, drove the enemy, at the point of the bayonet, through their camps ; and thousands took refuge on their transports on the river's edge. The troops, some of whom had never been armed as soldiers until three days before, flushed with victory, gave themselves up to rejoicing. Officers began making stump-speeches for the Union. There were no wagons to move the captured property ; and the rebel tents were fired, consuming their blankets and all their camp-equipage.

Major-Gen. Polk, who commanded at Columbus, opposite, had now decided that something must be done. The heavy fire from the guns which he had brought to bear had not stopped the victorious advance of Grant. He accordingly sent over three regiments under Gen. Pillow, and three more under Gen. Cheatham. The latter were landed between our troops and their boats to cut off their retreat. Grant had observed these movements, and had commenced his return-march to re-embark with his men disorganized by their victory. When the troops met in the woods the soldiers of Cheatham, they shouted, " We are surrounded !" and were thrown into confusion. A raw officer, in much excitement, made the announcement to Grant : —

" General, we are surrounded. What can we do ?"

" Cut our way out, sir, as we cut our way in," said Grant.

To some of the soldiers, who seemed to think themselves captured, Grant said, " We whipped them once, and we can whip them again."

Grant, here and always, acted on the principle so well expressed by an Irish soldier in the Ninth Massachusetts, who on one occasion, after being informed several times, by a comrade at his side, that they were defeated, at last shouted impatiently, " Niver b'leive y're whipped, man, till y're whipped yourself !" ·

Logan, who afterwards became so distinguished, placed the colors in front, and moved at once upon the enemy.*

* Hon. John A. Logan was a Douglas Democrat, a member of Congress from Illinois, at the opening of the war. On the day of the first battle at Bull Run, he rode down from Washington as a visitor, but, on reaching the

The fight was furious; but the old flag steadily advanced, and by five o'clock in the afternoon, our troops, having driven the enemy before them, reached their boats.

While the troops were embarking, Grant sent out a detachment to bring in the wounded. He had posted a battalion in the morning as a reserve, who, when they saw the main body returning, thought it proper for them to return also without special order. They had done so, and without reporting to any one, — so little were our citizen-soldiers then accustomed to military forms. They could fight and die for the good cause; but military experience they did not possess. Grant, supposing them still in position, rode back, with only a single member of his staff, to order their return. Suddenly he came upon the whole rebel line, now re-formed to advance, and not fifty yards distant. He was an excellent mark for the rebel sharpshooters; but he stopped, looked at the situation, then turned his horse, and rode slowly back to avoid an appearance of haste. Gen. Polk, who had seen him, called to his men, "There is a Yankee, if you want to try your aim!" But the bullet destined to kill Grant was not there; and he rode slowly back until nearing the boats, when the leaden rain hurried his horse into a gallop; the animal fairly sliding down the river's bank on his haunches.

A plank was quickly thrown out from one of the boats, over which he trotted his horse; the balls now

field, borrowed a rifle, asked permission to join a Michigan regiment, and fought in its ranks throughout the day. He is now Grand Commander of the Army of the Republic.

flying around him in all directions. The transports moved off towards Cairo; and the gunboats, by way of farewell, opened on the rebel force, now thronging the shore, with grape, canister, and five-second shells, which scattered them with terrible slaughter. The Federal loss was about four hundred men. The Rebel force was about seven thousand: their loss, as admitted by Pollard, was about seven hundred killed, and one hundred and seventy-five more taken prisoners.

The battle was of much importance: it gave our fresh recruits confidence in themselves and in their leader. One incident in connection with this battle shows the nature of civil wars, which place friend against friend. Col. Wright of Tennessee, and Col. Fouke, had been friends in Congress. When they separated at Washington the preceding spring, Wright said, " Fouke, I expect our next meeting will be on the battle-field." They parted: one followed the flag of treason; the other, the flag of his country. Their next meeting was on the field of Belmont, where Wright was killed, and sixty of his men taken prisoners by Col. Fouke's regiment.

The next day, the following order was read to the troops: —

The general commanding this military district returns his thanks to the troops under his command at the battle of Belmont on yesterday.

It has been his fortune to have been in all the battles fought in Mexico by Generals Scott and Taylor, save Buena Vista; and he never saw one more hotly contested, or where troops behaved with more gallantry.

Such courage will insure victory wherever our flag may be borne and protected by such a class of men.

To the brave who fell the sympathy of the country is due, and will be manifested in a manner unmistakable.

U. S. GRANT, *Brig.-Gen. commanding.*

The same day, Grant wrote a private letter to his father, giving an account of the battle, from which the following extracts are taken : —

"The whole command, with the exception of a small reserve, was then deployed in like manner, and ordered forward. The order was obeyed with great alacrity; the men all showing great courage. I can say with great gratification, that every colonel, without a single exception, set an example to their commands, that inspired a confidence that will always insure victory when there is, the slightest possibility of gaining one. I feel truly proud to command such men.

.   .   .   .

"The object of the expedition was to prevent the enemy from sending a force into Missouri to cut off troops I had sent there for a special purpose, and to prevent re-enforcing Price.

"Besides being well fortified at Columbus, their numbers far exceeded ours; and it would have been folly to have attacked them. We found the Confederates well armed and brave. On our return, stragglers that had been left in our rear (now front) fired into us, and more recrossed the river, and gave us battle for a full mile, and afterwards at the boats when we were embarking.

"There was no hasty retreating or running away. Taking into account the object of the expedition, the victory was complete. It has given us confidence in the officers and men of this command, that will enable us to lead them in any future engagement, without fear of the result."

Much importance had been attached at the War Department to retaining the recruits in camps, and making no movements until they had been thoroughly drilled and manœuvred : but, after the battle of Belmont, Grant always entertained and acted on the opinion that such delay was useless ; that, where both parties are inexperienced, nothing is gained by delay.

CHAPTER III.

ON the 31st of August, Fremont issued his celebrated order, declaring the slaves of rebels free
men, as follows: —

" The property, real and personal, of all persons in the State
of Missouri who shall take up arms against the United States, or
shall be directly proven to have taken active part with their enemies in the field, is declared to be confiscated to the public use;
and their slaves, if any they have, are declared to be *free men.*"

This was a blow aimed directly at the very heart of
the Rebellion. Fremont was born in South Carolina,
and knew slavery thoroughly. But the country was
not ready for this. The Union must be preserved; but
slavery must not be harmed. President Lincoln directed the withdrawal of the order. Fremont requested that this should be done by the commander-in-chief;
and Mr. Lincoln accordingly overruled it. Three
years more of war and suffering were required before
it was seen that God had his purposes in this civil
conflict; and one of these was to " let the oppressed go
free."

Two days after the battle of Belmont, Nov. 9, Gen.
Fremont was superseded by Gen. H. W. Halleck,

who soon after issued his equally celebrated Order No. 3, excluding " unauthorized persons " from entering the army-lines.   It was as follows : —

"It has been represented that important information respecting the number of our forces is conveyed to the enemy by means of fugitive slaves who are admitted within our lines. In order to remedy this evil, it is directed that no such persons be hereafter permitted to enter the lines of any camp, or of any forces on the march; that any now within such lines be immediately excluded therefrom. No fugitive slaves will therefore be admitted within our lines or camps, except when especially ordered by the general commanding."

The Mississippi, the Tennessee, and the Cumberland, are the only rivers which were navigable from the southern lines of the free States into the States in rebellion.

The rebels had, with great foresight, stretched a strategic line east from Columbus, on the Mississippi, which had been strongly fortified, two hundred miles to Bowling Green, in the centre of Kentucky; crossing both the two last-named rivers at a right angle. Bowling Green was at the junction of the Memphis and Ohio and Louisville and Nashville Railroads.

About the centre of this line, near the boundary of Kentucky and Tennessee, the Cumberland and Tennessee Rivers approach within twelve miles of each other. Here the rebels had erected two strong forts with great skill and labor, — Fort Donelson on the Cumberland, Fort Henry on the Tennessee. But the forts were south of Columbus and Bowling Green; so that these strongholds must both be evacuated when the forts were taken.

Grant perceived all this, of course, but had been required for two months to drill and organize his men. Late in January, 1862, he visited St. Louis in person to obtain permission to take these forts; but the plan was not entertained. After his return, Grant telegraphed to St. Louis, Jan. 28, " With permission, I will take and hold Fort Henry on the Tennessee, and establish and hold a large camp there." On the same day, Com. Foote, commanding the gunboats in that region, by a happy coincidence telegraphed as follows : —

CAIRO, Jan. 28, 1862.

Major-Gen. H. W. HALLECK, St. Louis, Mo., commanding, —

Gen. Grant and myself are of opinion that Fort Henry, on the Tennessee River, can be carried with four iron-clad gunboats, and troops to permanently occupy. Have we your authority to move for that purpose when ready ?

A. H. FOOTE, Flag-Officer.

The reader can judge whether Gen. Grant requested Foote to send this despatch in aid of his request.

Permission to move arrived on the 1st of February. The next day, Grant had left Cairo with seventeen thousand men on transports, accompanied by Foote with several gunboats. They sailed up the Ohio to the mouth of the Tennessee, then up the latter to within about eight miles of the fort where Gen. McClernand had selected a landing ; but Grant himself pushed up the river on one of the gunboats to draw the fire from the fort and ascertain the range of their guns, which he satisfactorily learned by a thirty-two-pound shot passing through the boat.

He now determined to move his troops four miles up

the river, to Bailey's Ferry; and there they debarked. Both sides of the river were found to be fortified. The principal works were on the east side. A bastioned* front, with seventeen heavy gun embrasures, had been formed with sand-bags on the parapets between the guns. On the land-front, there was a camp protected by a commanding line of rifle-pits, filled by Western sharpshooters. The fort enclosed about three acres. There were about three thousand rebel troops, under Brig-Gen. Tilghman.

McClernand was ordered to move at eleven o'clock on the 6th to the rear of Fort Henry, on the road to Fort Donelson, to cut off retreat and re-enforcements. Gen. Smith was to seize Fort Heiman on the west bank of the river; and the gunboats were to advance in two lines, and attack from the river.

Com. Foote well knew that thousands of troops could not march as rapidly as his boats could steam up the river, and was by no means unwilling to do the principal part of the bloody work before the land-force could arrive. Unlike Atlantis, who lingered in the race that she might be overtaken by her lover, Foote, emulous of glory, secretly rejoiced that he could not be overtaken or passed by the army; and at the last moment, unable to conceal his anticipated success, he said to Grant, with a smile and bright twinkle in his eye, " I shall take Fort Henry before the troops arrive."

The little fleet was composed of " The Cincinnati,"

---

* BASTION, a projecting part of the main fort. EMBRASURE, an opening in a parapet for cannon. PARAPET, a breastwork for covering soldiers. MINE, a cavity under a fort, filled with powder. TRENCH, an excavation made to cover troops advancing in a siege. PARALLEL, a wide trench for communication between batteries. MOAT, a canal around a fort.

" Essex," " Carondelet," " St. Louis," " Conestoga,"
" Tyler," and " Lexington,"—the first three iron-clads,
the last wooden vessels. They engaged the forts at six
hundred yards, opening a terrific cannonade, which was
continued for nearly an hour with unabated fury. But
the gallant commodore had ordered the men to " aim
carefully," " fire steadily," and to " make every shot
tell ; " and they did. At last, a twenty-eight-pound
shot struck " The Essex " in a weak spot, and pierced
her boiler. In an instant, the vessel was filled with
scalding steam, killing and wounding nearly forty men ;
among them Capt. W. D. Porter and both pilots. For
a moment, the scene on board was appalling. The
little vessel trembled in every timber, and now, struck
in a vital part, like a strong man pierced in the heart,
drifted slowly out of the fight. The rebels, thinking
the attack repulsed, now made the welkin ring with
their shouts. But the remaining vessels continued
their fire, as if determined to lift the fort, and ground
which held it, bodily from the earth. In an hour and
fifteen minutes the white flag was seen, upon which a
boat was lowered ; and soon the national ensign was
raised over this stronghold of treason amid long-continued cheers. The short time within which the fort
had been captured was a surprise to both Foote and
Grant. The troops had been compelled to march eight
miles around, through muddy roads, cutting their way
through the woods, building bridges across several
streams ; and were unable to arrive until nearly an hour
after Tilghman's surrender. This delay had permitted
most of the garrison to escape. Gen. Tilghman, eleven
on his staff, seventy men, sixteen invalids, barracks and

tents for fifteen thousand soldiers, were captured. Grant instantly sent forward his cavalry on the road to Fort Donelson; but they took only twenty or thirty men and a few guns.

That Foote should at once have all the honor he deserved, Grant immediately telegraphed to Halleck, "Fort Henry is ours! The gunboats silenced the batteries before the investment was completed. I shall take and destroy Fort Donelson on the 8th, and return to Fort Henry." The reader will remember that he had only asked permission to attack Fort Henry; no allusion being made to Fort Donelson. And Foote, with the same spirit, reported as follows: "The plan of the attack, so far as the army reaching the rear of the fort to make a demonstration simultaneously with the navy, was frustrated by the excessively muddy roads and the high stage of the water preventing the arrival of our troops until some time after I had taken possession of the fort." *

Grant, although he had received no orders to that effect, determined to move at once upon Fort Donelson, and ordered his entire force to be "ready to march by daylight" the next day. But the windows of heaven opened, and the floods came; the streams were rivers, the roads mires; the ground seemed turned into swamps.

The gunboats had steamed up into the interior as far as Florence, Ala., some two hundred miles, and within two hundred and fifty miles of Montgomery, the capital of the so-called Confederacy. The novel sight drew the inhabitants to the river by thousands. Men, women, and children lined the shores; and the old flag was often saluted with loud huzzas, and tears of joy.

---

* Foote's Report.

Some of the scenes among the people were referred
to in the following lines published at the time : —

> " Massa ! Massa ! Hallelujah !
>   The flag's come back to Tennessee ! "

> " Pompey, hold me on your shoulder,
>   Help me stand on foot once more,
> That I may salute the colors
>   As they pass my cabin-door.
> Here's the paper signed that frees you;
>   Give a freeman's shout with me :
> ' God and Union ' be our watchword
>   Evermore in Tennessee ! "

3

CHAPTER IV.

CAPTURE OF FORT DONELSON.

ON the 10th of February, Grant wrote to Foote, " I have been waiting very patiently for the return of the gunboats under Com. Phelps, to go around on the Cumberland, whilst I march my land-forces across to make a simultaneous attack upon Fort Donelson."

It was six days before the army could be moved. Fort Donelson was a far more formidable place than Fort Henry. It enclosed nearly a hundred acres, on a bluff a hundred feet high. It was defended by sixty-five guns, among them a ten-inch Columbiad, sixty-four and thirty-two pounders, water-batteries on the river, and on land felled timbers breast-high, — the whole garrisoned by about twenty-one thousand men. It was one of the strongest works in the South or North.

Generals Buckner, Pillow, and Floyd were in command.

After the fall of Fort Henry, the men had worked day and night to enlarge and render the works impregnable. Its importance to the Confederacy was well understood by the rebel government. It was the key to Nashville, the capital of Tennessee. It had been made a large dépôt of supplies; and its fall would compel the evacuation of Bowling Green, which had even then been partially weakened to re-enforce Donelson, so important was it deemed to hold the latter at all hazards.

On the morning of the 12th, the army began its march: the bands played patriotic airs, the flags danced in the sunlight, and the men were determined to conquer or die. Grant carried no tents or baggage; he took only bullets, guns, and rations; he threw up no intrenchments; his picks were pickets; his spades were those described as having been used in the burial of Sir John Moore on the Heights of Coruña, —

> " We buried him darkly at dead of night,
> *The sods with our bayonets turning.*"

The exact number of the rebels was then unknown; and, after giving directions as fully as possible, Grant added in his field-order, in regard to the details of the attack, "*The necessary orders will be given on the field.*"

Gen. C. F. Smith had the left, and Gen J. A. McClernand had the right, of the national line, which was gradually extended to nearly three miles in length, in the form of a crescent.

The men bivouacked in line of battle with their arms in their hands, and were constantly under fire from the rebel breastworks. Many of the men had thoughtlessly thrown away their blankets. No fires could be lighted; and near daylight there was a severe snow-storm. Through the night, the rebels dropped shells frequently over our lines; and the suffering of our troops was very great.

Before daylight, on Friday the 14th, the welcome sound of the gunboats was heard on the river, and Com. Foote arrived with four ironclads and two wooden gunboats. At three o'clock in the afternoon, they moved up to within four hundred yards of the heaviest guns of the fort. There, until half-past four, they maintained a most unequal fight. The elevation and number of the rebel guns, their great weight of metal, both from the fort and the water-batteries, placed the boats at a great disadvantage. At last, the wheel of " The St. Louis " and the tiller of " The Louisville " were shot away, and they were rendered useless; a rifled gun exploded upon another boat; " The Carondelet " received a 120-pounder in one of her forward ports; Com. Foote was wounded; and the disabled fleet was compelled to fall back out of the range of the guns.

Grant then wrote, " Appearances now are that we shall have a protracted siege here. . . . I fear the result of an attempt to carry the place by storm with new troops. I feel great confidence, however, of ultimately reducing the place."

Another night of piercing wind, snow, and sleet, came down upon the devoted soldiers.

No regrets were heard, no impatience manifested. They only seemed eager for the hour when they could show traitors how brave men could fight and die for the land they loved. Grant seemed omnipresent. Without food or sleep he was everywhere, and yet appeared to be exactly at the place where required at the proper moment.

At two o'clock at night, he received the following note from the wounded commodore : —

FLAGSHIP " St. Louis," Feb. 14, 1862.

Gen. GRANT, commanding United-States Forces.

DEAR GENERAL, — Will you do me the favor to come on board at your earliest convenience? As I am disabled from walking, from a contusion, I cannot possibly get to see you about the disposition of these vessels, all of which are more or less disabled.

A. S. FOOTE, *Flag-Officer*.

The rebels, seeing the gunboats retire, were greatly encouraged, and determined to move out early Saturday morning, drive back the Union line, overwhelm Grant's army, and win one of the greatest victories of the war.

At daylight, Floyd massed his troops heavily on the left, who advanced under Gen. Pillow against McArthur's brigade, on our extreme right, where our line was thin and weakest. They came on with a daring and bravery worthy of a better cause; and for two hours the fighting was terrific. At this time, two or three of our regiments were broken, and one or two more were out of ammunition; and the Union line wavered. Gen. McClernand sent word back that Buckner had joined Pillow, and he should be destroyed unless re-enforced.

Gen. W. H. L. Wallace, who commanded the centre, now advanced to his support, accompanied by Logan. Both were fearless, and both were magnetic men, who inspired their soldiers with their own indomitable spirit. They and their troops fought with a courage which drew forth the admiration of their enemies. But one regiment, misdirected by a guide, took the wrong road, and was delayed; the ammunition was getting short; and, after long and heavy fighting, the whole right wing had been pushed back by the furious and long-continued assaults of the rebel columns.

Until this time, Grant had been in consultation with Foote, on the gunboat, three or four miles distant.

He was now returning, and was met by an aide on full gallop to inform him of the state of affairs. Soon after, he met Gen. C. F. Smith, and decided that the rebels had probably massed almost their whole force for the attack against McClernand and Wallace. The battle was thought to be lost. So it was at Marengo. "I see the battle is lost," said Dessaix to Napoleon as he arrived on the field. "I suppose I can do no more than secure your retreat." — "By no means," replied Napoleon: "the battle is gained. Charge with your columns. The disabled troops will rally in your rear."

Grant immediately ordered Gen. Smith on our left, who had not been engaged, to hold himself ready to advance with his whole force against the rebel right. He also sent back the following note to Foote, who had advised him to fortify, and wait until the fleet could be repaired and return: "A terrible conflict ensued in my absence, which has demoralized a portion of my command. I think the enemy is much more so. If the gunboats do not appear, it will re-assure the enemy, and still further demoralize our troops. Must order a charge to save appearances. I do not expect the gunboats to go into action."

The men were getting weary and exhausted with the fatigue and prodigious efforts of the last few days and nights. Grant always had a theory, that there comes a time like this in every hard-fought battle, when tired nature begins to yield, and that whichever party rallies and attacks at this time wins. But for two or three days to look over a field of a hundred thousand men, and amid the din, roar, and confusion of a battle, to weigh as in the hollow of the hand the rising and falling enthusiasm of the contending hosts, and then, with un-erring judgment, to select the one auspicious moment which leads to victory, — this is given only to the few great soldiers in the world's history. And then the fixed purpose, the unconquerable will to do or die, to scorn the weakness of the flesh, must always be there; and they were there.

It was noticed that the rebels had put on their knap-sacks and haversacks, instead of leaving them in the fort; and some of our troops near Grant spoke of this, and said, " They have come out to stay for a battle of several days."

" Are the haversacks filled, or empty ? " said Grant. No one could answer.

" Examine some of the prisoners," said he.

" They are filled ; they have three days' rations," was the report.

" Nothing is little in the world," said Dr. Johnson, " to him who properly understands it."

As soon as the report was made, Grant said, " Then they are trying to cut their way out : they do not mean to stay and fight. Whoever attacks now wins. They'll be quick if they beat me."

And, dashing his spurs into his horse's flanks, he gal-loped off to Smith's division on the left, occasionally explaining to the officers and men as he passed, " They are whipped ; they are fighting to be allowed to retreat." He explained briefly, that he wished to attack them on their weakened right. It was thus Napoleon on the morning of Austerlitz, in almost the only instance in his life, explained to the French soldiers his plan of attacking the Russian centre on the Heights of Prutzen.

Grant knew well that his bayonets reasoned; that American soldiers could *think* as well as fight, and would understand and appreciate this confidence. He knew the war was a war of ideas; and that the serious, intelligent convictions of men would carry them through a forlorn hope, or into a deadly breach spouting with fire, where the mere martial ardor of a military machine would quail to follow. Hamlet said, " Conscience makes cowards of us all; " but " conscience also makes *heroes* of us all." *

Grant now ordered Smith to advance, at the same time sending word to McClernand and Wallace to close up and be ready to attack. The men rallied; the weary and the laggard in the rear came forward; wounds were forgotten; all caught the spirit of their leader.

Gen. Smith was a veteran soldier: he had followed the stars and stripes through the battles of Mexico to " the halls of the Montezumas." He was a man sixty years old, his hair white as the snow on the ground. As he rode down his line, forming his division for the attack, he was a fine target for the rebel rifles; but the bullets showered unnoticed about him. His column was formed of Lauman's brigade; the Second Iowa infantry having the front, followed by the Seventh, Fourteenth, and Twenty-fifth Indiana. He also told the soldiers what was to be done. This reciprocal confidence between the general and his soldiers was like that of a father and his sons; and the enthusiasm of the soldiers was unbounded. As he took his place to lead the advance, his colors by his side, years seemed to drop from him like a mantle. Those near him said his countenance

* Coleridge.

blazed with the fire of youth: he was young again. Putting his çap on the point of his sword, he flung it toward the rebel intrenchments, and dashed forward into the thickest of the fight. So Marlborough, with a soldier's ardor, flung his marshal's *bâton* over the French lines, sure of recovering it again.

Nothing could withstand the onset. Without firing a gun, they charged directly on the intrenchments, carried them at the point of the bayonet, and forced their way to the summit of a hill, where artillery could be planted, and which was the key to the fort.* Wallace, too, had regained his lost ground, and driven Buckner back to within a hundred and fifty yards of his intrenchments.

Night now settled down on the field, with a battle undecided. Smith, maintaining his commanding position, in vain protested that one half-hour more of daylight would give us the victory.

How many men, on how many battle-fields, have coveted the power of Joshua of old, — to stay the sun in the heavens!

Both parties had now been nearly four days and nights under arms, and with almost continuous fighting. Some even had slept as they stood in line of battle, as McDowell, completely overcome, had dropped to sleep while writing in the telegraph-office his despatch to Washington after the first battle of Bull Run.

And now the living lay down with the wounded, the dying, and the dead. Smith, wrapped in his cloak, rested among his men on the frozen ground.

Grant found shelter in a negro hut. Here, during

* McPherson's Report.

the night, a fugitive slave who had escaped through the rebel lines made his way to him to tell him that the enemy were retreating across the river, and desired to give him an account of their condition and the position of their forces. Grant was still under Halleck. Orders No. 3 and No. 13 were his military law: "Unauthorized persons must not be admitted within our lines." Should Grant admit the man, and talk with him, or read Order No. 3, call the guard, and have him arrested and sent back to his owner? One thing was not then, and is not now, generally known. When the war opened, Mrs. Grant, through her father, owned three slaves in Missouri. Grant privately, without talk, in his own right, issued three "emancipation proclamations," — one to each slave, telling them to go free. This man was unauthorized by Order No. 3 to go to headquarters; but he was authorized to go by a "higher law," and that was his hatred of slavery and the love of freedom which God has planted in the soul of every human being. When Nelson, in the battle of Copenhagen, was told that his commander had signalled for him to take his ship out of action, he put his spyglass to his blind eye, and said, "I don't see it: fire away!" Then, turning to an officer, he said, "I have a right to be blind sometimes." So Grant did not read or obey Order No. 3, but acted like a man of common sense, and received the fugitive, listened to his story, and questioned him carefully. One officer suggested that perhaps the fellow was lying, and had been sent to entrap Grant in some manner; but the man said, —

"You may whip me, shoot me, cut me to pieces, if it ain't as I tells you."

Within the fort a strange scene was enacting. Floyd called a council of war. The midnight conclave were to decide whether they should surrender, or renew the battle in the morning. Smith, at the south-west angle of the fort, could take other intrenchments in reverse. Buckner, opposite Smith's division, said he could not withstand any attack half an hour. It was evident they must surrender; but now Floyd declared that he would not do this.

History delights to tell us of the wounded Cambrone at Waterloo, who shouted, in defeat, "The Guard dies, but never surrenders!" "I can desert, but not surrender!" would have been the more appropriate exclamation of Floyd. This was a becoming episode in Floyd's history. He had been Secretary of War under James Buchanan, and had been guilty of a "financial irregularity," by which the government had lost nearly nine hundred thousand dollars, — an operation for which, in England, he would have been furnished with a passage to Botany Bay at government expense ; but, that Gov. Floyd might rival the citizens of that celebrated colony, he united treason to theft, and now added to these desertion to the flag he had chosen and the soldiers who had fought by his side.

Gen. Pillow followed his example ; both declaring that "personal reasons controlled them;" meaning, probably, the fear that they would be hung if they fell into the hands of the United States. Floyd turned his command over to Pillow, and Pillow to Gen. Buckner, who, like a soldier, had determined to share the fate of his men. He immediately sent a note in diplomatic style to Grant, suggesting an armistice. Without waiting an answer, Floyd and Pillow stole out in the dark, hoping to get on board a boat, unknown to the soldiers; but the men had rumors of what their commanders were doing, and now crowded to the landing, where they greeted them with hisses and curses loud and deep.*

A while after, with the first streak of daylight, as Grant was preparing to attack, a white flag was seen flying from the ramparts of Fort Donelson; and Grant received the following letter under a flag of truce: —

HEADQUARTERS, FORT DONELSON, Feb. 18, 1862.

SIR, — In consideration of all the circumstances governing the present situation of affairs at this station, I propose to the commanding officer of the Federal forces the appointment of commissioners to agree upon terms of capitulation of the forces I hold under my command; and, in that view, suggest an armistice until twelve o'clock to-day.

S. B. BUCKNER, *Brig.-Gen. C. S. A.*

To Brig.-Gen. GRANT, commanding U. S. Forces, Fort Donelson.

But Grant had learned during the night the true state of affairs, and instantly replied as follows: —

HEADQUARTERS, ARMY IN THE FIELD,
CAMP NEAR DONELSON, Feb. 14, 1862.

To Gen. S. B. BUCKNER, Confederate Army, —

Yours of this date, proposing an armistice, and appointment of commissioners to settle terms of capitulation, is just received. No

---

* " Such was the want of all order and discipline by this time on shore, that a wild rush was made at the boat, which the captain said would swamp her unless he pushed off immediately. This was done; and about sunrise, the boat on which I was — the other having gone — left the shore. By this precise mode I effected my escape; and, after leaving the wharf, the *department will be pleased to hear that I encountered no dangers whatever from the enemy.*" — *Floyd's Report.*

terms other than *an unconditional and immediate surrender* can be accepted. *I propose to move immediately upon your works.*

I am, sir, very respectfully your obedient servant,

U. S. Grant, *Brig.-Gen. U. S. A. commanding.*

Gen. Buckner accepted these terms in the following reply : —

Headquarters, Dover, Tenn., Feb. 15, 1862.

To Brig.-Gen. U. S. Grant, U. S. A.

Sir, — The distribution of forces under my command incident to an unexpected change of commanders, and the overwhelming force under your command, compel me, notwithstanding the brilliant success of the Confederate arms yesterday, to accept the ungenerous and unchivalrous terms which you propose.

I am, sir, your very obedient servant,

S. B. Buckner, *Brig.-Gen. C. S. A.*

The results of this victory were sixty-five guns, seventeen thousand six hundred small-arms, nearly fifteen thousand soldiers, with horses, mules, and army supplies. Our loss was about two thousand men.

After the surrender, up went the stars and stripes, greeted by tumultuous cheers ; and the sun shone bright and warm as if to illumine the victory.

As the different divisions marched into the works, their regimental banners from different States, the music, the loud huzzas, the proud steps of the victorious soldiers, made one of the grand historic pictures of the war.

Gen. Grant made his headquarters upon a boat which happened to have the significant name of " New Uncle Sam ; " and it was in the cabin of this steamer that the formal surrender was made.

The interview between Grant and Buckner was social. They had been classmates at West Point. Grant stated that he had no desire to humiliate the prisoners; that the officers might retain their side-arms, but horses and public property must be given up. Gen. Buckner acknowledged that it had been the intention of those in command to cut their way out; but they were defeated by Grant's movements.

When the transports were about to leave for the North with the rebel prisoners, Gen. Buckner asked Gen. Grant to visit his men, and, as they crowded around, told them that their victor had treated them with magnanimity and kindness.

After a while, at a signal from Com. Foote, the boat with Gen. Grant and staff on board, followed by the gunboat " Flotilla," steamed up past the fort to Dover, all the guns firing the national salute.

Gen. Grant issued the following congratulatory order to his troops : —

HEADQUARTERS, DISTRICT OF WEST TENNESSEE,
FORT DONELSON, Feb. 14, 1862.

The general commanding takes great pleasure in congratulating the troops of this command for the triumph over rebellion, gained by their valor, on the 13th, 14th, and 15th instant.

For four successive nights, without shelter, during the most inclement weather known in this latitude, they faced an enemy in large force, in a position chosen by himself. Though strongly fortified by nature, all the additional safeguards suggested by science were added. Without a murmur this was borne; prepared at all times to receive an attack, and with continuous skirmishing by day, resulting, ultimately, in forcing the enemy to surrender without conditions.

The victory achieved is not only great in the effect it will have in breaking down rebellion, but has secured the greatest number of prisoners of war ever taken in any battle on this continent.

Fort Donelson will hereafter be marked in capitals on the map of our united country; and the men who fought the battle will live in the memory of a grateful people.

U. S. Grant, *Brig.-Gen. commanding.*

Many interesting and amusing scenes occurred. It was here, on one of the transports laden with prisoners, that probably the first slaveholders' objection to reconstruction was made. A tall, raw-boned, red-haired, blustering Mississippi captain had found that the hands on board the boat would not take his secesh paper for whiskey or food. When he could not control himself any longer, he rushed up to a Northern man, a stranger, who was conversing near him, and said, "Look here: this is a d——d pretty business. They talk of reconstructing the Union, and begin by rejecting our money; and I can get nothing to eat." * It was evident to his mind that reconstruction must stop.

Buckner, on meeting Smith, congratulated him on his splendid charge. "Yes," said the old soldier, "it was well done, considering how small a force I had. But no congratulations are due to me: I simply obeyed orders."

On the arrival of the news at Washington, Grant was immediately nominated as a major-general, and confirmed by the Senate the same day; his commission being dated on the 16th, the day of the surrender of Fort Donelson.

Mr. Stanton, Secretary of War, published a letter, in which he spoke of the victory in the following

---

* C. C. Coffin.

terms : " We may well rejoice at the recent victories ;
for they teach us that battles are to be won now, and by
us, in the same and only manner that they were ever
won by any people, or in any age, since the days of
Joshua, — by boldly pursuing and striking the foe.
What, under the blessings of Providence, I conceive
to be the true organization of victory and military
combination to end this war, was declared in a few
words by Gen. Grant's message to Gen. Buckner, — '*I
propose to move immediately upon your works.*' "

Grant, who had spoken in the highest terms in his
special report of " the brilliant charge of Gen. Smith,"
recommended ' him also for promotion to a · major-
generalcy ; and he was accordingly appointed, and
confirmed by the Senate.

Gen. Smith died in about two months after the capture of Donelson, from disease contracted in the Mexican War and the exposures of this campaign. It
illustrates the characters of both Gen. Grant and Gen.
Smith to mention that Gen. Smith was commandant
at West Point when Grant was a cadet. He was also
so much Grant's senior in years, that, when the latter
found Gen. Smith under his command, he felt a little
delicacy in issuing orders to his old instructor. Smith
at once perceived this ; and, with the instinct of the
gentleman and the soldier, said to Gen. Grant, " Let
nothing in our past relations embarrass you in issuing
to me any orders you think best : I am a soldier, and
know my duty."

" Thus," says Wordsworth, " these two things, con-
tradictory as they seem, must go together, — manly
dependence and manly independence."

While these events were transpiring in camp, how different was the scene at the same hour in the peaceful cities and villages of the North! It was a Sabbath morning when Fort Donelson surrendered; the church-bells were ringing: and thousands of fathers, mothers, sisters, and brothers, were remembering and praying for their loved ones, far away on the tented field; little thinking, that, in a few hours, their cheeks would blanch and their hearts sicken at the tidings that the dear ones would come home no more. Already, on the banks of the Cumberland, they were sleeping the sleep of the brave.

> " There are glad hearts and sad hearts
>   By millions to-day,
>   As over the wires the magical fires
> Are flashing the tidings of Donelson's fray, —
>   Hearts swelling with rapture
>   For Donelson's capture,
>   Hearts breaking with aching
>   For Donelson's slain."

4

CHAPTER V.

BATTLE OF SHILOH.

THE capture of Fort Donelson and its troops produced a great effect throughout the whole country. It was the largest number of soldiers ever captured in any battle on the continent, and first drew the attention of the nation to Gen. Grant as the "coming man."

The North welcomed the victory as establishing a new era in the war, — the era of active, offensive, persistent attack. Grant's words, "I propose to move immediately on your works," were everywhere quoted, and became a watchword throughout the country.

The Cumberland and Tennessee Rivers were opened; Nashville, the capital of Tennessee, fell; Columbus was abandoned; Bowling Green evacuated; and the States of Kentucky and Tennessee were rescued from the rebel armies.

While preparing for the attack on Fort Donelson, Grant had asked Sherman, with whom he was not then on any terms of special intimacy, for troops and supplies. Sherman forwarded them with great vigor, and, although the senior officer, wrote to Grant as follows: "I will do every thing in my power to hurry forward your re-enforcements and supplies; and, if I could be of service myself, would gladly come without making any question of rank with you or Gen. Smith."

These two distinguished men, thus brought together, ever after acted in entire harmony; no envy, no jealousy, except for the honor of each other. Their natures were different, but well formed to act together. Their official relations ripened into a personal friendship, never yet interrupted, and fortunate alike for their own fame and their country's glory.

Gen. Grant was assigned to the district of West Tennessee, and on the 23d of February issued the following order : —

The major-general commanding this department desires to impress upon all officers the importance of preserving good order and discipline among these troops and the armies of the West during their advance into Tennessee and the Southern States.

Let us show to our fellow-citizens of these States that we come merely to crush out this rebellion, and to restore to them peace and the benefits of the Constitution and the Union, of which they have been deprived by selfish and unprincipled leaders. They have been told that we come to oppress and plunder. By our acts we will undeceive them. We will prove to them that we come to restore, not violate, the Constitution and the laws. In restoring to them the glorious flag of the Union, we will assure them that they shall enjoy under its folds the same protection of life and property as in former days.

Soldiers, let no excesses on your part tarnish the glory of our arms. The orders heretofore issued from this department in regard to pillaging, marauding, and the destruction of private property, and the stealing and concealment of slaves, must be strictly enforced. It does not belong to the military to decide upon the relation of master and slave. Such questions must be settled by the civil courts. No fugitive slave will, therefore, be admitted within our lines or camps, except when especially ordered by the general commanding. Women and children, merchants, farmers, and all persons not in arms, are to be regarded as non-combatants ; and are not to be molested, either in their persons or property. If, however, they assist and aid the enemy, they become belligerents, and will be treated as such. As they violate the laws of war, they will be made to suffer the penalties of such violation.

Military stores and public property of the enemy must be surrendered ; and any attempt to conceal such property, by fraudulent transfer or otherwise, will be punished. But no private property will be touched, unless by order of the general commanding.

Whenever it becomes necessary, forced contributions for supplies and subsistence for our troops will be made. Such levies will be made as light as possible, and be so distributed as to produce no distress among the people. All property so taken must be receipted fully, and accepted for as heretofore directed.

These orders will be read at the head of every regiment, and all officers are commanded strictly to enforce them.

By command of Major-Gen. Halleck.

W. II. McLean, *Adjutant-General.*

By order of Maj.-Gen. U. S. Grant.

J. A. Rawlins, *A. A. G.*

At this time, a coldness occurred between Gen. Halleck and Gen. Grant, which the former afterwards explained to have been caused partly by the failure of colonels of regiments to report to him on their arrival, and partly from an interruption of telegraphic communication. During the few weeks in which it continued, Gen. Grant submitted to the displeasure of his superior in the best temper and spirit, and telegraphed from day to day as follows : —

"I am not aware of ever having disobeyed any order from your headquarters, — certainly never intended such a thing. . . . In conclusion, I will say that you may rely on my carrying out your instructions in every particular, to the best of my ability. . . . I did all I could to get you returns of the strength of my command. Every move I made was reported daily to your chief of staff, who must have failed to keep you properly posted. I have done my very best to obey orders, and to carry out the interests of the service. If my course is not satisfactory, remove me at once. I do not wish in any way to impede the success of our arms. . . . I do not feel that I have neglected a single duty."

The regimental officers at Fort Henry, on the ground, and appreciating the true state of the case, on the 12th of March presented Gen. Grant with a magnificent sword, the blade of the finest steel, the handle of ivory mounted with gold, with two scabbards, one of polished steel for service, one of gilt for parade, all appropriately inscribed.

On the 17th, Grant established his headquarters at Savannah, on the Tennessee River, a hundred and seventy-five miles south of Nashville, and near the northern corner of Alabama and Mississippi. There were with him Generals McClernand, Wallace, Smith, Hurlbut, and Sherman. Eight miles down the river is Pittsburg Landing; three miles south of it is Shiloh; sixteen miles beyond is Corinth.

When the rebels were compelled to evacuate Columbus, they fortified Corinth, just over the line of the State of Mississippi, east of Memphis, at the junction of the Memphis and Charleston and Mobile and Ohio Railroads. It was one of the most important points in the whole South-west, from Memphis to the Gulf of Mexico. From there a rebel force could advance into Kentucky, cross the Ohio River, and move north. It was the centre of the vast network of railroads in the South-western States.

Gen. Albert Sidney Johnston, one of the ablest, if not the ablest, of the rebel generals, had been placed in command; and rumor gave him from fifty to a hundred thousand troops. With him were Beauregard, Polk, Hardee, and Breckinridge. He was near the cotton States, the hot-bed of secession, in a region whose resources were then untouched by the war.

Sherman and Hurlbut were at Shiloh; Wallace at Crump's Landing, five miles below. This was their position when Grant arrived. Within an hour, he issued orders for them to concentrate; and McClernand and Smith were moving up to Pittsburg Landing. Grant remained for a few days to superintend the forwarding of supplies and re-enforcements. When his arrangements were made to move his headquarters to Pittsburg Landing, Gen. Buell, who was advancing from Nashville, telegraphed him to remain at Savannah, to meet him in consultation April 5.

Grant had apprehended an early movement by Johnston, but was ordered not to bring on a general engagement until Buell should arrive.

On the 3d and 4th, there was skirmishing on Sherman's front; but he thought there would be no battle immediately. Grant visited him on the 4th, and agreed in his opinion. It was in returning at night from this visit that Grant's horse slipped on a log, and fell on his rider, injuring him so severely that he did not recover for some time. This accident is said to have originated the slanders in regard to Grant's habits. Both Grant and Sherman were in error. But the skirmishing required watchfulness. Grant ordered W. H. L. Wallace to hold himself ready to support Lewis Wallace, and said, —

"Should you find danger of this sort, re-enforce him at once with your entire divisi

To Sherman he wrote, —

"Information just received would indicate that the enemy are sending a force to Purdy.

.   .   .   .

" I should advise, therefore, that you advise your advance guards to keep a sharp lookout for any movement in that direction ; and, should such a thing be attempted, give all the support of your division, and Gen. Hurlbut's, if necessary."

To Halleck, on the 5th, he wrote, —

" Our outposts had been attacked by the enemy, apparently in considerable force. I immediately went up, but found all quiet. . . . I have scarcely the faintest idea of an attack (general one) being made upon us, *but will be prepared should such a thing take place.*"

The field of Shiloh was bounded east by the Tennessee River, west by Owl Creek, north by Snake Creek, and south by Lick Creek, and was about three miles in area between the boundary-lines. The enemy advanced from the south.

Johnston's force comprised about seventy thousand men. This was stated by all the prisoners, spies, and deserters. Beauregard acknowledged to have had over forty-three thousand after the defeat. The whole Union army was about thirty thousand. Buell was ordered to re-enforce Grant from Nashville with forty thousand men, and was hourly expected.

Sherman was in front with Prentiss and Stuart ; McClernand was partly behind Sherman, in a diagonal line, the left of which extended between Sherman and Prentiss ; Hurlbut was some distance in the rear of Prentiss, toward Pittsburg Landing. This was the position of affairs, Sunday morning, April 6.

Grant was at Savannah, waiting for Buell. Buell was a *slow* man, a good officer when he arrived, a good tactician, handled his men in fine style on the field; but he had not learned the value of *time* in war. He ordered the divisions of his army to move six miles apart. There are men who are always *late*. They were late at school, late at their wedding, late in their business appointments, late at the cars, late at their meals; in a word, behind time on all occasions, private and public. They can be honest in all things but the time and patience of others; and that they constantly pilfer. Buell was one of this class.

The rebels knew this; and they planned to advance and crush Grant with his little army before Buell arrived, and then crush Buell. Sabbath morning, Grant's horse stood saddled at the door of his tent; and he was about starting to see if he could not find Buell, and hurry him up, when he heard heavy firing in the direction of Shiloh. The first few guns told him the story, and he instantly started the following note to Buell: —

"Heavy firing is heard up the river, indicating plainly that an attack has been made upon our most advanced positions. I have been looking for this, but did not believe the attack could be made before Monday or Tuesday. This necessitates my joining the forces up the river, instead of meeting you to-day, as I had contemplated. I have directed Gen. Wilson to move to the river with his division. He can march to opposite Pittsburg."

He stopped on his way at Crump's Landing, and told Lewis Wallace that a battle had begun. He then rode to Sherman's headquarters, where he arrived about eight o'clock.

The night previous, Johnston had moved up in front

of Sherman, with double guards in his own front, ordered to shoot any man who attempted to pass; and at
early day had precipitated his whole army upon the
two feeble divisions of Sherman and Prentiss. But
Sherman was there, and during the day showed that he
was an army in himself.

In the morning, Beaureguard promised his cavalry
that "they should water their horses in the Tennessee
before sunset." The Cossacks, on leaving Russia,
threatened that theirs should "drink of the Seine, beneath the windows of the Tuileries." The Cossacks
kept their word.

Our troops were many of them raw, and had never
been under fire. Some even had gone out without
cartridges, and early fell back against the overwhelming
odds. This alarmed others: a panic ensued; and five
or six thousand men began falling back towards the
landing. Sherman and Prentiss did all that men could
do, but without avail. Sherman was shot in the hand;
but, winding a handkerchief about the wound, he rode
on. His horse was shot under him: he jumped on another, and continued his efforts to rally and re-form the
troops.

As Grant hurried to the front, he encountered the
fugitives, and was everywhere told, "We are beaten!
we are beaten!" "Our regiment is cut to pieces!"
"The battle is lost!" But he did not see it. No.
Fate seemed determined that Grant should be at a distance when his great battles began, — on duty, it is true,
but absent, as if to show what the addition of one man
to a hundred thousand amounts to. Wellington said,
"I consider the presence of Napoleon on any battle-

field equal to a re-enforcement of forty thousand troops." Often during the war there were calls for two and three hundred thousand men. After a while, it came to be seen that there was only *one* man more wanted.

Grant made his way to the front, where he found Sherman riding about among rifle-balls, cannon-shot, and shells, as if he bore a charmed life. Wherever the shot fell the fastest and the thickest, there was Sherman. He was untiring in his efforts; cool, daring, and full of fight.

Grant congratulated him on the stand he had made: things looked badly; but the army was not to be whipped. Grant, before starting, had thoughtfully given orders to forward all day supplies of ammunition. Messengers were sent again and again to the commanders in the rear to come up. He endeavored during the forenoon to re-form the broken regiments, to put the disorganized troops into position. Meanwhile the rebels, greatly encouraged by their first success, steadily advanced. The conflict was deadly, and raged with increasing fury. It recalled Lannes' description of the battle of Montebello: "I could hear the bones crash in my division like glass in a hail-storm."

At half-past four, in the afternoon, our forces had been driven to within half a mile of the landing. Grant listened for Buell's guns. About this time, Gen. Buell, who had heard the firing at a great distance, had ridden on with his staff in advance of his army, and reached the field. Seeing the desperate state of affairs, he asked Grant, —

"What preparations have you made to secure your retreat, general?"

"We shall not retreat, sir."

"But it is possible," added Buell; "and a prudent general always provides for contingencies."

"Well, there are the boats," said Grant.

"The boats!" said Buell. "But they will not hold over ten thousand men, and we have thirty thousand."

"They will hold more than we shall retreat with. We shall whip them yet," was Grant's characteristic reply.

Hurlbut's and W. H. L. Wallace's commands fought with stubborn valor. They could be forced back slowly by the rebel host; but they covered the ground with their own and the enemy's dead as they receded; and among them, at last, Wallace himself fell.

Late in the afternoon, when all seemed lost, on a ravine not far from the landing, Col. Webster of Grant's staff, a splendid artillery-officer, collected a battery of twenty-two guns in a semicircle, which the rebels did not silence. Gunners were called for; and a surgeon of one of the Missouri regiments, Dr. Cornyn, thought his professional experience in surgery was no disqualification, and insisted on taking a place at the guns.

Rebel batteries were moved up, and opened fire; but now the gunboats " Tyler " and " Lexington " joined in the fight with 7-inch shell and 64-pound shot. Buell arrived, but too late.

At this time, Beauregard telegraphed to Richmond as follows : —

We have this morning attacked the enemy in strong position in front of Pittsburg; and after a severe battle of ten hours, thanks to Almighty God! gained a complete victory, driving the enemy from every position.

The loss on both sides is heavy, including our commander-in-chief, Gen. Albert Sidney Johnston, who fell, gallantly leading his troops into the thickest of the fight.

G. T. BEAUREGARD, *General commanding.*

It was at this time that Grant made about the only attempt at rhyme of which we have any record. The excellent staff-surgeon, Dr. Hewitt, seeing the vast numbers of the wounded, was disposed to take a desponding view, and expressed a belief that the enemy would drive us. Grant tried to rally those about him into good spirits, and said, —

> " Major Hewitt
>   Says they can do it :
> General Grant
>   Says they can't ! "

It was then, too, that Grant, as Sherman afterwards related,* told him the story of Donelson, of the disasters early in the day ; and expounded to Sherman, no doubt an easy convert, his ever-favorite theory of the mutual exhaustion of both armies in every great battle, when, by some vast power, you must rouse your own, and go in to triumph. He thought the rebels were about in the right condition then, and, if it were not night, should attack ; but gave orders that they " *should be attacked at daylight.*"

It must be owned, it is difficult to defeat such a man : because he assumes that you will fight hard and fight long; that both armies will do all that mortal men can be expected to do ; but that then he will select a moment when his own shall do something more. But that he,

* Sherman's Letter to the Army and Navy Gazette.

or those following him, shall be the party to fail, he never believes. There are men in whom this would seem to be conceit and over-weening self-confidence ; but there is a class of men in whom it is the natural fruit of conscious power. Be careful how you encounter them.

" Who sails with me comes to shore," said Cæsar.

. " You never were on a boat with me before, I think," said Jackson to a nervous gentleman on a rickety steamer in a dangerous storm.

It had been a terrible battle, one of the most bloody that occurred in the war. Gen. Johnston, the rebel leader, had been killed, but, with the intrepidity of the American soldier, sat motionless on his horse after he was shot, not moving until he was lifted out of his saddle. Beauregard was in command. W. H. L. Wallace was mortally wounded Prentiss was captured with two thousand men. Grant had been struck, but not injured ; and the wounded, the dying, and the dead, of both armies, covered the field to the number of about twenty thousand men. The Federal camp was in possession of the enemy.

The shells from the gunboats, dropping into the woods during the night, set them on fire ; and the sufferings of the helpless wounded were terrible, and would have been aggravated but for the copious rain, which partly quenched the fire, and mitigated their anguish.

Few except eye-witnesses can form a conception of the sufferings of a battle-field. " What a glorious sight must be a great victory! " said a lady to Wellington. " The saddest sight in the world, madam, except a defeat," was the reply.

It is not generally known, that, among the wounded, the most acute anguish is from thirst. A man will live longer without food than without water. Water is essential to all vital existence, except that of mosses. Indeed, the ancients believed that water was the parent of all things.*

The torture of thirst is always increased tenfold by the loss of blood. And these poor beings, unable to move, were compelled to lie all night: sometimes the flames were crackling about them; sometimes they would throw their heads back, and thrust out their tongues, hoping to catch a few drops of the falling rain. Here was a headless body; there was a disembowelled corpse; near would be a man weakly struggling to

* This theory was partly drawn from the Mosaic account of the creation. The same is taught in the Koran. And Milton, in "Paradise Lost," accepting this belief, writes, —

> " On the watery calm
> His brooding wings the Spirit of God outspread,
> And vital virtue infused, and vital warmth,
> Throughout the fluid mass."

It was chosen in the parable to represent with most power to the minds of men the unutterable torture of the lost: "Let him dip the tip of his finger in water, and cool my tongue." It was the only bodily suffering which extorted utterance amid the agonies of the crucifixion, — "I thirst;" and the cruel refusal to mitigate it was all that was needed to wring from the convulsed lips of the dying, "It is finished." Children have remembered through life a glass of water given them on some occasion when enduring extreme thirst; and invalids nursed in homes of comfort and luxury have described for years the sensation of cold water, given to them when burning and parched with fever, rendering literally as well as poetically true the lines of Talfourd : —

> " Its draught
> Of cool refreshment, drained by fevered lips,
> Will give a shock of pleasure to the frame
> More exquisite than when nectarian juice
> Renews the life of joy in happiest hours."

free himself from a pile of corpses. Men, horses, mules, mingled in every form of mutilation; the shells screeching and the cannon-balls flying above them, the flames threatening to burn them alive. At times, the field seeming to be a bed of fire, except where drowned with pools of blood, — friends unable to reach them. And so those who survived wore the long hours of the night away. A vast field of carnage and woe! If angels weep, there were tears in heaven. And this was war, but only one scene in a war made and continued for four years, that a few men might buy and sell human beings.

But, when the morning dawned, these brave men again welcomed the old flag with cheers as they saw the advancing re-enforcements of Buell's divisions, and regiment after regiment marched into position for the final struggle.

CHAPTER VI.

TOWARD morning, Gen. Grant lay down on the ground in the storm, with a log for his pillow, and " slept soundly." Thus Alexander slept on the night before the battle of Arbela ; so Condé slept on the eve of the battle of Rocroi ; so Napoleon slept on the field of Bautzen.

The talent for sleeping soundly when great events are impending is not one of the least elements of success. The power of going without sleep, or of commanding it when needed, which some men possess, is a great gift. That commander is more to be dreaded who comes to the field with all the energies of his body and mind restored by refreshing sleep, than the nervous, excitable man who is jaded out with restlessness and anxiety. The affairs of life look very differently in the morning to the man who has slept soundly than they do to the man who has tossed in feverish worry. Success in life is often as much an affair of the body as the mind.*

* " As a torch gives a better light, a sweeter smell, according to the matter it is made of, so doth our soul perform all her actions, better or worse, as her organs are disposed ; or, as wine savors of the cask wherein it is kept, the soul receives a tincture from the body through which it works." — *Burton's Anatomy of Melancholy.*

During the night, some of Buell's men had crossed over the river in the rain : and the line now had Lewis Wallace on the right; then Sherman, McClernand, Hurlbut, with the heroes of Fort Donelson; and McCook, Crittenden, and Nelson, on the left. Grant ordered an attack at daylight, on Monday the 7th, along his whole line, as if there had been no fighting for three months. The ball was opened by Nelson's division, which soon drew upon itself the fire of almost the whole rebel force. His artillery not having come up, his men suffered severely from the rebel batteries, until silenced by those of Capts. Mendenhall and Terrill, whom Grant sent to Nelson's support. Opposite Wallace was the famous Crescent Regiment from New Orleans, and the Washington Artillery of Manassas renown.

Beauregard could be seen riding in front, and exciting them to the utmost.

Sherman now steadily pressed forward to a point about fifteen hundred feet east of Shiloh Church, from which he had been driven on Sunday morning, and where Beauregard slept on Sunday night. Here the rebel army was plainly seen re-forming, regimental colors flying, and bands playing. A rebel battery was pounding grape and canister into our forces with terrible effect. Two brigades, under T. Kirby Smith and Rousseau, charged, and carried it at the point of the bayonet.

By two o'clock, Grant had driven the enemy, all the while fighting stubbornly, nearly five miles beyond his own line of battle on Sunday. An "impressed New-Yorker," who was with the Confederate army, wrote,—

· " No heroism of officers or men could avail to stay the advance of the Federal troops."

Late in the afternoon, Grant, standing on a little knoll, saw the First Ohio marching to another portion of the field. One of our regiments, in line of battle, had been so thinned and weakened, that it was evident that it must give way soon, although fighting to drive the enemy from one of the last important positions which ·they held. Grant saw the time for the final blow had come : he instantly halted the regiment, and showed himself to the men, who received him with ringing cheers. He, drawing his sword, placed himself at their head, and shouting, " Now's the time to drive them ! " led them across the field, while the cannon-balls were falling like hail-stones around him. The enfeebled regiment, seeing the determined gallantry of their leader, closed up, joined in the charge as if just arrived on the field, and swept the enemy from their last stronghold.

The rebels were now evidently retreating. Grant, like Blucher, was anxious to send "the last man and the last gun after them." But it was represented to him that the roads were almost impassable, and that the condition of the men was such that some rest was absolutely indispensable. After twenty hours' fighting, he reluctantly yielded to these representations for a few hours of repose. They encamped on the field from which they had first been driven. Early the next morning, however, cavalry were sent out on the road to Corinth to follow the retreating army. They found the route strewn with haversacks, muskets, blankets, and all the evidences of a flying foe.

Grant's loss had been about twelve thousand. Beauregard admitted his to be about eleven thousand; but those who buried the rebel dead estimated his loss far larger, — some even as high as twenty thousand.

The battle was mainly decided at night, on Sunday, when our forces repulsed the last rebel assault at the ravine.

Beauregard, in his report of Sunday's battle, says, " Our troops fought bravely, but with the want of that animation and spirit which characterized them the preceding day."

The slaughter on both sides was terrific. Sherman described it as the most dreadful which he saw in the war. Grant says he only saw its equal in the Wilderness. In some divisions, the killed and wounded were thirty per cent of the numbers who went into the action. Regiments, in some instances, were commanded by lieutenants, and brigades by majors.

Yet the determination and endurance were truly wonderful. A ball was extracted from the brain of one soldier, who, three days after, was on duty with the bullet in his pocket. A rifle-ball passed through the head of a member of the First Missouri Artillery without killing him.*

The battle-field and the dead were in the possession of the victors.

Gen Grant issued the following congratulatory order : —

HEADQUARTERS, DISTRICT OF WEST TENNESSEE,
PITTSBURG, April 8, 1862.

GENERAL ORDERS, No. 34.

The general commanding congratulates the troops who so gallantly maintained their position, repulsed and routed a numerically

---

* Surgical Reports.

superior force of the enemy, composed of the flower of the Southern army, commanded by their ablest generals, and fought by them with all the desperation of despair.

In numbers engaged, no such contest ever took place on this continent; in importance of result, but few such have taken place in the history of the world.

Whilst congratulating the brave and gallant soldiers, it becomes the duty of the general commanding to make special notice of the brave wounded and those killed on the field. Whilst they leave friends and relations to mourn their loss, they have won a nation to gratitude, and undying laurels not to be forgotten by future generations, who will enjoy the blessings of the best government the sun ever shone upon, preserved by their valor.

By command of Major-Gen. GRANT.

JOHN A. RAWLINS, *A. A. G.*

Of Gen. Sherman he said in his official report, " I was greatly indebted for his promptness in forwarding to me, during the siege of Fort Donelson, re-enforcements and supplies from Paducah. At the battle of Shiloh, on the first day, he held with raw troops the key-point to the landing. To his individual efforts I am indebted for the success of that battle. Twice hit, and several (I think three) horses shot under him, on that day, he maintained his position with raw troops. It is no disparagement to any other officer to say that I do not believe that there was another division commander in the field who had the skill and experience to have done it."

Tuesday morning, Beauregard asked permission to bury his dead, as follows: —

HEADQUARTERS, DEPARTMENT OF MISSISSIPPI,
. MONTEREY, April 8, 1862.

SIR, — At the close of the conflict yesterday, my forces being exhausted by the extraordinary length of the time during which they were engaged with yours on that and the preceding day, and it being apparent that you had received re-enforcements, I felt it to be my duty to withdraw my troops from the immediate scene of the conflict. Under these circumstances, in accordance with the usages of war, I shall transmit this, under a flag of truce, to ask permission to send a mounted party to the battle-field of Shiloh for the purpose of giving decent interment to my dead. Certain gentlemen wishing to avail themselves of this opportunity to remove the remains of their sons and friends, I must request for them the privilege of accompanying the burial-party; and in this connection I deem it proper to say, I am asking what I have extended to your own countrymen under similar circumstances.

Respectfully, general, your obedient servant,

P. G. T. Beauregard, *General commanding.*

To Major-Gen. U. S. Grant, commanding U. S. Forces, Pittsburg.

Grant, in reply, sent the following: —

Headquarters, Army in the Field,
Pittsburg, April 9, 1862.

To Gen. P. G. T. Beauregard, Commanding Confederate Army on Mississippi, Monterey, Tenn., —

Your despatch of yesterday is just received. Owing to the warmth of the weather, I deemed it advisable to have the dead of both parties buried immediately. Heavy details were made for this purpose, and it is now accomplished. There cannot, therefore, be any necessity of admitting within our lines the parties you desired to send, on the grounds asked. I shall always be glad to extend any courtesy consistent with duty, and especially so when dictated by humanity.

I am, general, respectfully your obedient servant,

U. S. Grant, *Major-General commanding.*

The immense numbers wounded and slain during these two days called forth the beneficent operations of the Sanitary Commission, which were continued throughout the war on a gigantic scale. Steamers crowded with physicians and nurses, and loaded with all necessaries and delicacies for the sick, were immediately despatched to the scene of battle, and every effort made to mitigate the sufferings of the wounded.

This commission was one of the wonderful demonstrations of the war, and received Gen. Grant's earnest support and co-operation. The civilization and Christianity of Europe had for centuries beheld contending hosts march out and deluge the earth with their blood; but the care of the wounded was restricted to the army officials, and such limited aid as they could render. It was reserved for the people of America to exhibit to the world the most majestic proof of love and devotion to their country; giving a million and a half of men to its service; then following in the wake of its armies with thousands of volunteer surgeons, physicians, and nurses, — women and men bountifully supplied with every comfort and luxury of the sick-chamber, eager to dress the wounded, care for the sick, write messages of love for the helpless, pray with the dying, — shrinking from no office that poor humanity could need; and, when all was over, tenderly embalming and forwarding their lifeless remains to the homes they had left. Such a people could not be conquered.

Sherman said, "It was necessary that a combat fierce and bitter, to test the manhood of the two armies, should come off; and that was as good a place as any." The battle made the North and South better acquainted with the character of the Northern and Southern soldiers. It showed the North that the Southern soldier who could brag could also fight; it showed the South that the Northern soldier could " stand, and, having done all, stand." There was less talk after that of " one

Southerner whipping five Yankees,"—the bluster with which the rebels opened the war. They found that the "mudsills" of the North, as Senator Hammond of South Carolina called the men who held the plough and handled the trowel, shoved the jackplane and swung the sledge, did not fear in battle the face of animated dust. The Southern soldier had the ardor, the vehemence, the enthusiasm, the self-assertion, of the French,—the same which carried the French cavalry up to the enemy's ranks until they rattled their sabres upon their muskets. They came on with terrific "yells," which seemed to demand a victory as a thing of course; but they had not the "hold-on,"—the grip which yields only to death itself. They wanted to carry every thing with a dash, and, if resisted firmly, after a while gave way.

The Northern soldiers did not "yell,"—they "cheered," and oftener *after* victory than before. Like the Spartans of old, who did not need martial strains to excite them, but could march into battle "to the Dorian mood of flutes and soft recorders," the Northern men in making a charge would grit their teeth, compress their lips, slope their bayonets, then silently rush on with a power that swept every thing before it. It was like the Norman and Saxon blood on the battle-fields of Europe. "These English," said Napoleon to Soult on the morning at Waterloo, as he first swept the field with his glass,—"these English: at last we have them!" —"I know them, sire," said Soult, who had been in Spain,—"I know them; and they will die where they stand!" The news of the victory was telegraphed over the country. It was read to both houses of Congress, then in session. Salutes were fired; and everywhere the news was received with great rejoicing.

This battle, or rather the two battles of Shiloh and Pittsburg Landing, were fought April 6 and 7, 1862. They were important in many ways, but not the least in the entire change which they made in the views of the man who was finally to wield the whole force of all the Union armies against the Rebellion. He had believed that the South, after a few defeats, would relinquish the purpose of actually destroying the government, and fastening anarchy upon the whole nation; but that they would use their position to negotiate upon the questions in dispute, and ultimately return to the Union. He was now convinced that he had not fathomed their purpose, and that the words of the secession leader at Washington, as reported by Judge Douglas, were true: "If you give us a sheet of white paper to write our own terms, we will not remain in the Union." He became convinced that the leaders of the Rebellion had "resolved, in the gloomy recesses of minds capacious of such things," to overthrow the liberties of their country, and erect on its ruins a vast empire to extend and perpetuate human slavery. He saw that it was a life-and-death struggle; that the government must exterminate the Rebellion, or be exterminated by it; that, with the capture of forts and the surrender of armies, the slaveholders were not willing to yield the accustomed fruits of victory. Men often mark the progress of our race by battles, sieges, the dismemberment of old and the creation of new empires; but the silent, still birth of a *thought*, an *opinion*, in the mind of a single man, has often shaken the earth with the force of an earthquake.

Grant now formed a belief that it was not by marching and countermarching of armies, by taking Fort

Sumter or Montgomery, by holding this city or blockading that harbor, by "crushing, anaconda strategy,"
such as Scott first recommended, that the Rebellion was
to be put down; but that the Rebellion was in the hearts
and minds of the slaveholders; that its power was with
Lee and the unnumbered bayonets that followed him:
and thereafter his policy was to pursue the rebel armies,
and constantly strike, strike. This opinion he ever after
acted upon, as far as his power went, until the final surrender at Appomattox Court House. He acted on the
doctrine that political metaphysics, armies, slavery, every
thing, should be destroyed which resisted the triumph
of the right. And here was one great secret of his
success where others had failed.

Gen. Halleck, who was at St. Louis, now came down
and took command.

The North claimed a great victory at first; but, very
soon, dissatisfaction was expressed. Gen. Grant, it was
said, "had not properly chosen his battle-field; he should
have had Buell's army on the ground on the first day of
the fighting; his habits were bad, or the army would not
have been driven back to the Landing on Sunday; it
was a defeat which Buell only prevented from becoming
a rout." Such were some of the wise criticisms made.

Gen. Halleck, after investigating the facts, issued an
order, thanking Gen. Grant and Gen. Buell, their officers
and men, "for the bravery and endurance with which
they sustained the general attacks of the enemy on the
5th, and for the heroic manner in which, on the 7th,
they defeated and routed the entire rebel army."

In regard to the selection of the field, Gen. Sherman
wrote as follows: —

"I will avail myself of this occasion to correct another very common mistake in attributing to Gen. Grant the selection of that battle-field. It was chosen by that veteran soldier, Major-Gen. Charles F. Smith, who ordered my division to disembark there, and strike for the Charleston Railroad. It was Gen. Smith who selected that field of battle; and it was well chosen. On any other we surely should have been overwhelmed, as both Lick and Snake Creeks forced the enemy to confine his movements to a direct front attack, which raw troops are better qualified to resist than where the flanks are exposed to a real or chimerical danger. Even the divisions of the army were arranged in that camp by Gen. Smith's order, before Gen. Grant succeeded him to the command of all the forces up the Tennessee. If there were any error in putting that army on the west side of the Tennessee, exposed to the superior force of the enemy, also assembling at Corinth, the mistake was not Gen. Grant's; but there was *no* mistake."

Hon. E. B. Washburne, member of Congress from Illinois, thus noticed the attacks on Gen. Grant in an able speech in the House of Representatives, May 2, 1862:—

"But there is a more grievous suggestion touching the general's habits. It is a suggestion that has infused itself into the public mind everywhere. There never was a more cruel and atrocious slander upon a brave and a noble-minded man. There is no more temperate man in the army than Gen. Grant. He never indulges in the use of intoxicating liquors at all. He is an example of courage, honor, fortitude, activity, temperance, and modesty; for he is as modest as he is brave and incorruptible. It is almost vain to hope that full justice will ever be done to men who have been thus attacked. Truth is slow upon the heels of falsehood. It has been well said that 'falsehood will travel from Maine to Georgia while truth is putting on its boots.'

"Though living in the same town with myself, Gen. Grant has no political claims on me; for, so far as he is a politician, he belongs to a different party."

It has long been thought very difficult to describe a battle : the man who is with the right wing describes what happened there ; the man who is with the left, what happened there ; and the man with the centre describes something different from either.

In reading what was said of the battles of April 6 and 7, Gen. Grant might adopt as his own the remark which Gen. Taylor, in the latter part of his life, was accustomed to make when the battle of Buena Vista was spoken of: " I used to think I was at Buena Vista. I certainly did the day of the battle ; but I have heard so much about it since, that I often doubt if I ever was there at all."

A member of Gen. Grant's staff, an eye-witness to the cruel injustice which was done in these criticisms, wrote some letters in his defence, and sent them to Gen. Grant's father for publication. One only was published. As soon as the general learned of this, he wrote, asking that no defence should be made. Conscious of having done his duty, and his whole duty, he preferred to bide his time for a just judgment upon his conduct.

CHAPTER VII.

SIEGE OF CORINTH.

GRANT was for an immediate attack: but Halleck decided otherwise; and he determined to advance toward Corinth, where the rebels had concentrated, and lay siege to the place. Gen. Halleck ordered up an immense army to his camp, until a hundred and twenty thousand bayonets could be put in line. It was called the "Grand Army of the Tennessee." Shovels and spades appeared by thousands. He threw up forty miles of intrenchments. Wells were sunk, as if the army itself was besieged. He dragged heavy siege-guns through the mud; he threw up sodded earthworks, all constructed upon the highest principles of military art.

Bomb-proof magazines were carefully built; roads were cut in every direction. He advanced cautiously about two and a half miles a week for six weeks; the enemy, meanwhile, making no attack. They were satisfied as long as they were "let alone."

Gen. Halleck carried out faithfully his Order No. 3. No "unauthorized persons" were allowed within his lines: the stories of fugitive slaves about the movements of Beauregard's army were disbelieved. Corinth was to be approached, besieged, and taken with dignity; and week after week he advanced, moving forward his own camp, now a perfect Sevastopol. Grant was of opinion, meanwhile, that the enemy were dividing their forces, and evacuating Corinth. He examined their works, and became satisfied, that on their extreme left, opposite to or a little west of Sherman's line, was their weakest spot; and that there they could be carried at once by assault. The digging and intrenching, as if besieged, had a depressing effect on the national troops. They had driven the enemy, flushed with victory, from the ravine at Pittsburg Landing, with deadly slaughter, five miles back to Shiloh Church. The enemy were retreating, with every sign of disorder, to Corinth; and the Union army stopped six weeks to intrench, and protect itself from an attack. Grant ventured modestly to express some of these views in the briefest manner to Gen. Halleck, and suggested an attack, which he had urged the morning after the victory at Pittsburg Landing; but Gen. Halleck did not agree in these opinions, and intimated to Gen. Grant that he need not offer his advice unless solicited.

Gen. Grant never intruded his opinions again.

On the last of May, Gen. Halleck was confident that he should be attacked. On the 3d he announced, "There is every indication that the enemy will attack our left this morning;" and his magnificent army, one of the finest seen during the war, was put in line of battle, and waited an attack: but the enemy never came. Halleck had sent Col. Elliott to cut the Mobile and Ohio Railroad on the 27th, in Beauregard's rear. The whole country had watched daily, for weeks, the siege of Corinth, and looked for the capture of Beauregard and his grand army. On the night of the 3d of May, the sentinels heard a great rumbling and rolling of cars in Corinth, and reported it. It continued all night long. Toward morning, loud explosions were heard. What could it all mean? Perhaps re-enforcements were pouring in to the enemy. Halleck said to Sherman, "I cannot explain it;" and ordered him to "advance and feel the enemy, if still in his front." Sherman advanced and advanced; but there was no enemy to "feel." He entered Corinth: it was a deserted town. There were a few worthless tents, some wooden guns, and a few stragglers firing the public buildings; but the enemy had left. It now appeared, that, for nearly a month, the enemy had been planning to leave the place. Orders were issued to move in the direction of Danville and Booneville. The works were formidable in appearance only, and could easily have been carried. Grant at once rode to the rebel left, the point at which he had advised an attack, to ascertain if he had been correct in his judgment; and found that this was the weak point in Beauregard's line, and, if attacked, could have been carried, and the whole army probably captured.

For two or three days, Beauregard had been sending his sick and his most valuable stores toward Mobile, with the greatest part of his ordnance: the troops had gone to the south and west. The magazines and storehouses had been blown up, and were a mass of ruins.

It is not necessary now to censure any one for this result. Gen. Halleck was a military scholar: he was an over-cautious man. He would have all, but venture nothing. The general who will never move an army of a hundred thousand men until every linch-pin of every wagon has been examined and reported to him will never move. Such a body of men will never all be ready. The campaign was ended as far as results were concerned. It had been a campaign of laborious idleness.

Halleck was doubtless acting under the impulse of opinions formed at St. Louis when he first heard of the attack at Shiloh,—that Grant should have been intrenched; and he came down at once, and began intrenching.

On the contrary, Grant had been on the ground all the time: he considered the battle of Shiloh and of Pittsburg Landing as substantially one battle, in which the victory was with him and his troops; that with Buell's army of fresh troops, the rebel army weakened by two days of fighting, our troops should have followed them at once, and destroyed them; that, if·this had been done, the whole campaign in the Valley of the Mississippi could have been terminated in thirty days. Grant's plan was not engineering and mining and counter-mining, but an advance, a battle, and a victory. Subsequent events showed the correctness of this judgment. Beauregard had expected a vigorous pursuit, and had sent to Breckinridge, in command of the rear-guard, " This retreat must not be a rout." As soon as he arrived at Corinth, he telegraphed in cipher to Richmond for re-enforcements, and said, "*If defeated here, we lose the Mississippi Valley, and probably our cause.*" And so it was: in a few days, New Orleans was captured, and Memphis fell. Grant's war policy, in a word, was expressed in his letter to Buckner, "*I propose to move immediately on your works:*" and it is evident there was one man who. agreed with him that this policy would be the most disastrous to the rebel forces; and that was Beauregard. The rebel army was now to be pursued. Grant was there, and Sherman was there; but Buell was sent.

On the 10th of June, he took seventy thousand men, and moved south, toward Booneville. It was a *cautious* man sending a *slow* man in pursuit. Buell had doubtless, too, become inspired with the importance of caution as well as deliberation. He went thirty miles, to Booneville, with his splendid army; and, finding no enemy, threw up lines of defence, and waited for them to attack. It was evident to the soldiers the enemy had fled; but Buell, on whom rested the responsibility, did not perceive this.

After a few days, however, he was compelled to march back to Corinth. The rebels were fifty miles distant by the nearest railroad, and seventy miles by wagon-road; and the campaign was ended. The opinion was freely expressed by military men, that, if Gen. Halleck had remained in St. Louis, Grant would have captured Beauregard and his whole army.

On the 17th of July, Halleck was called to Washington as commander-in-chief, and Grant was left in command. Soon after, four divisions of his army were ordered to join Buell, towards Chattanooga.

Grant at once strengthened and improved the works which Beauregard had left.

CHAPTER VIII.

BATTLE OF IUKA. — BATTLE OF CORINTH.

A RE-ORGANIZATION of military departments now gave to Gen. Grant the Department of West Tennessee, stretching from the west bank of the Mississippi to the west shores of the Tennessee. This included Memphis, which was now occupied by the Union forces. Gen. Grant now visited that city, and took measures to prevent the sending of letters, fire-arms, goods, and ammunition out of the city. He rented unoccupied buildings owned by traitors, and directed the rent paid to the United States. He notified the families of rebels that they would be required to move from the city unless they signed a parole that they had, in no form whatever, aided the rebel government, and would not do so; that captured guerillas would not be treated as prisoners of war; and that the property of traitors would be sold to indemnify the government for all losses caused by the depredations of outlaws.

Notwithstanding the surrender of the city, and its occupation by the Union army, the rebel press was constantly endeavoring to stir up and keep alive the most bitter hatred toward the Union citizens and soldiers. Gen. Grant found it necessary to stop this; and one of the most rancorous of the rebel sheets received the following very explicit order : —

HEADQUARTERS, DISTRICT OF WEST TENNESSEE,
OFFICE PROVOST-MARSHAL-GENERAL,
MEMPHIS, TENN., July 1, 1862.

Messrs. WILLS, BINGHAM, & Co., Proprietors of the Memphis Avalanche, —

You will suspend the further publication of your paper. The spirit with which it is conducted is regarded as both incendiary and treasonable, and its issue cannot longer be tolerated.

This order will be strictly observed from the time of its reception.

By command of Major.-Gen. U. S. GRANT.

WM. S. HILLYER, Provost-Marshal-General.

MEMPHIS, July 1, 1862.

" The Avalanche " can continue by the withdrawal of the author of the obnoxious article, under the caption of " Mischief-makers," and the editorial allusion to the same.

U. S. GRANT, Major-General.

The guerilla warfare was continued by the rebels with fierceness and cruelty; and Gen. Grant found it necessary to issue still more severe orders, to one of which the following is a reply : —

TRENTON, TENN., July 29, 1862.

GENERAL, — The man who guided the rebels to the bridge that was burned was hung to-day. He had taken the oath. The houses of four others who aided have been burned to the ground.

    (Signed)   G. M. DODGE, Brigadier-General.

Slaves in large numbers had early sought refuge within the Union lines; but the government was not yet prepared to enlist them as soldiers. In one instance in Missouri, slaves having given valuable information to the Union forces had been seized by their rebel owner, to be sent within the rebel lines; upon which they were taken by an Iowa officer, and the circumstance reported to headquarters. The slaves soon after, understanding the full import of Gen. Halleck's Order No. 3, attempted to escape: they were pursued by a detachment of Missouri militia in the pay of the United States; and one was actually shot by the pursuing party.

Senator Wilson of Massachusetts had introduced a bill in Congress forbidding all officers from returning fugitive slaves; and this was followed by legislation of a similar character.

Gen. Grant forthwith gladly issued orders that fugitive slaves should be enrolled, and regulated the relation of these refugees to the army within his department.

During the summer, Gen. Grant, by active and constant cavalry reconnoissances, kept himself thoroughly posted as to the position and movements of the rebel forces; and had for some time been secretly forwarding troops north in aid of movements for the protection of Cincinnati and Kentucky before it was known to the enemy. Early in September, the rebel commanders in the South-west determined to unite in an attack on Grant's position. Gen. Braxton Bragg, as a piece of consummate strategy, while really at Chattanooga in Tennessee preparing to move towards the Ohio River, issued an order dated at Sparta, a small town in the south of Alabama. The warlike associations with the name of Sparta perhaps secured for it the honor of being used by Gen. Bragg for the purpose of deceiving the Union commander.

But Gen. Grant, though not a resident of the ancient

city or the modern village, was too much of a Spartan by nature to be in the least deceived by the order or its author. He immediately telegraphed to Rosecrans at Tuscumbia, putting him on his guard.

Van Dorn and Price, early in September, began moving toward the Tennessee; Price striking east of Grant, as if for Kentucky; while Van Dorn threatened Corinth.

On the 18th of September, Gen. Grant ordered Generals Rosecrans and Ord to advance upon Iuka, where a severe engagement took place on the afternoon of the 19th. Gen. Grant had intended that Ord and Rosecrans should unite early in the morning of that day: but Rosecrans had been deceived and misled by a rebel spy who had secured his confidence, and remained with him until an hour or two before the fight; and he was also detained by the terrible condition of the roads and the thickly-wooded country. The troops fought well; held their ground: and in the night the enemy fled with a loss of 1,438, our army entering Iuka the next morning. But Grant, owing to the fact that Rosecrans and Ord did not unite as expected, failed to destroy Price's whole force as he had intended. Price was prevented from advancing into Kentucky, or holding his force in full strength until Van Dorn could join him in a united attack on Corinth.

The North at this time was threatened with invasions in Maryland and Ohio. Pope and McClellan were superseding each other on the Potomac; and Grant's troops were constantly being ordered east to their support. This weakened and embarrassed him; and to hold his own with diminished forces caused him the greatest anxiety and perplexity, as his despatches at this time abundantly testify.

Price retreated to Ripley, Miss., united with Van Dorn, and, on the 2d of October, appeared before Corinth with thirty-eight thousand men, where Rosecrans was now stationed with nineteen thousand men. Grant was at his headquarters at Jackson. On the 3d of October, they attacked Corinth with full force. Grant had ordered Rosecrans to attack; but the enemy were so confident of victory, they did not wait for this, but attacked, and drove Rosecrans back to the defences, of which Grant's quick eye had seen the need on first examining the position of Corinth, and which he had constructed as soon as Halleck left for Washington. The rebel attack was renewed on the 4th with great confidence and valor; but it was everywhere repulsed. Rosecrans had skilfully placed his guns, and induced the enemy to attack, where, when they opened, their men would go down in swaths. On they came; then the guns with their grape and canister, a flash, a loud report, and the rebels went down in hundreds. It was hard iron shells and balls ploughing through soft, warm flesh and blood. But on they came. "The rebel soldiers," said an eye-witness, "marched steadily to death, with their faces averted like men striving to protect themselves against a driving storm of hail."

The Confederate Congress had recently substituted the new rebel flag, — the stars on a cross, instead of the "stars and bars" first used. The new flags were borne that day. The Parrott guns make terrible slaughter. A Texan, Col. Rogers, is about to charge at the head of his regiment. He seizes the new flag in one hand, and,.

with a revolver in the other, rushes forward at the head of his men. He has not been hit: he mounts the parapet, waves the new flag, and falls headlong a corpse into the Union intrenchment, with five men by his side, riddled with bullets.

Grant, though "absent in body, was present in mind." He had ordered McPherson to march from Jackson with re-enforcements for Rosecrans : he arrived during the fight, in the rear of Price and Van Dorn ; and, by eleven o'clock in the forenoon, the defeat of the enemy was complete.

Grant had anticipated this, even, and had sent Hurlbut and Ord, four thousand strong, to the Hatchie River, forty miles away, to strike them in flank as they retreated ; which was done on the 5th with fine effect, capturing a battery of artillery and several hundred men. Grant had determined to capture Van Dorn and his whole army, and would be satisfied with nothing less. He had informed Rosecrans of the march of Ord and Hurlbut to Hatchie River, and directed him to pursue immediately, even as far as Bolivar. The character of commanders is often seen in the energy with which the fruits of a well-earned victory are seized and followed up. The army that is allowed to " fight and run away can fight another day," but, if mercilessly pursued, is often demoralized, scattered, and broken up. Rosecrans' men had fought two days (though mostly behind their intrenchments), and were fatigued, hungry, and weary; but Grant had ordered them to pursue. One day of pursuit would give them peace and rest for a long time. Rosecrans reported, " I rode all over our lines, announcing the result of the fight in person ;" ordered the troops " to rest, and start the next morning in pursuit." This was eleven o'clock on the 4th. " The next morning"! But will Price and Van Dorn wait at Hatchie's Run to be captured? will they not escape from Ord and Hurlbut during all the afternoon and night? It was even so. The next morning, Rosecrans started out, but, being misinformed, took a road which led him eight miles away from Hatchie's Run before the mistake was discovered. Meanwhile, Ord and Hurlbut had had their fight, at a disadvantage, with Price and Van Dorn, who had made a wide circuit round, crossed the Hatchie several miles south at Crown's Bridge, burning the bridge after them.

Grant was displeased and chagrined at the failure to obey his orders implicitly. It did not quite suit his taste either for a commander to ride about his army, announcing his victory in person, at any time, and especially when under orders to advance and follow up the retreating enemy. He did not wish any one to eat or sleep, or glorify a victory, until all had been wrung from it that it could possibly be made to yield. Pursue, disperse the enemy, take the last prisoner, the last musket, before you rest or sleep. This spirit animated Grant in all his battles on the Tennessee, the Cumberland, the Potomac. It made him Lieutenant-General, and carried him in triumph to the final scene on the Appomattox. " The longer I live," said Fowell Buxton, " the more I am certain that the great difference between men, between the feeble and the powerful, the great and the insignificant, is *energy, invincible determination*, a purpose once fixed, and then death or victory ! That quality will do any thing that can be done in this world; and no talents, no circumstances, no opportunities, will make a two-legged creature a man without it."

But Rosecrans and his men had fought nobly, and received the gratitude of the country. The Union loss was about 2,359; of whom 315 were killed, the remainder wounded and missing. "Our loss," says Pollard, "was probably double that of the Federal forces."

President Lincoln telegraphed as follows : —

WASHINGTON, D.C., Oct. 8, 1862.

MAJOR-GEN. GRANT, — I congratulate you, and all concerned, in your recent battles and victories. How does it all sum up? I especially regret the death of Gen. Hackelman; and am anxious to know the condition of Gen. Oglesby, who is an intimate personal friend. A. LINCOLN.

Gen. Rosecrans was made a major-general of volunteers, and ordered to Cincinnati to supersede Gen. Buell as commander of the Army of the Cumberland. The battles of Iuka and Corinth had both been planned and fought by Grant, in his brain, before the armies met: the victories were the result of his orders. If they had been more strictly obeyed, the results would have been far larger. But he was quiet, and put forth no claims: he did not stand tiptoe, and shout, "I did it!" He did not receive the credit he deserved. The victory was ours: who had won it was of less consequence to Grant. He was not a demonstrative man. He had about him no "fuss and feathers," — not enough to attract early notice. His words were few, his manners simple: he assumed nothing. As soon as he had won a great victory, he set to work planning how to win another, and

did not get leave of absence to run up to show himself in
the hotels at Cincinnati and Washington. Such a man
was so great a novelty, that he had to be observed and
studied to be appreciated. But his time was coming: not
even his own modesty, great as it is, could conceal his
merits. " The truth is, that Grant's extreme simplicity of
behavior, and directness of expression, imposed on various
officers both above and below him. They thought him
a good, plain man, who had blundered into one or two
successes, and who, therefore, could not be immediately
removed; but they deemed it unnecessary to regard his
judgment, or to count. upon his ability. His superiors
made their plans invariably without consulting him; and
his subordinates sometimes sought to carry out their own
campaigns in opposition or indifference to his orders,
not doubting, that, with their superior intelligence, they
could conceive and execute triumphs which would excuse or even vindicate their course." *

On the 16th of October, Gen. Grant's department
was designated as the " Department of the Tennessee,"
and was extended to include the State of Mississippi, in
which was Vicksburg.

It was divided by Gen. Grant into four districts, under
Generals Sherman, Hurlbut, Hamilton, and Davies.

The Administration was desirous that the State of
Tennessee should resume her loyal position. It was
thought that Gen. Grant's victories rendered it an auspicious time to address the people. The following docu-
ment, written by Abraham Lincoln, united, perhaps for
the first time, the names of Gen. Grant and Andrew
Johnson ; and, in view of recent events and the discus-

---

* Badeau.

sions on reconstruction, will be read with interest. The remarks about "*peace again upon the old terms of the Constitution*" sound strangely now after the great and irrevocable events we have witnessed.

EXECUTIVE MANSION, WASHINGTON, Oct. 21, 1862.

Major-Gen. GRANT, Gov. JOHNSON, and all having military, naval, and civil authority under the United States within the State of Tennessee,—

The bearer of this, Thomas R. Smith, a citizen of Tennessee, goes to that State, seeking to have such of the people thereof as desire to avoid the unsatisfactory prospect before them, and to have *peace again upon the old terms under the Constitution* of the United States, to manifest such desire by elections of members to the Congress of the United States, particularly; and perhaps a legislature, State officers, and a United-States senator, friendly to their object. I shall be glad for you, and each of you, to aid him and all others acting for this object as much as possible. *In all available ways, give the people a chance to express their wishes at these elections. Follow law, and forms of law, as far as convenient; but, at all events, get the expression of the largest number of the people possible.* All see how much such action will connect with and effect the proclamation of Sept. 22. Of course, the men elected should be gentlemen of character, willing to swear support to the Constitution as of old, and known to be above reasonable suspicion of duplicity.

Yours very respectfully, ·

A. LINCOLN.

The Emancipation Proclamation of President Lincoln was issued in January, 1863; and was thus cordially welcomed by Gen. Grant:—

GENERAL ORDERS, NO. 25.   MILLIKEN'S BEND, LA.

Corps, division, and post commanders will afford all facilities for the completion of the negro regiments now organizing in this department. Commissaries will issue supplies, and quartermasters will furnish stores, on the same requisitions and returns as are required from other troops.

It is expected that all commanders will especially exert themselves in carrying out the policy of the Administration, not only in organizing colored regiments and rendering them efficient, but also in removing prejudice against them.

By order of Major-Gen. U. S. GRANT.

JOHN A. RAWLINS, *A. A. G.*

CHAPTER IX.

THE VICKSBURG CAMPAIGN.

IT had long been predicted that the Valley of the Mississippi would be the seat of future empire in America. When Napoleon was negotiating the cession of Louisiana, he said, "The nation which controls the Valley of the Mississippi will eventually rule the world." Its importance in a civil war was early seen. "The Valley of the Mississippi," says De Tocqueville, "is the most magnificent dwelling-place prepared by God for man's abode." The river enriches an area of nearly one million and a half of square miles, — six times the size of the empire of France. Fifty-seven rivers, some of them a thousand miles in length, contribute to swell its waters. It is the monarch of rivers. The Indians called it " the Father of Waters." "The possession of the Mississippi River is the possession of America," said Gen. Sherman. "Assist in preserving the Mississippi River," said Jefferson Davis to the citizens of Mississippi, at Jackson, " that great artery of the Confederacy, and thus *conduce, more than in any other way, to the perpetuation of the Confederacy* and the success of the cause." " There is not one drop of rain that falls over the whole vast expanse of the North-west that does not find its home in the bosom of the Gulf," said Vallandigham, in his speech declaring the inability of the government to conquer the Rebellion, and the determination of the North-west to go with the South if a separation took place. But other men of the North-west saw different means of preserving their right of way on the great river besides receiving it as a gift from a few slaveholding rebels. Among them was Logan, who could talk eloquently as well as fight bravely. He said, " If the rebels undertake to control the Mississippi, the men of the North-west will hew their way to the Gulf, and make New Orleans a fishpond." Aside from Grant's appreciation, as a military commander, of the importance of the river, he was a Western man, born on the banks of the Ohio; and he sympathized thoroughly with the invincible determination which burned and glowed in the hearts of the people of the North-west to hold their way unchallenged to the sea.*

The rebels, very early in the Rebellion, seized and fortified the most important points, — Columbus, Fort Pillow, Island No. 10, Vicksburg, and Port Hudson. The first three had fallen before Vicksburg was included in Gen. Grant's department. All that the Confederacy had of engineering skill and experience was

---

* In the summer of 1857, the writer, visiting St. Louis for the first time, happened to cross the river on the ferry-boat in the same carriage with Judge Douglas. The public mind was then full of the discussions in regard to Kansas. Judge Douglas turned to a Boston gentleman, and, pointing out of the window to the river, said, " As you are a stranger here, sir, I will show you a natural curiosity. The waters of the Missouri and Mississippi flow side by side here without intermingling, and with different colors, — one clear, one dark and muddy." — " Perhaps," was the reply, " it is to represent the free soil and slave soil through which they flow." — " Perhaps so," said the judge with a smile. " I didn't think of that."

exhausted in rendering Vicksburg the Gibraltar of America. Nature and Art combined made it almost impregnable. It is four hundred miles above New Orleans, is situated on high ground, and had a population of four or five thousand.

. The military results of the victories of Donelson and Shiloh had been to open the Mississippi from Cairo to Memphis, — a distance of two hundred and forty miles.

Early in June, 1862, Farragut, after his brilliant victory at the mouth of the river, sent a part of his squadron up the river under Com. Lee, who found the city too strong to be taken with gunboats or mortar-boats.

An attempt was made to move Vicksburg six miles from the river by cutting a canal in a bend in the Mississippi opposite. In former years, the course of this fickle and meandering stream had been changed in a single night by running a furrow with a plough across a neck of land. The canal was three miles and a half long, six feet deep, ten feet wide. The project deeply interested Mr. Lincoln, and attracted great attention throughout Europe. Several thousand men were engaged in this work for a number of weeks. It was nearly completed, when the river rose suddenly, burst the dam at the head of the canal, and, instead of confining itself to the prepared channel, overflowed in all directions. Camps were submerged, horses drowned: the canal was a failure. Vicksburg was not to be displaced from the river-bank in that manner. For seventy days, from about the middle of May till the last of July, 1862, Vicksburg had been besieged ; and twenty-five thousand shot and shell were thrown into the city by the fleet, without impairing its defences.

It was attempted to cut a way from the river to Lake Providence, seventy miles north of Vicksburg, and formerly a part of the old channel; thence into the Tensas, Washita, and Red Rivers, into the Mississippi, above Port Hudson. It was a long and winding way; could only be used by steamers of light draught; had no depth of water when the river was low; and was finally abandoned.

Twelve miles north of Vicksburg, on the east side, is the mouth of the Yazoo River. Up this river the rebels had extemporized a navy-yard, and built there gunboats, and a powerful steam-ram and a water-battery. The mouth of the river was strongly fortified, especially at Haine's Bluff. One hundred and fifty miles north of Vicksburg, on the east side, is Moon Lake: from this lake the Yazoo Pass extends to the Coldwater River, thence to the Tallahatchie River, thence to the Yazoo River, — all parallel to the Mississippi. The Yazoo Pass was a tortuous bayou, thirty feet deep, six miles long. In former years, this route had been used by small trading-vessels; but, as the whole country between the two rivers was often overflowed, the State of Mississippi had constructed a dam at the entrance to the pass. A mine was exploded; the dam was thrown open; and, in two days, a river a mile in. length was pouring into Moon Lake, allowing the largest steamers to pass. But the rebels were not idle below. The banks of the rivers were lined with gigantic trees, — sycamores, cottonwood, oak, elm, and pecan-wood. These trees were felled in large numbers across the stream, mainly by enforced slave-labor. One barricade was a mile and a quarter in length. Some of these primeval giants, which were old when the Mississippi was first seen by white men, weighed twenty tons. These had to be hauled out by cables; men working in parties of five hundred in the water. After an almost incredible amount of labor, the pass was opened from Moon Lake to the Coldwater River. But, while the Union army had been opening the northern end of the new route, the rebels had been as diligently closing the lower end.

Gen. Ross with forty-five hundred men, on twenty-two transports, preceded by two iron-clads under Lieut.-Commander Watson, entered the Coldwater, twenty-five miles from the Mississippi, on the 2d of March. The river is about forty miles long, one hundred feet wide, and runs through a wilderness till it enters the Tallahatchie, a river of similar character, and both too deep to be easily obstructed. This long passage of two hundred and forty miles was made cautiously; the boats moving slowly by daylight, and being tied to the shore at night. It was an exploring expedition through an unknown region, filled with active and unrelenting enemies; but it was safely completed on the 10th of March.

Its success inspired the hope that the whole army might be transported through this circuitous route, nine hundred miles in length, and landed near Haine's Bluff, a few miles above Vicksburg. But the difficulty was to obtain at once, in sufficient numbers, steamers of light draught only. At first, only one division, under Gen. Quimby, could be sent; then the corps of Mc-

Pherson, and a division of Hurlbut, were ordered to follow as fast as transportation could be obtained.

Near where the Tallahatchie flows into the Yazoo, a third river, the Yallabusha, enters it at the town of Greenwood. Opposite Greenwood, the rebels had erected Fort Pemberton. The land was so low as to be almost surrounded by water, too deep for a land-attack by infantry, and not deep enough for boats to get within short range. The expedition depended wholly upon the insufficient naval force for success. The boats could not get within less than twenty-seven hundred feet of the battery. The attack was made, but was unsuccessful. One boat was disabled, six men killed, and twenty-five wounded. The rebel loss was one man killed.

It was now attempted to drown out the garrison, only twenty-four inches above the water, by cutting a levee three hundred miles distant, at Austin, near Helena, and turning the floods of the Mississippi in that direction ; but the lordly and capricious Father of Waters, as if determined that the dwellers on its banks should themselves settle forever their right of way to the sea, could neither be coaxed nor forced from its usual channel, and left Fort Pemberton unharmed. The course of the river was one of " non-intervention."

But Ross was in peril, and must be relieved. The Union gunboats held the mouth of the Yazoo. On this river, before reaching Haine's Bluff, Steele's Bayou opens, runs north, circles around Fort Pemberton, and re-enters the Yazoo sixty miles above a trackless and labyrinthine maze ; adopting on its devious course of one hundred and fifty miles, as if to elude detection, the *aliases* of Black Bayou, Deer Creek, Rolling Fork, and Big Sunflower. Grant accompanied Admiral Porter on a reconnoissance on the 15th of March. On the 16th, he sent forward Sherman and a division of troops. He ardently hoped, not only to relieve Ross, but to find some base from which to prosecute his campaign on dry land.

Sherman's troops were sent up the Mississippi, on transports, to Eagle Bend; marched about a mile over to the transports in the bayou, building bridges across the swamp. The gunboats became entangled in the drift-timber, and could with difficulty force their way along, sometimes moving only four miles in twenty-four hours. Trees had to be pulled up by the roots, stumps sawed off under water. The bayous were crooked, covered with a thicket of trees overhead, and filled with saplings in the channels. With incredible difficulty, they advanced slowly; but it was found, at last, that the troops must be disembarked from the transports, and put on coal-barges and tugs, the way for steamers becoming impassable. The progress of the infantry was now much slower than that of the naval vessels; and Admiral Porter arrived at Rolling Fork, March 30, much in advance of the troops. The rebels here were felling trees across the stream in great numbers, and compelling slaves to aid them at the point of the bayonet: they were doing the same farther down in the rear of the boats. The labor of removing these obstructions was pursued day and night, under fire of a cloud of sharpshooters, and was toilsome beyond description. The heavy guns of the little fleet were not available in such a warfare to any great extent. It became apparent that the fleet was in danger; and Admiral Porter sent word by a slave, who succeeded in making his way thirty miles back to Sherman, to come to his support. The promptitude of Blucher's movements gave him among the Prussian soldiers the name of "Marshal Forwards." A like spirit was in Sherman. It was night when this message came; but at once the army was started, and moved up along the narrow, slimy, treacherous path, on the river's bank, through almost impenetrable canebrakes, guided by lighted torches; the indomitable general leading the way. It was the first "torchlight procession" ever seen in that desolate region. He found Porter's boats about three feet below the river bank, unable to reach the rebel force, and their sharpshooters, of whom there were about four thousand, and a battery of artillery, in the swamps. But Sherman's men soon changed the appearance of all this, drove off the enemy, and saved the fleet.

But it was found necessary to abandon the route. The character of the country, the blockading of the creek by the rebels, now thoroughly aroused to the importance of the movement, compelled a return of the expedition. The gunboats unshipped their rudders, and backed down the narrow streams, where there was not room to swing around; and, thumping over the trees, finally returned in safety to their starting-point. Grant had ordered a concentration of forces at Milliken's Bend; and by the last of March the army were back there, baffled in their main object, it is true, but hardened by exposure, better acquainted with the difficulties to be encountered, and commander and men inflexible in their determination to take Vicksburg.

All the elaborate and laborious schemes to take the city, some five in number, had failed; the rebels were jubilant, but still continued to strengthen the place by every means known and unknown to military science; the administration was discouraged; the Western State authorities were impatient. Grant had been compelled at times to stop all letters between the army and friends at home, lest the mails should be captured, and reveal to the enemy the location and movements of his forces. At these times, the anxiety of friends at home colored their fears. It was said the soldiers were dying by thousands in those pestilential swamps: fevers, dysenteries, and exposure were destroying what rebel rifles left in those impenetrable morasses, fit only for snakes and reptiles, and inaccessible to any ministrations to the sick and wounded. Grant was, after all, a failure. He had been "lucky," it was said, at Donelson and Corinth; but he had "taken to drinking," and should be removed. He still said quietly, "I shall take Vicksburg;" but this was regarded as mulish and unreasoning obstinacy, and only showed more clearly the necessity for removing him. The newspapers were filled with the spirit of these criticisms; and they produced, of course, a powerful influence at Washington; and various officers were urged for appointment as his successor.

And now was seen the sense of justice, and the marvellous power to judge of men, surpassing intuition, possessed by Abraham Lincoln. A strong friend of Gen. Grant, a member of Congress, who had been moved by these representations, but who now despaired of his success, called on the President to acknowledge, from a sense of duty, that the condition of affairs required another commander at Vicksburg. He received this answer: "I rather like the man. I think we will try him a little longer." This was not the least of the services which the beloved President rendered to the country. Meanwhile, Grant, though appreciating all the circumstances, preserved his usual silence: he transmitted regularly his official reports to the War Department; but he did not write, nor cause to be written, long arguments to show that Vicksburg ought to have fallen, and would have fallen, "if" the government had sustained him, had sent him more re-enforcements, or "if" this or that had been otherwise. He accepted the facts without any "ifs." In his own mind, he had never had great confidence in the success of any of these plans, though they might succeed. But the army could not remain idle; and the summer droughts were needed to carry out the other plans he had long contemplated.

The natural situation of Vicksburg, and the topography of the country around it, were its defences, as well as the skill, science, and courage of its defenders. It seemed to be, as Davis had pronounced it, "the Gibraltar of America." The European press re-echoed the censures of American journals. The administration telegraphed that "the President was getting impatient."

But, April 4, Grant telegraphed to Halleck, "The discipline and health of this army is now good, and I am satisfied the greatest confidence of success prevails." And success came.

CHAPTER X.

THE failure of the many attempts on Vicksburg had one good effect: it showed to the mind of the commander how it could *not* be taken, and so reduced the remaining alternatives from which a selection could be made.

Grant's army was at Milliken's Bend, on the west side of the Mississippi, above Vicksburg. His plan was to march the army down to New Carthage, cut a canal through the bayous, put the troops on barges and empty coal-boats, which should be drawn by tugs to some point south of the citadel. But this would leave the army on the west bank of the river, with no means of crossing. But this was to be remedied by the boats above running past the batteries in the night, and then ferrying the army over. Good roads would give him control of the country in the rear; and he would besiege Vicksburg by land, while the gunboats should prevent relief by the river.

It is undoubtedly an immense satisfaction to a commanding officer to know that his plans will be carried out, not merely according to the letter of the law, but without a constant looking for predicted failure; that they commend themselves to the judgment, if not to the

102

admiration, of his subordinates.   Before the battle of Aboukir, Nelson called his captains into his cabin, and explained to them his plan of battle by doubling on a portion of the enemy's fleet; and, as his officers began to understand it, Capt. Barry, in his enthusiasm, jumped to his feet, and exclaimed, " If we succeed, what will the world say of us ? "   Nelson, with equal enthusiasm, sprang up, and exclaimed, " But there is no *if* in the case: *we shall* succeed."   No one there uttered the opinion afterwards expressed by Cooper, — that with American vessels it would fail ; and the ardor and confidence of the officers was felt the next day by every man and powder-boy throughout the English fleet.

When Gen. Grant made known his plan to a council of his corps commanders, not one approved it.   The plan was opposed to military rule.   It severed his army from the North and its supplies.   If not an immediate success, it must end in overwhelming disaster.   All his officers — Sherman, McPherson, Logan, Wilson, all able men, all attached to their commander, and anxious he should not fail — argued the points against the project. Sherman, after reflecting, could not restrain himself from renewing the debate.   Grant knew his friendship, his sincerity, and his ability.   Sherman even rode up to Grant's headquarters the next day, and presented his views, respectfully of course, but earnestly, as an earnest man does every thing.

He assured Grant that the only way to take Vicksburg was to move on it from some high ground as a base, on the north.   " This," said Grant, " will require us to go back to Memphis."

" Exactly so," said Sherman, and set forth his reasons

with the intensity of conviction and the ingenuity and ability of an able soldier.

Grant replied, "I shall take no step backward: it would seem to the country, now discouraged, like a retreat. I have considered the plan, and have determined to carry it out."

Sherman left; but the strength of his convictions, the vast importance of the movement to the nation and the army, would not allow him to leave the subject thus; and he carefully committed his views to paper, and on the 8th of April forwarded them to headquarters, concluding with these noble words, so honorable to him as a patriot and a soldier: "I make these suggestions with the request that Gen. Grant simply read them, and give them, as I know he will, a share of his thoughts. I would prefer he should not answer them, but merely give them as much or as little weight as they deserve. Whatever plan of action he may adopt will receive from me the same zealous co-operation and energetic support as though conceived by myself."

And here is one of the points of moral grandeur in the career of Grant. Those who would understand his character should observe him at this juncture. This single man — newspapers, politicians, army officials at Washington, clamoring for his removal, he acknowledging his failure thus far, his present plan opposed earnestly by all his officers — sees the path of duty before him gleaming with light in the surrounding darkness, and walks in it with unfaltering step. How many men were there in the country who would have gone on?

It had been said early in the war that the North had no cavalry, and nothing to make cavalry out of; that

the Southern men were born riders; and in this arm of
the service, which Napoleon pronounced the most important in war,* the South would always be infinitely superior to their opponents.

Gen. Scott, whose opinions at the opening of the
war, whether with or without reason, were supreme,
declared we needed no cavalry; and, in consequence,
thousands of cavalry were refused when offering to
enlist. The few regiments accepted were attached to
different corps, and, when used, were generally sent out
in small numbers.

It was the fashion to ridicule the efficiency of the
cavalry. The sarcasm of a distinguished major-general
in asking, after a battle, " if any one ever saw a dead
cavalry-man," was often repeated. Under Grant, the
cavalry became a power, as it deserved to be; and
expeditions, ten and fifteen thousand strong, were sent
out, and used effectively until the close of the war.

While studying his campaign, Grant wrote to Hurlbut, " It seems to me that Grierson, with about five
hundred picked men, might succeed in cutting his way
south, and cut the railroad east of Jackson, Miss. The
undertaking would be a hazardous one; but it would
pay well if carried out."

This railroad was the principal artery for supplies to
Vicksburg. Col. B. H. Grierson of the Sixth Illinois
was at La Grange, Tenn., with seventeen hundred

---

* " My decided opinion," said Napoleon, " is that cavalry, if led by equally
brave and resolute men, must always break infantry." — *Las Casas*, vii. 184.

" It was by cavalry that Hannibal conquered at Ticino; a charge of
French horsemen at Marengo placed Napoleon on the consular throne; another of the English light dragoons on the flank of the Old Guard hurled
him to the rock of St. Helena." — *Alison.*

men, including the Sixth and Seventh Illinois and Second Iowa, with Col. Prince and Col. Hatch. Grierson started April 17; passed through Ripley, behind all the Confederate forces, through Pontatoc, Clear Spring, Louisville, Newton, burning bridges, cutting telegraph-wires, tearing up railroads, destroying property of the rebel government wherever found, passing through forests and swamps, and swimming rivers. At Newton, they turned south - west, towards Raleigh; thence to Gallatin, where they captured a 32-pound rifled Parrott and fourteen hundred pounds of powder; then to Union Church behind Natchez, where they had a skirmish; then to Brookhaven, where they burned the station-house, cars, and bridges of the New-Orleans and Jackson Railroad; thence to Greenburg, La., having a fight at Amite River.

May 2, the people of Baton Rouge were astounded at the arrival of a courier, who announced that a brigade of cavalry from Gen. Grant's army had cut their way through the whole of the State of Mississippi, and would arrive in an hour. They were met at the picket-line, and escorted into Gen. Banks's camp amid the vociferous cheers of their astonished friends.

In sixteen days they had ridden six hundred miles through the heart of one of the richest regions of the Confederacy, traversing the whole length of Mississippi; killed and wounded one hundred of the enemy; captured and paroled five hundred prisoners; destroyed three thousand stand of arms, and six million dollars' worth of Confederate supplies, and property of various kinds, with a loss of three men killed and twenty-five horses. Thousands of rebel cavalry were sent out from

Jackson and from Vicksburg; but the chivalry never could find them.

Grierson's expedition was one of the most brilliant cavalry exploits of the war, and will be long remembered.

The raid withdrew attention somewhat from Grant, and was of essential service to his army in its new movement.

On the 29th of March, Gen. McClernand, with the Thirteenth Army Corps, was ordered to move down to New Carthage. The winter overflow had hardly subsided, and the roads were wet and spongy.

On arrival, it was found that the levee of the Bayou Vidal, which here empties into the Mississippi, had broken, leaving New Carthage an island. It was found necessary, therefore, to march the army to Perkins's Plantation, twelve miles below, and thirty-five miles from Milliken's Bend. Four bridges, two of them six hundred feet long, were required during this march. Ammunition and provisions were carted along this route with incredible labor.

It was now determined to send three steamers and ten barges, loaded with rations and forage, past the batteries. Grant applied to Admiral Porter, who entered cordially into the undertaking. Grant wrote, " I am happy to say the admiral and myself have never yet disagreed upon any policy."

The passage would be a terrible one, — to many it might be like embarking on the river of death. Some of the captains and crews of the river-steamboats were unwilling to make the attempt; and the trip was so hazardous, that the officers preferred to call for volunteers rather than order men to the duty. But volunteers enough pressed forward to man twenty fleets. None would give way; and the places were at last assigned by lot. One boy, residing near Grant's home in Illinois, who had drawn a chance to go, was offered a hundred dollars for his place; but the post of danger was the post of honor. The boy indignantly refused the money; took his position, like young Casabianca at the battle of the Nile, and passed bravely through.

As soon as the wants of the service were known, the army seemed to swarm with boatmen, pilots, and engineers, as the Massachusetts regiments under Butler, in their first march to Washington, furnished at a moment's call men who could make steam-engines and build railroads.*

One officer wrote, that if orders were given, " Painters, present arms!" or "Poets, to the front!" or "Sculptors, charge bayonets!" dozens in every company would respond. Hundreds of young men in our colleges, nurtured in wealth and luxury, flung aside their books, cheerfully endured the privations and hardships of camp-life, and in battle bore themselves with inspiring gallantry, like young Lowell, who was shot on his fourteenth charger.†

It was the rare accomplishment in a private soldier,

---

* "Does any one here know any thing about this machine?" said Gen. Butler at Annapolis, when surveying a rusty and dilapidated locomotive. A soldier of the Massachusetts Eighth answered, "Our shop made that engine, general. I guess I can put her in order and run her;" and it was done.

† "As to the way in which some of our ensigns and lieutenants braved danger, — the boys just come from school, — it exceeds all belief. They ran as at cricket." — *Wellington on Waterloo.*

of being able to write, which first made Marshal Junot known to Napoleon. But the Union army was composed of men who could fight when fighting was to be done; and it furnished sailors, scholars, engineers, mechanics, for every exigency which war could require.

It was ten o'clock at night, on the 16th, when the fleet started down the river. There was no moon. The intrepid Porter led the way in "The Benton," followed by "The Lafayette," "Carondelet," "Pittsburg," "Tuscumbia," "Price," "Louisville," and "Mound City."

Between eleven and twelve, there was a flash on the high bluff above them; and in an instant the batteries along the whole water-front were thundering at the fleet, and kept up a terrific cannonade. The boats immediately replied with grape and shrapnel, which took effect on the city rather than on the batteries. Houses were soon blazing. The shells from the batteries lighted the hay on one or two of the large transports, the flames mounting up the sky. The transports were cut loose from the gunboats, and, floating down the river like great palaces of fire, were reflected on the dark waters beneath them. The flames, tossing and swaying in the midnight wind, looked like meteor-flags streaming out from battlement and tower. The whole heavens were lighted up so clearly, that the men at the guns and in the streets of Vicksburg were seen as plainly as at noonday. The population were out, watching a display of fireworks grand beyond description. For about three hours, nearly two hundred heavy guns were hurling their deadly missiles at the brave fleet, which passed triumphantly on.

Grant watched the operations with intense interest from a transport moored in the middle of the river, where the shot and shell fell thick about him.

Within two hours after the batteries had been passed, the whole scene was changed: the guns were silent; the dark river was flowing as peacefully, the stars were shining as brightly, as when the Indian first paddled his canoe along its waters.

As may be imagined, the fate of the expedition had been anxiously watched by McPherson's men below. The first herald was a transport burning to the water's edge, followed by the wreck of one of the barges. An old man, a wealthy rebel, on whose plantation McPherson had established his headquarters, could not conceal his delight from the Union officers, and confidently predicted the destruction of the whole Union fleet. The officers watched anxiously; and, soon after daybreak, one gunboat after another came steaming around a bend in the river, the old flag dancing in the early sunlight; and the cheers went up loud and long. It was in a double sense the dawning of a new day for that brave army. But it was too much for the old rebel; and that day, in his impotent wrath, he set fire to his splendid residence.

He had enriched himself on the unrequited toil of his slaves. The estate was one of the most princely in Louisiana. It seemed to realize Wirt's description of Blannerhassett's home: "He had reared upon it a palace, and decorated it with every embellishment of fancy. Shrubbery that Shenstone might have envied bloomed around him. Music that might have charmed Calypso and her nymphs was his." The elegant mansion, embowered in overarching trees, was situated on an eminence, and commanded a view of varied and surpassing loveliness. The majestic river in its windings seemed lingering to reflect and beautify the scene. Though spring, all around bespoke the luxury of early summer. The warm, genial air, vocal with song of birds, was laden with perfumes of the oleander and the blossoms of the magnolia. The broad savannas were waving with corn and cotton. Figs grew in the open air. .Nature seemed here to have spread a banquet of festal glory. But, in a few hours, all was changed. The house was a mass of blackened ruins. The grounds, which had smiled with a beauty which would " re-create the lost Eden anew," were transformed into a crowded and noisy camp.

Foolish old man! and yet in this act, which would have been denounced as vandalism in the Union army, he but imitated the leaders of the Rebellion, who sought to make themselves the architects of a far grander ruin, — the ruins of the temple of American liberty.

CHAPTER XI.

THE troops were now to be crossed over the river. It was decided to land them at the most southern point of the rebel batteries, — at Grand Gulf, seventy-five miles below Milliken's Bend. Reconnoissances had shown this to be the only practicable spot for landing. Transportation-boats were insufficient; and the army marched through mud and mire to a place appropriately called "Hard Times," opposite Grand Gulf.

The gunboats were to silence the batteries; and then the troops, ten thousand in number, were to be crossed in such boats as there were, and carry the works at the point of the bayonet.

At eight o'clock on the morning of the 29th, the iron-clads, seven in number, opened fire, and continued the bombardment for nearly six hours. The intrenchments were high up on the bluffs above them: the stream was too deep to anchor, and too rapid to lie still; thus compelling the boats to sail about as they fired.

The fleet did every thing that a fleet could do; but all in vain. The batteries were too high up to be damaged. Grant said, "Many times, it seemed to me the gunboats were within pistol-shot of the enemy's batteries." But, at half-past one, not a single gun had been silenced. It was a most unfortunate repulse.

Grant knew it would be simply a massacre of his men to lead them against such works; but he knew, also, no such word as "fail." His definition of the word "difficulty" was a thing to be overcome. He signalled to the admiral, and was immediately put on board the flagship, where he requested that the fleet would run the batteries the same night as a cover to the transports, while the troops marched farther down the river.

It was expected they would be obliged to march south as far as Rodney before they could effect a crossing; but a "contraband," during the night, told them of an excellent road at Bruinsburg, only half-way to Rodney, which led directly to Port Gibson, in the interior.

At this time, Grant desired an attack to be made on Haine's Bluff, above, to divert the attention of the enemy from his real movement, to the rear of Vicksburg; but it was only to be a feigned attack, and then the army were to withdraw. He hesitated to order Sherman to make an attack and fall back at this time. It would be misunderstood at the North. It would be published as another defeat, and stimulate still more the efforts for his removal. Sherman, as well as Grant, had been subjected to the harshest censures for the failures to take Vicksburg. But Grant wrote to him, still remaining at Milliken's Bend, "The effect of a heavy demonstration in that direction would be good so far as the enemy are concerned; but I am loath to order it, because it would be so hard to make our own troops understand that only a demonstration was intended, and our people at home would characterize it as a repulse."

8

But Sherman replied, "I believe a diversion at Haine's Bluff is proper and right, and will make it, let whatever reports of repulses be made."

This incident brings out in admirable light the rare friendship of these remarkable men.

Sherman at once moved ten regiments up the Yazoo, who were landed and disposed as if to make a formidable attack. The gunboats, which had been left at the bend, commenced a furious bombardment. These movements created great excitement in Vicksburg. "There was mounting in hot haste;" troops were hurried from one point to another. For two days and nights, Sherman kept up active preparations for an attack of the most threatening character, when he received the following from Grant: "Move up to Perkins's Plantation with two divisions of your corps as rapidly as possible."

He at once retired, and hurried down the river, not having lost a single man. The news went over the country of "another repulse at Haine's Bluff;" the rebels shouted over another victory won. Vicksburg is impregnable!

Grant had only passed Grand Gulf; had not begun his march to Jackson; and, while all seemed dark to others, he was full of confidence, and wrote to Halleck, "I feel now that the battle is *half over*." Four days after, he wrote, "In two weeks, I expect to be able to collect all my forces, and turn the enemy's left."

As the gunboats were now all at Grand Gulf, Gen. Grant was apprehensive that the rebels might send an armed steamer down the Big Black River, turn north, and attack him at Perkins's, where he had accumulated stores and ammunition. To meet any such emergency, he constructed a gunboat by placing some pieces of light artillery on board one of the transports, and had four 30-pound Parrott guns dragged by oxen to a commanding position on the river, ready for immediate service.

Port Gibson is in the rear of the works at Grand Gulf, about twelve miles from Bruinsburg, on the route to Jackson and also to Vicksburg. The capture of Port Gibson would carry also the fall of Grand Gulf.

Grant hurried his army across the river with the utmost speed, that he might advance before the enemy should be aware of his plans. To the quartermaster he wrote in regard to loading rations, " Do this with all expedition, in forty-eight hours : *time is of immense importance.*"

He thus cuts away the " red tape " of the chief commissary's department: " You will issue to the troops of this command, *without provision-returns,** for their subsistence the next *five* days, three rations."

Every tug, boat, and barge was crowded to its utmost in taking the men over the river, which is here a mile in width. And Admiral Porter, who also knew the value of time, offered the naval vessels for the unusual work of ferry-boats, and loaded them with men and guns, in cordial sympathy with Gen. Grant's energetic movements. The navy could not follow the army on dry land; but it could go with them to the water's edge, and bid them " God speed."

Not a single tent, nor any personal baggage, was

---

* " Provision-returns " are technical vouchers required of each officer drawing rations, involving formality and delay.

allowed to go over, not even the horses of the general and staff, until the troops were landed. Hon. Mr. Washburne, the early and eloquent friend of Gen. Grant, who was with the army at this time, thus writes : —

"In starting on the movement, the general disencumbered himself of every thing, setting an example to his officers and men. He took neither a horse nor a servant, overcoat nor blanket, nor tent nor camp-chest, nor even a clean shirt. *His only baggage consisted of a tooth-brush.* He always showed his teeth to the rebels. He shared all the hardships of the private soldier ; sleeping in the front and in the open air, and eating hard-tack and salt pork. He wore no sword, had on a low-crowned citizen's hat; and the only thing about him to mark him as a military man was his two stars on his undress military coat."

It was about an hour before sunset that the Thirteenth Corps led the way from the bluffs in this the last and successful expedition for the capture of Vicksburg. The scene was inspiring. Behind them was the broad river; around and before them was the verdure of midsummer. The air was loaded with perfumes, the corn was waving, the magnolia was in full blossom. The peaceful beauty of the landscape was in strange contrast with the glittering bayonets, the rolling drums, and the warlike appearance of the military array. The army advanced quietly until about two o'clock, when they encountered a rebel force of about eleven thousand men, in a strong position, under Gen. Bowen. After a light fire from the infantry, both armies waited the coming of daylight before opening battle. The nature of the ground was peculiar : the roads were on ridges, with ravines on each side choked up with magnolia trees and vines, and gave the rebels opportunity to contest with great advantage the advance of the Union army. On the right, McClernand advanced with Generals Carr, Hovey, and A. J. Smith; and the left was under the command of Osterhaus.

The right advanced steadily, pressing back the enemy; but an almost impassable ravine resisted the left wing. About noon, Grant ordered two brigades of Logan's division, and Smith's brigade, to attack and outflank the enemy on the left. Grant and McPherson both accompanied the advance. Soon after, a general charge was ordered; and the enemy gave way in all directions. Before sunset, the enemy were retreating toward Port Gibson, leaving their dead and wounded on the field.

They were pursued to within two miles of Port Gibson, when darkness and the danger of ambuscades rendered it necessary to rest till daylight. But, lest the enemy should attempt a retreat, Grant's orders to McClernand were, " Push the enemy, with skirmishers well thrown out, until it gets too dark to see him. Park your artillery so as to command the surrounding country, and renew the attack at early dawn. . . . No camp-fires should be allowed, unless in deep ravines and in rear of the troops."

Grant took six hundred and fifty prisoners, four flags, six field-guns; and nearly eight hundred of the enemy were killed or wounded. Among the former was Gen. Tracy. Our loss was one hundred and thirty killed, and about seven hundred wounded. The landing at Bruinsburg, and the rapid advance of the Federal troops, had surprised and disconcerted the enemy ; and Gen. Pemberton, in command of the department. telegraphed at once to Gen. J. E. Johnston, "A furious battle has been going on since daylight, just below Port Gibson. Enemy can cross all his army from Hard Times to Bruinsburg. I should have large re-enforcements. Enemy's movements threaten Jackson, and, if successful, cut off Vicksburg and Port Hudson."

To this, Johnston gave the best possible advice (no one could have given better) : " Unite your troops, and beat Grant : " its only infirmity was the difficulty of carrying it out.

In the morning, it was found that the enemy had evacuated Port Gibson, and burned the bridge, one hundred and twenty feet long, across Bayou Pierre, to prevent pursuit. It was rebuilt with great energy. Houses were torn down to furnish timber, and the men worked up to their waists in water. Meanwhile, a part of Logan's command succeeded in fording the stream, and pushed on with impatience after the retreating foe.

Crocker's division of McPherson's corps had been ferried over the river, had filled their haversacks with three days' rations, which were to last five days, and also hurried forward. Three miles beyond Port Gibson, the troops came upon some fifty thousand weight of hams in fine order, which the rebels had left by the road in their flight. The pursuit was kept up, with occasional skirmishing, to the Big Black River, fifteen miles beyond Port Gibson, and within eighteen miles of the city of Vicksburg. Pemberton might well ask for " large re-enforcements."

As Grant had foreseen, the capture of Port Gibson carried with it the fall of Grand Gulf; and the next morning he rode over to this place with a small cavalry escort to learn that the enemy had abandoned the whole country, from the Bayou Pierre to the Big Black River north. He at once took possession, and gave orders to make Grand Gulf his base of supplies, instead of Bruinsburg.

The magazines had been blown up, and the guns buried or spiked. They had not been removed by the enemy, for the following excellent reason, given in Gen. Pemberton's report: "*So rapid were his*" [Grant's] "*movements, that it was impracticable to withdraw the heavy guns.*"

Grant had not had his clothes off for three days and nights: his only baggage was a tooth-brush, his only indulgence a cigar. He now went on board one of the gunboats, borrowed a change of linen, and wrote until near morning.

To Gen. Halleck he announced the victory in the following modest terms: —

GRAND GULF, Miss., May 3, 1863.

Major-Gen. HALLECK, General-in-Chief, —

We landed at Bruinsburg, April 30; moved immediately on Port Gibson; met the enemy, eleven thousand strong, four miles south of Port Gibson, at two o'clock, A.M., on the 1st instant, and engaged him all day, entirely routing him, with the loss of many killed, and about five hundred prisoners, besides the wounded. Our loss is about one hundred killed, and five hundred wounded.

The enemy retreated towards Vicksburg, destroying the bridges over the two forks of the Bayou Pierre. These were rebuilt; and the pursuit has continued until the present time.

Besides the heavy artillery at the place, four field-pieces were captured, and some stores ; and the enemy were driven to destroy many more. The country is the most broken and difficult to operate in I ever saw. Our victory has been most complete, and the enemy is thoroughly demoralized.

But Gov. Yates of Illinois, who was with the army, had no disposition for such moderation ; and he telegraphed as follows : —

GRAND GULF, MISS., May 4, 1863.

Our arms are gloriously triumphant. *We have succeeded in winning a victory, which, in its results, must be the most important of the war.* The battle of May 1 lasted from eight o'clock in the morning until night, during all which time the enemy was driven back on the right, left, and centre. All day yesterday, our army was in pursuit of the rebels ; they giving us battle at almost every defensible point, and fighting with desperate valor. Last night, a large force of the enemy was driven across Black River ; and Gen. McClernand was driving another large force in the direction of Willow Springs. About two o'clock yesterday, I left Gen. Logan with his division, in pursuit of the enemy, to join Gen. Grant at Grand Gulf, which the enemy had evacuated in the morning ; first blowing up their magazines, spiking their cannon, destroying tents, &c. *On my way to Grand Gulf, I saw guns scattered all along the road, which the enemy had left in their retreat.* The rebels were scattered through the woods in every direction. *This army of the rebels was considered, as I now learn, invincible ; but it quailed before the irresistible assaults of North-western valor.*

I consider Vicksburg as ours in a short time, and the Mississippi River is destined to be open from its source to its mouth.

I have been side by side with our boys in battle, and can bear witness to the unfaltering courage and prowess of our brave Illinoisians.

CHAPTER XII.

G RANT had now obtained a foothold on the high
ground he had been fighting for during five
months. He had captured Grand Gulf, one of the strong
outworks of Vicksburg. He had won a splendid victory.
It was the beginning of the end. The foregoing despatches show the style in which the achievements were
narrated by Grant and by an impartial observer.

Grant had now to decide on his plan of operations.
He had thirty-five thousand men in his command, of
whom he wrote, " My army is composed of hardy and
disciplined men, who know no defeat, and are not willing
to learn what it is."

He was in the State of Mississippi, the home of Jefferson Davis, in a region wholly given over to secession.
Shall he advance at once on Vicksburg, and begin the
siege where Pemberton, by his report, has 59,411 men ?
or shall he go north and east, and meet the force gathering
under Gen. Gregg with numbers unknown ? If he sits
down to besiege Vicksburg, Gregg will be upon his rear ;
if he attacks Gregg, Pemberton will be upon his rear.
Gen. Joseph E. Johnston, who had entire command of
the rebel armies in that region, was moving toward
Jackson, the capital of the State, and only fifty miles

distant, with railroad communication in various directions. The question must be decided at once.

Grant determined to move east, to Jackson; attack and beat Gregg and the army there, before Pemberton should know of his plan, or could march to interfere with him; then return, and beat Pemberton; or, if he retired into Vicksburg, besiege and capture it. But to do this before the rebel armies can unite and overwhelm him requires energy and speed not often exhibited. The army must be hurled with its whole force, first in one direction, then in another, as with the will of a single man.

He cannot leave part of his force to watch and fight Pemberton while he goes east to fight Gregg. This would require two armies, and he has but one.

But, if he strikes out with thirty-five thousand men into the heart of the Confederacy, how is he to feed them? His supplies, brought from Milliken's Bend, are now to be sent from Grand Gulf. But Pemberton can easily send a force to intervene between his army and its base.

Grant determined to take what supplies he could, leave his base to care for itself, feed his army from the country through which he moved, fight his battles as fast as possible, then turn west, and return to Vicksburg. But he knew well that the cautious mind of Gen. Halleck, sitting in his office at Washington, would never sympathize with his views; and he thought his only method was to do it, and ask permission afterward. So he proclaimed no plans in advance, but reported regularly results as they occurred. We shall see that he judged correctly. They were studying the maps in

Washington at this time, and telling him where he ought to go. But there was no telegraph beyond Cairo, and it was a long way for letters to be sent from Cairo to the interior of Mississippi; and he would act so rapidly, that, when they arrived, they would be found to relate to past events. It is well to contemplate him here. Gen. Badeau says,—

"So Grant was alone. His most trusted associates besought him to change his plans; while his superiors were astounded by his temerity, and strove to interfere. Soldiers of reputation, and civilians in high place, condemned in advance a campaign that seemed to them as hopeless as it was unprecedented. If he failed, the country would concur with the government and the generals. Grant knew all this, and appreciated his danger, but was as invulnerable to the apprehensions of ambition as to the entreaties of friendship, or the anxieties even of patriotism. That quiet confidence which never forsook him, and which amounted, indeed, almost to a feeling of fate, was uninterrupted. Having once determined in a matter that required irreversible decision, he never reversed, nor even misgave, but was steadily loyal to himself and his plans. This absolute and implicit faith was, however, as far as possible from conceit or enthusiasm. It was simply a consciousness, or conviction rather, which brought the very strength it believed in; which was itself strength; and which inspired others with a trust in him, because he was able thus to trust himself."

At midnight of the 3d he had taken farewell of Grand Gulf in his own mind, and was on his way to Hankinson's Ferry, on the Big Black River. But his orders show his state of mind. Sherman's corps was hurried across the river. Supplies were wagoned sixty miles from Milliken's Bend, ferried over the river, and carted eighteen miles farther.

To Sherman he wrote, "Order forward immediately

your remaining division, leaving only two regiments (to guard Richmond), as required in previous orders. Have all the men leave the west bank of the river with three days' rations in haversacks, and make all possible despatch to Grand Gulf."

To Hurlbut he orders, " Four regiments to Milliken's Bend with the utmost despatch." " Take them from the troops most convenient to transportation."

To the commissary at Grand Gulf, " You will load all teams presenting themselves for rations with promptness and despatch, regardless of requisitions or provision-returns. There must be no delay on account of either lack of energy or formality."

To one of his staff superintending affairs at Grand Gulf he says, " See that the commissary at Grand Gulf loads all the wagons presenting themselves for stores with great promptness. Issue any order in my name that may be necessary to secure the greatest promptness in this respect. . . . Every day's delay is worth two thousand men to the enemy."

To the same officer, two or three days after, " Send me a report of about the number of rations on hand, and send forward to Grand Gulf. Send also to McFeely and Bingham, and remind them of the importance of rushing forward rations with all despatch. . . . How many teams have been loaded with rations and sent forward? I want to know, as near as possible, how we stand, in every particular, for supplies. How many wagons have you ferried over the river? How many are still to bring over? What teams have gone back for rations ? "

To Hurlbut, who was to remain at Memphis, he

wrote, " You will have a large force of cavalry: use it as much as possible in attracting attention from this direction. Impress upon the cavalry the necessity of keeping out of people's houses, or of taking what is of no use to them in a military point of view. .... They must live as far as possible off the country through which they pass, and destroy corn, wheat-crops, and every thing that can be made use of by the enemy in prolonging the war. Mules and horses are to be taken to supply all our own wants; and, when it does not cause too much delay, agricultural implements may be destroyed: in other words, cripple in every way, without insulting women and children, or taking their clothes, jewelry, &c."

These, and many other despatches that could be quoted, show, better than could any comments, the varied and multitudinous cares which pressed upon the mind of Gen. Grant at this time. They show, that, while major-general, he could be quartermaster, commissary, ordnance-officer, and even ferryman. Nothing essential to the one grand object, *success*, was too great or too small for him to grasp with all his energy. He pressed his orders with all the more force and exact-ness because he knew that the campaign was in defiance of rules: it was his own.

Near the battle-field of Leuthen, the traveller is still shown the tree under which Frederick the Great assem-bled his generals, and said, " The moment for courage has come. I am resolved, *against all rules of the art of war*, to attack *the army* of Charles of Lorraine *wherever I may find it.* There is no question of the number of the enemy or the strength of his position.

*We must beat them, or find our graves before their bat-
teries.*"

It was not until his arrival at Hankinson's Ferry
that the personal baggage and horses of Gen. Grant
and staff arrived. Previous to this he had slept in the
porch of the nearest house, and eaten at the table of
the officer near whom he happened to be. He ordered
reconnoissances to be made by the cavalry on the roads
leading up to Vicksburg, to keep alive in the enemy the
belief that he intended to march in that direction.

On the 8th, Grant had his headquarters at Rocky
Springs. Sherman, who was still solicitous about the
result of the campaign, did not see the possibility of the
army abandoning its base; and wrote from Hankinson's
in regard to the crowd of men, wagons, and trains, urging him to " stop all troops till your army is partially
supplied with wagons, and then act as quick as possible;
for this road will be jammed, as sure as life, if you
attempt to supply fifty thousand men by one single
road."

To this Grant replied, " I do not calculate upon the
possibility of supplying the army with full rations from
Grand Gulf. · I know it will be impossible without constructing additional roads. What I do expect, however,
is to get up what rations of hard-bread, coffee, and salt,
we can, and make the country furnish the balance. . . .
You are in a country where the troops have already
lived off the people for some days, and may find provisions more scarce; but, as we get upon new soil,
they are more abundant, particularly in corn and
cattle."

Grant was here acting on the policy which he determined to be the only one practicable to end the Rebellion ; and that was, to make the Rebellion furnish the supplies for the Union army. He had never, in the earliest days of the war, sent back a trembling fugitive with his compliments to his master. He had never detailed soldiers along the line of his march to guard the flowers and fruit of rebel officers. The rebels themselves had taught him that the Government must bring the war home to the slaveholders of the South, and compel them to feel the consequences of their acts in consuming power. It was his belief, that, the quicker this was done, the quicker the war would end.

On the 11th of May, Grant sent word to Halleck, "My forces will be this evening as far advanced towards Jackson as Fourteen-mile Creek. As *I shall communicate with Grand Gulf no more*, except it becomes necessary to send a train with heavy escort, *you may not hear from me again for several days.*"

The same day, and almost the same hour, Halleck, from his desk at Washington, was ordering Grant on a far different expedition, as follows. He said, " If possible, the forces of yourself and Banks should be united between Vicksburg and Port Hudson, so as to attack these places separately with the combined forces." Singular position in which a commanding general finds it necessary to use strategy both with the enemy and his superior at Washington !

At this time, the Hon. J. J. Pettus, Governor of Mississippi, determined to test the effects of a proclamation addressed to the whole State, in retarding the advance of the Union armies. The principal portions are as follow : —

> EXECUTIVE OFFICE, JACKSON, MISS., May 5, 1863.
>
> TO THE PEOPLE OF MISSISSIPPI, —
>
> Recent events, familiar to you all, impel me, as your chief magistrate, to appeal to your patriotism *for united effort in expelling our enemies from the soil of Mississippi. It can and must be done.* Let no man capable of bearing arms withhold from his State his services in repelling the invasion. Duty, interest, our common safety, demand every sacrifice necessary for the protection of our homes, our honor, liberty itself. . . . Awake, then, arouse, Mississippians, young and old, from your fertile plains, your beautiful towns and cities, your once quiet and happy, but now desecrated, homes! Come and join your brothers in arms, your sons and neighbors, who are now baring their bosoms to the storm of battle at your very doors, and in defence of all you hold dear. . . .
>
> *Fathers, brothers, Mississippians, while your sons and kindred are bravely fighting your battles on other fields, and shedding new lustre on your name, the burning disgrace of successful invasion of their homes, of insult and injury to their wives, mothers, and sisters, of rapine and ruin, with God's help, and by your assistance, shall never be written while a Mississippian lives to feel in his proud heart the scorching degradation! . . . Let no man forego the proud distinction of being one of his country's defenders, or hereafter wear the disgraceful badge of the dastardly traitor who refused to defend his home and his country!*
>
> JOHN J. PETTUS, *Governor of Mississippi.*

Notwithstanding the proclamation of Gov. Pettus, the army advanced toward Jackson. It moved in two columns; Generals Sherman and McClernand on the right, and Gen. McPherson on the left.

About half-past three o'clock on the morning of the 12th, Gen. Logan's division encountered the rebel vedettes near Raymond, under Gen. Gregg. Regiments were deployed, the cavalry called in, and preparations made for battle. A few hours later, the enemy were encountered, about six thousand strong, within two miles of Raymond, strongly posted. Their artillery swept a bridge which it was necessary McPherson should cross: the infantry were posted on a range of hills to the right and left, and among ravines in front.

The battle was to be fought here. Orders were sent back to clear the road of all trains, and move up the troops to the front. Before they could arrive, the enemy were beaten.

As usual, they came on with a " yell," and with great fury rushed at De Golyer's (Eighth Michigan) battery, but were driven back with grape and canister. The Twentieth, Sixty-eighth, and Seventy-eighth Ohio, and Thirteenth Illinois, were closely engaged with the enemy. Later, the rebels still holding their position, a charge was ordered by Gen. McPherson ; and the Eighth Illinois, led by Col. Sturgis, went in with fixed bayonets in fine style, broke their line, and drove them in disorder. During the battle, the Eighth Illinois and Seventh Texas Regiments, which had opposed each other at Fort Donelson, met again, and fought with unflinching ardor. The Eighth Missouri, an Irish regiment, fought with determined bravery. At Winchester, two Irish regiments which had been pressed into the rebel service, refused, when brought on to the field, to fire on the American flag ; and at Fredericksburg the Irish troops piled up their dead within forty feet of the muzzles of the rebel cannon. For centuries, at Fontenoy, at Albuera, at Waterloo, the valor of Irishmen has shed lustre on the flag of England in war, which has returned them only persecution in peace.

Logan, with the advance, pressed the retiring enemy,

and at five o'clock entered Raymond in triumph.
Generals McPherson and Logan were constantly under
fire, animating the troops; the latter having his horse
shot under him.

The enemy retreated toward Jackson. The rebel
loss was one hundred and three killed, and seven hundred and twenty wounded and taken prisoners. Our
loss was sixty-nine killed, and about three hundred and
sixty wounded and missing.

At Raymond, the Union officers found newspapers
published in Jackson the day previous, from which they
learned, to their surprise, that the " Yankees had been
whipped at Grand Gulf and Port Gibson, and were
falling back to seek the protection of their gunboats."
It was by such falsehoods that the rebel press sought to
deceive the people of the South.

Pemberton had been entirely deceived by Grant and
by himself.

He had an invincible reluctance to change his
base, and could not imagine that Grant had launched
his columns into the country, to find their base in
their haversacks and in the supplies around them. By
advancing to Raymond, Grant exposed, of course, his
line of communication with Grand Gulf; and Pemberton thought it the highest generalship to move south
to Raymond, and seize this line, which he believed
indispensable to Grant's army. Pemberton said, " My
own views were expressed as unfavorable to any movement which would remove me from my base, which
was and is Vicksburg."

But Pemberton, it is seen, was about to assail a line
of communication which did not exist. Grant had

said, " I shall communicate with Grand Gulf no more."
He would open a line of communication again with the
North ; but it would not be until he had placed the old
flag on the capitol of Mississippi, and driven Pemberton
and his army fifty miles back, within the intrenchments
at Vicksburg.

CHAPTER XIII.

BATTLE AT JACKSON.

PEMBERTON now advanced his army to Edward's Station. On the 12th, he had telegraphed to Johnston, "The enemy is apparently moving his heavy force towards Edward's Dépôt. *That will be the battle-place.*"

Without knowledge of this telegram, of course, Grant, the same day (the 12th), wrote to McClernand, "Edward's Station is evidently the point on the railroad the enemy have most prepared for receiving us. I therefore want to keep up *appearances* of moving upon that place." The day Pemberton was thus theorizing, Grant fought and won the battle of Raymond against Gregg, far on the road to Jackson ; and that night he ordered McPherson to "march at daylight for Clinton and Jackson." And to Sherman he wrote, "You will march at four, A.M., in the morning, and follow McPherson." At the same hour, he sent to McClernand, "Start with your three divisions as soon as possible, and *on to Raymond.*"

McPherson, as ordered, had advanced on Clinton, where he arrived about two o'clock, and immediately burned the bridges, tore up the railroad-track, and destroyed the telegraph.

Sherman and his column arrived about the same time. That night, the 13th, Gen. Johnston, a soldier of genius and vigor, had arrived at Jackson to command the forces which were constantly forwarded there with all the energy of the leaders of the Rebellion. Before he slept, he sent orders to Pemberton to attack the Federal troops at Clinton, saying, " To beat such a detachment would be of immense value. Time is all-important." Even Johnston did not understand that it was no " detachment " they would meet.

The same night, Grant ordered the army to move at early dawn upon Jackson. On the morning of the 14th, he sent word to Gen. Halleck of the battle at Raymond, and said, in closing his despatch, " I will attack the State capital to-day." Pemberton and his troops were busily strengthening Edward's Station, deceived by McClernand's pickets, and expecting an attack there; but Grant and Pemberton were planning campaigns for different armies.

It had rained hard during the night, increasing all the difficulties of the movement; but the soldiers felt that they were marching from one victory at Raymond to another at Jackson, and pushed on in fine spirits. It was nine o'clock on the morning of the 14th when the rebel pickets were met and driven in about five miles out from Jackson. The army advanced, and found the enemy in force nearly two miles and a half beyond.

Johnston was in command, with the flower of the Southern soldiery. Regiments were there from South Carolina and Georgia. Their batteries were posted on a semicircular ridge in the rear, and the infantry in front, in ravines traversed by a fence.

While the regiments were moving into position, the rain was so violent, that every cartridge-box opened was filled with water. It was eleven o'clock before the artillery commenced the battle. Our skirmishers were met by so heavy a fire, that they were called in; and Gen. Crocker was ordered to charge. At once, the whole line swept forward with muskets loaded, bayonets fixed. The loud cheers ring out. On they go, through the ravine, and up the hill, to the muzzles of the rebel guns. The enemy broke, and fled back to their defences, a mile and a half in the rear. Here an effective fire of artillery was opened; and officers were sent out to reconnoitre the works.

Sherman, who had advanced in another direction from McPherson, also found intrenchments to the left as far as could be seen, from which a sharp artillery-fire was maintained. Grant ordered an examination to the extreme right, the flanks of these intrenchments. Those sent not returning as soon as he desired, he started himself, followed only by his staff, and rode until he found that the enemy had evacuated the town. The route was open, and he rode on. His son, a boy of thirteen, who was with him as they neared the town, started his horse on a gallop, and was the first to enter the streets.

But McPherson also learned that the rebels had evacuated the works, and marched inside of them on one flank, while Sherman marched in on the other, meeting midway amid prolonged shouts of victory.

By three o'clock, the national ensign, raised by the Fifty-ninth Indiana, was waving from the dome of the capitol.

The leading secessionists of the place had left with the rebel army, including the State Treasurer with the funds, and Gov. Pettus with all the most valuable State papers except the copies of his proclamation. But history will preserve this.

Before four o'clock, Grant was issuing orders to his corps commanders in the governor's room at the capitol. Sherman was ordered to occupy the rifle-pits, and destroy the railroads, bridges, and telegraphs in all directions, except towards Vicksburg. Factories and arsenals were burned. A public house called the " Confederate Hotel " was fired by some of the soldiers before the guard could take possession of the city. On investigation, it appeared that some of the Union troops had been transported through Jackson, some months before, as prisoners on cattle-cars, which were stopped in front of this hotel. The captives, who had suffered long from thirst, asked for a little water, but were refused with brutal and insulting taunts by those in the hotel. They had been exchanged, and returned to the army in time to assist in the capture of Jackson, and exhibited in the first moments of victory a vivid recollection of the inhumanity of their former treatment. The officers regretted the unauthorized destruction of private property ; but the soldiers probably thought that one burning wrong was in this case not unfitly avenged by another.

That night, Grant occupied the elegant mansion of a wealthy rebel, which had been Johnston's headquarters. The indications were, that the rebel generals the night before had celebrated with a banquet the victory they expected to achieve over Grant ; but their victory was in anticipation only.

It was

> " A banquet-hall deserted:
>   Its lights were fled,
>   Its garlands dead,
> And all but (Grant) departed."

Johnston retreated several miles, and at once wrote to Pemberton, asking, " Can Grant supply himself from the Mississippi? Can you not cut him off from it? And above all, should he be compelled to fall back for want of supplies, beat him." The idea that Grant had left his base still distressed both these distinguished generals, and gave them unnecessary solicitude.

Grant at once issued orders for McPherson to start at daylight, and return; marching to Bolton, twenty miles on the road to Vicksburg. Orders were also despatched to McClernand and Gen. Frank Blair to concentrate at the same point. The object now was to return and defeat Pemberton before Johnston and his army could join him. A courier was sent back to Grand Gulf with despatches for Gen. Halleck, announcing the victory at Jackson.

By half-past nine o'clock, the advance of Osterhaus's Federal cavalry was driving in the rebel pickets, and picking up prisoners in the town of Bolton. The troops were pressing on as fast as possible over the muddy roads, now badly cut up by the artillery and baggage-wagons. But the soldiers saw that quick movements and rapid marches enabled them to outnumber the enemy at the point of attack; and they hurried forward with increased confidence in the genius of their leader.

" I am happy to see you," said the Emperor Alexander to Gen. Savary the night after the battle of

Austerlitz. "This day has been one of glory to the Emperor Napoleon. I confess, the rapidity of his manœuvres never gave me time to succor the menaced points. Everywhere you were double the number of our forces." — "Sire," said Savary, "our force was twenty-five thousand less than yours, and the whole of that was not engaged; but the same division combated at different points. *Therein lies the art of war.* The emperor has seen forty pitched battles, and is never wanting in that particular."

The rank and file thoroughly understood Gen. Grant's desire to spare human life, and enable them to fight their battles with their legs rather than with the deadly missiles of war.

While Grant was attacking Jackson, Pemberton was in council with his generals, deciding whether he should adopt Gen. Johnston's suggestion to move east, and attack the Federal troops at Clinton. He decided that it was not so important as to "cut Grant's line of communication with Grand Gulf," a desire which never forsook him; and he accordingly moved south towards Dillon to sever Grant from his base. At forty minutes past five, P.M., May 14, he wrote to Johnston, " I shall move, as early to-morrow as practicable, a column of seventeen thousand on Dillon's. The object is to cut the enemy's communication." Such had been the masterly strategy of Gen. Grant in this campaign, that the extraordinary sight was now witnessed of three rebel armies marching south, north, and east away from him, while he was converging between them, from three different quarters, his united army, flushed with victory. This is the art of war.

But Pemberton now learned more of Grant's movements, and perceived, that in moving from Edward's Station, on the direct road from Vicksburg to Jackson, he had simply moved out of Grant's path, and left the way open to Vicksburg. His object now was to return as soon as possible; but this must be done with care, or he would find himself passing in front of Grant's columns. Grant was marching from east to west for Edward's Station; and Pemberton was returning from the south to the north, toward the same line.

About five o'clock on the morning of the 15th, Grant learned from a couple of men employed on the Jackson and Vicksburg Railroad, who had passed through Pemberton's army, that the enemy were near Edward's Station with about twenty-five thousand men.

In thirty minutes, a courier was on the road to Jackson with the following order to Sherman: "Start one of your divisions on the road at once with their ammunition-wagons.

.   .   .   .

"I have evidence that the entire force of the enemy was at Edward's Dépôt at seven, P.M., last night, and was still advancing. The fight may therefore be brought on at any moment."

In one hour after this order was received, Sherman's troops were in motion.

Pemberton, who had been educated at West Point, had selected his battle-field with the eye of a trained soldier. Champion's Hill, half-way between Vicksburg and Jackson, rises sixty or seventy feet above the surrounding country: its summit, free from woods, afforded an admirable position for artillery; but the sides over

which our troops must move were covered with thick
underbrush, and seamed with ravines. Here Pemberton
had placed his army of twenty-five thousand men.
Loring had the right, Bowen the centre, and Stevens
the left, of the rebel line. Pemberton was ignorant that
Grant's entire army was in the vicinity around him.
Hovey's troops were nearest to Pemberton; but Grant
preferred that the action should not be opened until the
divisions in the rear could be moved up. By eleven
o'clock, the battle had commenced: McClernand, with
four divisions, was advancing from Raymond, and had
been ordered to hurry forward, but had not arrived.
Hovey's division moved against the hill toward the
west, supported by two brigades of Logan, which were
within four hundred yards of the enemy.

The fire raged along the whole line of battle. Cannon, shot, shell, and rifle-balls swept the field in every
direction. But Hovey's division pressed through the
storm of death, and slowly mounted the hill; the living
closing their ranks as the dead dropped beside them.
They drove the enemy back six hundred yards, and captured eleven guns and three hundred prisoners. The
stars and stripes, and the State flags of Ohio, Indiana,
Iowa, and Wisconsin, were flying on the crest of the
hill. But here it was found that the road over the hill
was so cut as to afford a natural breastwork, which the
rebels at once used to their great advantage. Pemberton re-enforced the position; and Hovey's men, in spite
of all their heroic efforts, were pressed slowly back,
fighting every inch of the ground, but losing the
captured guns. Where is McClernand with his four
divisions of fifteen thousand men?

Officer after officer had been despatched to hurry him up. Grant, who had watched the battle with his son by his side, repeatedly looked toward Raymond, and listened for McClernand's guns as Napoleon listened for the cannon of Davoust beyond the Tower of Ncuisedel at Wagram. But Hovey was giving way against overwhelming odds; and Grant ordered a brigade of Crocker's division to his support, and they held their ground.

Meanwhile, Logan had pressed the left of the rebel line with such terrible effect, that he was working into their rear; which they soon discovered. At this time, a battery on the Union right opened upon them with fearful slaughter; McPherson moved on the rebel right front; Hovey and Crocker's divisions once more advanced with Logan's men; the enemy gave way; five of the guns were recaptured; the battle was won.

The enemy retreated over the Big Black River, and were followed till night. This was the severest battle of the campaign. Our loss, in killed, wounded, and missing, was 2,457. The rebel loss was between three and four thousand in killed and wounded, and nearly three thousand taken prisoners; fifteen or twenty guns, eleven of them captured by Logan's command. Among the rebel dead was Gen. Tighlman, who was captured the year previous at Fort Henry. The pursuit by Grant after the battle was so quick, that Gen. Loring's division was separated from Pemberton's main army, and was never able to join the garrison of Vicksburg.

The nature of the ground had required the Union troops to ascend the hill in column, and offer their solid masses to be ploughed by the enemy's artillery,

GRANT AND HIS SON AT CHAMPION'S HILL. — Page 140.

which was worked with deadly skill. The soldiers
called it the "Hill of Death:" but it was also the hill
of victory; for, in reality, it decided the fate of Vicksburg.

> "They never fail who die
> In a great cause: the block may soak their gore;
> Their heads may sodden in the sun; their limbs
> Be strung to city gates and castle walls:
> But still their spirits walk abroad."

That no incident might be wanting to render the day
remarkable, Grant now received orders from Gen. Halleck, dated the 11th, to move down the river instead
of marching into the interior. "If possible," he said,
"the forces of yourself and Banks should be united
between Vicksburg and Port Hudson. The same
thing has been urged on Banks." It was well that
Grant had broken up his line of communication with
his superior, as well as with Grand Gulf, before these
orders arrived. He was now marching back to the
Mississippi; but it was to enter Vicksburg as a conqueror.

Grant and his staff rode on with the pursuing column,
until, late in the night, he found himself too far in advance, and rode back to bivouac with his soldiers. He
slept on the piazza of a house which was used as a
hospital for the rebel wounded. The battle was fought
on Saturday: the evening brought the close of the
week and the approach of the sabbath. It was a
beautiful night. Though yet spring, the air in that
Southern clime was touched by the fervors of midsummer; and, not unnaturally, the hearts of all were softened by thoughts of home and loved ones far away.

The Twenty-fourth Iowa was called the " Methodist Regiment," as a large portion of its officers and men were of that denomination ; and all at once, as if by common impulse, the men began singing " Old Hundred: " others joined ; and, as the strains of the grand old hymn went up on the voices of thousands, it seemed both a requiem for comrades slain, and a song of thanksgiving for the victory won.

CHAPTER XIV.

BATTLE AT BIG BLACK RIVER.

ON the morning of the 17th, McClernand's forces found the enemy strongly posted on both sides of the Big Black River, at the railroad-bridge. In front of the eastern bank was a wide bayou, nearly twenty feet across: this was a natural wet ditch, behind which were rifle-pits. The west bank was a high bluff, with twenty pieces of artillery in position to command the east bank and the approaching Federal forces. Trees had been felled to form an abatis. Engineering science could have hardly constructed a more formidable position than Nature here offered for defence. Here Pemberton took his stand with four thousand men. He said, " So strong was the position, that my greatest, almost my only, apprehension was a flank movement by Bridgeport or Baldwin's Ferry, which would have endangered my communications with Vicksburg." But he had against him the men who had been at Donelson, at Corinth, and at Champion's Hill.

The artillery-firing and skirmishing continued for two or three hours; when Gen. Lawler — who was rushing around in his shirt-sleeves, determined to cross somewhere — discovered a spot on the left of the rebel defences, where, by moving a portion of his brigade through a piece of woods, he thought an assault might be made.   The supporting troops, seeing a part of Lawler's men start, animated by their repeated victories, dashed after them without waiting for orders, and rushed over the bayou in the midst of a murderous fire, which swept down a hundred and fifty of their number.   On reaching the end of the rebel parapet, a place was seen wide enough for four men to walk abreast: through this the assaulting party rushed with fixed bayonets and loud cheers.   The astonished rebels, accustomed to defeat, as Pemberton said, " did not wait to receive them, but broke, and fled precipitately." A panic ensued. The rebels fired the western end of the bridge, regardless of their troops on the other side. Many jumped into the river to escape; some attempted to cross amid the flames; some ran wildly up and down the banks of the river; others surrendered. An entire brigade was taken prisoners.   The rebel army, now little better than a mob, began its hurried flight to Vicksburg, where their unexpected arrival and utterly demoralized condition filled the city with terror and dismay.

Our loss was twenty-nine killed and two hundred and forty-two wounded. Seventeen hundred and fifty-one prisoners were captured, eighteen cannon, five stand of colors, and large quantities of commissary-stores. All the roads to Vicksburg were opened.

Grant immediately ordered bridges to be built; and cotton-gins, boards, timbers from the farm-houses, and cotton-bales, were brought into requisition for this purpose. At one point, an ingenious bridge was thrown over by simply felling large trees on both sides so as to unite their tops in the middle of the stream.

That night, Sherman, who had the pontoon-train, was ordered to cross the river at Bridgeport, north of the railroad; Grant adding, "We will move in three columns, if roads can be found to move on; and either have Vicksburg or Haine's Bluff to-morrow night."

Early the next morning, McPherson and McClernand, with their columns, were moving on Vicksburg, now fifteen miles distant. At daylight, Sherman's division also crossed the river higher up, and struck for Walnut Hills, north of Vicksburg, between it and Haine's Bluff, and commanding the entrance to the Yazoo River.

By half-past nine o'clock, the head of Gen. Sherman's columns halted within three miles and a half of Vicksburg for the remainder of the force to come up.

During this campaign, for thirteen days the men had only six days' rations and such supplies as the country afforded; grinding their own corn, and marching without tents or cooking-utensils: yet all were prompt and cheerful in the discharge of their duty.*

In eighteen days, Grant had marched two hundred miles, fought five battles, taken six thousand and five hundred prisoners, killed and wounded six thousand more, taken twenty-seven cannon and sixty-one pieces of field-artillery. He had compelled the evacuation of Grand Gulf, captured the capital of the State of Mississippi, and destroyed its network of railroads for more than thirty miles in all directions.

His losses were six hundred and ninety-eight killed, three thousand four hundred and seven wounded, and two hundred and thirty missing.

He had subsisted his army on the enemy's territory.

10

* McClernand's Report.

The whole campaign was a new thing in war, and was the model of "the great march to the sea." This was the first instance in history of an army marching into an enemy's country, and depending on their haversacks for daily supplies. Napoleon had levied contributions on cities and countries; but they were often in money, always ordered in advance, and, in many instances, months before his army left Paris.

And here a strange scene took place. The friendship of Grant and Sherman will live in history as one of the many remarkable incidents of the war. It has for centuries been observed that great men seldom choose friends so much for mental as for social qualities. Heroes rarely seek companions in their equals. Eagles fly alone. Achilles does not seek friendship with Ajax, but the gentle Patroclus; and Æneas soothes himself with the affection of Achates, and not the companionship of Diomed. It was not Ney, "the bravest of the brave," but the unknown Col. Muiron, whom Napoleon loved, and whose name he wished to wear in his exile at St. Helena. Grant and Sherman rode out alone on the summit of one of the highest of the Walnut Hills, and gazed in silence on the panorama at their feet,— the river; the city; the great prizes of the campaign; the Yazoo, along whose banks Sherman had led his column by torchlight; Haine's Bluff, which had tossed back the Federal troops as the rocky shore flings back the ocean spray; and the long line of batteries unassailable by the navy. Neither spoke. The letter of Sherman to Grant, remonstrating against the campaign so earnestly, had never been mentioned. Sherman now turned suddenly to Grant, and said, "Until this moment, I never thought your expedition a success. I never could see the end clearly until now. But this is a campaign. This is a success if we never take the town."

Haine's Bluff was abandoned by the enemy, and its garrison joined that of Vicksburg. Communication was opened with the river at the foot of Walnut Hills, and supplies of all kinds were forwarded to the troops.

CHAPTER XV.

THE SIEGE OF VICKSBURG.

BY the 19th of May, Vicksburg, "the city of a hundred hills," was closely invested; and its fall was only a question of time. The city was about four or five miles long, and nearly two miles wide. The defences consisted of detached redoubts connected by rifle-pits. The works on the land-side were eight miles long, with about four miles of heavy batteries on the water-front. It was intersected by ravines and ridges covered by an impenetrable growth of cane and vines; and, in front, heavy trees had been felled. It was a vast intrenched camp, with two hundred cannon mounted in commanding positions, and bristling with forty thousand bayonets in the hands of brave and determined men.

Johnston had sent word to Pemberton, "If Haine's Bluff is untenable, Vicksburg is of no value," and urging him to save his army. Pemberton was holding a council of war to determine what he should do, when the guns of the Union army announced that Grant had already decided this question, and that escape was impossible.

His expectation now was, that the Confederate Government would relieve him before the place could be taken.

Johnston was gathering an army to attack Grant in the rear. Grant had no force equal to besieging Pemberton, preventing a *sortie* of his army, and at the same time fighting a battle with thirty thousand under Johnston. The army was impatient for an assault before settling down to the dull, tedious labor of engineering; and at this time it was not supposed that Pemberton had over twelve or fifteen thousand men. His full force was not known until their surrender.

It was determined to make an assault at two o'clock on the 19th; which was done with great bravery. The Thirteenth United-States Infantry planted their colors on the outer works. The Eighty-third Indiana and the Hundred and Twenty-seventh Illinois reached a similar position at the same time. Gen. Blair secured and held an advanced position until ordered to fall back. But the strength of the works was too great to be carried in that manner before night settled down over the scene; and the troops fell back.

The bombardment, especially from the mortar-boats, was so severe, that the people began digging caves in the sides of the hills; and Pemberton, unable to feed his horses and mules, drove them outside his lines.

On the 22d, it was determined to make one more attempt to carry Vicksburg by storm. Gen. Grant knew that Johnston was concentrating a large army at Canton; and he was desirous of capturing Vicksburg, so that he could attack this army, and drive the rebels out of the State, giving to the government the railroads and military highways west of the Tombigbee, before the heat of summer came on. He was anxious also to save the necessity of sending to him any re-enforcements which were needed so much elsewhere. The troops also were fully persuaded that the works, which were only four hundred yards distant, could be carried by storm, and would have been disheartened to enter the trenches for a prolonged siege until this was settled.

A commander is unwise who wholly disregards the convictions of an army of thirty thousand intelligent men in such a case, even if they do not wholly agree with his mature judgment.

Orders were given for a general assault at ten o'clock on the 22d. "Promptly at the hour designated, all will start at quick time, with bayonet fixed, and march immediately upon the enemy, without firing a gun until the outer works are carried."

Watches of the corps commanders were compared, and set by that of the general commanding. At five minutes before ten, the bugles sounded to prepare for a charge; and at ten precisely the three army corps of McClernand, McPherson, and Sherman, moved on the works. Gen. Grant was in a commanding position near Sherman's corps, which gave him the best view of the advancing columns.

A forlorn hope of a hundred and fifty men, with poles and boards, was to bridge the ditch in the face of the concentrated fire of five batteries. Not a man or rifle of the rebels was seen until the storming-parties began to ascend the ridge, when along the whole line they opened a most murderous fire, against which it was simply self-murder to persist.

Regiment after regiment pushed on, and at different points placed their colors on the outer slopes of the enemy's works. At one point, a handful of men led by Sergeant Griffith, a lad not twenty years old, of the Twenty-second Iowa, entered one bastion; but all were captured except the brave Griffith, who secured thirteen rebels as prisoners. While this was going on, the fleet and mortar-boats, with 100-pound Parrotts mounted on rafts, were filling the air with their deadly missiles, and raining shot, shell, fire, and death upon the city from the river. The sight was awful and sublime. The constant booming of so many hundred heavy cannon, the shells screeching and exploding, and the tens of thousands of Minie-balls whizzing through the air in every direction, drove to desperation the enraged combatants.

There were deeds of unsurpassed bravery throughout the day. White's Chicago Mercantile Battery actually put their ammunition in their haversacks, and dragged their heavy guns by hand, while under constant fire, down one slope and up another, and fired into one of the embrasures.

But all in vain. The inner works commanded the outer. The natural and artificial strength of the place was too great, and the army defending it too large, for an army of only equal numbers to carry it by assault.

The long wars of Napoleon showed no such daring assault. It was fifty-one thousand Englishmen under Wellington at Badajos that assaulted five thousand French, and it was thirty-five thousand English at Ciudad Rodrigo that assaulted seventeen hundred French.

It was now evident that Vicksburg could only be taken by regular siege; and this was commenced without a day's delay. Hurlbut and Prentiss were ordered to send forward " every available man that could possibly be spared." " The siege of Vicksburg is going to occupy time, contrary to my expectations when I arrived near it. . . . Contract every thing on the line of the route from Memphis to Corinth, and keep your cavalry well out south of there : by this means, you ought to be able to send here quite a large force."

And now earthworks and covered ways were erected; and the soldiers took practical lessons in engineering, and became learned in the technicalities of the science. Trenches, revets, salients, gabions, banquettes, boyau, mining, and counter-mining were the order of the day. " Vicksburg must be taken." The labor in the trenches was greatly aided by large numbers of negroes. The length of all the trenches was twelve miles. Eighty-nine batteries were constructed; and by the 3d of June two hundred and twenty guns were in position. The very small number of professional engineers with the army required Gen. Grant to give personal supervision to the details of the siege in different sections of the work almost from hour to hour. Occasionally the rebels would open mines, and sometimes make a *sortie*, but with little effect. Their desire seemed to be to save their men, and wait for relief from Johnston. At one point, the pickets of the besieged and besiegers agreed not to fire on each other at night, when the principal labor was done, and allotted the ground between them so that working-parties were not ten yards apart. The amount of labor performed night and day was prodigious. Those not in the trenches were picking off the rebels by sharpshooting whenever a head was seen ; or working the artillery, which never seemed to be silent. On the 4th of June, Johnston had collected, by his own report, an army of about twenty-seven thousand men, which he was endeavoring to increase to forty thousand. Grant really had two armies on his hands. Expeditions were sent east to the Big Black River to destroy bridges and forage, and to bring in cattle and every thing which could be of use to Johnston's army.

Gen. Blair was sent with twelve thousand men to drive off the enemy between the Yazoo and the Big Black River, where Johnston was gathering large supplies. Grant was attacking Pemberton on the west, and at the same time carefully preparing to defend himself from Johnston on the east. While besieging, he was threatened with a siege. Pemberton now conceived the idea of tearing down the houses of Vicksburg to build two thousand boats with which his army might escape over the river; and Vicksburg was turned into a sort of navy-yard "*ad interim*." But the boats, if boats they could be called, never touched the river. After the capture of the city, many of them were examined by our soldiers as curious specimens of marine architecture.

On the 22d, it was expected that Johnston would advance. Sherman was ordered to look after him: and Grant said, " They seem to put a great deal of faith in the Lord and Joe Johnston; but *you* must whip Johnston at least fifteen miles from here." To Herron and A. J. Smith he wrote, " Should Johnston come, we want to whip him, if the siege has to be raised to do it." To Parke he wrote, " We want to whip Johnston at least fifteen miles off if possible." To McClernand, " Hold and fight the enemy *wherever he presents himself*, from the extreme right to the extreme left. The movements of an enemy necessarily determine counter-movements." To another, " *Certainly, use the negroes, and every thing within your command*, to the best advantage. Travel with as little baggage as possible, and use your teams as an ordnance and supply train." To Ord, " Keep Smith's division sleeping under arms to-night. Notify Lauman to be in readiness all night." To Washburne, " Make the detail with reference to the competency of the colonel who will command the expedition. He must be a live and active man."

To maintain himself thus between two armies, required, as may well be imagined, the most constant and untiring vigilance ; and Johnston, after a full study of the situation, wrote to the Secretary of War at Richmond, " Grant's position, naturally very strong, is intrenched, and protected by powerful artillery, and the roads obstructed. . . . The Big Black covers him from attack, and would cut off our retreat if defeated."

Pemberton was writing, " Enemy bombards day and night from seven mortars. He also keeps up constant fire on our line with artillery and musketry." Again he says, " On the Graveyard Road [significant name to the rebel army], the enemy's works are within twenty-five feet of our redan. My men have been thirty-four days and nights in the trenches without relief, and the enemy within conversation-distance."

On the 25th, a mine which had been prepared was exploded. The mine contained two thousand two hundred pounds of powder. At three o'clock, word was brought that all was ready. Two hundred men from the Forty-fifth Illinois and the Twenty-third Indiana were to lead the forlorn hope. Many were in their shirt-sleeves, and carrying nothing but their guns and cartridge-boxes, prepared for close and hard fighting. These men were in view of thousands whom the thrilling excitement of the moment hushed into silence. A few moments, and the fuses exploded, and the earth was lifted to the skies as with the power of an earthquake. The vast mass of powder blazed up; the chasm yawned, and showed a sea of surging flame, as if the globe itself had opened to spout out its great central fires. Sods, earth, rocks, cannon, broken gun-carriages, mangled remains of men, all mingled in confusion, were hurled a hundred feet into the air. Strange to say, some of the rebels were carried over and landed alive within the Union lines. Simultaneously, twelve miles of artillery and rifles opened with their dread roar. The cavity made in the earth was large enough to hold two thousand men, into which the combatants rushed with maddened fury. The soldiers called it "the death-hole." There, with rifles, bayonets, clubbed muskets, hand-grenades, revolvers, the struggling mass fought until after nightfall. The Union soldiers were unable to enter the inner lines, but held their ground; and the next day extended rifle-pits across the opening.

Thus the siege progressed. Pemberton especially, after Grant's successes in the opening of the campaign, was accused of "selling Vicksburg," and made the most determined efforts to hold the city. He had early made a speech to the citizens and soldiers, in which he said, "You have heard that I am incompetent, and a

traitor; and that it was my intention to sell Vicksburg.
Follow me, and you will see the cost at which I will
sell Vicksburg. When the last pound of beef, bacon,
and flour, the last grain of corn, the last cow and hog,
and horse and dog, shall have been consumed, and the
last man shall have perished in the trenches, — then,
and only then, will I sell Vicksburg."

Forty-seven days and nights the work went on.
Seven thousand mortar-shells, and four thousand five
hundred shells from the gunboats, had been thrown into
the devoted city. The houses burned, and torn to
pieces, the citizens had been obliged to find shelter in
holes dug in the earth in the sides of the hills; and here
parents died, and children were born. Flour was a
thousand dollars a barrel (rebel money); meal, a hundred and forty dollars a bushel; mule-meat, one dollar a
pound. Mule-soup was a luxury. The rich had eaten
their last crust; and now rich and poor were meeting
starvation together. The soldiers were living on bran-
bread, and half-rations at that. The heats of summer
were now filling the exhausted and worn-out frames of
the soldiers with the pestilence of the swamps. Nature
was undermining the rebel camp more surely than the
art of man.

A rebel woman living in the outskirts, who had
remained in her battered tenement, asked Gen. Grant
one day, when he stopped for some water, if he ever
expected to take Vicksburg. He said, " Yes."

" But when ? " said the woman.

" I don't know *when;* but I shall take it if I stay
here thirty years." His determination had greater
longevity than she had imagined.

To illustrate the character of this civil war: The pickets of the two armies at one point were accustomed at last to meet at night at a well between the lines, where they would discuss the cause of the war, the rights of the South and slavery; and, when debate grew excited, they would part, as they said, "to avoid getting into a fight on the subject." It was, in truth, a war of *ideas*, — an "irrepressible conflict" between liberty and slavery.

Meanwhile, parlor-soldiers, solemn croakers, who opened their papers at quiet firesides, and read daily, "Siege of Vicksburg progressing," shook their wise heads, and said, "They'll never take that place: it's a perfect Gibraltar."

At this time, Grant was not only confident of success, but mentally reaching forward to other operations. To Gen. Banks he writes, "Should it be my fortune, general, to get into Vicksburg while you are still investing Port Hudson, I will commence immediately shipping troops to you, and will send such number as you may indicate as being necessary." To Halleck, who had aided him with energy as far as possible since his campaign became pronounced, he wrote, "There is no doubt of the fall of this place ultimately." Later he says, "The enemy are now undoubtedly in our grasp. The fall of Vicksburg, and the capture of most of the garrison, can only be a question of time."

On the 30th of June he writes, "The troops of this command are in excellent health and spirits. There is not the slightest indication of despondency either among officers or men."

The walls of fire were steadily closing around Vicksburg, day by day, hour by hour. On the 1st of July, Grant was preparing another assault; when, on the morning of the 3d, a white flag was seen flying from the rebel lines; and Gen. Bowen, and Col. Montgomery of Gen. Pemberton's staff, left for the Union camp. The rebel soldiers imagined a surrender was to be made, and were much excited. Gen. Bowen was the bearer of a letter to Gen. Grant. After being blindfolded, these officers were conducted to Gen. Smith's quarters, where the following letter from Gen. Pemberton was delivered : —

" I have the honor to propose to you an armistice of —— hours, with a view to arranging terms for the capitulation of Vicksburg. To this end, if agreeable to you, I will appoint three commissioners to meet a like number to be named by yourself at such place and hour as you may find convenient. I make this proposition to save the further effusion of blood, which must otherwise be shed to a frightful extent; feeling myself fully able to maintain my position for a yet indefinite period. This communication will be handed you, under a flag of truce, by Major-Gen. J. S. Bowen.

To which Gen. Grant returned the following reply : —

" Your note of this date is just received, proposing an armistice for several hours for the purpose of arranging terms of capitulation through commissioners to be appointed, &c. The effusion of blood you propose stopping by this course can be ended at any time you may choose *by an unconditional surrender of the city and garrison.* Men who have shown so much endurance and courage as those now in Vicksburg will always challenge the respect due them as prisoners of war. I do not favor the proposition of appointing commissioners to arrange terms of capitulation, *because I have no other terms than those indicated above.*"

Gen. Bowen desired a personal interview with Gen.

Grant; which the latter declined. Upon the suggestion of the former, an interview between the two commanders was arranged for three o'clock that day.

At three o'clock, a signal-gun was fired; and Gen. Pemberton, with Gen. Bowen and Col. Montgomery, left the rebel works. Gen. Grant rode through the Union trenches to an outlet leading to a spot of green earth which had not been trod by either army, about two hundred feet from the rebel lines. With him were Generals McPherson, Logan, Ord, and Smith, and one or two of Grant's staff. The two commanders, having never met, were introduced, and exchanged the salutation of gentlemen.

The interview was witnessed by thousands of both armies, who crowded the parapets unarmed, and gazed with deep and silent interest on the scene. The day was sultry, and the summer air as still as if it had never for centuries resounded to the voice of war.

After a moment's silence, Gen. Pemberton said, —

" Gen. Grant, I meet you in order to arrange terms for the capitulation of the city of Vicksburg and its garrison. What terms do you demand ? "

" Unconditional surrender," said Grant.

" If this is all," said Pemberton with assumed impatience and *hauteur*, " the conference may terminate, and hostilities be resumed immediately."

" Very well," said Gen. Grant, and turned to walk away.

The acquaintance of the men had not been long enough to show to Pemberton that Grant was a man who wasted no words, but who said what he meant, and meant what he said.

Gen. Bowen now ventured to suggest that two of the subordinates should confer, and present some basis of negotiation for their chiefs. Grant said he had no objections, but should be bound by no such action, and should be governed by his own sense of duty.

Bowen and Smith conversed a few moments; while Grant and Pemberton stepped aside, and engaged in conversation under a large oak-tree. Very soon, Gen. Bowen proposed that the rebels should march out from Vicksburg with honors of war; taking their muskets and field-guns, but leaving their heavy artillery. Grant smiled at this proposal, and said it was inadmissible. It was finally agreed that he should send his terms in writing before ten o'clock that night. Meanwhile hostilities were not to be resumed until negotiations were at an end.

He returned to his tent, and for the first time summoned his corps commanders and generals to a council of war as to the terms which should be offered; but none of them, with a single exception, proposed terms which he was willing to accept.

He finally sent the following letter to Gen. Pemberton : —

"In conformity with agreement of this afternoon, I will submit the following proposition for the surrender of the city of Vicksburg, public stores, &c. On your accepting the terms proposed, I will march in one division as a guard, to take possession at eight o'clock, A.M., to-morrow. As soon as rolls can be made out, and paroles signed by officers and men, you will be allowed to march out of our lines, — the officers with their side-arms and clothing; and the field, staff, and cavalry officers, one horse each. The rank and file will be allowed all their clothing, but no other property. If these conditions are accepted, any amount of rations you may deem necessary can be taken from the stores you now have, and also all the necessary cooking utensils for preparing them. Thirty wagons also, counting two-horse or mule teams as one, will be allowed to transport such articles as cannot be carried along. The same conditions will be allowed to all sick and wounded officers and soldiers, as fast as they become able to travel. The paroles for these latter must be signed, however, while officers are present authorized to sign the roll of prisoners."

Pemberton submitted these terms to a council of his officers, all of whom, with one exception, advised their acceptance ; and late at night he sent the following to Gen Grant : —

"I have the honor of acknowledging the receipt of your communication of this date, proposing terms of capitulation for this garrison and post. In the main, your terms are accepted ; but, in justice both to the honor and spirit of my troops manifested in the defence of Vicksburg, I have to submit the following amendments, which, if acceded to by you, will perfect the agreement between us.

"At ten o'clock, A.M., to-morrow, I propose to evacuate the works in and around Vicksburg, and to surrender the city and garrison under my command, by marching out with my colors and arms, stacking them in front of my present lines ; after which you will take possession. Officers to retain their side-arms and personal property, and the rights and property of citizens to be respected."

This was not received until midnight ; but Grant replied immediately as follows : —

"I have the honor to acknowledge the receipt of your communication of the 3d of July. The amendment proposed by you cannot be acceded to in full. It will be necessary to furnish every officer and man with a parole signed by himself, which, with the completion of the roll of prisoners, will necessarily take some time.

"Again: I can make no stipulations with regard to the treatment of citizens and their private property. While I do not propose to cause them any undue annoyance or loss, I cannot consent to leave myself under any restraint by stipulations. The property which officers will be allowed to take with them will be as stated in my proposition of last evening; that is, officers will be allowed their private baggage and side-arms, and mounted officers one horse each.

"If you mean, by your proposition, for each brigade to march to the front of the lines now occupied by it, and stack arms at ten o'clock, A.M., and then return to the inside, and there remain as prisoners until properly paroled, I will make no objection to it. Should no notification be received of your acceptance of my terms by nine o'clock, A.M., I shall regard them as having been rejected, and shall act accordingly. Should these terms be accepted, white flags should be displayed along your lines to prevent such of my troops as may not have been notified from firing upon your men."

Gen. Pemberton returned an immediate answer as follows : —

"I have the honor to acknowledge the receipt of your communication of this day, and in reply to say that the terms proposed by you are accepted."

On receipt of Pemberton's *first* letter, while the correspondence was still progressing, Gen. Grant sent the following orders to Sherman : " There is little doubt but that the enemy will surrender to-night or in the morning. Make your calculations to attack Johnston, and destroy the road north of Jackson."

To Generals Steele and Ord, similar orders were issued. " I want," says Grant, " Johnston broken up as effectually as possible. You can make your own arrangements, and have all the troops of my command except one corps."

Nothing can show more clearly the unremitting energy of Gen. Grant's character than the issuing of these orders that night.

At ten o'clock on the morning of the 4th of July, regiment after regiment of the rebel army marched out in front of their breastworks, and, in view of the Union soldiers, laid down their arms and colors. It was not until afternoon that the army, preceded by Logan's division, marched into the city. The Forty-fifth Illinois raised the national ensign on the court-house; and, as it spread itself to the breeze, thousands of the troops greeted it with the well-known song, beginning, —

> "Yes, we'll rally round the flag, boys, we'll rally once again,
>   Shouting the battle-cry of freedom!"

Gen. Grant rode to Gen. Pemberton's headquarters, where it might be supposed he was entitled, under the circumstances, to the ordinary civilities of private life. He alighted at the porch; but there was no one to receive him. He made his way into the house, where he found Pemberton and his staff: no one gave him a seat. The day was exceedingly hot and dusty, and Gen. Grant asked for a glass of water. He was curtly told he could find it inside. He wandered about the premises, until the negro, ever present where a service could be done to a Union soldier, furnished the needed refreshment. Pemberton asked Gen. Grant to supply his famished soldiers with rations; which Grant at once did. Gen. Pemberton could be indebted to Gen. Grant's grace and favor for the sword he wore, could ask from his captor the honors of war for himself and his army, receive from his hands the bread they were to eat; but he could not return to him the ordinary civilities of society. By such means do little men show their littleness.

Admiral Porter with his glass had seen the national flag raised; and before night seventy steamers were lying at the levees, and more were coming. All was activity: the long embargo was removed. From a besieged garrison, Vicksburg had in appearance changed, in a few hours, to a thriving inland city.

The surrender of the city was a surprise to many, especially to the talking rebels. Some Union soldiers strolled into the office of "The Citizen," the valiant rebel newspaper. It had been printed on house-paper. The forms of the paper for the second day of July were still standing; and these words appeared: "The great Ulysses — the Yankee generalissimo, surnamed Grant — has expressed his intention of dining in Vicksburg on Saturday next, and celebrating the 4th of July by a grand dinner. Ulysses must get into the city before he dines in it. The way to cook a rabbit is 'first to catch the rabbit,'" &c. This inflated bluster was quite in keeping with the management of the Rebellion. The people of Vicksburg were starving, living in caves, exalting mule-soup and fricasseed kittens into luxuries; yet their resources for boasting were inexhaustible, and they printed their silly defiance on house-paper until the hour of surrender.

Some of our soldiers, whose fingers were as skilful with types as with rifles, added these words: "Two days bring about great changes. The banner of the

Union floats over Vicksburg. Gen. Grant has caught the rabbit: he has dined in Vicksburg." *

Gen. Grant saw Gen. McPherson in possession of elegant headquarters in the city, but at night went back to his tent in the canebrakes.

The tidings of the surrender were telegraphed to the principal towns and cities of the North in the afternoon, and, with the news of the battle at Gettysburg, illumined the closing hours of the great national holiday.

The results of the whole campaign were the defeat of the enemy in five battles; the occupation of Jackson, the capital of the State; a loss to the enemy of fifty-six thousand prisoners, and at least ten thousand killed and wounded. Arms and munitions of war for sixty thousand men, railroad-cars, locomotives, steamboats, were destroyed in large numbers. Thirty-one thousand and six hundred of the above prisoners were surrendered with Vicksburg, a hundred and seventy-two cannon, and thirty-five thousand rifles and muskets.

Grant had lost 943 killed, 7,095 wounded, 537 missing. Half the wounded in a few weeks recovered, and were on duty. He announced this great victory to the government in the following terms: " The enemy surrendered this morning. The only terms allowed is their parole as prisoners of war. This I regard as a great advantage to us at this moment. It saves, probably, several days in the capture, and leaves troops and

* When Moscow was occupied by the French, a monument was erected in Coblentz with this inscription: " In honor of the memorable campaign against the Russians in 1812." Two years after, Col. Mardeuke, the Russian commander at Coblentz, left the monument untouched, but caused the following words to be cut under the inscription: " Seen and approved by the Russian commander of Coblentz, 1814."

transports ready for immediate service. Sherman, with a large force, moves immediately upon Johnston to drive him from the State."

Gen. Grant had made the largest capture ever made in war. The nearest approach to it was by Napoleon at Ulm; but there only thirty thousand prisoners and sixty guns were taken, and by a much larger army than Grant's.

This was the heaviest blow the Rebellion had ever received, and was one from which it never recovered. The thirty-two thousand prisoners, who had been well treated by Gen. Grant after taking possession of Vicksburg, and had mingled freely with our soldiers, scattered through the South to spread the news of the great disaster and predict the future of the " lost cause." An entire army had been taken out of the Rebellion. The great river was opened: the Confederacy was rent in twain.

CHAPTER XVI.

GENERALS Sherman and McPherson were recommended for appointment as brigadier-generals in the regular army in these noble words : —

" The first reason for this is their great fitness for any command that it may ever become necessary to intrust to them. Second, their great purity of character, and disinterestedness in every thing except the faithful performance of their duty, and the success of every one engaged in the great battle for the preservation of the Union. Third, they have honorably won this distinction upon many well-fought battle-fields. The promotion of such men as Sherman and McPherson always adds strength to our army."

President Lincoln addressed the following letter to Gen. Grant, so characteristic for its candor and honesty. It was dated July 13, 1863, at the Executive Mansion.

DEAR GENERAL, — I do not remember that you and I ever met personally. I write now as a grateful acknowledgment for the almost inestimable service you have done the country. I wish to say further, when you first reached the vicinity of Vicksburg, I thought you should do what you finally did, — march the troops across the neck, run the batteries with the transports, and thus go below; and I never had any faith, except a general hope that you knew better than I, that the Yazoo-pass expedition and the like could succeed.   When you got better, and took Port Gibson, Great Gulf, and the vicinity, I thought you should go down the river, and join Gen. Banks; and when you turned northward, east of the Big Black, I feared it was a mistake.   I now wish to make a personal acknowledgment that you was right, and I was wrong.

Yours very truly,

A. LINCOLN.

It was about this time that an ardent temperance man, in speaking of Gen. Grant's successes to President Lincoln, repeated some of the stories in regard to Gen. Grant's habits; adding, —

"It's a pity he is such a drunkard."

Mr. Lincoln, who had never countenanced these attacks, asked, —

"Do you know what *kind* of liquor he drinks?"

"No, sir," was the answer; "and I don't know that *that* is essential."

"The reason I asked," said Mr. Lincoln with a twinkle in his eye, but without moving a muscle of his face, "was, that, if I knew, I should like to send some of the same liquor to some of our other generals." *

President Lincoln was a rigid temperance man himself.   He refused to furnish or allow others to offer wine at his house to the committee who went to Springfield to inform him of his nomination for President.   His visitor saw that Mr. Lincoln wished to show the absurdity of thinking that a man could possibly do what Grant had accomplished in that campaign while debauched and enfeebled by intemperance.

---

* Some one was lamenting to old George II. that the war-office had placed confidence in such a red-haired, daring, hot-brained young officer as Gen. Wolfe, and sent him to Quebec; adding, "Wolfe is mad, your Majesty."—"Is he?" said the king. "I wish he would *bite* some of my other generals."

Port Hudson, which had been invested for some weeks by Gen. Banks and his army, surrendered on the 9th of July; and the Mississippi, as Mr. Lincoln expressed it, "rolled unvexed to the sea."

On the evening of the 4th, Ord and Steele had moved out of camp; and on the 6th Sherman was able to cross the Big Black River with not less than fifty thousand men. "I want you," said Grant, "to drive Johnston from the Mississippi Central Railroad, destroy the bridges as far north as Grenada with your cavalry, and do the enemy all the harm possible."

They were to march through places not easily forgotten. "They came," said Grant, "by Black-river Bridge, Edward's Station, and Champion's Hill. That is the route they now go." To Sherman he says again, "I have no suggestion or orders to give. I want you to drive Johnston out in your own way, and inflict on the enemy all the punishment you can. I will support you to the last man that can be spared."

Johnston fell back toward Jackson, where, on the 9th, Sherman found him. The works here had been strengthened, and extended toward Pearl River, both above and below the city. Johnston was anxious that Sherman should attack him, and telegraphed to Jefferson Davis, "If the enemy will not attack, we must, or at the last moment withdraw." For similar reasons, Sherman would not attack. He sent out cavalry for sixty or seventy miles in every direction, destroying every thing that could aid the rebel army, and bringing the war home to the people who were sustaining it.*

* It was during one of these raids that our cavalry overhauled the library and correspondence of Jefferson Davis, finding a gold-headed cane

On the 12th, Sherman's heavy guns commanded every part of the city, and more were being placed in position. Johnston saw the inevitable result; and on the night of the 5th he quietly moved his army out across Pearl River, and Jackson was once more in the hands of our forces.

Sherman decided that enough would not be gained by pursuit to warrant him in following Johnston a hundred miles across the country at that season of the year, in that climate; and he completed the work of destruction around Jackson. He rendered it impracticable for Johnston to return and annoy Grant; issued flour and pork to the starving families at Jackson and Clinton, who had been stripped by the demands of two armies; and returned to Vicksburg.

On the 11th of July, Gen. Grant wrote to the War Department, in regard to colored troops, as follows: " I am anxious to get as many of these negro regiments as possible, and to have them full, and completely equipped. . . . I am particularly desirous of organizing a regiment of heavy artillerists from the negroes to garrison this place, and shall do so as soon as possible."

On the 24th of July, " The negro troops are easier to preserve discipline among than our white troops,

---

sent to him by Ex-President Franklin Pierce, and various letters from Northern men, encouraging the Rebellion; among them the letter of Pierce in which he says, " And if, through the madness of Northern abolitionists, that dire calamity must come, the fighting will not be along Mason and Dixon's line merely. It will be within our own borders, in our own streets, between the two classes of citizens to whom I have referred. Those who defy law, and scout constitutional obligations, will, if we ever reach the arbitrament of arms, find occupation enough at home."

and I doubt not will prove equally good for garrison-duty. All that have been tried have fought bravely."

After the Emancipation Proclamation was issued, orders were sent from Richmond to the rebel armies to "give no quarter" to black troops and their officers. It was held by the South that the black soldiers were runaway slaves, and the officers found with them were thieves; and neither were entitled to the treatment of prisoners of war. In Grant's department and at Milliken's Bend occurred one of the first instances in which the rebels sought to carry out this theory. Grant, as we have seen, had never been technically an "abolitionist;" but he recognized the events which the war revealed. He had long determined that war should support war. He had organized camps for fugitives, protected them from abuse, received and acted on the information which they often brought him, and supported the policy of Mr. Lincoln on the question of "contrabands" as fast as it was pronounced. He did not anticipate the President and Congress in making a policy for them, but obeyed orders from time to time as they were issued.

But his private opinions were none the less clear, statesman-like, and decided. As early as Aug. 30, 1862, and before the Emancipation Proclamation was issued, he wrote to the Hon. E. B. Washburne of Illinois as follows: —

"The people of the North need not quarrel over the institution of slavery. What Vice-President Stevens acknowledges the corner-stone of the Confederacy is already knocked out. Slavery is already dead, and cannot be resurrected. It would take a standing army to maintain slavery in the South, if we were to make peace to-day, guaranteeing to the South all their former constitutional privileges. I never was an abolitionist, not even what could be called antislavery; but I try to judge fairly and honestly; and it became patent to my mind, early in the Rebellion, that the North and South could never live at peace with each other except as one nation, and that without slavery. As anxious as I am to see peace established, I would not, therefore, be willing to see any settlement until this question is forever settled."

In nothing was the arrogance of the slave-power more clearly seen than in their reasoning upon the relations of slaves to the war. They said, " Slaves are *property:* black soldiers shall be treated as fugitives, and their officers as having stolen them." But it is a universally acknowledged law of war, that the *property* of the enemy can be used or destroyed. Horses, mules, cotton, hay, grain, cattle, could be seized, because they are " property." But slaves are property, — a species of property vital to the support of the Rebellion, — and should therefore be used by the government. But here the slaveholders instantly pleaded their rights under the Constitution which they were seeking to destroy. When the Union was assailed, the Constitution, in the eyes of slaveholders, was only a " compact," a piece of paper of no binding effect; but, when slavery was assailed, the Constitution loomed up at once as " the great charter of our liberties," " a sacred bond," " a solemn covenant," to be obeyed though the heavens fell.

Slaves could be made to work at the point of the bayonet, by thousands, on rebel fortifications; and this was " constitutional;" but for the government to allow slaves in the armies of the Union was " unconstitutional," said rebels and their Northern apologists.

In an attack on Milliken's Bend during the Vicksburg campaign, it was rumored that several negro soldiers who had been captured were hung by the rebels. Gen. Grant addressed Gen. Richard Taylor on the subject in the following style: "I feel no inclination to retaliate for offences of irresponsible persons; but if it is the policy of any general intrusted with the command of troops to show no quarter, or to punish with death prisoners taken in battle, I will accept the issue. It may be that you propose a different line of policy towards black troops, and officers commanding them, to that practised towards white troops: if so, I can assure you that these colored troops are regularly mustered into the service of the United States. The government, and all officers under the government, are bound to give the same protection to these troops that they do to any other troops."

Gen. Grant also issued the following orders for the care and protection of the freedmen in his department: —

" At all military posts in States within this department where slavery has been abolished by the proclamation of the President of the United States, camps will be established for such freed people of color as are out of employment.

" Commanders of posts or districts will detail suitable officers from the army as superintendents of such camps.

" It will be the duty of such superintendents to see that suitable rations are drawn from the subsistence department for such people as are confided to their care.

" All such persons supported by the government will be employed in every practicable way, so as to avoid as far as possible their becoming a burden upon the government. They may be hired to planters or other citizens, on proper assurance that negroes so hired will not be run off beyond the military jurisdiction of the United States. They may be employed upon any public works, in gathering crops from abandoned plantations, and generally in any manner local commanders may deem for the best interests of the government, in compliance with the law and the policy of the Administration.

" It will be the duty of the provost-marshal at every military post to see that every negro within the jurisdiction of the military authority is employed by some white person, or is sent to the camps provided for freed people.

" Citizens may make contracts with freed persons of color for their labor, giving wages per month in money ; or employ families of them by the year on plantations, &c., feeding, clothing, and supporting the infirm as well as the able-bodied, and giving a portion, not less than one-twentieth, of the commercial part of their crops in payment for such service.

" Where negroes are employed under this authority, the parties employing will register with the provost-marshal their names, occupation, and residence, and the number of negroes so employed ; they will enter into such bonds as the provost-marshal, with the approval of the local commander, may require for the kind treatment and proper care of those employed, and as security against their being carried beyond the employé's jurisdiction. Nothing of this order is to be construed to embarrass the employment of such colored persons as may be required by the government."

" By order of Major-Gen. U. S. Grant."

It was at Milliken's Bend and Port Hudson that the bravery of the black soldiers first answered the question, " Will the negroes fight ? " Gen. Banks, in his report, said, " The position occupied by these troops was one of importance, and called for the utmost steadiness and bravery in those to whom it was confided. It gives me pleasure to report that they answered every expectation : in many respects, their conduct was heroic. No troops could be more determined or more daring. They made during the day three charges upon the batteries of the enemy, suffering very heavy losses, and holding their position at nightfall with the other troops on the right of our line."

The following lines by Mr. Boker were published about this time : —

> " Hundreds on hundreds fell :
> But they are resting well;
> Scourges and shackles strong
> Never shall do them wrong.
> Oh! to the living few,
> Soldiers, be just and true;
> Hail them as comrades tried;
> Fight with them side by side:
> Never, in field or tent,
> Scorn the black regiment."

CHAPTER XVII.

GRANT now understood perfectly the character of the war, and urged a vigorous use of all the recognized means of weakening the enemy. Until the battle at Pittsburg Landing, he believed the difficulties could be settled by negotiations between the sections; but, after he became satisfied of his mistake, he went for war with all its terrible realities.

"Feed your armies on the country which makes the war;" "Destroy every thing useful to the enemy;" "Seize every thing useful to your own forces." Have no measures of half war and half peace. If you blockade the rebel ports, and shut the South out from trade, shut them out wholly. Draw the cord so tight, that all commerce with them shall be strangled. Let there be no half trade and half non-intercourse. It was in this spirit that Gen. Grant thus wrote to Washington in answer to suggestions for partial trading: "No matter what the restrictions thrown around trade, if any whatever is allowed, it will be made the means of supplying the enemy with all they want. Restrictions, if lived up to, make trade unprofitable; and hence none but dishonest men go into it. I will venture that no honest man has made money in West Tennessee in the last year; whilst many fortunes have been made there during that time. The people in the Mississippi Valley are now nearly subjugated. Keep trade out but a few months, and I doubt not but that the work of subjugation will be so complete, that trade can be opened freely with the States of Arkansas, Louisiana, and Mississippi." He concluded, "*No theory of my own will ever stand in the way of my executing in good faith any order I may receive from those in authority over me:* but my position has given me an opportunity of seeing what could not be known by persons away from the scene of war; and I venture, therefore, great caution in opening trade with rebels."

Gen. Halleck perceived fully the vast importance of the results achieved, and generously wrote to Grant, —

"Your narration of the campaign, like the operations themselves, is brief, soldierly, and in every respect creditable and satisfactory. In boldness of plan, rapidity of execution, and brilliancy of routes, these operations will compare most favorably with those of Napoleon about Ulm. You and your army have well deserved the gratitude of your country; and it will be the boast of your children that their fathers were of the heroic army which re-opened the Mississippi River."

The rank of major-general in the regular army was conferred upon Gen. Grant; and the country everywhere rejoiced in the success of his armies.

On the 26th of July he writes, "I am very much opposed to any trade whatever until the Rebellion in this part of the country is entirely crushed out."

On the 13th of August, "My opinion is, that all trade with any enemy with whom we are at war is calculated to weaken us indirectly. I am opposed to selling or buying from them whilst war exists, except those within our lines."

Still later he says, " If trade is opened under any general rule, all sorts of dishonest men will engage in it ; taking any oath or obligation necessary to secure the privilege. Smuggling will at once commence, as it did at Memphis, Helena, and every other place where trade has been allowed within the disloyal States ; and the armed enemy will be enabled to procure from Northern markets every article they require."

Yet, at the same time, application was made to Gen. Grant for medicines by the rebel sick at Raymond, and subsistence for some families who were in extreme suffering ; and he ordered supplies forwarded at once.

He acted in the spirit of a father, and wrote, " It should be our policy now to make as favorable an impression upon the people of this State as possible. Impress upon the men the importance of going through the State in an orderly manner, refraining from taking any thing not absolutely necessary for their subsistence while travelling. They should try to create as favorable an impression as possible upon the people ; and advise them, if it will do any good, to make efforts to have law and order established within the Union."

There could be no wiser policy than this. A movement was soon after made by citizens near Pearl River to bring Mississippi back into the Union ; but it was premature.

Grant now advised that Mobile should be taken, the expedition starting from Lake Pontchartrain. If this advice had been followed, and an attack been made at once, there is little doubt that Mobile would have fallen, and the war have been shortened by a year. But this was not done. The President himself wrote to Grant, " I see by a despatch of yours that you incline strongly towards an expedition against Mobile. This would appear tempting to me also, were it not, that, in view of recent events in Mexico, I am greatly impressed with the importance of re-establishing the national authority in Western Texas.

The truth was, that the government at this time was greatly embarrassed by the movements of England and France in Mexico, and desired to strengthen itself on the border-line between Mexico and Texas. It was impossible to foretell what the hostility of the English Government might prompt them to do.

The policy of England had fastened slavery upon us as colonies, and her people had waxed rich upon the profits of the slave-trade. Within fifty years, a million and a half of its inhabitants were stolen from the coast of Africa by English ships, a quarter of a million of whom died from the horrors of the voyage ; and their floating corpses showed the track of the vessels.

Their orators and writers never failed to denounce the crime of American slavery ; yet, when slavery made war upon the Republic, they hastened to bestow belligerent rights upon the slaveholders before the American minister could present himself at her court.

In all the varieties of argument, ridicule, and persuasion, the war for the Union was denounced in its causes, its objects, and the methods of its pursuit, by the statesmen, the press, and the writers of England.

Her people carried on a civil war for nearly a hundred years, until massacre and devastation had well-nigh destroyed the land, on the question, whether, if the king died without a child, he should be followed by his brother, or the son of his brother.

Yet a nation three thousand miles distant from their shores, carrying on a war for four years to maintain its national life, and uphold human liberty, was execrated as exhibiting the " bloodiest picture in the book of time."

Englishmen dethroned seven of their kings, and beheaded another; drove into exile the house of Stuart; and imported aliens from Germany, ignorant of their language and their laws, to play for them the part of royalty; and sneered at Americans because they had " no personal representative of loyalty."

For years, the scaffolds of England were red with the blood of the noblest martyrs to liberty in Church and State; and yet they sermonized to Americans on " toleration in political differences."

England built ships for the rebel navy, forged their guns, crowded their decks with sailors, furnished them with supplies, welcomed and protected them in their ports, rejoiced in the destruction of our unarmed merchantmen, sorrowed at rebel defeats, mourned over the sinking of " The Alabama " as if it were a national disaster, and boasted to us of their " strict neutrality."

In India, England seized upon that vast country and its wealth; and, when its rapacity and oppression for long years had goaded its people to resistance, they blew the rebel Sepoys in pieces from the mouths of their cannon, and preached to Americans of " magnanimity to rebels."

In Ireland, England has robbed and plundered the inhabitants for five hundred years, and driven them like exiles beyond the seas, and discourses to Americans of " moderation in politics." *

During the campaign, furloughs had been granted only in extreme cases and for short periods. Now Grant ordered furloughs to be issued for thirty days to five per cent of the non-commissioned officers and privates, except those who had shirked duty, or straggled on the march or from camps. All sick soldiers were also sent home. Gen. Grant had a special hatred of jobbing, speculating, or making money out of the war, but particularly out of the necessities of the soldiers. As a practical illustration of the effect of " trade following the flag," and his care of the soldiers, the following fact may be mentioned : As soon as the river was opened, steamers came to Vicksburg to convey furloughed troops up the river at extortionate charges, demanding twenty-five and thirty dollars for a passage from Vicksburg to Cairo.

One steamer had its decks crowded with soldiers. Grant asked a man standing on the wheel-house, and giving orders loudly, " Are you the captain of this boat ? "

" Yes, general."

" How many soldiers have you on board ? "

" About twelve hundred and fifty."

" What have you charged for fare to Cairo ? "

" From ten to twenty-five dollars each, general."

" Ten to twenty-five dollars each ! Is that all ? Why,

* No State paper issued during the war presented the conduct of the English Government toward America with more clearness, force, and eloquence, than the eulogy on President Lincoln by Hon. Charles Sumner, whose pen, as Johnson said of Goldsmith's, touches nothing it does not adorn.

that is too moderate! It is a pity you should have to take the boys for so small a sum. You had better wait a while." Speaking to the officer on guard, he walked away. The steam whistled, the bell rung, the wheels began to move slowly; but, for some reason, she was not cast off. The men could not understand it, until, in a few moments, an order came for the guard to keep the steamer until the captain paid back all over seven dollars taken for fare from each officer, and all over five dollars from each soldier; and the order was obeyed.

The men knew they had been victimized, but felt helpless. When they learned what the general had done, they gave "three cheers for Grant" with a will.

Grant said to one of his staff, "I'll teach these steam-boat-men that the boys who have opened the river for them are not to be plundered of their hard earnings on their first trip home. If 'trade is to follow the flag' so soon, it shall be honest trade, so far as I can control it."

It was necessary for Grant soon after to visit Memphis. Before leaving, the officers who had been witnesses of the incessant care and anxiety which Grant had given to the campaign desired to offer some testimonial of their personal appreciation of his services to the country and to the army. They presented him with a splendid sword; the handle representing a young giant crushing the Rebellion, elaborately designed; the scabbard of solid silver; the whole appropriately inscribed, and enclosed in an elegant rosewood box bound with ivory and lined with satin.

Gen. Grant arrived at Memphis on the 25th of August, and was at once waited on by a committee of the citizens, and invited to a public reception and dinner.

Though disliking all display, Grant did not feel at liberty to decline such a manifestation of loyalty on the part of the citizens, and accepted. He addressed to the committee the following admirable letter : —

I received a copy of the resolutions passed by the loyal citizens of Memphis at the meeting held at the rooms of the Chamber of Commerce, Aug. 25, 1863, tendering me a public reception. In accepting this proposal, which I do at a great sacrifice of my personal feelings, I simply desire to pay a tribute to the first public exhibition in Memphis of loyalty to the government, which I represent in the Department of Tennessee. I should dislike to refuse, for considerations of personal convenience, to acknowledge everywhere, or in any form, the existence of sentiments which I have so long and ardently desired to see manifested in this department. The stability of this government and the unity of this nation depend solely on the cordial support and the earnest loyalty of the people. While, therefore, I thank you sincerely for the kind expressions you have used towards myself, I am profoundly gratified at this public recognition, in the city of Memphis, of the power and authority of the government of the United States. I thank you, too, in the name of the noble army which I have the honor to command. It is composed of men whose loyalty is proved by their deeds of heroism and their willing sacrifices of life and health. They will rejoice with me that the miserable adherents of the Rebellion, whom their bayonets have driven from this fair field, are being replaced by men who acknowledge *human liberty as the only true foundation of human government.*

May your efforts to restore your city to the cause of the Union be as successful as have been theirs to reclaim it from the despotic rule of the leaders of the Rebellion!

I have the honor to be, gentlemen, your very obedient servant,

U. S. Grant, *Major-General.*

At the dinner, when the toast in honor of Gen. Grant was given, he declined to make a speech ; and Surgeon Hewitt of his staff said, " I am instructed by

Gen. Grant to say, that, as he has never been given to public speaking, you will have to excuse him on this occasion; and, as I am the only member of his staff present, I therefore feel it to be my duty to thank you for this manifestation of your good will, as also for the numerous other kindnesses of which he has been the recipient ever since his arrival among you. Gen. Grant believes, that, in all he has done, he has no more than accomplished a duty, and one, too, for which no particular honor is due. But the world, as you do, will accord otherwise."

Gen. Grant could fight; he could write: but he could not make a speech. "If you want a man to *talk*," said the Greeks, " get an Athenian; if you want a man to *act*, get a Spartan."

Gen. Grant went down to New Orleans to confer with Gen. Banks in regard to affairs in Texas, stopping at Natchez, and inspecting this and other posts in his department.

The following day, it was officially announced that trade on the river, throughout its length, was free from all restrictions.

A day or two after, Sept. 4, there was a grand review of the troops. An eye-witness thus describes the departure of Gen. Grant from his hotel: " Gen. Banks, accompanied by a numerous staff, was at the St. Charles Hotel as early as eight o'clock; and at nine o'clock both generals left for Carrollton, where the review took place. The street was crowded to witness the departure of these officers; all present being desirous of seeing Gen. Grant. He was in undress uniform, without sword, sash, or belt; coat unbuttoned; a low-crowned black felt hat, without any mark upon it of military rank; a pair of kid gloves; and a cigar in his mouth."

It seems often to be an indispensable part of the honor done to a public man in giving him a reception to provide him with an elegant horse which will do his best to break his neck. Washington, Lafayette, Jackson, Kossuth, had narrow escapes in this way. Virginians said that Washington had such power of muscle, that, with a good bit, he could jerk a horse back on his haunches. Kossuth had been so much annoyed by vicious but good-looking horses, that he once ventured, in arranging for a review, to ask of the committee " *a quiet horse.*" This was instantly telegraphed over the country by the papers opposed to him as proof that he was a coward.

Gen. Grant's horse became excited on his return from the review; ran against a car, and injured him so much, that he had to be placed on a litter. His breast-bone was said to have been crushed, three ribs broken, and he was confined to his bed for three weeks. He did not walk without crutches for two months. It was feared at one time that he would never be able to take the field again.

As soon as he was partially recovered, he moved up the Mississippi on a steamer, stopping at different places as the public service required. On the 16th of October, he received at Cairo the following telegraphic despatch from Gen. Halleck: " You will immediately proceed to the Galt House, Louisville, Ky., where you will meet an officer of the War Department with your orders and instructions. You will take with you your staff, &c., for immediate operations in the field."

Grant immediately started for Louisville, but was met at Indianapolis by Hon. Mr. Stanton, Secretary of War, who accompanied him on his journey.

At the Galt House, the distinguished general attracted much notice. Among the stalwart Kentuckians was one from the " rural districts," who seemed to be disappointed that he was not a giant in size.

" Is that the great Gen. Grant?" said he to a gentleman.

" Yes, sir: that is Gen. Grant."

" Well! I thought he was a *large* man. He would be considered a small chance of a fighter if he lived in Kentucky." The Kentuckian had not learned that generals fight battles with their brains.

CHAPTER XVIII.

BATTLE AT WAUHATCHIE.

GEN. GRANT now found himself appointed to a department newly created, reaching from the Alleghanies to the Mississippi, and called the "Department of the Mississippi." It embraced the departments before known as the Cumberland, the Ohio, and the Tennessee. It included the States of Michigan, Illinois, Indiana, Ohio, Kentucky, Tennessee, Mississippi, Northern Alabama, and North-western Georgia. It contained two hundred thousand soldiers, and stretched a thousand miles from east to west. In uniting these departments under one commander, the government was adopting the policy which Grant had always recommended, of placing the military power of the nation under one head, and not subdivided into half a dozen armies, marching and fighting each on its own plan. If half a dozen divisions, under half a dozen different generals, were to meet on any one battle-field, and all were to attack the enemy here and there, without plan, as the judgment of each prompted, it would be thought absurd, and sure to end in disaster. But the whole country was one battle-field: its armies were only divisions of one grand army, and should be subjected to one brain, and wielded by one will.

The command now tendered to Grant was the largest ever given to any officer. It was worthy of any man's ambition : it was equal to any man's abilities.

The national forces had met with a severe repulse at Chickamauga, Sept. 23, and had fallen back to Chattanooga under circumstances which caused great depression. Grant had thought it not improbable that Sherman might be called to the command of the Army of the Cumberland; and he had written to Sherman, "I have constantly had the feeling that I shall lose you from this command -entirely. Of course, I do not object to seeing your sphere of usefulness enlarged, and think it should have been enlarged long ago, having an eye to the public good alone; but it needs no assurance ·from me, general, that taking a more selfish view, while I would heartily approve such a change, I would deeply regret it on my own account."

Sherman was at Memphis when he heard that Grant had been ordered North; and at once wrote him, " Accept the command of the great army of the centre : dòn't hesitate. By your presence at Nashville, you will unite all discordant elements, and impress the enemy in proportion. All success and honor to you ! "

There are noble things in human nature with all its frailties.

The government feared that Chattanooga, which was short of provisions, would be abandoned before Gen. Grant could arrive there : and he was directed to assume command at once by telegraphing to Rosecrans, Thomas, and Burnside, which he did; the former being in command at Chattanooga. The country had yet to be studied by him, the condition of the army to be learned in detail. He gathered what he could from maps and the full statements of Mr. Stanton. But, the moment his mind began to grasp the great facts, it is curious to see how it leaped into the work; how impatient he grew to stay results until he could arrive in the midst of them. He was in the hotel at Louisville, Ky. At half-past eleven o'clock at night, he telegraphed eagerly to Gen. Thomas, " Hold Chattanooga at all hazards. I will be there as soon as possible." How noble and how gratifying the reply which was immediately flashed over the wires by Thomas, " I will hold the town till we starve "!

Early the next morning, Oct. 20, Grant started by steam, and reached Nashville at night. But, during the day, his mind had been incessantly revolving the affairs of his unseen command; and he at once telegraphed to Burnside, who was at Knoxville, Tenn., in command of the Department of the Ohio, but in circumstances creating great anxiety at Washington, " Have you tools for fortifying? Important points in East Tennessee should be put in condition to be held by the smallest number of men as soon as possible. . . . I will be in Stevenson to-morrow night, and Chattanooga the next night."

To Admiral Porter at Cairo he telegraphed, " Gen. Sherman's advance was at Eastport on the 15th. The sooner a gunboat can be got to him, the better. Boats must now be on the way from St. Louis with supplies to go up the Tennessee for Sherman."

To Thomas, whose great difficulty of obtaining supplies he fully appreciates, he telegraphs, " Should not large working-parties be put upon the road between Bridgeport and Chattanooga at once?" Farther on the road, at Bridgeport, he telegraphs to Nashville, "Send to the front, as speedily as possible, vegetables for the army. Beans and hominy are especially required."

His restless energy was overflowing wherever on the route he could find lightning to carry his commands. Every hour, every moment, was precious. It was evidently the same man at work at the telegraph-wires, who could not find time for three days and nights to take off his clothes when starting from Bruinsburg on his Vicksburg campaign; whose orders were everywhere, — in the hands of his staff, the ordnance-officers, commissaries, corps commanders,—and were everywhere obeyed. During the evening, both here and at Louisville, a large crowd gathered at the hotel, and called for a speech; but he declined. He was making more effective speeches over the wires to his generals. On his journey, he met for a few moments Gen. Rosecrans, whom he had superseded. Rosecrans was polite, and gave such information as the interview permitted of the condition of the army. At Bridgeport, Grant and his staff mounted horses. The rain poured in floods. They made their way as best they could over roads torn up by the mountain-torrents, and strewed with fragments of army-wagons, dead mules and horses. Parts of the road were so bad, that Grant, who was still lame and suffering from his injuries at New Orleans, had to be carried by some of the soldiers in their arms. But by steam-power, horse-power, and man-power, he was constantly moving, without a moment's rest, to the post of duty. Of such stuff, heroes are made.

It was night when Gen. Grant, cold, weary, and hungry, reached Chattanooga, and proceeded to Gen. Thomas's tent. He was at first scarcely recognized.

It reminds us of a scene on the retreat of the French from Russia. "Who are you?" said Gen. Dumas to an officer who suddenly entered his quarters, his beard unshaved, his face black with gunpowder.

"Do you not know me?" was the answer. "I am the rear-guard of the Grand Army, the last man to leave Russia, — Marshal Ney."

Grant came at night, without the thunders of artillery, and with only the members of his staff; but the army was re-enforced that hour with a power that was soon to overwhelm the enemy with irretrievable disaster.

Gen. Thomas, whose valor well-nigh saved the day at Chickamauga, received his commander with the courtesy of the gentleman and the nobleness of the soldier. There had been rumors that Thomas himself would be appointed to the command. He assured Grant he was glad the post had been given to "a successful man;" and he promised him at once the most cordial support.

The next morning, Grant and Thomas rode out together.

Chattanooga, the Indian name for "eagle's nest," is situated at a bend of the Tennessee River, two hundred and fifty miles by water below Knoxville, near the corners of the States of Georgia, Alabama, and Tennessee. It is the junction of the Memphis and Charleston, and Richmond and Nashville Railroads, connecting with the chief towns of Georgia. Three miles west of the town is Lookout Mountain, twenty-two hundred feet high, about a mile and a half across. West of this is Raccoon Mountain. Lookout River flows in the valley between them. South and west of Chattanooga is Missionary Ridge, about three miles distant, and four hundred feet high. It was so named because it was the boundary beyond which the missionaries were not allowed to pass by the Indians. The rebels, with their batteries, held all of these heights, completely commanding the town and plain below. It commanded the passage south into the cotton States.

The Indians had determined that this valley and these mountains should be the outposts beyond which the white man should not carry the blessings of civilization and Christianity. In a similar spirit, slavery now sought at the same barriers to stay the great tide of freedom and free labor which was sweeping on to the shores of the Pacific. It was a position of vast natural strength and of untold importance to the Southern Confederacy.

The national army, by the defeat at Chickamauga, had been entirely shut in, with no means of feeding itself except by carting supplies sixty miles over the mountains from Nashville.

The whole army was on half-rations; three thousand were in the hospitals; ten thousand horses and mules had died around the town; there was only ammunition for one battle. The men were cheerless, feeble from lack of food, and disheartened by recent defeat.

Gen. Bragg, holding the route by which re-enforcements must come, felt that famine and despair were conquering the national army faster than he could by pitched battles. It was late in October. The nights were cold; and the soldiers were, many of them, without overcoats and blankets.

It was conceded that affairs could continue thus but a few days longer without the ruin of the army. Grant determined to open the valley route to Bridgeport. He ordered Gen. Hooker, who had been sent to the aid of Rosecrans with the Eleventh and Twelfth Corps from the Army of the Potomac, to cross the river at Bridgeport, and advance up Lookout Valley to Wauhatchie, threatening an attack on Bragg's flank. A force under Gen. Palmer was also to cross the river opposite Chattanooga, and march down the north side of the river to a point opposite Whitesides, to Hooker's support. Meantime, a force under Gen. W. F. Smith, of four thousand men, was to seize by surprise the range of hills at the north of Lookout Valley, which commanded a road from Kelley's Ferry to Bridgeport. Thus supplies could be received by steamers or by ordinary teams.

The vast importance of obtaining control of the road from this ferry to Bridgeport had been proposed, admitted, discussed, and contemplated: but it remained for Grant to issue orders that the work be done; and this he did on the first day he arrived, after examining the ground. At three o'clock in the morning, on the 27th, sixty pontoon-boats, each containing thirty men, floated quietly out from Chattanooga. They were under command of Brig.-Gen. Hazen.

They had nine miles to pass, in seven of which they would be exposed to the fire of the rebel pickets. But the night was very dark, the current swift, rendering oars less necessary; and, by hugging the northern shore of the river, they hoped to pass without discovery. Secrecy and surprise were important to the success of the undertaking; because, if the enemy had time to concentrate, it would be almost impossible, from the nature of the ground, for our men to attack successfully. The boats floated as silently down the river as the boats of Wolfe glided down the St. Lawrence to the Heights of Abraham. Not a man spoke, not a gunlock clicked, not an oar was stirred; but every eye was strained to the mountain-side in the distance. As the men came nearer, the rebel camp-fires could be seen blazing far up in the darkness; and now and then the rebel pickets were heard singing, "Way down in Dixie!" They rounded the foot of the mountain, touched the south side of the river at Brown's Ferry, leaped ashore, surprised a rebel picket, rushed up the steep, slippery ridge, three hundred feet high; and the first point was gained.

Another portion of Smith's force had crossed at Brown's Ferry, moved down the north bank of the river; and by five o'clock the whole command were so securely placed, that only a very large force could drive them out. The men who had crossed at Brown's Ferry began constructing a bridge; and by ten o'clock an excellent pontoon-bridge was in working-order, and artillery were placed to command the roads around the base of the mountain to the enemy's camps on the other side. Supplies could now be brought from Bridgeport to Kelley's Ferry without trouble.

Hooker had crossed the Tennessee at Bridgeport, accompanied by Gen. Howard and Brig.-Gen. Geary, and marched along the line of the Nashville and Chattanooga Railroad to Wauhatchie,— a small station on this road in Lookout Valley, about twelve miles from Chattanooga. He drove the rebel pickets in, meeting no serious opposition. He had with him about seven thousand men. At night, the advance with Howard halted near Brown's Ferry. Geary's smaller portion of the force was at Wauhatchie, some three miles distant, to hold the road up the valley from Kelley's Ferry. The rebels had seen the day's proceedings from the heights, and understood their import; but were not strong enough there to descend, and encounter the whole force. A division of Longstreet's celebrated corps was there; and it was determined that they should attack Geary at one o'clock at night with superior numbers, trusting to the terrors of a night-assault, in an unknown region, to destroy him.

But they were bravely met. Howard hurried down his nearest division to Geary's support; and the enemy found, after a desperate fight of two or three hours, that the Union troops had come to stay. In the darkness and confusion, some of the mules from the army-wagons broke loose, and ran pell-mell toward the enemy, who at first thought it a charge of cavalry; creating a panic, and increasing the confusion inseparable, to some extent, from a night-assault.

By four o'clock the enemy withdrew, leaving one hundred and fifty-three dead.

The sun did not more surely lift the fogs from the valleys around Chattanooga than did Grant's genius lift the clouds of gloom from the national army. In five days after his arrival, steamers, loaded with food, clothing, blankets, shoes, were plying on the Tennessee from Bridgeport to Kelley's Ferry. Horses, forage, and ammunition were forwarded to Chattanooga, full rations were issued to the half-starved troops, all was changed; in a word, it was hope, courage, and well-fed soldiers, in place of starvation and despair. From being, as Bragg expressed it, "at the mercy of the rebel force," this despondent army were now becoming the assailants.

When Rosecrans was removed, the rebels sneered at the appointment of Grant to the command at Chattanooga, and said, "The Federals have taken away one general" [Rosecrans], "and put two fools" [Grant and Thomas] "in his place." Some one at this time showed the rebel paper containing this attempt at wit to Mr. Lincoln. He was "reminded of the story" of the Irishman, who, when buying a cooking-stove, being told, "This one stove will save half your fuel," answered, "Faith, then I'll take two stoves, and save the whole!" He said, "If one fool like Grant can win such victories, and accomplish what he has, I don't object to two; for they will certainly wipe out the rest of this Rebellion."

At this time, "The Richmond Enquirer" thought the movements at Chattanooga were not such as they should be on the part of Gen. Bragg. It said, "The enemy were out-fought at Chickamauga; (thanks to the army!) but the present position of affairs looks as though we had been out-generaled at Chattanooga." By no means an unwise conclusion. The people in the mountains of East Tennessee, of Northern Georgia and North Carolina, with Northern Alabama, had never imbibed the poison of treason. Like mountaineers the world over, they loved freedom, and were inured to hardy toil. Their mountain-fastnesses were not fit homes for slaves. It has not been the sterile mountain-passes clad with snow and ice, but the warm and fertile plains covered with waving and golden harvests, and flowing with oil and wine, which in all ages have invited and yielded to the arms of invasion.

The sufferings of the noble Union men in these regions, especially in Tennessee, had deeply moved the hearts of the North. They had been thrown into filthy prisons; they had been hung and shot; tied to logs, and whipped to death; their houses plundered, and burned over their heads; husbands murdered before their wives and children ; or, escaping this, they had fled to caves to die by starvation, or be fed by the hand of charity. These persecutions were continued in every form that the "barbarism of slavery" could devise to drive the people into support of the Rebellion, and fill the rebel armies; but all without avail.

Gen. Grant determined that this style of warfare should cease; and he issued orders, that, —

"For every act of violence to the person of an unarmed Union citizen, a secessionist will be arrested, and held as hostage for the delivery of the offender. For every dollar's worth of property taken from such citizens, or destroyed by raiders, an assessment will be made upon secessionists of the neighborhood, and collected by the nearest military forces, under the supervision of the commander thereof; and the amount thus collected paid over to the sufferers. When such assessments cannot be collected in money, property useful to the government may be taken at a fair valuation, and the amount paid in money by a disbursing officer of the government, who will take such property upon his returns. Wealthy secession citizens will be assessed in money and provisions for the support of Union refugees who have been or may be driven from their homes and into our lines by the acts of those with whom secession citizens are in sympathy. All collections and payments under this order will be made through the disbursing officers of the government, whose accounts must show all money and property received under it, and how disposed of.

"By order of Major-Gen. U. S. GRANT."

Gen. Grant's orders were not mere paper-orders to be read and forgotten, but were rigidly and strictly enforced.

Gen. Burnside, with twenty-five thousand men, was at Knoxville, short of rations and ammunition, and with no means of obtaining any without great delays and through long and circuitous routes.

His situation excited great anxiety at Washington, and the authorities were constantly urging Grant to "relieve Burnside;" but how to do so was the problem. Burnside himself was least concerned of all about his safety.

On the 3d of November, Bragg determined to send twenty thousand men under Longstreet to "drive Burnside out of East Tennessee, or, better, to capture or destroy him." He took with him eighty guns. They did not start till the 13th.

Grant had foreseen a movement of this nature, and had telegraphed his apprehensions to Burnside some time before.

Grant ordered an attack to be made on Bragg's positions at Missionary Ridge, as a diversion in favor of Burnside, and to bring Longstreet back: but it was ascertained by Gen. Thomas that he had no horses to move his artillery; and the condition of his army was not equal to so hazardous a movement; and he so reported.

Burnside was so isolated, and the means of communication so slow, that many evils were dreaded in his behalf, which a more rapid communication would have shown to be groundless.

Sherman was on his way from Memphis with the Fifteenth Army Corps; but he was to march four hundred miles across the country. It is a long journey from the Mississippi River to Chattanooga, when you make the distance on foot, step by step. There is nothing to be done, therefore, but for Burnside to hold on and hold out till Sherman's force can re-enforce Grant. But how hard for Grant to wait! Every day seems a week.

Bragg has reduced his strength to attack Burnside. If Grant could only now attack Bragg, he could defeat him, and then follow and defeat Longstreet. The contemplation of all these facts and possibilities stirs him to even unwonted activity in all directions. To Sherman he telegraphed as early as Oct. 24, the day after he arrived at Chattanooga, "Drop every thing east of Bear Creek, and remove with your entire force towards Stevenson until you receive further orders. The enemy are evidently moving a large force towards Cleveland, and may break through our lines, and move on Nashville; in which event, your troops are the only forces at command that could beat them there."

This was sent by a courier, who floated down the river, to Tuscumbia; and from there was sent to Sherman at Iuka.

Gen. Grant watched his march almost every hour

after this until his arrival; studying his route, anticipating and providing for the wants of his men, step by step. On the 7th he telegraphs, " Gen. Sherman will reach Fayetteville to-morrow without any thing to eat. See the shipping commissary, and direct him to secure transportation, and send one hundred thousand rations to-morrow morning."

Sherman was marching, fighting, and toiling on through the soft, glutinous roads, his teams often slumping in to their hubs; climbing mountains; fording streams; straining every nerve to reach his chief.

Meantime Grant is building bridges, repairing railroads, refitting steamboats, and watching over four armies, — three of his own, and one of the enemy. To Thomas he sent word, " The steamer ' Point of Rocks ' should by all means be got down to Brown's Ferry before morning, even if a house has to be torn down to get the necessary fuel."

To his adjutant-general at Nashville, in regard to the forwarding of supplies, he telegraphs, " Make any order necessary to secure the result in the promptest manner." To another he says, " Make contracts with different bridge-builders, so as to get this work done in the shortest possible time. Extra bridges should also be in readiness at all times to replace any that may be destroyed. Keep me advised of what you do in this matter."

But day after day passes, and Grant suffers the most intense anxiety to attack Bragg before Longstreet returns. Every hour, he can see the lofty summit of Missionary Ridge, and his eagerness to advance is consuming in its fervor; every hour, Longstreet may return;

every hour he hopes for Sherman's corps. But four hundred miles are just as long when in our impatience we would annihilate distance as when we move reluctantly to some undesired goal.

But such desire leaves its mark. "If I should die to-day," wrote Nelson to the admiralty, "'Want of frigates' would be found engraven on my heart."

As Sherman approaches nearer to Chattanooga, Grant's solicitude increases. He is picking out the best roads, and would doubtless level all the hills and fill up the valleys to make smooth travelling, and bring in his army in fine condition. On the 10th he writes, "I learn that by the way of New Market and Maysville you will avoid the heavy mountains, and find abundance of forage. If a part of your command is now at Winchester, and a part back, that portion behind had better be turned on the New-market route."

The preparations, which had been made on a gigantic scale, were about completed, and the drama was soon to open. The numbers to be engaged in the coming battle, the transcendent interests involved, the natural grandeur of the scene of the great contest, would forever render it one of the most memorable battles in the annals of our country.

CHAPTER XIX.

GEN. GRANT'S department was truly an imperial domain. As we have seen, it included ten States, covering nearly half a million square miles, and comprised more than eleven millions of people. It stretched from Lake Superior to Louisiana, and from Pennsylvania to the Valley of the Mississippi. It is not an exaggeration to say, that, during this time, there was scarcely a corner of this vast region, which, directly or indirectly, was not stirred by the preparations of the campaign. The cattle on a thousand hills were moving to feed the army; a million hands were at work to clothe it, furnaces glowed by night and day. The railroads from Lake Erie to Natchez toiled hourly with their enormous labor. The Mississippi, the Ohio, the Tennessee, the Cumberland Rivers, were crowded with fleets of steamers loaded with all the munitions of war; and tens of thousands of soldiers, who were to decide the contest, were winding in long lines over mountain and plain, but all marching to the field of glory or the grave of honor.

And the man whose active brain and indomitable will are organizing and directing this vast and complicated

Grant and Sherman at Missionary Ridge. — Page 203.

machinery is apparently all unconscious of his power. He looks sober; talks but little to any one. Not yet recovered from his recent accident, he limps around Chattanooga, smoking a brier-wood pipe, wearing a blouse and slouched hat. He often rides off to study the country, taking one or two of his staff with him; but with no plumed troops, and flying pennons, and gorgeous pageantry of war. But the inexorable will, the fixed purpose to do or die, are all there.

Sherman arrived at Chattanooga on the morning of the 15th in advance of his column, having reached Bridgeport the night previous. Grant, Sherman, and Thomas rode out on the high ground on the north of the Tennessee, whence the tents of the enemy and the whole theatre of operations were in full view, — "a mighty amphitheatre, where the actors were nearly ready to assume their parts, with distant mountains for spectators; while cloud-capped hills, and valleys shrouded in mist that was lifted to display the movements of armies, formed the stage." *

It was indeed a vast natural colosseum. Europe does not offer so grand a battle-field from Gibraltar to Moscow. It resembled more those granite gates of Greece of which fame has told us for two thousand years, where Leonidas and the three hundred sons of Sparta waited all night to offer up their lives with the morning's sun.

Here Sherman was shown the eastern extremity of Missionary Ridge, which he was to attack. He entered at once with enthusiasm into all Grant's plans, and, the

* Badeau.

same night, returned to Bridgeport to hurry up his troops; himself rowing a boat, in his impatience, down from Kelley's Ferry.

It was thought that Sherman's force could be brought up and put in position for battle by the 20th, and Grant gave orders to attack on the 21st; but the condition of the army after such a march, heavy rains, and the terrible state of the roads, rendered it impossible to be prepared before the 23d.

On the 20th, Gen. Bragg treated himself to the following sublimely impudent epistle to Gen. Grant: "General, as there may still be some non-combatants in Chattanooga, I deem it proper to notify you that prudence would dictate their early withdrawal." When Grant read this, he was convinced that Bragg felt that "prudence dictated his own early withdrawal." His suspicions were soon after confirmed by the statements of a deserter.

It was Grant's purpose to give Bragg the impression that Sherman's force was to be massed on his left; but in reality they were to attack on his right. As fast as they arrived, therefore, they were advanced to Whitesides, where they were pushed behind the hills, out of the enemy's sight, to our left; but the camp-fires were kept burning, and every art used to induce the belief that they were gathered where they first rested. They were constantly marching from Brown's Ferry, where they were seen by the enemy, up the river back of the hills, to a concealed camp. Once behind the hills, it was impossible for the enemy to know whether they had marched to Knoxville to relieve Burnside, or were still held on the north of the river. From this place

Sherman's force was to emerge, lay a pontoon-bridge across the Tennessee, and attack Bragg's right.

At noon on the 23d, Gen. Granger with the Fourth Corps advanced from our centre, held by Gen. Thomas, to ascertain the enemy's strength at this point. Howard's corps was formed in mass behind Granger, Sheridan's division on the right, and Woods's on the left.

It was a splendid day; and the different divisions marched into position with the steadiness and precision of a grand review, which the rebels at first supposed it to be. They looked at the evolutions from the lofty heights of Missionary Ridge, and said, in sneering allusion to Hooker's men who had come from the Potomac, "Now we shall have a Potomac parade." They considered the Army of the Potomac excellent at drilling, but poor at fighting.

From the national line to the rebel rifle-pits was about a mile. The highest point for observation was Fort Wood, near our centre ; and here Grant took his position with Gen. Thomas. The troops moved over the ground in grand style, drove in the enemy's pickets, and captured the first line of rifle-pits and two hundred prisoners. Our line now included a mound named "Orchard Knoll," which had been a redoubt of the rebel outer line. The troops began intrenching at once. About five o'clock, the enemy opened a furious discharge of shells, which was continued for some time without producing great effect. During the night, cannon were put in position, and our line greatly strengthened. The effect on the troops, of the afternoon's work, was inspiring. They had fought under the eye of the hero of Donelson and Champion's Hill and Vicksburg for the first time; and here they were, their flags a mile in advance of the old line.

They felt confident they should carry the summit whenever the order came to advance. The old Army of the Cumberland was itself again.

They were no longer starving, defeated men, but victorious soldiers. Grant had trusted them, took his stand with them; and they were proud to show him they were worthy of their leader. They no longer thought of Chickamauga, except to avenge it.

North Chickamauga Creek enters the Tennessee about five miles above the point on the river opposite, and in front of the hills behind which Sherman lay concealed. Here a hundred and sixteen pontoons were hidden with which to float down a portion of Sherman's men to land on the south side of the river, and commence the bridge on which Sherman's army was to cross. Seven hundred and fifty picked oarsmen were marched around behind the curtain of hills with Smith's brigade during the night of the 23d. By twelve o'clock at night, nearly three thousand five hundred soldiers were passing down the river so silently, that even our own pickets on the north bank of the river did not discover them.

Before daylight, they jumped ashore where Sherman's bridge was to be thrown across, and captured the enemy's astonished pickets before they fairly understood what had happened. The pontoons were sent back to be filled again, and returned. By daylight, Gen. Bragg found eight thousand men, well protected, putting a bridge over the river in front of his right, the northern end of Missionary Ridge. Opposite, another large force were at work in a similar manner. Cannon on both sides opened their fire; but the men worked as if nothing could stop them. At the same time, boats were crossing the river, which is here about fourteen hundred feet wide, each carrying about forty soldiers, and landing them on the southern side of the Tennessee. It is evident to Bragg that Sherman is to attack here. This was not expected; but it is too late now to prevent it.

Howard with three regiments had marched up the south bank of the river from Chattanooga; and now both ends of the bridge are rapidly building, and the intervening space is growing smaller and smaller. By twelve o'clock, the bridge is nearly completed. Sherman is impatient, and advances on the northern side, almost plank by plank, animating and directing the men, who work incessantly: he wears a long India-rubber over-coat, and is talking and gesturing. The space is narrowing. Howard has advanced from the other side, and introduced himself to Sherman across the little gulf. The gap is filled; and Sherman jumps across, and seizes Howard by the hand.

By one o'clock, men, horses, artillery, and cavalry in large numbers, were over, and were formed in three columns in *échelon;* the left under M. L. Smith, the centre under J. E. Smith, and the right under Ewing.

Sherman stands on a little mound, with his generals around, trying to light a cigar in the rain, when he quietly gives the order to advance. Grant is with Thomas in the centre, where the principal attack is to be made; and Hooker is at Lookout Mountain, thirteen miles from Sherman: but all are on the same battle-field, carrying out one plan.

Sherman fought his way steadily up; and by half-past three he had secured the heights at the north end of Missionary Ridge, called "Tunnel Hill." The enemy tried to drive him out with artillery; but he threw up breastworks, dragged guns up the heights, and threw up intrenchments. Heavy mists from the river concealed him from view, until during the night it grew cold, the air cleared, and his camp-fires were seen stretching around toward Thomas, and holding the coveted position.

Meanwhile, Hooker with fiery valor had assaulted Lookout Mountain. The mountain did not slope gradually from base to summit; but the first twenty-five or thirty feet were abrupt palisades. There were but two routes, — one a trail or footpath, the other a crooked road on the east side of the mountain. Hooker chose the road. Half-way up, the rebels had a line of earthworks, and rifle-pits in front of these.

A portion of his force, under Geary, advanced up the Valley of the Lookout, threw a bridge over Lookout Creek, and swept around the north side of the mountain; while another column attacked from the south and west side, pressing their way through the forests, and climbing cliffs, as best they could.

The enemy had been so attentively studying bridge-building as practised by Gen. Geary, that the advance of the column on the south-west was a surprise. Our batteries and those of the rebels kept up a terrific cannonade, and shrouded the whole hill in clouds of smoke. The enemy, taken in flank and rear, driven from their earthworks, kept up their fire from behind rocks and trees, but everywhere gave way. Prisoners were taken in large squads, who were found to be men who were paroled at Vicksburg, and had not been exchanged, though they had been so told by their officers.

By two o'clock, the clouds and darkness on the mountain caused a cessation of the battle to some extent. To those below, the flashes of fire, the thunder of the artillery, the rolling clouds of smoke, recalled the descriptions given of Mount Sinai of old, when " the smoke thereof ascended as the smoke of a furnace, and the whole mount quaked greatly." The loud cheers of our troops, sounding to their comrades' in the valley to come from the skies, told that the height was won. By four o'clock, Hooker reported to Grant his success. At half-past five, Grant ordered Brig.-Gen. Carlin of the Fourteenth Corps to cross Chattanooga Creek, and join Hooker on the left.

The rebels gradually withdrew to concentrate on Missionary Ridge; leaving twenty thousand rations, and camp-equipages for three brigades.

At six o'clock, Grant telegraphed in modest terms to Washington, " The fight to-day progressed favorably. Sherman carried the end of Missionary Ridge; and his right is now at the tunnel, and left at Chickamauga Creek. Troops from Lookout Valley carried the point of the mountain, and now hold the eastern point and slope high up. Hooker reports two thousand prisoners taken, besides which a small number have fallen into our hands from Missionary Ridge."

The President replied, " Your despatches as to fighting on Monday and Tuesday are here. Well done! Thanks to all. Remember Burnside."

By midnight the bugles were mute, the soldiers were sleeping, and the sentinels paced their weary round; but there was no rest for their commander, who was busy despatching his orders for the next day's battle.

CHAPTER XX.

GRANT was not a general who issued orders for a battle of two or three days' continuance, and then looked on to see it carried out, and was disconcerted and defeated if the programme was interfered with. He fought the battle, and issued orders as the battle developed. He fought his battles by military rules; but he applied the rules as the exigencies changed on the field. No two battles are alike; and his staff said it was not his habit to discuss the details and muse over the evolutions of celebrated battles, and speculate on what might have been if this had been so, and that had been otherwise.

When the board was ready and the pieces placed, he played to win, as his own position and that of the enemy appeared to require. When the sun rose on the morning of the 25th, the whole scene was spread out like a map. At the extreme right, on the lofty summit of Lookout Mountain, the national flag was seen flying, having been raised by the Eighth Kentucky Volunteers. In front was Missionary Ridge, four hundred feet high, seven miles long, where the rebel hosts, numbering forty-five thousand men, were now united. In the centre, Bragg's headquarters were plainly seen; far off on the left, Sherman's drums were heard on the crests he had won the afternoon before. Trees, houses, fences, had all been removed; and the field was clear for the day's great work.

Grant, with Thomas and some of his division generals, was on Orchard Knoll, the highest point of observation along the Union lines. Hooker had descended from Lookout Mountain, crossed the valley, and was at the south end of Missionary Ridge.

Grant's plan was to attack the enemy on both flanks until he was compelled to weaken his centre to support them; when the centre was to be broken, and the ridge carried.

The eminence which Sherman had carried was not continuous with the whole ridge; but ravines and gorges intervened, and each was strongly fortified and defended, — those behind rising above those in front, and affording a chance for the rebel artillery to play upon our advancing columns with great effect. Sherman had been in his saddle since daylight. It was now sunrise. The men were quiet: some of them were writing little notes in their diaries, and replacing them in their pockets, thinking, perhaps, they would, before night, be read by other eyes than theirs. The bugles sound the advance; and Gen. Corse, Gen. Morgan L. Smith, and Col. Smith, with their brigades, move on. The Fortieth Illinois, and the Twentieth and Forty-sixth Ohio, march down the slope, and up to within eighty yards of the rebel intrenchments. The fighting is very severe; hand to hand it is maintained, now advancing, and now receding a little. The fire of the rebel artillery is murderous with grape and canister; the blood

flows in torrents: our soldiers charged up to within
pistol-shot of the rebel works; but, in the main, each
party held its position. But Sherman's attack threat-
ens Bragg's rear, and must be repulsed, or all is lost.
He orders first one column and then another from his
centre to repel Sherman ; but Sherman is not to be
driven off, if he cannot advance against great odds.
Still more troops move off to the left of Bragg.

Grant saw all this with eagle eye as he watched the
movements of the enemy. Thomas's four divisions,
who were with him in the centre, had been impatiently
waiting all day for orders to " go in ; " and now the
moment had come.

Sheridan (then fighting for the first time under
Grant's eye), Johnson, Baird, and Wood were ordered
to advance to the enemy's rifle-pits, clear them, then
re-form, and ascend the ridge. It was about nine hundred yards to the rebel rifle-pits; and there was not
an inch of the ground that was not swept by the artillery from the ridge.

But the men moved steadily without firing a gun,
then dashed on at the double-quick ; and the rifle-pits
were carried. Some of the rebels threw themselves
down and surrendered as the line approached ; others
fled up the hill. Sheridan said he " happened to be in
advance ; " and, as he looked back at the twenty thousand gleaming bayonets, he was impressed by the sight
of their terrible power. The rebels could not resist
the effect on their imagination ; and many surrendered
at once. A thousand prisoners were captured, and
hurried to the rear. The men could not now be
halted to re-form as had been agreed ; but along the

whole line the loud shouts of triumph rang out, and on they pressed up the hill crowned with cannon and crowded with rifles. The rebels loaded their guns with canister and grape. But our troops clung to the hill, sometimes lying on their faces to let the storm drive over them, and swarmed up the hill.· The flags constantly advancing, first one and then another, up they went through that storm of death.

The whole ridge seems heaving with volcanic fires.

> " From peak to peak, the rattling crags among,
> Leaps the live thunder."

Baird, Wood, Granger, Johnson, are everywhere active and cool. Color-bearers fall; but on go the flags. The men press steadily through the ‚sheet of flame. Bullets are as thick as snow-flakes in a winter storm. The rebels light fuses, and roll shells down the hill: they hurl rocks even, and load their guns with handfuls of cartridges in their hurry. But nothing breaks the line of blue-coats: they swarm up; the flags still ascend. There is a long, loud cheer from thousands of victorious men: the ridge is won.

For a few minutes, the bloody struggle continues between the masses of infuriated troops. Artillerists are bayoneted at their guns, and the guns turned on the retreating foe. Whole regiments surrender: others fling themselves down the mountain-side, followed by clouds of rifle-bullets. The rebel centre is broken; the wings are doubling up in confusion; the victory is complete. It had only been a march of fifty-five minutes; but in those minutes thousands of heroic men had taken their last, long march to the realms of death.

> " On Fame's eternal camping-ground
> Their silent tents are spread ;
> And Glory guards with solemn round
> The bivouac of the dead."

Gen. Grant, who had been under fire all day, was now recognized on the hill ; and the men greeted him with loud cheers wherever he moved.

Bragg, powerless to resist, was retiring, probably in the spirit of his note to Grant,—that "prudence required non-combatants to leave." He was astonished. " It was a position," he said, " which a line of skirmishers ought to have maintained against any assault."

The German soldiers engaged fought with the steadiness and courage with which their race, battling for fatherland, conquered Napoleon at Leipsic, and drove his victorious legions beyond the banks of the Rhine.

Grant captured over six thousand prisoners, forty pieces of artillery, and seven thousand stand of arms,—the largest capture which had been made on any open field during the war. Our loss in killed and wounded was five thousand.

At seven o'clock in the evening, Gen. Grant sent the following modest despatch to Washington, making no mention of himself in any manner : —

Although the battle lasted from early dawn till dark this evening, I believe I am not premature in announcing a complete victory over Bragg. Lookout-mountain top, all the rifle-pits in Chattanooga Valley, and Missionary Ridge entire, have been carried, and are now held by us.

U. S. GRANT, *Major-General.*

Gen. Meigs, the Quarter-Master-General of the United-States army, who was at Chattanooga at this time, and an eye-witness of the battle, wrote a full account of these military operations to Gen. Halleck, in which he said, "Probably not so well-directed, so well-ordered a battle has taken place during the war. Kentucky and Tennessee are rescued; Georgia and the South-east are threatened in the rear; and another victory is added to the chapter of '*unconditional-sur-render Grant*.'" The victory was worthy of such announcement. Jefferson Davis was a very vain man; and, when a great battle was about to be fought, he would hurry to the scene of the contest, and interfere with the plans of his generals. If a victory ensued, he claimed it as the result of his advice; if a defeat, he alleged it was because he could not remain and person-ally direct the carrying-out of his plans.

Only a few weeks before the great battle at Chatta-nooga, he stood on the lofty summit of Missionary Ridge, and surveyed the field of the impending contest, with Generals Bragg and Pemberton.

As he looked down on the Union camps in the valley, he said exultingly, "The Federals are in just the trap I set for them. The green fields of Tennessee will soon be ours."

Gen. Pemberton, whose remembrance of Vicksburg was still fresh, replied, "Mr. Davis, you are command-er-in-chief, and, of course, will direct as you judge best. I have been blamed for not attacking the enemy when they were drawing around me at Vicksburg; but do you order an attack on these troops now, and, my life on it, not a single man will ever come back over the valley, except as a prisoner." But Davis predicted only conquest. The reader of sacred history will be reminded of another arch-rebel, who once ascended "an exceeding high mountain," and promised dominion and power over broad regions he did not possess, and never conquered. A high rock from which the Confederate President addressed the troops has since been called " The Devil's Pulpit."

CHAPTER XXI.

IT was not Gen. Grant's disposition to rest satisfied with the first-fruits of victory; and Sheridan was ordered to pursue the retreating enemy, which he did with such vigor, that Bragg barely escaped capture with his whole staff.

About a mile in the rear of the battle-field was a hill, on which the rebels planted a formidable battery, and endeavored to rally their broken columns; but Sheridan and his men charged with the same bayonets and the same impetuosity which had carried them up the heights of Missionary Ridge.

"It was now dark; and, just as the head of one of these columns reached the summit of the hill, the moon rose from behind, and a medallion view of the column was disclosed as it crossed the disk of the moon and attacked the enemy. Outflanked on right and left, the rebels fled, leaving the coveted artillery and trains. Those who escaped capture were driven across Chickamauga Creek, where they burned the bridges almost while they passed." *

Early the next morning, the army pushed on to destroy the enemy, and to relieve Burnside at Knox-

* Badeau.

ville, — an object now of the first importance. Sherman's force advanced toward Chickamauga, and Hooker and Palmer moved toward Ringgold. Gen. Grant was at the front, directing the pursuing columns. At eleven o'clock, our advance was at Chickamauga Dépôt. Here was witnessed a scene such as is only found in war. The station was in flames, and the vast stores of the enemy had been fired. Corn, bacon, gun-carriages, cheeses, pork, flour, molasses, powder, sugar, broken muskets, and pontoon-trains, — every thing used in an army, — had been given up by the enemy, who had not time to complete their destruction. Large and valuable captures of stores were made by our forces. Among them, one pontoon-train of fifteen boats, twenty army-wagons, sixty thousand rations of corn, fifty thousand of corn-meal, two sixty-four-pounder rifled siege-guns, one thousand pounds of bacon, six forges, some ordnance-stores, artillery and small-arm ammunition. The rebel loss by fire alone amounted to fifty thousand dollars' worth of property.

All day long, the pursuit was continued. "Tramp, tramp, tramp, the boys were marching;" and everywhere were the evidences of a defeated and routed army. Guns and ammunition thrown away, abandoned ambulances, tents, wagons, caissons, strewed along the road, told of the hurried flight. The rebel camps of the previous night were passed, the bivouac-fires still blazing.

Just at night, a sharp engagement took place between the rear-guard of the enemy and the advanced guard of our forces, in which the enemy gave way, and our army bivouacked for the night.

Ringgold, a small place of twenty-five hundred

inhabitants, — the county-seat of Catoosa County, Ga., — was five miles distant. It is situated at the base of the White-oak-mountain ridge. In the rear of the town is a gap, or gorge, about a hundred yards wide, with abrupt ridges on both sides rising five hundred feet high, and half a mile or more in length. Artillery planted on these ridges completely commanded the pass, and, manned by even a few hundred men, could hold an army of thousands.

The enemy seized upon the natural advantages of this place, and determined to make here a desperate stand. The forests which fringed the ridges were filled with sharpshooters and four thousand of the enemy, disposed in a manner to offer a most effective resistance.

Our guns were not yet up; but our men were flushed with victory, and impatient of delay: and, soon after eight o'clock, Gen. Hooker ordered an attack by Oster-haus, who led the advance, followed by Geary and Craft.

The troops advanced with determined bravery; but the enemy opened with musketry, and poured shot and shell from the ridges above them. After a time, our men were compelled to fall back. The enemy, surprised and delighted with their success, followed with great ardor. Several attempts were made to carry the position, but in vain. It was too strong to be carried without artillery; but the men were unwilling to be delayed even for a few hours by an enemy so recently beaten, and fought with reckless gallantry. The Thirteenth Illinois was specially distinguished for its bravery; and the Seventh Ohio lost all its officers, coming out of action under command of a lieutenant.

But our men were being slaughtered without gaining adequate advantage; and it was decided to wait the arrival of the artillery, which had not been able to cross the west fork of the Chickamauga.

About twelve o'clock, a section of howitzers was brought to bear on the enemy in the gap; artillery were sent to the southern side of the river; and Grant sent orders to Sherman to place a force on the east side of the ridge, and turn his position. But the artillery had done the work. The guns told with terrible effect. Osterhaus and Geary again advanced; and, before one o'clock, the rebels had taken up the line of retreat.

They were quickly followed, and three pieces of artillery, and two hundred and thirty prisoners, captured. One hundred and thirty rebels were found dead on the field. Our loss was sixty-five killed, and three hundred and seventy-seven wounded.

The railroad at Ringgold was destroyed; mills and military materials of various kinds; also a large tannery, which was not likely to escape Grant's eye.

Hooker followed the enemy toward Dalton, Ga., for several miles, but only to find pictures of the unwritten miseries of war, — wounded and dying men, broken wagons, caissons, and corpses, lining the roads where the enemy marched.

The pursuit would have been continued, but for Grant's solicitude, which never ceased, to relieve Burnside at Knoxville.

To Thomas he wrote, " Direct Granger to start at once, marching as rapidly as possible, to the relief of Burnside."

A despatch to Burnside was sent in duplicate; one

copy to be delivered to Gen. Burnside, the other to be allowed to fall into the hands of the enemy.

Gen. Grant became impatient with all delays; and on the 29th he placed the whole force moving on Knoxville, under command of the most energetic of his generals, Sherman. He wrote to him, "Push as rapidly as you can to the Hiswassee, and determine for yourself what force to take with you from that point. Granger has his corps with him, from which you will select, in conjunction with the forces now with you. In plain words, you will assume command of all the forces now moving up the Tennessee."

In our next chapter, we shall see the results of this march.

CHAPTER XXII

THE SIEGE OF KNOXVILLE.

KNOXVILLE, formerly the capital of Tennessee, is beautifully situated on the Holston River, a hundred and eighty-five miles east of Nashville. It is located on high ground, commanding a fine view of the river and the blue mountains of Chilhowee, thirty miles distant.

Gen. Burnside had thrown up a line of works around the city, from the river on the left to the river on the right. He had about twelve thousand six hundred men, and three or four thousand more loyal Tennesseeans. Longstreet had with him about twenty-two thousand men of all arms. Beef, cattle, and hogs had been driven into the city, and slaughtered and salted. Useless animals were killed, rations were reduced ; and the works were put in the best possible condition. Farmers, and Union citizens from the country, volunteered to work in the trenches, and did so bravely. Negroes cheerfully worked early and late, and many disloyal men were compelled to aid in protecting the city from assault. The farmers loaded flat-boats with grain and provisions of all kinds, and sent them down the river, under cover of the autumn fogs, at night. Formidable ditches were made; abatis, and all the usual devices for withstanding a siege, were constructed.

At the north-east corner of the works, on high ground west of Knoxville, was an eminence named "Fort Saunders." A battery crowned the summit. It was protected by traverses; and every effort had been made to render it impregnable to assault. If carried, it permitted the destruction or capture of Knoxville.

Both Burnside and Longstreet, who was a very able military man, knew that really the siege of Knoxville was to be decided on the heights of Missionary Ridge. If Knoxville could not be carried at once, he would find himself between Burnside's intrenchments in front, and Grant's victorious legions in his rear.

He determined to make one more fight for rebel dominion in Tennessee, and ordered an assault on the morning of the 29th of November. Late in the night of the 26th, the rebels advanced, and sunk rifle-pits along the whole line to aid the assaulting columns. Four brigades of picked regiments were chosen to make the assault: they were compelled to advance over a piece of ground two or three hundred yards wide.

Sunday morning the 29th, the artillery of the enemy opened with a terrible cannonade upon the fort, which our guns received in ominous silence. It was continued for half an hour. Every gun on the fort was loaded, every man at his post; but not a gun was fired. At last, a solid column of rebels moved out on the open space, and advanced to the assault at a double-quick. Numbers fell over the wires which had been stretched across the ground: but the column pressed forward; and, when near the ditch, the guns from the fort all opened, loaded with triple rounds of canister. The slaughter was fearful beyond description. Forces were stationed also on the flanks of the fort, which gave them a cross-fire over the same masses.

The front ranks fell like grass before the scythe; but the column pressed up, trampling over the bodies of their dead and dying comrades. Those who succeeded in crossing the ditch found themselves at the foot of the parapet, where hand-grenades were thrown over among them. Every head that appeared was instantly pierced by a rifle-bullet, or beaten to pieces with the butts of infantry muskets. It was a scene of carnage and blood beyond the power of words to describe. Five hundred were captured; and a thousand rebels lay dead in front of the fort, who, an hour before, were glowing with manly life, — each one of them an American; each one with some heart to love him, and sorrow for his loss; but each one fighting in a war for slavery, and meeting at last a traitor's death.

The moans of the dying, the piteous cries of the wounded, rose up to heaven on the still sabbath air.

As soon as it was evident that the foe had retired from the assault, Gen. Burnside himself, with becoming humanity, offered a flag of truce, under which they could bury their dead and care for the sufferings of the wounded.

"Not wholly lost, O Father! is this evil world of ours:
  Upward through its blood and ashes spring afresh the Eden
     flowers:
  From its smoking hell of battle, Love and Pity send their
     prayer;
  And still thy white-winged angels hover dimly in our air."

Gen. Burnside had lost only thirteen men. The works were admirably constructed by the engineering skill of Generals O. E. Babcock and O. M. Poe; and the whole defence inspired by the spirit and valor of Lieut. Samuel Benjamin, commander of the fort, who was supported by the utmost coolness on the part of detachments of three hundred men from the Seventy-ninth New-York and Second Michigan Volunteers. These men reserved their terrible fire until the enemy were actually at the ditch, and then made every shot a messenger of death.

Half an hour after Burnside tendered to Longstreet the flag of truce, the latter received a message from Jefferson Davis, announcing Bragg's defeat at Mission-ary Ridge, and ordering him to unite with the latter. But Longstreet had more military skill than Davis, and decided to aid Bragg by continuing the siege. He would thus call off Grant from the pursuit of Bragg; or, if Grant followed Bragg without relieving Burnside, he would, after a few days more, have starvation as his powerful ally in the siege of Knoxville.

Longstreet now received the despatch from Grant to Burnside written for his perusal, and put in the way of the rebel scouts. From this, Longstreet learned of Sherman's advance; that he was cut off from his sup-plies; and, if he would escape capture, he must hurry toward Virginia. He accordingly raised the siege, and, on the night of the 4th of December, began his retreat.

The next morning, Sherman sent to Burnside as follows: "I am here, and can bring twenty-five thou-sand men into Knoxville to-morrow: but, Longstreet having retreated, I feel disposed to stop; for a stern chase is a long one. But I will do all that is possible. Without you specify that you want troops, I will let mine rest to-morrow, and ride to see you."

The next morning, Sherman rode over to Knoxville, and held an interview with Gen. Burnside. They arranged for the pursuit of Longstreet, and that Sherman should return to Grant's support, lest Bragg should venture to attack Grant with his now-reduced force.

On the 6th, Gen. Halleck, in a report to the Secretary of War, said, "Considering the strength of the rebel position, and the difficulty of storming his intrenchments, the battle of Chattanooga must be considered the most remarkable in history."

On the 10th of December, Gen. Grant issued the following eloquent order to his victorious soldiers: —

"The general commanding takes the opportunity of returning his sincere thanks and congratulations to the brave armies of the Cumberland, the Ohio, and the Tennessee, and their comrades from the Potomac, for the recent splendid and decisive successes achieved over the enemy. In a short time, you have recovered from him the control of the Tennessee River from Bridgeport to Knoxville. You dislodged him from his great stronghold upon Lookout Mountain; drove him from Chattanooga Valley; wrested from his determined grasp the possession of Missionary Ridge; repelled, with heavy loss to him, his repeated assaults upon Knoxville; forced him to raise the siege there; driving him at all points, utterly routed and discomfited, beyond the limits of the State.

"By your noble heroism and determined courage, you have most effectually defeated the plans of the enemy for regaining possession of the States of Kentucky and Tennessee. You have secured positions from which no rebellious power can drive or dislodge you. For all this, the general commanding thanks you collectively and individually. The loyal people of the United States thank and bless you. Their hopes and prayers against this unholy Rebellion are with you daily. Their faith in you will not be in vain. Their hopes will not be blasted. Their prayers to Almighty God will be answered. You will yet go to other fields of strife; and, with the invincible bravery and unflinching loyalty to justice and right which have characterized you in the past, you will prove that no enemy can withstand you, and that no defences, however formidable, can check your onward march."

The battle of Chattanooga will ever be regarded as one of the most romantic and interesting in the annals of war.

CHAPTER XXIII.

THE campaign was indeed extraordinary. The war in the South-west was substantially closed. The opening of the Mississippi had severed the Confederacy, and separated its armies from their great supplies of cattle in Texas; and they were now shut out from the rich granaries of Tennessee and Kentucky. With the exception of Virginia, the Rebellion was dethroned when its proud army was hurled from the summit of Missionary Ridge. There was historic grace and fitness, therefore, that, in the closing drama, the men of the Valley of the Mississippi, of the North-west, and the descendants of those who conquered at Bunker Hill and Saratoga, should unite in achieving this transcendent victory. Their blood, mingling there in a common libation, gave hope that the Union would be immortal.

The national standard flying from the peak on Lookout Mountain signalled Sherman's great march to the sea.

Upon the assembling of Congress on the 8th of December, on motion of Hon. Mr. Washburne, the thanks of Congress, and a gold medal, were voted to Gen. Grant. The medal was ordered to be "presented to him in the name of the people of the United States of America."

The Legislatures of Ohio, New York, and other States, passed votes of thanks for his public services. Various religious bodies of high character, among them the Methodist Missionary Society of the Cincinnati Conference, elected him to honorary membership.

While these honors were being showered by his grateful countrymen on Gen. Grant, he was busily occupied in visiting the outposts of his army, preparing reports, and submitting plans to the government for future operations. He visited Nashville and Knoxville, crossing the country by the Cumberland Gap on horseback, that he might see the country for himself, and examine the routes for supplying his army. The snow was deeper than had been known for thirty years; and the party often waded through deep drifts, driving their half-frozen horses before them. He could have gone by a shorter and easier route; but such was the temperament of the man, that no route seemed to him long or difficult which gave him the most valuable information in regard to his army and his duties.

Wherever he went, crowds thronged to greet him; but everywhere he seemed unconscious of his great achievements. His manners were simple and natural. Various efforts were made to induce him to make speeches, but never with success. At Lexington, Gen. Leslie Coombs said to the crowd, " Gen. Grant has told me in confidence that he never made a speech, knows nothing about speech-making, and has no disposition to learn."

It was on his return from this tour, that Gen. Grant, in one of his communications to the War Department, foreshadowed the march of Sherman through the South. He said, —

"I look upon the next line for me to secure to be *that from Chattanooga to Mobile;* Montgomery and Atlanta being the important *intermediate* points. To do this, large supplies must be secured on the Tennessee River, so as to *be independent of the railroad from here (Nashville) to the Tennessee for a considerable length of time.* Mobile would be a second base. The destruction which Sherman will do to the roads around Meridian will be of material importance to us in preventing the enemy from drawing supplies from Mississippi, and in clearing that section of all large bodies of rebel troops. . . . I do not look upon any points, except Mobile in the south, and the Tennessee River in the north, as presenting practicable starting-points from which to operate against Atlanta and Montgomery."

On the 24th of January, Gen. Grant was informed by telegraph that his oldest son, who had accompanied him through his Vicksburg campaign, was lying dangerously sick at St. Louis; and he obtained leave to visit him for a few days.

He arrived unheralded, unannounced; and the first intimation the citizens of St. Louis had that the hero of Vicksburg and Chattanooga was among them was on seeing on the hotel-register the name of "U. S. Grant, Chattanooga."

Men show their characters in small matters. The citizens would have been glad to escort him into the city with a cavalcade, under waving flags, beneath smiling balconies, and through applauding thousands; but he had given no opportunity for display.

He was at once invited to a public dinner.

The banquet was sumptuous and elegant in all respects. At the toast, " Our disinterested guest, Major-Gen. Grant," the band struck up, " Hail to the Chief."

Gen. Grant rose, and said, " Gentlemen, in response, it will be impossible to do more than thank you."

During the evening, he was serenaded; and the hotel was surrounded by thousands anxious to see him, and shouting, "Speech, speech!" Gen. Grant stepped out upon the balcony, and was welcomed by the most flattering cheers. He instantly removed his hat, bowed, and, amid profound silence, said, "Gentlemen, I thank you for this honor. I cannot make a speech; it is something I have never done, and never intend to do: and I beg you will excuse me."

But the crowd were not so easily satisfied, and continued shouting loudly, "Speech, speech!"

Several gentlemen urged him to address the people; but he declined. At last, one said, "General, tell them you can fight for them, but cannot talk to them: do tell them that."

But Grant could not glorify himself; and he immediately answered, "Some one else must say that if it is to be said."

But the multitude thinking he only needed urging, and continuing their shouts, he leaned over the balcony, and said deliberately, "Gentlemen, making speeches is not my business. I never did it in my life, and never will. I thank you, however, for your attendance here."

He then bowed and retired.

While in the city, he visited the university, and was also invited to attend a meeting in aid of the Sanitary Commission. He took the occasion to express his grateful appreciation of the great and beneficent work done by the commission for the soldiers in an eloquent letter.

CHAPTER XXIV.

GEN. GRANT had rendered a great service to the country in the victories he had achieved. He had captured ninety thousand prisoners, four hundred and seventy-two cannon, and small-arms unnumbered. But he had also done a great service in demonstrating what could be done in a department embracing ten States, by uniting its military power under one head. What the will of one man had accomplished west of the Alleghanies, showed what unity of plan, and concentration of action, could accomplish throughout the country. The war was taxing the resources and patience of the people as it continued year after year. A victory in one section was offset by a defeat in another.

While these views were generally entertained, Hon. Mr. Washburne of Illinois introduced into Congress a bill to revive the grade of Lieutenant-General. But two men had ever held this position. In 1798, the country was apprehensive of a war with France, then passing through its great revolution ; and President John Adams appointed George Washington " Lieutenant-General of the armies of the United States." In 1855, the office was conferred by brevet upon Major-Gen. Winfield Scott.

The bill was passed on the 26th of February, 1864. On the 2d of March, President Lincoln nominated Gen. Grant as Lieutenant-General, and he was confirmed the following day by the Senate. By the bill, he was " authorized, under the direction of the President, to command the armies of the United States."

The same day, he was ordered to Washington, and started the next morning, March 4.

At this time, Gen. Sherman was at Memphis. Grant's intention was to return, and accompany the army through the heart of the rebel States on its march to the sea. Before leaving, Gen. Grant wrote the following letter to Gen. Sherman, honorable alike to the writer and to the friend to whom it was addressed. No biography of these distinguished men, and no history of our war, is complete without them.

DEAR SHERMAN, — The bill reviving the grade of Lieutenant-General has become a law; and my name has been sent to the Senate for the place. I now receive orders to report to Washington immediately in person; which indicates a confirmation, or a likelihood of confirmation. I start in the morning to comply with the order.

Whilst I have been eminently successful in this war, in at least gaining the confidence of the public, no one feels more than I how much of this success is due to the energy, skill, and the harmonious putting-forth of that energy and skill, of those whom it has been my good fortune to have occupying subordinate positions under me.

There are many officers to whom these remarks are applicable to a greater or less degree, proportionate to their ability as soldiers; but what I want is to express my thanks to you and McPherson, as the men to whom, above all others, I feel indebted for whatever I have had of success.

How far your advice and assistance have been of help to me, you know. How far your execution of whatever has been given you to do entitles you to the reward I am receiving, you cannot know as well as I.

I feel all the gratitude this letter would express, giving it the most flattering construction. The word *you* I use in the plural, intending it for McPherson also. I would write to him, and will some day; but, starting in the morning, I do not know that I shall find time just now. Your friend,

U. S. GRANT.

The following is Gen. Sherman's reply : —

DEAR GENERAL, — I have your more than kind and characteristic letter of the 4th instant. I will send a copy to Gen. McPherson at once.

You do yourself injustice, and us too much honor, in assigning to us too large a share of the merits which have led to your high advancement. I know you approve the friendship I have ever proffered to you, and will permit me to continue, as heretofore, to manifest it on all proper occasions.

You are now Washington's legitimate successor, and occupy a position of almost dangerous elevation ;. but if you can continue, as heretofore, to be yourself, — simple, honest, and unpretending, — you will enjoy through life the respect and love of friends, and the homage of millions of human beings, who will award you a large share in securing to them and their descendants a government of law and stability.

I repeat, you do Gen. McPherson and myself too much honor. At Belmont, you manifested your traits; neither of us being near. At Donelson, also, you illustrated your whole character. I was not near, and Gen. McPherson was in too subordinate a capacity to influence you.

Until you had won Donelson, I confess I was almost cowed by the terrible array of anarchical elements that presented themselves at every point; but that admitted a ray of light I have followed since. I believe you are as brave, patriotic, and just as the great prototype, Washington; as unselfish, kind-hearted, and honest as a man should be : but the chief characteristic is the simple faith in success you have always manifested, which I can liken to nothing else than the faith a Christian has in the Saviour.

This faith gave you the victory at Shiloh and at Vicksburg. Also, when you have completed your best preparations, you go into battle without hesitation, as at Chattanooga, — no doubts, no reserves; and I tell you it was this which made us act with confidence.

My only point of doubt was in your knowledge of grand strategy, and of books of science and of history; but I confess, your common sense seems to have supplied all these. ·

Now, as to the future. Don't stay in Washington. Come West. Take to yourself the whole Mississippi Valley. Let us make it dead sure; and I tell you the Atlantic slopes and Pacific shores will follow its destiny as surely as the limbs of a tree live or die with the main trunk. We have done much; but still much remains. Time and time's influence are with us. We could almost afford to sit still, and let these influences work.

Here lies the seat of the coming empire; and from the West, when our task is done, we will make short work of Charleston and Richmond and the impoverished coast of the Atlantic.

Your sincere friend,

W. T. SHERMAN.

The appointment of Gen. Grant touched the heart of the whole nation; and, although he travelled rapidly, wherever the people heard of his coming they thronged to the railway stations, and ratified and indorsed the action of the government by cordial greetings and tumultuous cheers.

On arriving at Washington, he went to Willard's Hotel, and soon after walked quietly into the dining-room with his son, without escort or staff, wearing a blue coat which had evidently seen service. He had been there some time unnoticed, when he was recognized by a gentlemen who had seen him in New Orleans. He announced that Lieut.-Gen. Grant was present; and the whole company, ladies and gentlemen, at once rose to their feet, and greeted him with welcoming applause. The homage was spontaneous and hearty.

In the evening, he attended the usual levee of the President. He walked into the reception-room unannounced, but was immediately recognized and cordially received by Mr. Lincoln. The east room adjoining was, as usual on such occasions, crowded with members of Congress and their families, officers of the army and navy, and distinguished strangers in Washington.

As soon as Gen. Grant entered, and his presence became known, the enthusiasm was very great. The company crowded around him ; and he was finally compelled to mount a sofa, where he was saluted with cheer upon cheer. But it was apparent that it was not wholly pleasant to the general to be the object of such marked attention. He afterwards escorted Mrs. Lincoln through the rooms, and retired. He remarked to a friend before leaving, " This is the *warmest campaign* I have had during the war. I must get away from Washington soon. I do not fancy this show-business."

At one o'clock the next day, Gen. Grant was formally received by the President in the Executive Chamber, and presented with his commission as Lieutenant-General. There were present all the members of the cabinet, Gen. Halleck, one or two other gentlemen, and Gen. Grant's son.

President Lincoln rose from his chair, and said, —

" GENERAL GRANT, — The nation's approbation of what you have already done, and its reliance on you for what remains to do, in the existing great struggle, is now presented, with this commission constituting you *Lieutenant-General* of the Army of the United States. With this high honor devolves on you a corresponding responsibility. As the country here intrusts you, so, under God, it will sustain you. I scarcely need add, that with what I here speak for the nation goes my own hearty personal concurrence."

Gen. Grant, receiving the commission, replied,—

"MR. PRESIDENT,—I accept this commission with gratitude for the high honor conferred. With the aid of the noble armies who have fought on so many fields for our common country, it will be my earnest endeavor not to disappoint your expectations. I feel the full weight of the responsibility now devolving upon me. I know, that, if it is properly met, it will be due to these armies, . and, above all, to the favor of that Providence which leads both nations and men."

Gen. Grant was then presented to the members of the cabinet. That evening he had a long consultation with Gen. Halleck on military affairs, and the next morning, in company with Gen. Meade, visited the Army of the Potomac. It was evident to all, that the new Lieutenant-General was not disposed to spend much time over ceremonials at Washington.

CHAPTER XXV.

RE-ORGANIZATION OF THE ARMY. — THE ADVANCE.

THE weeks of March and April were passed in re-organizing the army and preparing for the spring campaign. Gen. Halleck was made chief of staff, and stationed at Washington. Gen. Sherman was put in command of the West. Gen. Meade remained in immediate command of the Army of the Potomac, with whom Gen. Grant established his headquarters in the field.

The number of the army corps was reduced to three; and Major-Generals Hancock, Warren, and Sedgwick were in command. The cavalry, with ten thousand sabres, was under the command of Gen. Sheridan. Gen. Banks was to open a campaign in Louisiana; Gen. Sherman was to commence operations in Northern Georgia; while Gen. Steele was to move against Sterling Price in Arkansas, and Gen. Butler was to threaten Richmond from Bermuda Hundred. Thus it will be perceived that Gen. Grant's combinations covered a theatre of war whose magnitude has been seldom equalled. But he addressed himself to the vast undertaking with his wonted energy, calmness, and perseverance. "Success was a duty."

The topography of Virginia was remarkable. The

whole State was little less than a vast fortress for the rebels, manned by the most splendid of the Southern armies, and commanded by the ablest of the rebel generals.

Its bastions were mountains, its trenches were valleys, its moats were rivers, its embrasures were mountain-gorges. Its natural features offered in every direction the most formidable obstacles to our advance, and, at the same time, were easily defended.

Richmond was one hundred and seventeen miles from Washington on the James River, and ordinarily contained a population of sixty thousand. Beauregard and the engineers of the rebel army had exhausted their skill and resources upon its fortifications, until it had become one of the strongest citadels in the world. Culpeper Court House, ten miles north of the Rapidan and seventy-five miles south of Washington, was the headquarters of Gen. Grant. Lee with his veterans was at Orange Court House, ten miles south of the Rapidan. The two armies were twenty miles distant from each other.

Grant now issued the death-warrant of the Rebellion in giving orders for a general advance of the army.

Crossing the Rapidan. — Page 241.

CHAPTER XXVI.

CAMPAIGN IN THE WILDERNESS.

ON the afternoon of the 3d of May, 1864, the tents of the Union army were struck; and that night, beneath the starlight, troops began crossing the Rapidan at Germania and Ely's Fords. The crossing was continued during the next day. The force numbered a hundred thousand men. The day was warm, the sun was bright; and as column after column wound its way down the river's bank, over the bridges, and spread out in marching order on the opposite side, banners and bayonets disappearing in the distance, the scene, both as a picture and for its moral associations, was deeply impressive. Grant said, "This is a wonderfully-fine appearing army; but it has seemed to me it never fought its battles *through*."

They marched toward the Wilderness. This is a wild, desolate tract of country in Spottsylvania County, about five miles wide, and twelve miles long. It is an immense jungle. The wood has been burned off for miners: its surface is uneven, and covered with stumps, bushes, and an undergrowth of pines and scrub-oaks. Artillery and cavalry are at a great disadvantage in such a labyrinth. Fires were seen blazing on the hill-tops to signal our advance to Gen. Lee.

Unlike most generals in both armies, Lee did not generally approve of fighting an army at a river's bank to prevent its crossing, but preferred to allow it to cross in almost all cases.   Lee determined to attack Grant in the Wilderness, where he and his men were perfectly familiar, and, if possible, destroy his army in the opening of the campaign.   He had seen six generals start for Richmond; but he was now to meet the man who was to go there.

Gen. Warren was with the advance, and had his headquarters at the house of a Major Lacy, where Stonewall Jackson lay after being shot at Chancellorsville.   It was on a little eminence west of the old Wilderness Tavern, on the Orange Turnpike; and here Grant took his station.   Warren's corps was attacked about noon on Thursday, May 5.   Beginning with picket-firing and skirmishing, by twelve o'clock the battle was fully opened.

Lee, with his hosts concealed in the forests, could mass his troops, and hurl them on any point of the Union line which he chose to attack.   The enemy came on, confident of victory, and fought with the most determined bravery.   Our men, largely outnumbered at this point, slowly fell back, until early in the afternoon they were re-enforced, rallied, and drove the enemy with terrible slaughter.   Hour after hour, the bloody conflict raged.   The bodies of thousands were borne to the rear in every form of mutilation.   Bright eyes that welcomed the morning's sun with hope and gladness were closed forever.   Toward night, the rebels had been repulsed so generally, that Grant ordered an advance along our whole line; but darkness settled down over the scene before the final arrangements were completed. The hospitals were crowded, and surgeons and attendants were at work all night. Parties were engaged burying the dead; while, at headquarters, Grant and his generals were occupied in preparing for a renewal of the battle at daylight. " Attack along the whole line at five in the morning " was Grant's order.

The enemy were also making similar preparations; and, at a quarter before five o'clock in the morning of Friday, a furious onset was made upon Gen. Sedgwick's corps.

But Gen. Lee was now dealing with a man who was not to be " bluffed " or disconcerted. Grant's preparations were neither hurried, delayed, nor changed by Gen. Lee. He began his movements at five o'clock precisely as he had ordered. The line of battle was now some five miles in length, running north and south. The attack on Sedgwick was a feint. The real attack was to be made on Hancock's corps, on our left, by Longstreet and his veterans. Hancock advanced on both sides of the Orange Plank-road, the troops fighting with unsurpassed bravery. The contest was desperate; for the rebels fought with reckless heroism: but nothing could resist the valor of our soldiers; and they steadily drove the enemy in confusion nearly two miles, killing, wounding, and taking prisoners. Some of the terrified enemy fled even to the headquarters of Gen. Lee.

But the victorious advance disordered our men; and the movement through the woods had disarranged their formation.

When once the line is badly broken, soldiers begin to feel as if each man is fighting by himself, or in a crowd or mob: the sensation of being part of an army, and that fifty thousand men are striking with him, is lost. The line was re-formed, and again advanced; but the enemy were now greatly strengthened. Gen. Lee, to re-assure his soldiers and excite them to the utmost, rode to the front of a brigade of Texans, where he was instantly recognized, and, seizing a flag, ordered them to follow him in a charge. But the men, like the rank and file of every army who have a brave commander, loved their chief, and did not move. A bronzed veteran in the ranks, with a clarion voice, shouted that they would not stir till he had gone to his place in the rear: the shout was re-echoed by the whole brigade, until he was forced to retire.

But the rebel line was now so strong, that it was impossible to break it. A few hours after, the enemy themselves attacked, and flung their columns upon our lines with such terrific power, now here and now there, that our line was pressed back some distance. Gen. Wadsworth of New York, seeking to stem the tide, was shot through the head.

Again our troops rallied, and amid fearful carnage forced the enemy back with heavy loss, and took up their former position.

Night again closed over the bloody field. Neither party had won a decided triumph. Some of the soldiers thought the army would retreat the next day across the Rapidan, and call for re-enforcements; but Grant had come out to fight, and took no step backward. He was at headquarters, quiet and determined, issuing his orders. He claimed no victory, smoked constantly, and remarked, " I have noticed that these Southerners fight desperately at first; yet, *when we hang on for a day or two, we whip them awfully.*"

Thousands more had been wounded, and thousands slain. The dead were to be buried.

In narrating the history of battles, it is impossible not to mention prominently the names of leading generals; but it can never be done without deep emotion at thought of the private soldiers, the unnamed heroes, who went down unheralded to death, each of them with a life precious to him and to those who loved him. Sorrow was flying that night to thousands of afflicted homes, which its shadow would darken for years; and these brave men were to find their graves, not beneath sculptured marble, not among kindred where flowers would bloom over their dust, but in this dreary region of darkness and gloom.

But the spirit of the private soldiers of the Union armies inspired the war, and achieved its victories. A regenerated nation is their mausoleum. Wherever they lie, whether in the solitude of the wilderness, in the lonely mountain-pass, or beneath the beautiful magnolia's blossoms, the place of their last repose will be hallowed till the end of time.

Saturday morning came; but it was apparent that the unparalleled exertions of the previous days had told upon the powers of the men in both armies. There was skirmishing: some guns on our right opened; but there was no reply. Each was willing to be attacked, but disinclined to attack. Gen. Grant did not assault, because he had not intended to fight in the Wilderness:

he was merely passing through it. It was Gen. Lee who had required that it should be made a battle-field; and it was Gen. Lee who was now leaving it. At noon, it was found he was in full retreat to Spottsylvania Court House. Pursuit was immediately begun, which soon changed into a race, as both parties desired to secure the high ground around Spottsylvania Court House, fifteen miles distant. Gen. Grant rode forward to the advance; and, as he passed with his staff by the side of the troops, he was greeted by the soldiers with the wildest enthusiasm.

But the enemy had the start, and were in position when our forces arrived on Sunday morning.

Part of the day was occupied in examining the position which the enemy held, putting the divisions of the army in proper place as they arrived, and locating batteries. On Monday, while directing some of his artillery-men, Gen. Sedgwick noticed them watching with a little uneasiness the bullets of the sharpshooters, and said in a joking way, " Oh! they couldn't hit an elephant at this distance." He had hardly uttered the words, when a Minie-ball tore through his brain, and he fell dead into the arms of one of his aides, — another costly sacrifice in the cause of the Union. A brave man, and a splendid officer, he gave his life freely to his country in the day of its peril.

During Monday and Tuesday, the tide of battle surged like the ocean, — now advancing, now receding. The scenes were similar to those frequently described in preceding pages. Assaults on the enemy's intrenchments were made with unsurpassed heroism, and met by the most stubborn courage. The battle raged with unabated fury. The roar of artillery, the sharp rattle of musketry, the shrieking of bursting shells, were mingled with the groans of the wounded. The dying and dead covered the field by thousands. During the afternoon of Tuesday, a dash was made from our left by Gen. Wright's division, capturing nine hundred prisoners and several guns.

Later in the afternoon, Gen. Lee massed his troops in front of our centre, with the intention of hurling them with overwhelming strength upon that part of our line. To disguise his purpose, he sent two brigades to attack our right: but Grant had too recently employed the same tactics against Bragg at Chattanooga to be deceived by Lee ; and, by a singular coincidence, he was at the same time strengthening his own centre, preparatory to attacking Lee. Both generals had determined to assault each other on the same plan at the same time. The result was a desperate attempt on either side to break the line of the other.

On Wednesday, the battle was renewed ; and Gen. Grant sent to Washington his well-known despatch : —

"We have now ended the sixth day of very heavy fighting. The result to this time is much in our favor. Our losses have been heavy as well as those of the enemy. I think the loss of the enemy must be greater. We have taken over five thousand prisoners by battle, whilst he has taken from us but few except stragglers. *I propose to fight it out on this line if it takes all summer.*"

Grant determined to attack the enemy's right centre ; and during the night, under cover of a fog, a portion of the troops under Hancock, Barlow, and Gibbon, were advanced to within twelve hundred yards of the position they were to storm.

At half-past four o'clock, Thursday morning, they advanced at the double-quick, and, with cheers which echoed to the skies, rushed over the enemy's works, and engaged in a hand-to-hand fight with bayonets and clubbed muskets with the astonished foe. The fight was short, but sharp, and ended in the capture of thirty guns, twenty colors, and over three thousand prisoners, among them Generals Johnson and Stewart. Lee himself also narrowly escaped capture, although this was not known at the time.

The position won by our men was hotly contested throughout the day. Lee seemed determined to retake it at any sacrifice of the life of his men. Five times the most savage assaults were made by the rebels, and five times they were repulsed with fearful slaughter. At times, the rival flags would be seen for a few moments on opposite sides of the same breastworks. The fighting was as fierce and deadly as any that occurred during the whole war. The carnage on both sides was frightful.*

During the day, an incident occurred showing Gen. Grant's coolness, and readiness to apply the results of his military training. A shell fell near where Gen. Grant and some of his officers were standing; and, while the latter were stepping out of the way, Grant drew a small compass from his pocket, examined the course of the shell, ascertained the location of the battery, and at once gave orders for a few of our guns to reply in a

---

* "In the vicious phraseology commonly employed by those who undertake to describe military operations, and especially by those who never witnessed a battle-field, 'piles of dead' figure much more frequently than they exist in reality. The phrase is here no figure of speech, as can be attested by thousands who witnessed the ghastly scene." — *Campaigns of the Army of the Potomac.*

direction which soon rained a shower of shells upon the annoying rebel battery.

Brig.-Gen. Rice of Michigan was among those mortally wounded. "Turn me," said he a few moments before he expired, — "turn me, that I may die with my face to the enemy!" After his wish had been complied with, he said, "Tell my wife and children I died for my country." — "How does the great Captain of salvation appear to you now?" said the chaplain.

"Oh! Jesus is near and very dear," said the dying man, and soon after ceased to breathe. And thus another of the army of Christian heroes went up from the ensanguined fields of our war for freedom.

Hour after hour, the bloody havoc went on, until twenty thousand more precious lives were added to the costly sacrifice which slavery demanded with insatiable cruelty and voracity.

The army surgeons, the chaplains, the agents and nurses of the Sanitary and Christian Commissions, followed the reaper Death as he gathered his harvests of woe, binding up the wounds of the suffering, and ministering consolation to the dying.

> " In dust the vanquished and the victor lie :
>   With copious slaughter all the fields are red,
>   And heaped with growing mountains of the dead.
>   So fought each host, with thirst of glory fired ;
>   And crowds on crowds triumphantly expired."*

* Pope's Homer.

CHAPTER XXVII.

BATTLE OF COLD HARBOR.

AN order was read to the army, announcing the victorious march of Sherman, through Georgia, to the sea. The cheers with which it was received rang out above the din of battle, and were heard all along the rebel lines.

May 9, Sheridan had been sent, with Merritt, Custer, and a force of cavalry, on a raid to Richmond. At Beaver Dam, on the Virginia Central Railroad, they destroyed the station, ten miles of track, three trains of cars, a million and a half of rations, and liberated four hundred Union soldiers taken in the Wilderness, and then on the way to Libby Prison. At Yellow Tavern, a few miles north of Richmond, they had a battle with the rebel cavalry under Gen. Stuart, who was mortally wounded. Sheridan now dashed down the road to Richmond; and Custer carried the outer defences, capturing one hundred prisoners. But Richmond could not be taken by cavalry. He rejoined the army on the 25th of May.

The army manœuvred for several days with a view to find a vulnerable point of attack in Lee's intrenchments, and finally, on the 20th, began a flank-march to turn the enemy's position, and compel him to leave his intrenchments. It is one of the most difficult operations in war, and especially so in the presence of an able tactician like Gen. Lee; yet it was executed with complete success. But at midnight the rebels, under Longstreet, started south in the hope of interposing again between Gen. Grant and Richmond.

The two armies were again on a race, this time for the banks of the North Anna River; but, as Lee already held the shortest road, there was every chance that he would make the quickest journey.

The march was through a portion of the State which showed the great fertility of soil and the immense natural resources of Virginia. The weather was perfect, and scattered along the route were the stately mansions and broad acres of the Virginia gentlemen of the olden time. The region had not been swept by the tornado of war, and offered a beautiful picture of the Old Dominion in the days when McDowell, and Tom Marshall, and T. J. Randolph, had denounced slavery as "a curse," "a cancer," and predicted ruin and desolation for their native State unless she entered on a policy of emancipation. Their prediction was fulfilled.

On Monday, the 23d of May, the army had reached the north bank of the North Anna; but the columns of the enemy were already on the opposite side. On the 24th, our army crossed in full force; but, after carefully examining the rebel intrenchments, Gen. Grant became satisfied that they could not be carried by storm without a loss of life which he would not incur.

On the night of the 26th, with great skill, and unknown to the enemy, Gen. Grant again crossed the river, and marched south toward the Pamunkey River and the city of Richmond. Not a shot had been fired, nor any sound made to disturb the rebel pickets. When daylight came, Gen. Lee discovered that the Union army was already on its way to Richmond.

On the 27th, our army reached the Pamunkey at Hanovertown. Thus, with masterly ability, Grant had compelled Lee to leave his intrenchments. He had placed himself within fifteen miles of Richmond, and established a new and convenient base for supplies for his army by the York River and Chesapeake Bay, and opened communication with the columns of Gen. Butler on the James River.

He held command of the peninsula without having exposed Washington, or allowing Lee to keep a quarter of our army marching back and forth to protect that city.

The places in the vicinity were familiar to the old Army of the Potomac who had served under Gen. McClellan. The slimy swamps of the Chickahominy, where so many thousands had been sacrificed; Fair Oaks, from which Gen. Hooker had trotted down to within four miles of Richmond unopposed, until ordered back; Mechanicsville, which, after a victorious and bloody repulse of Lee's army, had been suddenly evacuated by our perplexed and doubting commander; Gaines's Mill, where one wing of the army had driven back the rebel hosts, while sixty thousand Union soldiers stood idle near at hand because their general could not decide whether to unite or divide his forces, — these spots were all within a short distance, and the thunder of our cannon could be distinctly heard at Richmond.

Gen. Grant had not yet taken Richmond; but he was fighting the rebel army. He was appalled by no visions of a rebel force two hundred thousand strong, which demanded daily re-enforcements from Washington at every halt; and he never, in a single instance, telegraphed to President Lincoln as another had done, " If I save this army now, I tell you plainly that I *owe no thanks to you or to any persons in Washington: you have done your best to sacrifice this army.*" *

Gen. Grant determined to force a passage across the Chickahominy. But a direct assault on the enemy's formidable works would lead to fearful loss of life; and he therefore determined to extend toward the left, and cross the river below at Cold Harbor. The place had no *harbor*, but was a small inland town at the junction of several roads, and of great importance to the enemy. Lee had been re-enforced by the garrison at Richmond, and was prepared to offer the most desperate

---

* A governor of one of the New-England States stated in the hearing of the writer, that, soon after Pope's defeat at Bull Run, he, with a few others, was conversing with President Lincoln concerning the prospects of the war, and remarked that " the people of his State were willing to do every thing possible to benefit the government; but they were *not* willing to bury their sons and brothers in the swamps of the Chickahominy to no purpose." One gentleman present intimated that Gen. McClellan could not be sincere in his determination to conquer, and must be disloyal. Mr. Lincoln said, " No: I have watched McClellan very carefully. I do not think he is disloyal; but he is constitutionally an over-cautious man. This and his indecision prevent all permanent success. For instance, the rebels lately, in moving into Maryland, advanced rapidly. Gen. McClellan was urged to do the same: but no; he insisted upon moving his whole army, day by day, in complete battle-array, ready to resist attack at any moment. Nothing we could say would induce him to value time and move with speed. He was a week or more in going the distance the rebels travelled in two days. Now, the result shows, if he had only saved half his time, he would have destroyed Lee's army, and ended the war."

resistance to Gen. Grant's advance. The rebel line was about six miles in length; and orders were given to attack the whole front at daylight on the morning of June 1. The assault was made by the Sixth Corps and Gen. Smith's command, which had just arrived from Butler's army. Gen. Burnside attacked the enemy's left. The first line of works was carried and held. The record of the day's fighting was like that often given. Our soldiers advanced to the muzzles of the enemy's guns with a bravery and patriotism that smiled at death in defence of their country; and they were met by a courage as fearless as it was misplaced. Fierce assaults were made upon each of our corps not engaged in the principal attack; but, in every instance, were repulsed.

Our loss in the battles at and around Cold Harbor was numbered by thousands.

Among the killed was Brig.-Gen. Peter A. Porter of New York. His patriotism had descended to him from a distinguished father, — Gen. Porter of Niagara Falls, who served with honor in the war of 1812. When the Rebellion broke out, Gen. Porter left a home of wealth and taste, embellished with every attraction which could be desired, and gave a noble life to the cause of his country. He was struck in the neck, and fell, but rose to his knees, when he was pierced by six bullets. His last words were, "Dress up to your colors!"

> "If there be, on this earthly sphere,
> A boon, an offering, Heaven holds dear,
> 'Tis the last libation Liberty draws
> From the heart that bleeds and breaks in her cause."

The whole series of brilliant military operations by which Gen. Grant had carried an army of a hundred thousand men in forty-three days from the Rapidan to the James, without the loss of a wagon, compelling his able antagonist to race at his side for the safety of the rebel capital, will never cease to be the study and admiration of the military student.

CHAPTER XXVIII

SIEGE OF PETERSBURG.

GEN. GRANT now determined to adopt the other alternative, which had from the first been in his mind, and transfer his army by flank-marches to the south side of the James River. This operation, in the face of an enemy always alert and energetic, Napoleon pronounced "the ablest manœuvre taught by military art." To conceal his purpose, strong demonstrations were made at Meadow Bridge and two or three other points, as if with a view of crossing the Chickahominy; and Gen. Lee commenced strengthening these points by defensive works. But on Sunday, the 12th of June, the army of more than a hundred thousand men, including cavalry, artillery, and infantry, began their march; and so skilful had been the arrangements, that, though within a short distance of an enemy in nearly equal numbers and a vigilant commander, Gen. Lee knew nothing of the movement, until, on the morning of the 13th, he found that his adroit and active enemy was far on the way to his rear.

The host pressed on night and day with untiring energy. Across rivers and mountains, through valleys and plains, the army moved, until, almost without halting, they were, in thirty-six hours, on the south bank of the James, fifty-five miles from Cold Harbor.

This extraordinary movement, in the secrecy, quickness, and perfect success with which it was executed, has excited the unqualified admiration of every historian of the war, North and South.

Petersburg is twenty-two miles south of Richmond, on the Appomattox; and is the centre of all the railroads connecting Richmond and the Southern States.

Gen. Butler had, on the 10th, sent a force of infantry and cavalry to capture the place if possible, and to destroy the railroads and bridges over the Appomattox.

The work was gallantly done, but with partial success. The defences on the south side were carried, and our men penetrated some distance into the town: but the works were too strong to be carried by assault; and Gen. Gilmore, in command of the expedition, retired.

Gen. Lee, astonished to find Gen. Grant fifty miles south of him, had hurried his army with all haste to the defence of Petersburg, rushing through Richmond to the amazement of its citizens. They succeeded in arriving a few hours before the assault on the 15th.

In this whole movement of Gen. Grant to the south of Richmond, he evinced a moral courage and self-reliance scarcely surpassed by his determination to move south of Vicksburg against the advice of all his generals. The Administration had no desire to interfere with his plans; but it was well known it was exceedingly anxious that the army should be kept between Washington and Lee's army, and not beyond and south of it. The government was well aware of the supreme importance which in Europe is attached to the cap-

ture of a nation's capital. Vienna in possession of the
French army was Austria conquered. Paris in the
hands of the allied sovereigns was France subjugated.
The capture of Washington would lead to immediate
and most embarrassing complications in our foreign
relations.

But, confident in the right, Gen. Grant "took the
responsibility." He had intended to take Petersburg
before Lee could arrive ; and had ordered Gen. Butler
to send forward Gen. Smith's corps for this purpose as
soon as it arrived from the Chickahominy, which was
promptly done : but Smith, moving in the deliberate
style of the former campaigns of the Potomac Army,
lost several hours of time, which never returned ; and,
when the advance was made, Lee and his veterans had
arrived in force.

During the week following, several assaults were
made with unparalleled heroism by the troops under
Generals Meade, Burnside, Butler, Warren, Hancock,
and other commanders ; but it was demonstrated that
the hosts of Lee, securely intrenched behind their formidable works, could resist fivefold their numbers.
Petersburg was only to be taken by siege.

June 22, Gen. Wilson, with six thousand cavalry,
was sent to destroy the railroad communications south
of Petersburg. He struck the Weldon Railroad at
Ream's Station, and destroyed sixty miles of track, with
dépôts, bridges, cars, locomotives, blacksmith-shops, and
mills.. He brought in four hundred negroes, and large
numbers of horses and mules.

The army, which had now been fighting and marching, almost without intermission, for two months of

extreme heat, enjoyed some days of comparative rest: still the Union lines were steadily closing around Petersburg, which was practically an outwork of Richmond.

Our lines now embraced a circuit of thirty miles. The main body of our army was south of and in front of Petersburg; while Gen. Foster was at Deep Bottom, and Gen. Butler was at Bermuda Hundred.

The labors of Gen. Grant were multiform and unceasing, — studying his plans, conferring with his engineers, receiving reports, and issuing orders at headquarters, riding to the outposts, superintending the works, speaking a cheering word to the pickets. Night and day, he was unwearied and unwearying in his care for his army and his watchfulness of the enemy; always plainly dressed, often attended only by a single orderly. The soldiers observed all these things, appreciated their general, and gave him their entire confidence. Officers and men said, " Gen. Grant is so easy to approach! " He always endeavored to set an example of earnest work, of avoiding show, and laying aside all official airs.

Sometimes the lessons which he gave in a quiet way to pompous subordinates were very effective. He happened to be one day on the wharf at City Point, plainly dressed, as usual, where a young second lieutenant, with very bright buttons and a very faultless blue coat, was directing some colored men in rolling a hogshead on board of a boat. It was so heavy, the men could not move it at first; when the young officer shouted gruffly, " Come, niggers, hurry up your work, or get another man to help you! "

A man who stood near, with a faded blue coat on,

turned up his sleeves, joined the negroes in pushing the hogshead on to the boat, then, without speaking a word to any one, walked away. It was the Lieutenant-General of the United States, as the young officer soon learned to his amazement.

It was probably of no consequence whether the boat was loaded five minutes sooner or later ; but it *was* of great consequence to show sympathy with the humble labor of the humblest man in carrying forward the great campaign, and to rebuke snobbery and laziness in high and low.

The soldiers saw, that with all his attention to the great plans, the mighty machinery of the campaign, he provided thoughtfully and with energy for the small comforts of his soldiers. The men expressed a determination to work and fight, because " it is Grant's job, and we are going to put it through for him." Such conduct in all armies always endears a commander to his soldiers.

" What is under my head ? " said Sir Ralph Abercromby, when dying at the siege of Alexandria, in Egypt.

" A blanket." — " Whose blanket ? " — " It is only one of the men's," was the answer.

" I want to know whose blanket it is." — " Duncan Roy's of the Forty-second, Sir Ralph."

" Then see that Duncan Roy has his blanket to-night." The next day an army wept, and a nation mourned.

Gen. Grant inspired his soldiers by his bravery, won their confidence by his skill, and their love by his kindness.

On the 21st of June, President Lincoln visited Gen. Grant.

For several weeks, the Forty-eighth Pennsylvania had been at work on a mine opposite the corps of Gen. Burnside, who had originally suggested the undertaking.

A gallery was dug out five hundred feet in length: at its end were two side-galleries, each forty feet long, directly under one of the rebel forts. In these side-galleries, four tons of powder were placed. The whole work was done with such entire secrecy, that no suspicion of its existence was created.

Some deserter or prisoner had published the fact in a Richmond paper; but, after examination, it was disbelieved in the rebel army.

The morning of July 30 was fixed upon as the time for the explosion. The rebels were strolling about, laughing, talking; some of them singing, " Maryland, my Maryland! " — little thinking that they would soon be numbered with the dead.

The mine was ready; the match was lighted; the siege-guns were loaded, ready to open their heavy fire to protect the storming column : but the mine did not explode. Lieut. J. Douty and Sergeant Reese of the Forty-eighth Pennsylvania volunteered to enter the gallery, and ascertain the cause of the delay. The fuse was found to be damp. Another was lighted; and, a few moments after, there was a low rumbling of the earth : then came the terrible explosion. The fort was lifted two hundred feet into the air, and with it the torn and mangled bodies of three hundred men of South-Carolina regiments, cannon, rocks, camp-equipages, broken gun-carriages, mingled in the clouds of smoke, and sheets of fire, which soared up to the skies. At the same instant, the guns of all our batteries opened with a thunder which was heard at a distance of several miles. The explosion showed a chasm one hundred and fifty feet long, sixty feet wide, and thirty feet deep.

It was one of the many instances in war where *time* is every thing; where five minutes' delay will make all the difference between an exultant victory which cheers, or a mortifying defeat which saddens, a nation's heart.

The storming-party were in the middle of the chasm. The enemy were paralyzed with terror and confusion: another mine might explode in an instant under their feet. Invisible danger is always the most appalling. The very uncertainty magnified their fears. It was the moment to rush forward, while unopposed, to the crest of Cemetery Hill, only four hundred yards distant, which commanded the whole rebel works.

> " Seize, seize the hour
> Ere it slips from you.   Seldom comes the moment
> In life which is sublime and weighty." *

But the advancing column halted, the divisions which followed halted, for a few moments only; but it was too late. Confusion ensued; the rebels, recovered from their fright, opened fire from their guns with terrible effect. They threw up intrenchments, planted new batteries. Gen. Potter suceeeded in charging toward the crest; but the enemy now met him with a furious storm of grape and canister, and he was compelled to fall back.

Our loss in killed and captured was four thousand men, that of the enemy one thousand.

There were military courts of inquiry, and long

* Schiller's Wallenstein.

investigations by Congressional committees, as to the causes of the failure. There were long and elaborate reports to prove that the assault ought to have been a success; but none of them succeeded in recalling the few moments lost in the outset, or altering the fact of failure. Men who are to make such an assault should be the picked men of an army.

On the 4th of July, Gen. Grant united in the honors paid at Gettysburg to the fallen heroes who there died that their country might live.

Gen. Lee, wishing to relax the iron grip with which Grant was contracting his lines around Petersburg, sent Gen. Early with a strong force up the Valley of the Shenandoah to take Washington, invade Pennsylvania, capture Philadelphia, and do other fearful things. But Gen. Grant was not the man with whom such strategy could succeed. The day and the man for that had passed away.

Aug. 7, Gen. Grant did with the Departments of Washington, the Susquehanna, and West Virginia, what the government had done with the larger departments. He united them into the Middle Department, under one commander, — Gen. Philip H. Sheridan. He sent him two divisions of cavalry; raising Sheridan's force to more than twenty thousand men.

As to instructions, Gen. Grant says, "I left City Point on the 15th of September to visit him at his headquarters, to decide, after conference with him, what should be done. I saw there were but two words of instruction necessary, — 'Go in!'" He went in, and came out with the victories of Opequan, Fisher's Hill,

Cedar Creek, and Waynesborough, on his banners. His memorable ride from Winchester to Cedar Creek, and his unmatched prowess, which there, as in the twinkling of an eye, changed defeat and disaster into victory and renown, is not exceeded in splendor in all the brilliant annals of war. The rebels had made the rich Valley of the Shenandoah their stamping-ground, and from its inexhaustible fields had drawn immense supplies for their armies. They had rendered it absolutely necessary that it should be devastated in such a manner, that, as Grant expressed it, nothing should invite their return. Sheridan performed this painful duty in a way which left this beautiful region until the close of the war a monument of desolation, which realized Burke's picture of the tempest of destruction and woe with which Hyder Ali blasted the Plains of the Carnatic.

During the siege, there were operations north and west of Petersburg, attended with various degrees of success. Gen. Butler crossed the James, and, with the Tenth and Eighteenth Corps, attacked Fort Harrison, below Chapin's Farm, capturing fifteen guns and a large portion of the enemy's intrenchments.

A gallant attack was also made on Fort Gillmore. Fort Harrison was of such importance to Richmond, that several desperate assaults were made to recover it; but they were repulsed with great loss of life to the enemy.

Gen. Warren took possession of and held the Weldon Railroad. Gen. Lee attacked repeatedly with great force, but without success; and he was at last compelled to surrender this important line of communication. The soldiers built a branch railroad from the City Point and

Petersburg Railroad to the Weldon Road, which greatly aided in supplying the army.

In all the operations around Petersburg, the colored troops bore themselves in a manner which elicited universal commendation. They were patient in toil, cheerful under privations, and brave in the hour of danger.

The capture of Atlanta was announced to the army on the 4th of September, and was greeted in all the camps by long-continued and enthusiastic cheering. Afterwards, by way of saluting the victory, all the guns opened fire on the rebel works. The rebel guns replied; and, while the cannonade continued, earth and sky seemed to tremble with the deafening roar.

During the remainder of the time, until the opening of the spring campaign, operations were mainly confined to defending and extending our lines, and to crippling the enemy's lines of communication, as well as preventing him from sending any force south. Gen. Grant said to a friend at this time, when croakers were predicting failure, " I shall take Richmond, and Gen. Lee knows it." He exhibited the same faith when he drew his lines around Vicksburg.

Mr. Greeley, in his able history of " The American Conflict," says, —

" Grant's conduct of this campaign was not satisfactory to the Confederate critics, who gave a decided preference to the strategy of McClellan. The merit which may be fairly claimed for Grant is that of resolutely undertaking a very difficult and formidable task, and executing it to the best of his ability; at all events, *doing it.*"

But we must now turn to the movements of Sherman and his army.

CHAPTER XXIX.

IT must be remembered that the siege of Petersburg, and the care of the vast army which encircled it, was but one item in the multitudinous occupations of Gen. Grant. The military operations of all the Union armies were conducted by him. In Missouri, in Louisiana, in Tennessee, in Georgia, large armies were marching, halting, fighting, as he gave orders. The oversight of either one was enough to tax the mind and energy of any one man.

When the despatches were read by Gen. Grant which announced that Hood, leaving Georgia, had crossed the Tennessee, and was marching on Nashville, he said, "If I commanded both armies, I should not alter the route which Hood is pursuing." *

Gen. Hood was an impulsive man; and the object of his movements was not clear to either Generals Grant or Sherman, — perhaps not clear to his own mind. He doubtless thought he should find much more comfortable quarters in the hotels at Nashville than in his camp.

---

* "I was with Napoleon at Boulogne," said Talleyrand, "when he learned that Gen. Mack was at Ulm. ' If it were mine to place him,' said he, putting his finger on the map at Ulm, ' I would place him there.' In a few hours, the camp was broken up, and the whole army was on the route to Ulm."

Grant could now bring Sherman's army to Petersburg by the ordinary routes, or by a long sweep to the sea, and then up the Atlantic coast to some point south of Richmond. A march to the sea was determined on, resembling, on a gigantic scale, the march of Sheridan through the Valley of the Shenandoah.

Atlanta had been captured; and Gen. Sherman ordered its complete evacuation as a military post.

The mayor and city council remonstrated vehemently. Gen. Sherman's reply enters admirably and with no waste of words into the philosophy of the Rebellion. It was a wholesome preaching they were not accustomed to hear. In the course of his letter, he said, " *The only way the people of Atlanta can hope once more to live in peace and quiet at home is to stop this war ; which can alone be done by admitting that it began in error, and is perpetuated in pride. We do not want your negroes, or your horses, or your houses, or your land, or any thing you have; but we do want and will have a just obedience to the laws of the United States. That we will have; and, if it involve the destruction of your improvements, we cannot help it.*"

Atlanta on the 15th of November was a city without inhabitants. Its houses were empty, its population had gone. Flowers were blooming in the gardens; but solitude reigned over the doomed city. That night the heavens reflected a sea of fire, the sky was one broad sheet of lurid flames. Buildings covering an area of two hundred acres were burning. The immense warehouses where the munitions of war for the destruction of Union men had been stored were destroyed. The founderies where rebel cannon and shot and shell had been forged and cast were in ruins. Terrible retribution had come to this city, which had sent forth the instruments of death to so many thousands of loyal men.

Most of Sherman's army had started on its great march. A Massachusetts regiment was the last to leave; and, fitly enough, its band was playing, by the light of the burning city, "John Brown's soul goes marching on."

For twenty-four days, the army disappeared from Northern view into the very heart of the Rebellion. About sixty-five thousand men swept over the country in a track fifty miles wide, and advanced from ten to twenty miles a day. Of these about five thousand were cavalry, under Gen. Kilpatrick, who moved in front and on each flank. The army was organized in two grand divisions; one under Gen. Howard, the other under Gen. Slocum. Each of these had two corps under Generals Logan, Blair, Davis, and Williams. Accompanying the train were 3,500 wagons and 35,000 horses. 1,328 prisoners and 167 guns were taken. Our whole loss in killed was 63 men, and 245 wounded. 5,000 horses and 4,000 mules were appropriated for army service. 20,000 bales of cotton were burned, and 25,000 captured at Savannah. 13,000 head of cattle, 10,000,000 pounds of corn, 1,217,527 rations of meat, 919,000 of bread, 483,000 of coffee, 581,534 of sugar, 1,146,500 of soap, 137,000 of salt, and 10,000,000 of fodder, were taken. This was in addition to the rice and sweet-potatoes, with which the army supplied itself bountifully every day. Fourteen thousand negroes resigned their connection with "the peculiar institution," and followed the army in its march.

All railroads, dépôts, mills, founderies, factories, arsenals, machine-shops, were destroyed, and every thing laid in ruins which could aid the Rebellion. The damage in the State of Georgia alone was estimated at a hundred million dollars.

This teeming abundance was found in a country where thousands of Northern soldiers had been deliberately put to death by the lingering tortures of starvation; rebel officers, in some instances, looking at the poor beings as they actually gnawed the flesh from their arms in their dying agonies.

Charleston was evacuated; Columbia, the capital of South Carolina, captured; and, April 13, the army had moved north, and occupied Raleigh, the capital of North Carolina.

It was a just judgment which led the armed hosts of the Union, bearing the national ensign, through South Carolina, which had commenced the war, and brought this avenging punishment upon herself. "Woe unto the world because of offences! For it must needs be that offences come; but woe to that man by whom the offence cometh!"

Soon after Gen. Sherman began his march, Gen. Grant sent out two expeditions to prevent a concentration of troops against him, — one from Vicksburg to the Big Black River, which destroyed railroads, bridges, and military stores; and the other from Baton Rouge, threatening the safety of Mobile.

The march of Sherman was a means of education to the South much needed. It brought the war to the

homes of the authors of secession; it showed the
people, that, notwithstanding all their leaders had told
them to the contrary, there *was* a North, there *was* a
United-States Government, with the will and power to
make itself obeyed.

It also afforded valuable instruction to the men of
the Northern army: it showed to them with terrible
plainness the poverty, the ignorance, and the arrogance created by slavery.

A member of Gen. Sherman's staff met with an
original character in Georgia, a shrewd old fellow, who
expressed his views on reconstruction in the following
pithy and forcible manner: "It'll take the help of
Divine Providence, a heap of rain, and a deal of elbow-
grease, to fix things up again."

Gen. Grant was among the first to commend Gen.
Sherman's services, and give to them the most generous
appreciation. He forwarded a subscription of five
hundred dollars to some friends of Gen. Sherman in
Columbus, O., who were intending to present him with
a testimonial of gratitude and regard; commending the
general in highest terms as "a good and great man."

In his official report, he says, "Gen. Sherman's
movement from Chattanooga to Atlanta was prompt,
skilful, and brilliant. The history of his flank movements and battles during that memorable campaign
will ever be read with an interest unsurpassed by any
thing in history." Gen. Grant never evinced toward
any one who co-operated with him the spirit of envy or
disparagement, which belongs to a little nature.

Atlanta, the heart of the Rebellion, had fallen: it
now remained for Grant to take Richmond, its head.

CHAPTER XXX.

THE final overthrow of the Rebellion was near at hand. During the winter of 1863–4, Fort Fisher was taken, which closed the port of Wilmington, N.C., —about the only place open to the Confederacy for sending out cotton, and importing ordnance, and munitions of war, from abroad.

Major-Gen. Grierson, starting from Memphis, captured the rebel camp under Forest at Verona, Miss. He destroyed the Mobile and Ohio Railroad, thirty-two cars loaded with wagons and pontoons for Hood's army, a large amount of stores, and four thousand English carabines intended for the invasion of Ohio and Indiana. He also struck the Mississippi Central Railroad, destroying machine-shops, factories, stores, and thirty warehouses, filled with public property of various kinds and of great military value.

It would require another volume to narrate in detail all the particulars of each of the movements throughout the country by which Gen. Grant prepared for the final campaign.

Suffice it to say, that in March, 1864, Gen. Canby was advancing from New Orleans against Mobile. A cavalry expedition of fifteen thousand men was sent out from Middle Tennessee under Gen. J. H. Wilson, which entered Alabama, and, sweeping over the region watered by the Tombigbee and the Black Warrior Rivers, captured Selma, and Montgomery, Ala., the capital of the rebel Confederacy. An immense amount of property was destroyed by the expedition, and by the rebels to prevent it from seizure. At Montgomery alone, a hundred and twenty-five thousand bales of cotton were destroyed, and twenty-five thousand at Selma.

Gen. Grant was apprehensive that Gen. Lee might evacuate Richmond and unite with Johnston, or retire to Lynchburg, and thence move into Tennessee. Grant was anxious to decide the fate of the Rebellion at Richmond, — not because of any excessive importance attached to that city; but he felt that the power of the Confederacy was in Lee's camp; that his army must be annihilated; and he had no desire to follow him on a chase through the South to Texas. His purpose was to break the military power of the Rebellion.

Gen. Stoneman was sent from East Tennessee with a cavalry expedition toward South Carolina, to destroy railroads and military resources, and release our starving soldiers at the prison at Salisbury, N.C. He was ordered also to destroy the Tennessee Railroad as near to Lynchburg as possible. Thence he entered North Carolina, capturing the rebel prison-camp at Salisbury with 1,364 prisoners. Ten thousand small-arms, seven thousand bales of cotton, and large magazines of ammunition, and stores of provisions and clothing, were destroyed.

West of the Mississippi, Gen. Pope was opening a

spring campaign against the rebels Price and Kirby Smith. Gen. Hancock was at Winchester to guard against a raid north, or to advance south, as might be necessary.

Generals Sherman and Schofield were at Goldsborough, N. C., — near the rebel army under Gen. Johnston. Gen. Sheridan had attacked Early at Waynesborough, capturing sixteen hundred prisoners, eleven guns, seventeen flags, and two hundred loaded wagons. Early's force was completely used up; and Sheridan advanced to Whitehouse, where Gen. Grant had sent an infantry force and supplies to meet him. He soon after joined the army before Petersburg.

The Armies of the Potomac and the James were before the defences of Petersburg and Richmond. Gen. Grant was evidently crushing out the life of the Rebellion.

To appreciate the cares and responsibilities of Gen. Grant at this time, it must be remembered that his supervision of military movements extended from the Atlantic to the Indians on the Western wilds, and from the Lakes to the Gulf of Mexico.

On the 24th of March, Gen. Grant issued orders for a general advance, on the 29th, of all the armies operating against Richmond.

But, on the 25th, Gen. Lee resolved to make a desperate struggle to free himself from the inexorable power which was steadily closing around him. At daylight, two divisions attacked Fort Steadman, which was within one hundred and fifty yards of the rebel works. It was a square redoubt covering about one acre, and mounted nine guns. Twenty thousand troops stood ready to support the attack. The rush was sudden, the surprise complete; and, in a few moments, the guns of the fort were turned upon its defenders. The supporting force did not advance immediately. Our men soon rallied; and, as the fort was commanded by those on its flanks, the artillery opened, and the result was the capture of twenty-seven hundred prisoners.

The guns trained on the ground over which the rebels retreated sent forth such a tempest of grape, canister, and round-shot, that nearly as many more fell, wounded or killed.

To make this assault, troops had been brought from the left of the rebel line; and an attack was ordered along the front of the Second and Sixth Corps on this weakened point. The attack was made with great spirit: the strongly-intrenched picket-line was carried and permanently held by our men. The positions gained were of much importance; and desperate efforts were made to retake them, but without success. It was an offset for our failure at the explosion of the mine.

President Lincoln had arrived at Gen. Grant's head-quarters the day previous, and witnessed this battle. It had been intended by Gen. Grant to give the President a grand review; but, on account of the bloody contest in the morning, it was postponed. President Lincoln, speaking of the victory gained, said, "This is better than a review."

A council of war was held here, at which President Lincoln, Gen. Grant, Major-Generals Sherman, Meade, Sheridan, and Ord, were present. Soon after, Gen. Sherman left to rejoin his army.

Gen. Lee's dash at Fort Steadman did not change Gen. Grant's orders for an advance on the 29th. Troops were concentrated, and dispositions made for the grand advance on that day.

Grant's line now extended from the north side of the James to Hatcher's Run, forty miles in length.

At three o'clock in the morning, the Fifth Army Corps, under Warren, crossed Rowanay Creek: a few hours later, the Second Army Corps, under Humphrey, crossed Hatcher's Run, four miles above. Both faced north, and advanced toward the enemy's right.

When within about two miles of the Confederate lines, Warren was sharply assailed, and a battle ensued; the rebels leaving their killed and wounded on the field, and losing about a hundred prisoners.

Humphrey advanced unopposed. Sheridan . had pushed round to Dinwiddie Court House, several miles to the left of the infantry; where he bivouacked on the night of the 29th. Grant 'sent him the following despatch : —

I now feel like ending the matter, if it is possible to do so, before going back. I do not want you, therefore, to cut loose, and go after the enemy's roads at present. In the morning push around the enemy, if you can, and get on to his right rear. The movements of the enemy's cavalry may, of course, modify your action. We will act all together as one army here until it is seen what can be done with the enemy. The signal-officer at Cobb's Hill reported, at half-past eleven, A.M., that a cavalry column had passed that point from Richmond towards Petersburg, taking forty minutes to pass.   U. S. GRANT, *Lieutenant-General.*

Major-Gen. P. H. SHERIDAN.

On Thursday, the 30th, the rain fell in such torrents as to render the roads impassable. Friday the 31st,

Saturday and Sunday, April 1 and 2, the whole line was engaged in fierce and bloody contest.

On the afternoon of the 31st, Sheridan advanced to Five Forks, the key to the whole rebel line, and about eight miles from Dinwiddie Court House. The position was altogether too strong to be ridden over, and Sheridan was forced back: but he dismounted the troopers, placed them behind some slight breastworks, left his horses to the care of a few mounted men, and received the enemy with such a deadly fire from his carabines, that they gave way; and night soon after compelled a cessation of the fight.

Grant, learning of Sheridan's situation, sent down a division of the Second Corps (Warren's) to his support; and at daylight the battle was renewed.

Sheridan, mounted on his splendid black horse, Rienzi, so famed in the poem entitled "Sheridan's Ride," accompanied by his staff, with his beautiful head-quarter-flag, rode up and down the lines, directing the formation of his troops. He seemed the incarnation of enthusiasm, yet entirely self-possessed.

When giving an important order to an officer on the field, he had a way of leaning over the neck of his horse, and, as though there were plenty of time, repeating his directions slowly, as if hammering every word into his memory in a particular place.

The troops moved into battle magnificently, but with the air and tread of men conscious of coming victory. The enemy were steadily pressed back to their works. Here the cavalry held the front; while the infantry, charging in flank and rear, rushed over the intrench-ments with irresistible power; Ayres's division taking

in a few moments a thousand prisoners, and Griffin's
fifteen hundred more. The enemy fled toward the
west, but were charged and pursued with relentless
vigor until long after dark. The battle of Five Forks
was won, the victory was complete. Between five and
six thousand prisoners were taken; and all their artillery.

The action was in every respect one of the most brilliant, as it·was one of the most important, in the war.
Sheridan masked the movements of his infantry behind
his lines of cavalry. His bugles sounded as if for a
charge on the right; while his real blow was delivered
with invincible impetuosity on the enemy's left. The
infantry were moved as if to attack the front; when suddenly they were wheeled, and hurled with the force of
an avalanche upon the astounded enemy in their rear.
Large bodies of infantry and cavalry were handled on
the field with the skill of a master, and as easily as the
pawns on a chess-board.

Gen. Grant thought it possible the enemy might
leave their lines in the darkness of the night, concentrate
against Sheridan, and force him out of his position.
He therefore at once ordered the batteries to open fire
along the whole line; and a terrific bombardment
ensued, which was continued until four o'clock in the
morning. All night·long, the darkness blazed with the
bursting of thousands of shells, and the heavens resounded with the thunders of the heavy guns. It was
the majestic prelude to the last great battle of the
Rebellion. It was a swelling anthem which celebrated
the approaching death of the gigantic conspiracy.

Gen. Grant's plans were made known only as he

issued his orders. His reserve as to his intended movements was the same to those around his head-quarters as to the enemy. That night it was tele-graphed north that Sheridan was to make a raid to Burkesville; that the army were to move toward the South-side Railroad: but such plans never existed in the mind of the commander of our armies.

· At daylight, Sunday morning, April 2, Gen. Grant ordered an assault by Parke, Wright, and Ord, who held our intrenchments from the Appomattox to Hatch-er's Run.

Parke, with the old Ninth Corps, was opposite the strongest portion of the rebel works; but in a few moments they had with a shout carried the outer line of defences, and taken twenty-seven guns and sev-eral hundred prisoners.

Wright, with the Sixth Corps, advanced at the signal in gallant style, sweeping every thing before them to the Boydton Plank-road, capturing guns, flags, and sev-eral thousand prisoners.

Ord, with the Second Corps, had overcome every difficulty, and carried the lines near Hatcher's Run, and was marching to unite with Wright, and move towards Petersburg.

At this time, Gen. Grant, who had left his head-quarters at Dabney's Mills to overlook the movements at another point, rode hurriedly along the lines. The old Army of the Potomac had welcomed many commanders with loud cheers and bright hopes who were to lead them to Richmond; but their hopes had died in their hearts, and their cheers on their lips. Their days of cheering and sanguine confidence were gone. But now they saw that the old cry, "On to Richmond!" was to be realized in the fulness and splendor of long-sought victory. The man and the hour at last had come.

As Gen. Grant passed, they now greeted him with exultant and grateful shouts. Wild huzzas rang out from all sides. He lifted his hat, acknowledging the salute, but trotted rapidly on. The soldiers were evidently in magnificent spirits.

Lee was now being pressed back into the inner works immediately around Petersburg. The murderous fire of the Union cannon, and the line of glittering bayonets, were encircling the rebel army, from the Appomattox on the right to the Appomattox on the left.

Gen. A. P. Hill now led a desperate charge, to save, if possible, the waning fortunes of the enemy. The attack was made with the reckless and impetuous valor of the Southern soldiers. It was the last grand attack of Lee's army, and was inspired by such determined bravery, that our men were re-enforced at the point of attack; but they were met by indomitable heroism, and repulsed with terrible slaughter. Gen. Hill was killed. He was among the ablest and most daring of the rebel generals, and his division one of the most renowned in the Southern armies. The words, " Hill's division," were the last sounds murmured by Stonewall Jackson as his wandering mind seemed watching the tide of battle on some hard-fought field.

Large fires were now seen to be burning in Petersburg; and the signal-officers on the towers soon reported that Gen. Lee was in full retreat, in three columns, across the Appomattox River.

CHAPTER XXXI.

CAPTURE OF RICHMOND.

DURING the day, President Lincoln was at City Point, at Gen. Grant's headquarters, and from time to time sent despatches of the advancing tide of victories to the Secretary of War, Mr. Stanton, by whom they were telegraphed to the Northern and Western cities, everywhere rejoicing the hearts of loyal men. At the same time, Jefferson Davis was attending morning service at St. Paul's Church in Richmond. At eleven o'clock, an orderly entered, walked up the aisle, and handed Mr. Davis a despatch, which read as follows : —

"My lines are broken in three places. Richmond must be evacuated this evening. "R. E. LEE."

The intense anxiety prevailing among the people of Richmond was depicted in the countenances of the audience. He read it in silence, and went immediately out. The Confederate president was deposed.

It was a still Sabbath day in spring. The city was held by the rebel forces. No proclamation was made; no Union flags were in sight; no Federal guns were heard: but the news, in some way, unaccountably flew through the air, as news of great events sometimes will.

People rushed out of church, and whispered to each other that Richmond had fallen. Carts were driven to the offices of the departments, and loaded with papers: the banks opened, and began paying out money to depositors. Wagons, carriages, vehicles of every description, were soon in demand at enormous rates, and were driven to private houses and stores, and loaded with trunks and goods, and hurried to the railroad station.

Late at night, Gen. Ewell ordered the burning of four large warehouses filled with tobacco, which threatened the whole city with conflagration. The citizens remonstrated with the military authorities; but no notice was taken of them: and the people of Richmond were doomed to see their property destroyed, and their city laid in ashes, by the leaders whom they had trusted, and followed in the war upon the government. The conflagration spread until the banks, churches, stores, mills, all the business part of the city, were in flames. All the roads out of the city were crowded with fugitives on foot and in every kind of vehicle. Jefferson Davis hurried off on a special train in the afternoon. The city authorities had ordered all the liquor in the city destroyed, and it poured through the gutters in torrents. Enough, however, was secured to infuriate large numbers of lawless and reckless soldiers, who filled the city with terror and alarm. Stores were plundered, and families buried their silver-plate and jewelry.

These events were all unknown to Gen. Weitzel and our army near Richmond. Gen. Weitzel's force had been reduced about one-half by the departure of Gen. Ord for Petersburg; but he was ordered to " keep up appearances," and give every indication possible of the presence of a large army. In consequence, on Sunday evening, he ordered all the regimental bands to play; and " Yankee Doodle " and " Hail Columbia " sounded forth with and without variations. What soldiers were left cheered, shouted, and made all the commotion possible. But Gen. Ewell at Richmond, ignorant of all this, and wishing to conceal from Gen. Weitzel as long as possible that his army was evacuating Richmond, also ordered his bands to play; and the remnants of the two armies treated each other to music all night, until the musicians fell asleep exhausted.

Before daylight, loud explosions were heard in Richmond, as if the enemy were destroying ammunition. The fire was seen reflected on the sky. The rebel rams were blown up. Orders were given to capture a rebel picket. One was soon brought in who told what regiment he belonged to, but could not tell where his regiment or its commander was that night. Soon after, a deserter came in, who said he was on guard, but had not been relieved at the usual time, and he had concluded to leave the rebel service. These things confirmed the suspicions that Richmond was being evacuated. At four, A.M., the inevitable negro drove into our lines in a buggy, and stated the fact. At daylight, Weitzel sent out forty troopers of the Fourth Massachusetts Cavalry, under Major A. H. Stevens, to reconnoitre. They rode on and on, unmolested by any one, until they found themselves in the streets of Richmond. They trotted through the city, and, just as the sun was rising, planted their guidons on the capitol. It was a new day for Richmond, and a newly-risen morn to the nation.

At six o'clock, Gen. Weitzel with his army marched into Richmond, the colored regiments singing, —

" John Brown's body lies a-mouldering in the grave."

A national flag, formerly carried by the Twelfth Maine Regiment, which had floated over the St. Charles at New Orleans, was raised on the capitol of Virginia.

Gen. Shepley was appointed military governor. The flames were still burning; and efforts were at once made to extinguish the fire. It had already consumed a third of the city, covering thirty squares. The losses to private property could only be counted by millions. A thousand prisoners were taken: five thousand were found in the hospitals. Five hundred guns, five thousand small-arms, thirty locomotives, and three hundred cars, were left by the retreating army.

That forenoon, the telegraph carried the joyful tidings all over the North. Business by general consent was suspended, flags were raised, salutes fired, church-bells were rung, prayers of thanksgiving were offered, public meetings were held, and the people gave themselves up to gratitude and rejoicing.

Gen. Grant was a man who never omitted to wring from the enemy all the fruits of victory. When he once gained the advantage, he pressed the foe to the utmost. When Gen. Grant attacked Lee from the south, military critics said it was wrong: he should have attacked from the north. But, now that Lee was retreating, Grant's wisdom was shown; for he was directly in Lee's road to the south.

Monday morning, April 3, it was found that the enemy had evacuated Petersburg; and, while the right of our army was entering the city, the cavalry on the left, under Custer, were already on the track of the retreating enemy. Lee was moving up the north bank of the Appomattox, and Grant the south side. Lee's object was to reach Burkesville, fifty-two miles from Petersburg, at the junction of the Danville and South-side Railroads.

Lee was confident of making a successful retreat and a prolonged campaign.

Gen. Ord, with the troops of the Army of the James, was marching for Burkesville down the line of the South-side Railroad: Sheridan, on a parallel line north, was marching to strike the road north of Burkesville. Lee crossed the Appomattox, and reached Amelia Court House on the same railroad, where he had ordered supplies for his army to meet him. But the train which carried them had been ordered to Richmond to take away Davis and his friends, and went on without unloading the supplies, which were there burned by order of the rebel authorities. Lee was compelled to halt his famished men here during the 4th and 5th, to gather up food and forage. Meanwhile Sheridan had struck the railroad at Jettersville half-way between Amelia Court House and Burkesville, and was in position to dispute Lee's advance. Grant and Meade, with the Second and Sixth Corps, arrived at Jettersville on the 5th. That night, Lee left Amelia Court House for Farmville, thirty-five miles west, where he hoped to again cross the Appomattox, and reach the mountains beyond Lynchburg. But Gen. Davies had, with a mounted force, reached Paine's Cross-Roads, where he captured a hundred and eighty wagons, five guns, and several hundred prisoners.

Lee was now retreating toward Deatonsville, with one corps of our army in his rear, one north, and one south, of his army, moving on parallel routes.

Sheridan ordered his division commanders to attack Lee's army-trains when feasible, and, if the escort was too strong to be captured, to fight on until the division behind them could pass them, and attack the enemy farther on; and this division was to fight until it was passed by those in its rear; hoping in this manner to find the weak spot in the enemy's line where a grand result could be achieved.

At Sailor's Creek, a small tributary of the Appomattox, Lee made a stand to save his trains; but his line was pierced by Gen. Custer's division, supported by Crook and Devin. Four hundred wagons were destroyed; and sixteen pieces of artillery, and many prisoners, were captured. The attack had separated Ewell's corps from the main body of Lee's army, who could see the smoke of their burning train in the distance. They were charged by a brigade of the cavalry under Gen. Stagg, until the Sixth Corps could come up; when the enemy fell slowly back, but fighting so stubbornly, that, for a few moments, a part of our line recoiled from their deadly fire. But, soon after, an assault was made by the infantry in front; and the cavalry under Custer, who drew their sabres, spurred their horses into a full run, and, with bugles sounding, charged with enthusiastic shouts and cheers upon the enemy. The rebel artillery poured in shells and grape and canister; but the horses, sharing the excitement of their riders, rushed madly on. Sabres were dripping with blood; wagons, ambulances, forges, were taken; whole regiments surren-

dered.   Between six and seven thousand prisoners
were taken, including Lieut.-Gen. Ewell and several
other general officers: among them were Kershaw,
Custis, and Lee.

It was the destruction of the rear-guard of Lee's
army.   The pursuit was becoming a hunt.

CHAPTER XXXII.

THE SURRENDER OF GEN. LEE.

A T Farmville, the head of Lee's army attempted to cross the Appomattox; but here he was attacked by Brig.-Gen. Read, with only two regiments of infantry and a squadron of cavalry, regardless of the superior numbers of the enemy. But Lee's veteran soldiers were not even then to be turned aside by a handful of our men, however heroic. They pressed on in overwhelming force, and crossed the river. Our loss was comparatively heavy; the gallant Read being among the killed. The advance of Lee's army passed on; but, before the rear could cross, the van of our Second Corps was upon them, and saved one of the bridges from being burned.

Gen. Grant was with the Second and Sixth Corps, and crossed the Appomattox at Farmville.

But an enemy more dreadful even than Sheridan's cavalry, more appalling than the Union bayonets, was now uniting to destroy the army of Gen. Lee. The men were starving: they could not search for food or forage in the neighboring country while the Federal horse hung upon their flanks. It was the ghastly skeleton of a proud army which had sought their country's ruin. The sunken countenances of the men showed they were famishing. Men and horses gladly fed on the buds of the trees, or a few kernels of parched corn. They dropped by hundreds from exhaustion : thousands were too weak to carry their muskets. For four days, they had been marching and fighting without rations.

On the night of Thursday the 6th, the rebel generals held a council of war, and decided that surrender was inevitable. They deputed Gen. Pendleton to announce this judgment to their chief. Lee still hoped to cut his way through our cavalry.

Gen. Lee was now retreating toward Appomattox Court House, about fifty miles distant, at the head of the Appomattox River.

On Friday the 7th, Gen. Grant addressed to Gen. Lee the following letter, written at Farmville. It was delivered that night.

APRIL 7, 1865.

GENERAL, — The result of the last week must convince you of the hopelessness of further resistance on the part of the Army of Northern Virginia in this struggle. I feel that it is so, and regard it as my duty to shift from myself the responsibility of any further effusion of blood by asking of you the surrender of that portion of the Confederate-States army known as the " Army of Northern Virginia."

U. S. GRANT, *Lieutenant-General.*

Gen. R. E. LEE.

Early the next morning, before leaving his headquarters, he received the following vague and diplomatic reply : —

APRIL 7, 1865.

GENERAL, — I have received your note of this date. Though not entertaining the opinion you express on the hopelessness of further resistance on the part of the Army of Northern Virginia,

I reciprocate your desire to avoid useless effusion of blood, and therefore, before considering your proposition, ask the terms you will offer on condition of its surrender.

R. E. LEE, *General.*

Lieut.-Gen. U. S. GRANT.

Gen. Grant at once forwarded the following reply:—

APRIL 8, 1865.

GENERAL,— Your note of last evening, in reply to mine of same date, asking the condition on which I will accept the surrender of the Army of Northern Virginia, is just received. In reply, I would say, that, *peace* being my great desire, there is but one condition I would insist upon ; namely, that the men and officers surrendered shall be disqualified for taking up arms again against the Government of the United States until properly exchanged. I will meet you, or will designate officers to meet any officers you may name for the same purpose, at any point agreeable to you, for the purpose of arranging definitely the terms upon which the surrender of the Army of Northern Virginia will be received.

U. S. GRANT, *Lieutenant-General.*

Gen. R. E. LEE.

Sheridan had started for Appomattox Station, five miles south of Appomattox Court House, where Gen. Custer, who was in the advance, captured four trains laden with supplies for Lee's starving soldiers. He pushed on toward Appomattox Court House, fighting with Lee's advance, capturing twenty-five guns, a hospital-train, wagons, and many prisoners. Sheridan had hurried up his cavalry ; and Grant had sent forward by a forced march the Fifth, the Twenty-fourth, and a part of the Twenty-fifth Corps, where they arrived at daylight, Sunday morning, April 9.

Gen. Lee supposed that he confronted only cavalry, and had given orders to Gen. Gordon, " Cut your way through at all hazards."

Sunday morning, the rebel army attacked our cavalry with great vigor. Sheridan dismounted his men, and ordered them to fall back slowly, until the infantry could form behind them ; when, at the right moment, the bugles sounded to mount : the cavalry rode to the right, and disclosed the large masses of infantry and the thousands of gleaming bayonets. The impetuous Custer was with the advance, dressed somewhat in the gay taste of Murat ; his jacket shining with gold lace, a crimson silk scarf streaming from his neck, a revolver in the top of his cavalry boots, which he used for holsters, and an immensely heavy claymore hanging at his side.*

At the moment the order " Charge ! " was to be given, a horseman was seen bounding out from the rebel lines with a white flag, to ask for a truce till a surrender could be completed. He rode upon a full run, and was greeted by the wild cheers of the soldiers.

Gen. Sheridan agreed to a suspension of hostilities for half an hour, promising to meet Generals Gordon and Wilcox at Appomattox Court House when Gen. Grant arrived. The officers rode about, and exchanged congratulations. The men began making coffee, and rejoicing that those sabbath hours would probably witness the end of the Rebellion.

At the appointed hour, Gen. Sheridan and several of his principal officers rode over to Appomattox.

Appomattox Court House, where the surrender of Gen. Lee was made, is a small old town in Virginia, containing a court house, a tavern, and four or five houses ; the principal one being occupied by a Mr.

* Col. Newhall.

Wilmer McLean. There was one street in the town, and one end of that was boarded up to keep out the cows.

While waiting for the arrival of Gen. Grant, our officers and some of the Southern generals strolled about, and talked over the war and the approaching peace. Gen. Longstreet was there, his arm still in a sling from the wound accidentally given in the Wilderness by his own men. Gen. Rickett was there, who had received the heaviest of our attack at Five Forks. He related the audacity of a Yankee cavalry-man, mounted on a mule, who leaped over the breastworks near him, and ordered him to surrender.

About two o'clock, when Gen. Grant rode into the town, he saw Generals Sheridan and Ord at the end of the street. Addressing Gen. Sheridan in his usual quiet and undemonstrative manner, he said, " How are you, Sheridan ? " — " First-rate, thank you. How are you ? " — " Is Gen. Lee up there ? " said Grant. " Yes." — " Well, then, we'll go up."

Some men would have entered upon a little glorification ; but this was not Gen. Grant's style.

" When all was over at Waterloo," said Wellington, " Blucher and I met at La Maison Rouge. It was midnight when he came ; and, riding up, he threw his arms round me, and kissed me on both cheeks as I sat in the saddle."

On reaching Mr. McLean's house, where the interview was to take place, Gen. Lee was already waiting : his fine gray charger, in the care of an orderly, was nibbling the grass on the lawn. Gen. Grant, with one or two of his staff, passed into a large front room, where he found Gen. Lee, a tall, soldierly-looking man, about sixty, with gray hair and beard, and bright eyes. He was dressed in a new uniform of Confederate gray, and wore an elegant dress-sword presented to him by the State of Virginia.

Grant had ridden over thirty miles; wore his usual campaign suit, not free from dust, and splashes of mud; had no sword or sash, and no insignia of rank.

The two officers shook hands courteously, and commenced conversation. The first topic related to the ceremonies to be observed at the surrender. The pride of the chivalry was sensitive on this point. Gen. Grant, as he could afford to do, waived all ceremony, and agreed that the arms should be received by his officers, and that Lee's officers should retain their side-arms and private baggage.

Gen. Lee then said that many of his men owned their horses. Gen. Grant consented that they should retain these also; adding, "Some will need them at home in their spring-work." Gen. Lee expressed great gratification at the generous terms conceded; and they were embodied in the two following letters, written at a small pine-table in the room: —

APPOMATTOX COURT HOUSE, VA., April 9, 1865.

GENERAL, — In accordance with the substance of my letter to you of the 8th instant, I propose to receive the surrender of the Army of Northern Virginia on the following terms: to wit, rolls of all the officers and men to be made in duplicate; one copy to be given to an officer to be designated by me, the other to be retained by such officer or officers as you may designate. The officers to give their individual paroles not to take up arms against the Government of the United States until properly exchanged, and each company or regimental commander to sign a like parole for the men of their commands. The arms, artillery, and public property, to be parked and stacked, and turned over to the officers appointed by me to receive them. This will not embrace the side-arms of the officers, nor their private horses or baggage. This done, each officer and man will be allowed to return to his home, not to be disturbed by United-States authority so long as they observe their paroles, and the laws in force where they may reside.

U. S. GRANT, *Lieutenant-General.*

Gen. R. E. LEE.

HEADQUARTERS ARMY OF NORTHERN VIRGINIA,
April 9, 1865.

GENERAL, — I received your letter of this date, containing the terms of the surrender of the Army of Northern Virginia as proposed by you. As they are substantially the same as those expressed in your letter of the 8th instant, they are accepted. I will proceed to designate the proper officers to carry the stipulations into effect. R. E. LEE, *General.*

Lieut.-Gen. U. S. GRANT.

When Gen. Lee came out, as he stood for a few moments on the steps waiting for his horse, he looked over toward the valley where his army lay, and smote his hands together, apparently not noticing any thing until his horse was brought, when he mounted and rode off.

When Gen. Grant appeared, his countenance told nothing. His manner was quiet and unexcited as ever as he rode away to telegraph the joyful tidings to Washington.

Mr. McLean soon sold out his furniture at high prices to officers who wished to preserve relics of the memorable occasion. Sheridan gave him twenty dollars in gold for the little pine-table, and sent it to the wife of his friend Custer. Others plucked the flowers in the door-yard, and sent them that night, odorous of peace, to distant homes.

The news of the surrender was received by both armies with acclamations. That evening, Gen. Grant sent rations for twenty thousand men to the starving enemy; and, as fast as paroled, Gen. Lee's soldiers were furnished with food and transportation home by the government they had fought to destroy.

Gen. Grant proceeded direct to Washington without entering Richmond, or accepting ovations on the route. He arrived on the 13th of April, and at once advised that the draft be stopped, and expressed the opinion that the Rebellion was virtually ended. That day, orders were issued, in accordance with these views, to stop all recruiting, curtail the purchases of arms, ammunition, and supplies, and to reduce immediately all the expenses of the army.

It was announced in the Washington papers of April 14 that Gen. Grant would attend Ford's Theatre that evening, in company with President Lincoln; but he had made arrangements to visit his family that day, and was absent. President Lincoln was assassinated that evening; and the evidence at the trial of Payne showed that it was the intention of the conspirators to have murdered Gen. Grant at the same time and place.

But Providence had ordered it otherwise. Gen. Grant at once returned to Washington, and was one of the most sincere mourners at the funeral of his tried friend, the beloved and martyred Lincoln, which took place on the 19th of April, 1865, the anniversary of the shedding of the first blood in the war in the streets of Baltimore.

Soon after, Andrew Johnson, who had succeeded to the presidency on the death of Mr. Lincoln, issued a proclamation that the assassination of the President had been "incited, concerted, and procured by and between Jefferson Davis, late of Richmond," and other persons named; and offering a reward for his arrest. On leaving Richmond, Davis proceeded to Danville, where he issued a proclamation to the rebel Confederacy. Referring to the evacuation of Petersburg and Richmond, he said, with far more truth and point than he was aware of, "We have now entered upon a new phase of the struggle." In a few days after, he was amazed and bewildered to hear of still another "phase in the struggle," in the surrender of Lee and his whole army. He now fled south as best he could; hoping to reach the seacoast, and escape out of the country. He was taken, on the 11th of May, in a small rebel camp at Irwinsville, Ga. When captured, "the president" of the Confederacy was dressed in woman's clothes, endeavoring to make his way to a small spring, and elude the Federal cavalry which surrounded his tent.

On the 5th of April, Gen. Grant had written to Sherman that Lee must soon surrender, and directing him to advance, and "see if we cannot finish the job with Lee's and Johnston's armies."

On the 16th, Johnston requested an interview with Gen. Sherman, in which he offered terms of surrender, which Sherman positively refused. The next day, however, they were reluctantly accepted in a modified form.

When transmitted to the Government, they were at once rejected, and Gen. Grant ordered to proceed to Raleigh, with full powers to act in the premises. He did so, but with entire delicacy toward Sherman and the peculiar circumstances in which he was placed. He arrived on the 24th, and acquainted Sherman with the views of the President and cabinet. He refused to suspend Sherman as he was authorized to do, or to displace him in the negotiations; and they were renewed between Johnston and Sherman: and, the second day after his arrival at Raleigh, Grant telegraphed to Washington that Johnston had surrendered to Sherman on the same terms which were accorded to Lee and the army of Northern Virginia. On the 28th, Gen. Grant was again at his headquarters at Washington, engrossed in the duties of his office.

On the 4th of May, Gen. Taylor surrendered to Gen. Canby all the remaining rebel forces east of the Mississippi. On the 22d and 23d, the Union armies were reviewed at Washington by the President of the United States, the Secretary of War, and the Lieutenant-General. The splendid pageant was witnessed by all the members of the diplomatic corps, and by vast numbers of citizens from all parts of the Union, who united in this ovation to the patriot soldiers.

Gen. Sherman was directed to proceed to Texas, and take immediate command of our forces there; but, on the 26th of May, Gen. Kirby Smith surrendered his entire command west of the Mississippi to Major-Gen. Canby.

The war was thus terminated with the surrender of all the armies of the rebel government. The number of rebel soldiers who surrendered was 174,223: the number of prisoners was 98,802. The Union armies under the command of Gen. Grant numbered 1,000,516 soldiers. Their commander might well be proud of the great services, which, with him, they had performed for the country. He issued the following farewell address : —

"SOLDIERS OF THE ARMIES OF THE UNITED STATES, — By your patriotic devotion to your country in the hour of danger and alarm, your magnificent fighting, bravery, and endurance, you have maintained the supremacy of the Union and the Constitution, overthrown all armed opposition to the enforcement of the laws and the proclamations forever abolishing slavery, — the cause and pretext of the Rebellion, — and opened the way to the rightful authorities to restore order, and inaugurate peace on a permanent and enduring basis on every foot of American soil. Your marches, sieges, and battles, in distance, duration, resolution, and brilliancy of results, dim the lustre of the world's past military achievements, and will be the patriot's precedent in defence of liberty and right in all time to come. In obedience to your Country's call, you left your homes and families, and volunteered in her defence. Victory has crowned your valor, and secured the purpose of your patriotic hearts; and with the gratitude of your countrymen, and the highest honors a great and free nation can accord, you will soon be permitted to return to your homes and families, conscious of having discharged the highest duty of American citizens. To achieve these glorious triumphs, and secure to yourselves, fellow-countrymen, and posterity, the blessings of free institutions, tens of thousands of your gallant comrades have fallen, and sealed the priceless legacy with their blood. The graves of these a grateful nation bedews with tears, honors their memories, and will ever cherish and support their stricken families."

CHAPTER XXXIII.

GEN. GRANT SINCE THE WAR.

THE following figures, taken from various public documents, will probably give a better idea of the gigantic nature of the war, and the costly sacrifices demanded by slavery, than any description in words. The simple facts are a tribute to the patriotism, the courage, the enduring faith, of the nation, more eloquent than any language of eulogium.

The war had closed, and Gen. Grant now addressed himself with great energy to the works of peace.

By the 22d of August, he had succeeded in mustering out of the army 719,338; by Sept. 14, 741,107; and by Nov. 15, 1865, there had been returned to their homes 800,963 men. The work was rapidly followed every month, until, Nov. 1, 1,023,021 had been discharged, and the army reduced to 11,000 men. Horses and mules had been sold to the value of $15,-239,000; barracks and hospitals sold to the amount of $147,873. The sale of damaged clothing yielded $902,770. The military railroads, covering 2,630 miles, with 6,605 cars and 433 locomotives, were relinquished, and transferred to proper authorities. Railroad equipments were sold, amounting to $10,910,812. The military telegraph, which extended 15,389 miles, at a cost of

$3,219,400, was discontinued, the materials sold, and its employés discharged.

The whole number of men enlisted at different times during the war was 2,688,522. Of these, 56,000 were killed in battle; 219,000 died of wounds and disease in the military hospitals; and 80,000 died after discharge, from disease contracted during service: making a total loss of about 300,000 men. About 200,000 were crippled or permanently disabled. Of colored troops, 180,000 enlisted, and 30,000 died. More than $300,-000,000 was paid in bounties, and by states, towns, and cities for the support of the families of soldiers. The Sanitary Commission disbursed, in money and supplies, $14,000,000. The Christian Commission disbursed $4,500,000.

During the summer of 1865, Gen. Grant accepted invitations from various cities to visit New England. He returned through the Canadas; and subsequently went to Illinois, visiting the tomb of Lincoln and his old home at Galena. Wherever he went, the people showed him every demonstration of respect and affection.

In December, he made a rapid tour of inspection through several of the Southern States. He passed one day each in Raleigh, Savannah, and Augusta, and two days in Charleston.

On his return, President Johnson requested Gen. Grant to report the result of his observations during this flying political reconnoissance. In the course of his report, Gen. Grant says, —

" I did not meet any one, either those holding places under the government, or citizens of the Southern States, who thinks it practicable to withdraw the military from the South at present. The white and the black mutually require the protection of the General Government.

.   .   .   .

"It is to be regretted that there cannot be a greater commingling at this time between the citizens of the two sections, and particularly of those intrusted with the law-making power."

Congress passed a bill to revive the grade of "General of the Army of the United States;" and Gen. Grant was appointed to the position. The bill was passed in the House of Representatives with only eleven dissenting votes. It was advocated by leading Democrats, among whom was Hon. Mr. Rogers of New Jersey. He said, —

"I believe that the mantle of the illustrious Washington may well fall upon the shoulders of Gen. Grant. I believe that he has walked in the footsteps of the Father of his Country."

Hon. Mr. Fink of Ohio, also a prominent Democrat, said, —

"I honor him, sir, not only for his brilliant services in the field, but because of his magnanimity in the hour of triumph, and his genuine modesty. He has conducted himself throughout this war independent of party considerations or party intrigues, devoting himself to the vindication of the true honor of the country in maintaining the Constitution and preserving the Union."

The South was undergoing the convulsions incident to the close of a great civil war, an entire re-organization of society, and a change in the relations of master and slave. The disbanded officers and soldiers of the rebel armies had returned to the South, and sought to resume their former influence on political questions.

Gen. Sheridan reported the condition of affairs in

Texas to be "anomalous, singular, and unsatisfactory."
He added, —

"My own opinion is, that *the trial of a white man for the murder
of a freedman, in Texas, would be a farce; and, in making this
statement, I make it because truth compels me, and for no other
reason.*"

Gen. Grant made the following indorsement on this
communication : —

"*Respectfully forwarded to the Secretary of War.* — Attention
is invited to that portion of the within communication which
refers to the condition of the Union men and freedmen in Texas, .
and to the powerlessness of the military, in the present state of
affairs, to afford them protection. Even the moral effect of the
presence of troops is passing away; and, a few days ago, a squad
of soldiers on duty was fired on by citizens of Brownsville. In
my opinion, the great number of murders of Union men and freedmen in Texas, which not only as a rule are unpunished, but unin-
vestigated, constitute practically a state of insurrection; and
believing it to be the province and duty of every good government to afford protection to the lives, liberty, and property of its
citizens, I would recommend the declaration of martial law in
Texas to secure these. The necessity for governing any portion
of our territory by martial law is to be deplored. If resorted to,
it should be limited in its authority, and should leave all local
authorities and civil tribunals free and unobstructed until they
prove their inefficiency or unwillingness to perform their duties.
Martial law would give security, or comparatively so, to all classes
of citizens, without regard to race, color, or political opinions;
and could be continued until society was capable of protecting
itself, or until the State is returned to its full relation with the
Union. The application of martial law to one of these States
would be a warning to all, and, if necessary, can be extended to
others.   "U. S. GRANT, *General.*"

Gen. Grant, it is to be remembered, is not a politician.
When the war broke out, he had never acted with the

Republican party, but with the Democrats. But in nothing has his honesty and independence been shown more clearly than in his judgments of events growing out of the war. Prejudice, preconceived opinions, have given way to actual facts as they have arisen. "A foolish consistency is the hobgoblin of little minds." "Speak what you think now in hard words, and to-morrow speak what to-morrow thinks."

On the 11th of August, 1867, President Johnson determined to remove Mr. Stanton from the office of Secretary of War, whose views upon the question of reconstruction in the Southern States had become obnoxious to the President.

He conversed with Gen. Grant upon the subject, who earnestly remonstrated against the proceeding, and in the course of the day addressed to him a private letter to the same effect. He foresaw that the action contemplated by the President would lead to evil results.

This advice was wise, straightforward, and statesman-like. It would have been well if it had been followed; but the President was not to be influenced, and the next day sent to Gen. Grant a letter directing him to act as Secretary of War *ad interim*.

In taking the post assigned to him by the President as commander-in-chief, he well knew the misconstruction which would be put upon his action by thousands: but, conscious that he was only doing what duty required, he made no explanations; sought no newspaper defence; made no mention to any one of the private letter addressed to the President on the 12th; and the letter was not made public until Congress assembled the ensuing winter.

He addressed to Mr. Stanton a letter, written when notified that he was to supersede that gentleman, which expressed his high sense of the valuable services rendered by him to the country and to the army.

It is not within the scope of this work to write a history of the differences between President Johnson and Congress on the question of reconstruction in the rebel States, except so far as the action of Gen. Grant is concerned. Suffice it to say, that Mr. Johnson had been a life-long Democrat and slaveholder until the opening of the war. He then denounced secession, and supported the Union party in Tennessee. The Republicans nominated him for Vice-President, not mainly because of his superior fitness for the position, but from a desire to recognize liberally all men, of every shade of opinion, who sought to preserve the Union. He accepted the nomination, and indorsed the principles upon which it was made. When, by Mr. Lincoln's death, he entered on the duties of President, he said, " Treason should be made odious; " that, in the work of reconstruction, " traitors should take back seats."

The rebel States had overthrown their State governments, and now desired, after the war, to return to the Union, and be again represented in the National Legislature. Congress said, in substance, return, but provide first that you shall not deprive any citizen of equal rights before the law.

When the number of representatives in Congress from the Southern States was to be determined, the slaves were counted as part of the population ; but, when the voting was to be done, the white men alone had the power. Congress said, Slavery is abolished.

The vote of the rebel soldier at the South must not be allowed to count as equal to the votes of two men in the free States. Shall the one vote of Jefferson Davis count as much as the votes of both Gen. Grant and Gen. Sherman? If the negroes are not fit to vote in the rebel States, they are not fit to give power to those States in Congress.

Slavery being abolished, justice requires that the four or five millions of freedmen shall be counted as citizens, as voters, or not counted at all. If this population is to be represented in Congress, it is to be represented like any other portion of the people, and not exclusively by their former owners, who have attempted to overthrow the government and bring anarchy upon the whole country.

But the President differed from Congress. He was Commander-in-chief; he was " President." It was for him, and not the representatives of the people, to decide the terms of reconstruction. The President had " a policy " of his own, and used his influence to prevent the acceptance of these terms. The slave States were to come back from their lost battle-fields, from Andersonville and Salisbury, with all the excess of political power over the free States which they once held under the Constitution which they had defied and rejected. Here issue was joined. Congress passed bills, and the President vetoed them: they passed them over the veto; and the President sought to nullify their effect, though sworn to " execute " the laws.

The President went personally to the people, from the Hudson to the Mississippi, and denounced Congress as " a body hanging on the outskirts of the Government; " and the people decided against him by majorities varying in different States from five thousand to forty thousand votes. Now, if we concede entire sincerity and honesty to the President at this time, it must be admitted that some men would have hesitated, and said, "Possibly the loyal millions of the people who have sacrificed every thing to save the nation are right, and I am wrong. My sworn duty is to 'execute,' not to make the laws." But the President did far otherwise. He removed Mr. Stanton, who sustained the acts of Congress.

On the 17th of August, he ordered Gen. Grant to remove from command at New Orleans Gen. Sheridan, who had faithfully carried out the laws in Louisiana and Texas. In doing this, he asked Gen. Grant to make any suggestions in regard to the order. Gen. Grant replied in patriotic terms far above all partisan spirit. He said, —

"I am pleased to avail myself of this invitation to urge, earnestly urge, urge in the name of a patriotic people who have sacrificed hundreds of thousands of loyal lives and thousands of millions of treasure to preserve the integrity and union of this country, that this order be not insisted on. It is unmistakably the expressed wish of the country that Gen. Sheridan should not be removed from his present command.

"*This is a republic, where the will of the people is the law of the land.* I beg that their voice may be heard.

"Gen. Sheridan has performed his civil duties faithfully and intelligently. His removal will only be regarded as an effort to defeat the laws of Congress."

The order was for a time suspended; but Gen. Sheridan was afterwards removed.

Jan. 13, 1868, the Senate passed the following resolution : —

"*Resolved*, That having considered the evidence and reasons given by the President in his report of the 12th of December, 1867, for the suspension, from the office of Secretary of War, of Edwin M. Stanton, the Senate do not concur in such suspension."

As soon as Gen. Grant was informed of this action of the Senate, he notified the President that his duties as Secretary of War *ad interim* were ended. He surrendered the keys of the office to the Adjutant-General, the custodian of the building, and returned to his office at the headquarters of the army. This gentleman afterwards surrendered them to the demand of Mr. Stanton in person, who took possession of the office.

A long correspondence ensued, in which it was evident that the President desired to avail himself of Gen. Grant's popularity in carrying on his war with Congress, — to put Gen. Grant in the front of the battle, and use him for his own purposes. But Grant was not to be *used* in any such manner. He had obeyed the President's orders during the recess of Congress to act as Secretary of War *ad interim*, when Mr. Stanton retired under protest. He discharged the duties of the office with unsurpassed honesty, wisdom, and fidelity. In no position in which Gen. Grant has ever been placed has he shown more real ability than in his administration of the War Department. How he acquitted himself, let President Johnson himself bear witness. In his message to the Senate, Dec. 12, 1867, giving his reasons for suspending Mr. Stanton, he concludes with these words, —

" Salutary reforms have been introduced by the Secretary *ad interim* (Gen. Grant), and great reductions of expenses have been effected under his administration of the War Department, to the saving of millions to the treasury.   "ANDREW JOHNSON."

While the friends of Gen. Grant may differ as to the value of such a certificate of character, it is certainly not for his political opponents to deny its truth, or depreciate its worth.

When notified of the vote of the Senate, that, under the law, he could not legally continue to act, he refused to serve any longer.

In a closing letter to the President, defending his conduct, he uses the following plain language : —

"The course you have understood I agreed to pursue was in violation of law, and that without orders from you; while the course·I did pursue, and which I never doubted you fully understood, was in accordance with law, and not in disobedience of any orders of my superior. And now, Mr. President, when my honor as a soldier, and integrity as a man, have been so violently assailed, pardon me for saying that I can but regard this whole matter, from beginning to end, as an attempt to involve me in the resistance of law for which you hesitated to assume the responsibility, in order thus to destroy my character before the country. I am in a measure confirmed in this conclusion by your recent orders directing me to disobey orders from the Secretary of War, my superior, and your subordinate, without having countermanded his authority. I conclude with the assurance, Mr. President, that nothing less than a vindication of my personal honor and character could have induced this correspondence on my part.

"I have the honor to be, very respectfully,

"Your obedient servant,

"U. S. GRANT, *General.*"

Gen. Grant confined himself exclusively to his military duties as head of the armies of the United States.

On the 21st of May, 1868, the National Republican Convention assembled at Chicago. Every State and

Territory was represented. The delegates were men distinguished for their worth in almost all the walks of life. The opera-house where the convention assembled was crowded from floor to ceiling.

The chairman of the National Committee, Gov. Ward of New Jersey, opened the proceedings with a brief address of welcome. Fervent prayer was offered by Bishop Simpson, invoking the divine blessing on the deliberations of the assembly, and praying that its action might result in bringing peace and harmony to the people of all sections, and increase the prosperity and glory of our beloved country.

Gov. Hawley of Connecticut was elected president. The enthusiasm for Gen. Grant was unbounded, and several premature attempts were made to nominate him by acclamation ; but the convention decided to proceed with its business in regular order. The resolutions were reported and adopted unanimously; each resolution, as it was read, being greeted with applause.

The nomination of candidates for president being then in order, Gen. Logan, chairman of the delegation from Illinois, rose, and said, " In the name of the loyal citizens and soldiers and sailors of this great Republic of the United States of America ; in the name of loyalty, liberty, humanity, and justice ; in the name of the National Union Republican party, — I nominate as candidate for the Chief Magistracy of this nation ULYSSES S. GRANT."

The nomination was received with enthusiastic cheering. When quiet was restored, the vote of each State was called alphabetically, beginning with Alabama. The chairman of each delegation announced the number of its votes, and for whom given. California said she came ten thousand miles to give Grant ten votes. Connecticut " unconditionally surrendered " her vote to U. S. Grant. " Maryland, my Maryland," gave fourteen votes for Grant. The vote of Georgia was announced by Gov. Brown, who said that the Republicans of Georgia had many of them been secessionists, but acted on the maxim, " Enemies in war; in peace, friends." As the call of States proceeded, and the vote of each was announced with a few patriotic words, the applause of the convention was renewed, until, at the close, the president made the formal announcement, that " six hundred and fifty votes have been cast, all of which are for ULYSSES S. GRANT."

The convention and the vast audience, numbering some three thousand persons, now rose to their feet, and greeted the result with tumultuous cheering and every demonstration of applause, which continued, without interruption, for some minutes. The band played " Yankee Doodle ; " the convention again cheered ; the ladies waved their handkerchiefs, when the band struck up, " Rally round the Flag," which the whole audience joined in singing. The scene was one of the most impressive and heart-stirring which can be imagined. But it was not a mere noisy demonstration of an excited crowd. Amid the wild enthusiasm, it was evident that hearts were moved by the deep significance, the moral grandeur and importance, of the action of the convention, and the earnest hope and determination to give peace and harmony to a long-distracted nation.

The father of Gen. Grant, who was visiting relatives in Chicago, was present, seated on the platform, — a silent, but not an unmoved, spectator of the honors thus gratefully bestowed upon his distinguished son.

The day these events were transpiring in Chicago, Gen. Grant was at his office in Washington, occupied with his official duties.

When some friends brought him the telegraphic despatch announcing the action of the convention, he evinced but little curiosity about the vote for president, but asked with much interest for the resolutions, and read them with attentive and thoughtful care.

The same evening, a large concourse of the citizens of Washington serenaded Gen. Grant at his house. He was introduced to the people in a few brief and eloquent remarks by Hon. George S. Boutwell, and made the following apt response : —

" GENTLEMEN,—Being entirely unaccustomed to public speaking, and without the desire to cultivate that power [laughter], it is impossible for me to find appropriate language to thank you for this demonstration. All that I can say is, that, to whatever position I may be called by your will, I shall endeavor to discharge its duties with fidelity and honesty of purpose. Of my rectitude in the performance of public duties, you will have to judge for yourselves by my record before you."

On the 29th of May, the officers of the convention visited Washington, and formally made known to Gen. Grant his nomination as President. These proceedings took place at his residence, in the presence of a large assemblage of visitors.

The general was attired in citizen's dress, wearing a blue military vest; and his manner was calm and thoughtful.

It was observed, that, when Gov. Hawley began

reading his address, Gen. Grant chanced to be standing near a marble bust of President Lincoln, and leaning upon the pedestal on which it stood. It was thought a fortunate companionship. Gen. Grant replied briefly, but with evident emotion; and closed by saying, " If elected President, *I shall have no policy of my own to enforce against the will of the people.*"

He subsequently accepted the nomination in the following letter : —

Washington, D.C., May 29, 1868.

To Gen. Joseph R. Hawley, President of the National Union Republican Convention, —

In formally receiving the nomination of the National Union Republican Convention of the 21st of May instant, it seems proper that some statement of my views, beyond the mere acceptance of the nomination, should be expressed. The proceedings of the convention were marked with wisdom, moderation, and patriotism, and, I believe, express the feelings of the great mass of those who sustained the country through its recent trials. I indorse their resolutions. If elected to the office of President of the United States, it will be my endeavor to administer all the laws in good faith, with economy, and with the view of giving peace, quiet, and protection everywhere. In times like the present, it is impossible, or at least eminently improper, to lay down a policy to be adhered to, right or wrong, through an administration of four years. New political issues, not foreseen, are constantly arising; the views of the public on old ones are constantly changing; and a purely administrative officer should always be left free to execute the will of the people. I always have respected that will, and always shall. Peace, and universal prosperity, its sequence, with economy of administration, will lighten the burden of taxation, while it constantly reduces the national debt. Let us have peace.

With great respect,

Your obedient servant,

U. S. Grant.

On the same day, a committee of the Soldiers' and Sailors' Convention waited upon Gen. Grant, and presented a complimentary address, and a copy of the resolutions passed by the convention.   In his reply he said, " While it was never a desire of mine to be a candidate for political office, it affords me great gratification to feel that I have the support of those who were with me in the war.   If I did not feel that I had the confidence of those, I should feel less desirous of accepting the position.   Acceptance is not a matter of choice, but of duty."

This spirit is in keeping with the character of the man and the high destiny to which he has been called.

CHAPTER XXXIV.

CONCLUSION.

To one who has read what Gen. Grant has done, little need be said as to what manner of man he is. The outline of his life shows his ability. A Western boy, with only common advantages, he enters West Point without preparatory study, attracts notice in the Mexican War, and soon after retires from the service. At the breaking-out of the Rebellion, he is an unknown man, in the leather business, in Galena, Ill. He returns to the army as colonel of a regiment, and without friends or influence, in spite of all opposition, advances step by step on the path of victory, until the Government places in his hands the whole military power of the Union. Millions of men march at his bidding: hundreds of millions of treasure are expended by his order. He captures more prisoners than all other generals, and ends a war of four years by the overthrow of the Rebellion, amid the grateful acclamations of his countrymen, and with a world-wide renown. Such achievements are not the result of luck or accident: they are but seldom seen in history.

It is easy for military critics to say that this or that campaign by rule ought to have resulted differently. Some writers said that Badajos ought not to have been taken, and others that Missionary Ridge ought not to have been carried. But they *were* taken. Success in war is the real test of merit. Gen. Grant did not quote military text-books as often as others; but he did his work with a smaller staff, and secured larger results.

Gen. Grant's honesty has never been questioned by any one. He had only a small property when the war began, and he had abundant opportunities of enriching himself by what many would consider legitimate means; but his bitterest opponent has never accused him of any "financial irregularity." Throughout the war, he steadily opposed all schemes for jobbing and speculation. He opposed the granting of permits to bring out cotton in his department as aiding the Rebellion, and destructive of the public interests. When overruled, and asked to name the parties to whom the privilege should be granted, he answered immediately, "No; I will not do it: for in a week it would be thought I was sharing the profits."

His single purpose, pursued with a steadiness and tenacity which never once relaxed its constancy and power, was to defeat the rebel armies. To this he made all things subordinate, and in this he triumphed.

Gen. Grant is not what is usually termed a "brilliant genius;" but he has that which in a ruler is far better, — a sound judgment. If he does not startle by the coruscations, he does not disappoint by the eccentricities or infirmities of genius, so called. Almost all qualities are found in men oftener than good judgment; because this requires the harmonious balance and play of all the other powers. A man may be learned, eloquent, an able general, a powerful writer, have great attainments in some specialty, and yet his usefulness be greatly impaired, if not destroyed, by an unsound judgment. One could apply to Grant the words of Tennyson on the Duke of Wellington, whom he in many respects resembles: —

> " The statesman-warrior, moderate, resolute;
> Whole in himself, a common good;
> Our greatest, yet with least pretence;
> Great in council, and great in war;
> Foremost captain of his time;
> Rich in saving *common sense;*
> And, as the greatest only are,
> In his simplicity sublime."

Gen. Grant showed great ability in the war; but he has also shown wisdom, practical sagacity, and independence in the whirl of extraordinary, important, and exciting events which have occurred at Washington since the close of the war. Witness his insisting that the Government should not violate the parole it had accepted from Lee and his officers when this was suggested by President Johnson. When, also, he entered the War Department in August, 1867, on the withdrawal of Mr. Stanton, the act was misunderstood, and denounced by many influential journals in the country; but, conscious that he was doing his duty, nothing was done, not a word was spoken or published by him, to stay the tempest of censure. When Congress assembled in the winter, the correspondence of Gen. Grant with the President and with Mr. Stanton appeared at the call of Congress, and his true position was made known. Gen. Grant's independence of faction and party has given him praise and censure, during the last two years, from leading journals in both political parties. No higher commendation will be given him from any source than has been accorded to him by the ablest of his political opponents.*

Gen. Grant does not make speeches, and some consider oratory indispensable to statesmanship. But they demand entirely different qualities. One requires the power to persuade, the other the power to rule. The builder of sentences is often far other than the builder of States. A man may for years attack and defend various public measures with vast learning and dexterity: he will overflow with language in showing "how not to do it;" but is dumb when compelled to achieve an immediate, wise, and possible result.

Men of executive power, in all countries, have often been preferred by the people to brilliant writers and speakers. Washington, Jackson, Taylor, and Harrison were neither of them orators; but their contemporaries and rivals were among the most eloquent men of whom America can boast. "It is the nature of party in England," says Lord John Russell, "to ask the assistance of men of genius, but to follow the guidance of men of character." "Caress literary men and philosophers," said Napoleon; "but do not take them into your counsels."

---

* "Of the steadiness and stanchness of Gen. Grant's patriotism, or the uprightness and solidity of his character, no man in the country doubts, or affects to doubt.

.   .   .   .

"On the score of loyalty and solid public services, no man in the country can come into competition with this illustrious soldier." — *New-York World.*

But Gen. Grant *acts* eloquence: the brave words of other men he puts into deeds; what orators splendidly *say*, he silently *does*. " Speech is silver," says the proverb; " but silence is golden." More public men have been injured by the fatal facility of fluency than by voiceless action. The highway of political life is marked by the graves of eminent men whose epitaph might be written, " Died of a speech," or " Killed by writing a letter."

But, when Gen. Grant has a meaning to express, he has no difficulty in making himself understood. In war, in civil convulsions, there is little place for bookish pedantry or scholarly dandyism. State-papers are not prisms in which to look for the colors of the rainbow; they are not word-pictures or literary mosaics in which each phrase is selected for its prettiness. The effect of a cannon-ball is determined, not by its brightness or polish, but by its weight of metal, by the power with which it moves, and by its reaching ·the mark. Gen. Grant's words have always reached the mark. " I recognize no Southern Confederacy." "I propose to move immediately on your works." " No terms but unconditional surrender." " I shall have no policy to enforce against the will of the people." " Let us have peace." These are eloquent words, and easily understood. It is stated on the best authority,* that, throughout the war, Gen. Grant's despatches, orders, and letters of any importance, were written by him; that his staff never attempted to imitate or improve his style. And it is a striking fact, that, among all the writings on the war, the most concise and clearly written accounts of the cam-

---

* Badeau.

paigns are found in Gen. Grant's official reports. Where the narrative of other historians is obscure or confused, the official report is plain and intelligible.

Gen. Grant's reticence has sometimes been imputed to a desire to conceal his opinions; but silence is not duplicity. He does not resort to mental legerdemain. No man has been more frank in declaring his sentiments at proper times. He has not chosen to keep his opinions "on draught" for political tipplers to imbibe, and intoxicate themselves by quoting at pleasure; and in this he has shown only prudence and sagacity. While not a member of Congress, holding no civil office, but at the head of the army, if he had entered the political tournament, and every morning fulminated his sentiments on the agitating and exasperating questions of the day, he would have been accused of impertinence and presumption, or denounced as a "dictator." When an officious editor from the South-west called on him, and said, "General, our people want to run you for President," Grant changed the topic of conversation. But his visitor returned to the charge with the remark, "General, our people want to run you for President. What am I to say when I get home ?"—"Say nothing, sir. I want nothing said."

When censured, Gen. Grant has at all times preferred to be judged by his record, by his acts, rather than by any explanations or defence from his friends. He has been ably supported, and has evinced great discrimination and foresight in the selection of his generals. He has put "the right man in the right place," regardless of personal friendships, or powerful influence in behalf of inferior men.

It is to be commended in Gen. Grant that he declares he shall have " no policy to enforce against the will of the people." Mr. Lincoln was reproached that he had " no policy ; " but it is one of his enduring titles to our gratitude.

The mission of the reformer, and the duty of the chief magistrate of a republic, are not the same. The reformer, who goes far in advance of the people, may shape the opinions of the generation which is to follow him, not those of the generation in which he lives ; but this is not the work of the wise and successful magistrate, who must move with the people, or not move at all. The office of President of the United States is not a hobby-horse : it was not created to afford any man an opportunity to experiment with his peculiar crotchets in morals or politics. An enthusiast might have issued the Emancipation Proclamation the morning after the attack on Sumter, and, by so doing, destroyed all his influence for good during the first year of the war, and secured a Congress eager to oppose his wishes and defeat his plans. Time is an ally who will not be despised without taking fearful revenge. In a free government, the statute-book represents the will of the people ; and the Executive is under oath to " execute the laws," not nullify or evade them. What Sir Joshua Reynolds says of the domain of art is in a measure true in affairs of State, — " The present and future are rivals : he who solicits the one will be discountenanced by the other." Bulwer, in one of his essays, happily says, " Statesmen are valued while living, less according to the degree of their intellect than to its felicitous application to the public exigencies or the prevalent opinions. Time, like law, admits no excuse for the man who misunderstands it." When a man has committed himself to great principles, it is useless for him to declare the particular measures by which he will accomplish the result. Mr. Lincoln issued the Emancipation Proclamation; but the convention which nominated him averred that the party would not interfere with slavery in the States. A nation like ours cannot be adjusted to a fabled bed of Procrustes, and stretched or shortened against its will to fit any man's policy. The true American doctrine was never better expressed than by Gen. Grant when he said, "This is a republic, where the will of the people is the law of the land."

While opposing the Rebellion with his utmost vigor, Gen. Grant has exhibited towards its authors the greatest magnanimity in the hour of their defeat. In no single instance has he ever sought to humiliate or degrade the men of the South. His opposition to the Rebellion has been touched with no trace of personal malice, or revenge toward individuals. He has admitted, as did all the world, the marvellous devotion of the South to the theories it had espoused. It is doubtful if any nation in history has ever shown more enthusiasm, more heroism, more self-sacrifice, than the men, women, and children of the South to the worst cause for which a people ever fought and died. Without an army or navy or treasury, they successfully defied and resisted the Government for years. Gen. Grant recognized the political heresies in which Southern men had been educated; and, while defeating their insane purpose to destroy the Union, looked forward to the

time, when, freed from the curse of slavery, and yield-
ing obedience to the laws, they should share the duties
and partake the blessings of a regenerated republic.
These sentiments are admirably expressed by Gen.
Grant in the closing words of his report, in July, 1865.
Speaking of the armies of the East and West, he
says, "The splendid achievements of each have nation-
alized our victories, removed all sectional jealousies
(of which we have unfortunately experienced too
much), and the cause of crimination and recrimination
that might have followed had either section failed in
its duty. All have a proud record; and all sections can
well congratulate themselves and each other for having
done their full share in restoring the supremacy of law
over every foot of territory belonging to the United
States. Let them *hope for perpetual peace and harmony
with that enemy whose manhood, however mistaken the
cause, drew forth such herculean deeds of valor.*" This
is the utterance of a patriotism broad and wide as the
nation itself. It will be fortunate for our country if it
shall be guided by its wisdom and animated by its spirit.

21

BIOGRAPHICAL SKETCH

OF

SCHUYLER COLFAX.

CHAPTER I.

SCHUYLER. COLFAX was born in New-York City, March 23, 1823. His grandfather, Gen. William Colfax, married Hester Schuyler, a cousin of Gen. Philip Schuyler, and was commander of Gen. Washington's Life-Guard during the Revolution. Schuyler Colfax, the father of the candidate for Vice-President, was an officer of one of the New-York banks, and died before the birth of his son; leaving his family with limited means. At ten years of age, he was placed in a store in New York, that he might contribute to the support of the family. In 1836, his mother moved to Indiana, and settled in New Carlisle, St. Joseph County. He again entered mercantile life, as a clerk, until 1840; when, at the age of seventeen, he was appointed deputy county auditor. He soon after removed to South Bend, the county town, where he has continued to reside. He employed his leisure in studying the State laws very carefully; and, in 1845, he became editor and proprietor of a weekly paper, "The St. Joseph-valley Register." He has continued his connection with this paper until quite recently, writing from Washington a letter every week for publication in its columns.

A debating club was formed in the town, at which all the prominent questions of the day in morals and politics were discussed; and this became a college to young Colfax. He prepared himself for debate by reading and study; and the debate gave him ease and readiness in extemporaneous speaking. Henry 'Clay, when at the height of his fame, attributed his success in public life to the training he had received in a similar society; although in his first efforts he excited the laughter of his companions by saying, " Gentlemen of the jury," instead of addressing the presiding officer as " Mr. President."

Mr. Colfax conducted his paper with great fairness and courtesy toward his opponents. He espoused the side of temperance, morals, decency, and good order, in controverted questions. The tone of his paper was such, that it was a welcome visitor in all families. At this time he made the acquaintance of Hon. John D. Defrees, now superintendent of government printing, then editor of " The Indianapolis Journal." Mr. Colfax was Senate reporter for " The Journal " for a few years; and the friendship then formed has continued to the present time.

Like almost all young men of active minds at the West, Mr. Colfax took a deep interest in the political questions of the day; and in 1848 was a delegate to and secretary of the Whig National Convention which nominated Gen. Taylor for the Presidency. In 1850, he was a member of the Constitutional Convention of Indiana. He opposed with great earnestness the proposition to exclude free colored men from settling in that State. He opposed it on the broad principles of humanity and justice, and as inimical to the true interests of the State. His speeches on this question caused his defeat the following year in a closely-contested canvass for Congress; his opponent, a shrewd political manager, leading him, however, by only two hundred out of nearly nineteen thousand votes in the district, which was strongly Democratic.

In 1852, Mr. Colfax was a member of the Whig National Convention which nominated Gen. Scott for President, and subsequently took an active part in the campaign which resulted in the election of Franklin Pierce as President. President Pierce in his Inaugural Address congratulated the country on the entire settlement of the questions relating to slavery by the passage of the so-called Compromise Measures of 1850. He said, " I fervently hope that the question is at rest, and that no sectional or ambitious or fanatical excitement may again threaten the durability of our institutions, or obscure the light of our prosperity." In his first message to Congress, Dec. 5, 1853, after dwelling upon the importance and certainty of the same " settlement," he said, " That this repose is to suffer no shock during my official term, if I have power to avert it, those who placed me here may be assured." Five months after, he signed the bill to repeal the Missouri Compromise, which had existed for nearly a quarter of a century, prohibiting slavery north of latitude 36° 30′. This convulsed the country with an agitation never before seen, and finally led to the disruption of both the great Whig and Democratic parties.

Dr. Fitch, the representative in Congress from the district in which Mr. Colfax resided, followed the lead of his party, and voted for the repeal. Mr. Colfax was nominated for Congress in opposition to him; and, during the summer and autumn of 1854, the two candidates addressed the people together on the great question of slavery extension.

Kossuth, when in this country, declared that the American mass-meeting was the greatest field for eloquence the world had ever seen, and its requirements among the highest. The remark is doubtless true. A question of vast public importance to be discussed, in which all are interested; large and intelligent audiences, more or less informed upon the subject, each man wielding a vote bearing directly upon the result; the enthusiasm of all thoroughly aroused, — neither the forum at Rome, nor the bema at Athens, could give higher inspiration to the orator. At the West, both speakers generally address the same hearers, and a subject is presented in all its aspects. No tribunal is more exacting in its requirements than a Western mass-meeting, none more fearless in enforcing its demands. Every variety of taste is to be suited. The whole nature of men is to be addressed. The legal disquisition, the polished essay, will not answer. Neither facts, nor figures, nor rhetoric, nor pathos, nor humor, nor satire, nor argument, will avail; but *all* must be combined, and urged with the glowing fervor of earnest conviction. You must not only convince, but persuade and inspire. You cannot talk *at* such a multitude : you must talk *to* them and *with* them. Such were the great debates between Lincoln and Douglas. These were the conditions which Mr. Colfax was required to meet ; and he came out of the canvass with a majority of two thousand in his favor, the same voters having given one thousand Democratic majority at the previous election.

When Congress assembled, Mr. Colfax entered warmly into the protracted and exciting contest which resulted in the election of Mr. Banks as Speaker of the House.

In June, 1856, during the struggle for freedom in Kansas, Mr. Colfax made a speech in the House of Representatives on the "laws" imposed on the Territory by border ruffians, which produced a powerful effect. He quoted the provision against any person who should "say that persons have not the right to hold slaves in this Territory." He alluded to the penalty affixed to this crime, — that of "imprisonment at hard labor, with ball and chain ;" and exhibited to the House an iron ball, such as the law required, thirty pounds in weight, and a chain six feet long. He then quoted from Washington and Jefferson and the fathers of the Republic, and showed, that, if living in Kansas, their sentiments would bring upon them the infamous penalties of the slave code.

Mr. Colfax had been a great admirer of Henry Clay ; and, in concluding, he said, —

"The language of one of the noblest statesmen of the age, uttered six years ago at the other end of this Capitol, rises before my mind. I allude to the great statesman of Kentucky, Henry Clay.

And while the party, which, while he lived, lit the torch of slander at every avenue of his private life, and libelled him before the American people by every epithet that renders man infamous, — as a gambler, *débauché*, traitor, and enemy of his country, — are now engaged in shedding fictitious tears over his grave, and appealing to his o'd supporters to aid by their votes in shielding them from the indignatfon of an uprisen people, I ask them to read this language of his, which comes to us as from his tomb to-day. With the change of but a single geographical word in the place of 'Mexico,' how prophetically does it apply to the very scenes and issues of this year! And who can doubt with what party he would stand in the coming campaign, if he were restored to us from the damps of the grave, when they read the following, which fell from his lips in 1850, and with which, thanking the house for its attention, I conclude my remarks? —

"'But if, unhappily, we should be involved in war, in civil war, between the two parties of this confederacy, in which the effort upon the one side should be to restrain the introduction of slavery into the new Territories, and upon the other side to force its introduction there, what a spectacle should we present to the astonishment of mankind in an effort not to propagate wrongs in the territories thus acquired from Mexico! It would be a war in which we should have no sympathies, no good wishes; in which all mankind would be against us: for, from the commencement of the Revolution down to the present time, we have constantly reproached our British ancestors for the introduction of slavery into this country.'"

This speech of Mr. Colfax presented the views of the Republicans with so much force, that half a million copies were printed by subscription for general circulation.

In 1858, he was triumphantly re-elected over all opposition. When the Thirty-seventh Congress organized, he was appointed chairman of the Committee on Post-Offices and Post-Roads. He took a deep interest in opening new routes, and giving mail facilities to the West; and was specially active in favor of all measures aiding the Pacific Railroad.

In 1860, he was an early and ardent friend of Mr. Lincoln's nomination for President, and contributed largely to the triumph of Republican principles in the election of that year. He was urged by powerful influences for the position of Postmaster-General; but Mr. Lincoln had decided to appoint Hon. C. B. Smith of Indiana Secretary of the Interior, and this forbade a second appointment from that State. His relations with Mr. Lincoln were those of warm personal friendship; and it is well known that Mr. Lincoln relied confidently on his judgment in regard to some of the most important measures of his administration.

CHAPTER II.

IN December, 1863, Mr. Colfax was chosen Speaker
of the House of Representatives ; and has been subsequently re-chosen to the same office, which he now holds.
The position is one of great difficulty and responsibility ;
but Mr. Colfax has acquitted himself with unsurpassed
dignity and ability.   It is an office requiring great tact,
and characteristics the opposite of each other.   But the
qualifications of a presiding officer were probably never
so clearly and forcibly described as in the language of
Sir William Scott, afterwards Lord Stowell, in nominating Mr. Speaker Abbott for re-election as Speaker of
the House of Commons in 1802 : —

" To an enlargement of the mind capable of embracing the most
comprehensive subjects must be added the faculty of descending
with precision to the most minute ; to a tenacious respect for forms,
a liberal regard for principles; to habits of laborious research,
powers of prompt and instant decision; to a jealous affection for
the privileges of the house, an awful sense of its duties; to a
firmness that can resist solicitation, a suavity of nature that can
receive it without impatience; and to a dignity of public demeanor
suited to the quality of great affairs, and commanding the respect
that is requisite for conducting them, an urbanity of private manners that can soften the asperities of business, and adorn an office of
severe labor with the conciliatory elegance of a station of ease."

In April, 1865, Mr. Colfax went with a party of friends
on a journey across the continent, to San Francisco.

The evening before he started, he called at the White House to take leave of President Lincoln. Mr. Lincoln was going to Ford's Theatre, and had invited Mr. Colfax to accompany him ; but the latter was compelled to decline. It was the night of the assassination. The conversation naturally turned on the immense mineral wealth of the West ; and Mr. Lincoln said, " Tell the miners from me that their prosperity is the prosperity of the nation. We shall soon prove that we are the treasury of the world." When Mr. Lincoln rose to leave the Executive Mansion, as it proved for the last time, Mr. Colfax accompanied him to the door of his carriage, and received the beloved President's last " good-by." At the parting moment he turned, and said, " Don't forget, Colfax, to tell those miners that that is my speech to them. A pleasant journey to you ! I will telegraph you at San Francisco. Good-by ! " Within an hour and a half, the assassin had done his work.

Before leaving home for the Pacific, Mr. Colfax delivered a eulogy on the martyred President, at Chicago ; and afterwards, by invitation, repeated it in Colorado to the Mormons at Salt-lake City, and in California.

His whole journey was a complete ovation along the route at every town and city. He was invited to address the people ; and he did so, speaking on the war, the Pacific Railroad, the Mexican question, and the great interests of the rising nation on the Pacific slope.

At Salt-lake City Mr. Colfax was received with much attention, and passed a few days in carefully studying the Mormon organization. Brigham Young inquired of the speaker what the government intended to do about the question of polygamy. Mr. Colfax shrewdly replied, that he had hoped the prophet would receive a new revelation on that subject, which would relieve all embarrassment. The prophet took the remark pleasantly, and did not intimate that he could not receive such revelations as he thought best. He accepted an invitation to address the saints, and gave them some excellent advice as to the respective duties of government and citizens.

He thus alluded to the motives of his journey : —

"I have had a theory for years past, that it is the duty of men who are in public life, charged with a participation in the government of a great country like ours, to know as much as possible of the interests, development, and resources of the country whose destiny, comparatively, has been committed to their hands. And I said to my friends, if they would accompany me, we would travel over the New World till we could look from the shores of the Pacific towards the continent of Asia, the cradle of the human race. And therefore we are here, travelling night and day over your mountains and valleys, your deserts and plains, to see this region between the Rocky Mountains and the Pacific, where, as I believe the seat of empire in this republic ultimately is to be."

He also said, " The duty of an American citizen is condensed in a single sentence, as I said to your committee yesterday, — *allegiance to the constitution, obedience to laws, and devotion to the Union.*"

At San Francisco, he was tendered a magnificent banquet by the principal citizens, and, in addressing them, took occasion, with manly independence, to dissent from the feverish impulse then existing in the South-west to embroil the nation in a foreign war over the Maximilian government. He said, —

"It is beyond the limit of mortal conception to compass the grandeur of the future of our nation if prudence guides its course.

Napoleon has said in his day, after a bloody war, that his empire was peace. We can more truly say that this republic is peace. Peace is the mission of freedom, and freedom is the primal principle of the American Republic. It is not by the glory and triumphs of aggressive war that its destiny is to be realized, but by peace.

" I am here among you, people of California, apparently a welcome guest. You have placed full confidence in my honesty of purpose; and I would not appear before you to speak only those words which you would applaud, when I really differed from you. I know how you feel on the Monroe Doctrine, and driving out Maximilian. I do not agree with you on these subjects. I will be frank with you. I am opposed to war for any purpose or for any cause, except for the vindication of the national honor or the salvation of the Union. I am for such a war, if it should occupy four, ten, or forty years; but to war in any other cause, that can be honorably avoided, I am opposed."

In his farewell speech at San Francisco, Sept. 1, 1865, he alluded to American manufacturing interests in the following words : —

" We have examined with interest many of your manufactures; and reared, as I was, in the school of Henry Clay, to believe in American manufactures, I am prouder of the suit in which I am clothed to-night, of California cloth, from wool on the back of California sheep, woven by the Mission Woollen Mills, and made here, than of the finest suit of French broadcloth I ever owned. I would urge you, in these last words, to foster manufactures, which are the backbone of national, of state prosperity and independence. Even if they should not be profitable as a pecuniary investment, every triumph of mechanical or manufacturing industry here is another spoke in the wheel of your progress. Develop and foster commerce on your great Pacific sea : for Raleigh spoke truly when he said, ' Those who command the sea command the trade of the world; those who command the trade of the world command the riches of the world, and thus command the world itself.' "

On the 21st of May, 1868, the National Republican Convention assembled at Chicago; and, after unanimously nominating Gen. U. S. Grant for President, nominated Hon. Schuyler Colfax for Vice-President. The nomination was made unanimous amid the most unbounded enthusiasm.

In response to a serenade given to him by the citizens of Washington on the evening of May 22, he said, —

"MY FRIENDS, — I thank you with all the emotions of a grateful heart for this flattering manifestation of your confidence and regard. I congratulate you on the auspicious opening of an eventful campaign on which we are entering. The Chicago Convention, representing the entire continental area of the republic, of every State, of every Territory, every district, and every delegate, from ocean to ocean, declared that their first and only choice for President was Ulysses S. Grant. Brave, and yet unassuming; reticent, and yet, when necessary, firm as the eternal hills; with every thought and hope and aspiration for his country; with modesty only equalled by his merits, — it is not extravagant for me to say that he is to-day, of all other men in this land, first in war, first in peace, and first in the hearts of his countrymen. His name is the very synonyme of victory; and he will lead the Union hosts to triumph at the polls as he led the Union armies to triumph in the field. But greater even than the conqueror of Vicksburg and destroyer of the Rebellion is the glorious inspiration of our principles animated by the sublime truths of the Declaration of Independence. Our banner bears an inscription more magnetic than the names of its standard-bearers, which the whole world can see as it floats to the breeze, — 'Liberty and Loyalty, Justice and Public Safety.' Defying all prejudices, we are for uplifting the lowly, and protecting the oppressed. History records, to the immortal honor of our organization, that it saved the nation, and emancipated the race. We struck the fetter from the limb of the slave, and lifted millions into the glorious sunlight of liberty. We placed the emancipated slave on his feet as a man, and put into his right hand the ballot to protect his manhood and his rights. We staked our political existence on the reconstruction of the revolted States, on the sure and eternal corner-stone of loyalty; and we shall triumph. I know there is no holiday contest before us; but with energy and zeal, with principles that humanity will prove, and that I believe God will bless, we shall go through the contest, conquering and to conquer; and, on the fourth day of next March, the people's champion will be borne by the people's vote to yonder White House, that, I regret to say, is now dishonored by its unworthy occupant. Then, with peace and confidence, we may expect our blessed country to enter upon a career of prosperity which shall eclipse the most brilliant annals of the past. I bid you God-speed in this work. And now good-night."

On the afternoon of May 29, a committee from a national convention of soldiers and sailors, which had recently assembled at Chicago, called on Speaker Colfax to pay their respects, and to present him with a copy of the resolutions of the convention. They were received in the Speaker's room at the Capitol; and after a few remarks by Mr. Alliman, the chairman of the committee, Mr. Colfax briefly replied.

He alluded in striking terms to the perils by land and sea which were endured by the soldiers and sailors of the Union in defence of the Constitution and flag of their country. "Great as were the obligations of the nation to those at home who stood by the Government in its hour of trial, greater still was the debt of gratitude it owed to those, who, leaving their homes, families, and all, at the risk of their lives and limbs, to save the republic from destruction, went forth from every position of the republic, — some in the freshness of life, and some in the ripe maturity of life. · The land, South and North, is filled with the graves of the nation's patriot sons. Their memory will ever be inscribed in all patriotic hearts as long as time shall last or republics endure." Thanking the committee, who represented the survivors of the heroic defenders of the Union, for this expression of their esteem and regard, he closed with the assurance, that, if the ballot-box should ratify the nominations at Chicago, his fidelity to principle and devotion to the Union would show that their confidence had not been misplaced.

A copy of the platform of principles was presented to him, and the committee retired. Bancroft Library.

The president and other officers of the convention visited Washington, formally to announce their nominations to Gen. Grant and Speaker Colfax. This was done on the evening of Friday, May 29, at the residence of Gen. Grant, in the presence of a large assembly of distinguished citizens. After the nomination for President had been accepted by Gen. Grant, and the enthusiasm with which his remarks were received had subsided, Gov. Hawley, president of the convention, informed Mr. Colfax of his nomination for Vice-President. Mr. Colfax replied, —

"Mr. President Hawley and Gentlemen, — History has already proclaimed that the victories of the party you represent during the recent struggle were always increased by a confidence in the national cause, while its reverses and disasters always increased the national peril. It is no light tribute, therefore, to the millions of Republicans of the forty-two States and Territories represented in the Chicago Convention, that our organization has been so inseparably woven with the best interests of the nation, that the triumphs and reverses of the one were the triumphs and reverses of the other. Since the general of our armies, with his heroic followers, crushed the Rebellion, the key-note of our policy — that loyalty should govern what loyalty preserved — has been worthy of our honored record in the war.

"Cordially agreeing with you in the platform of principles adopted at the Chicago Convention, and with the resolutions thereto attached, I accept the nomination with which I have been honored, and will hereafter indicate to you that acceptance in the more formal manner which usage seems to require."

On the 30th of May, Mr. Colfax wrote the following letter in acceptance of the nomination as Vice-President: —

WASHINGTON, D.C., May 30, 1868.

To the Hon. J. R. HAWLEY, President of the National Union Republican Convention.

DEAR SIR, — The platform adopted by the patriotic convention over which you presided, and the resolutions which so happily supplement it, so entirely agree with my views as to a just national policy, that my thanks are due to the delegates as much for this clear and auspicious declaration of principles as for the nomination with which I have been honored, and which I gratefully accept.

When the Great Rebellion which imperilled the national existence was at last overthrown, the duty of all others devolving on those intrusted with the responsibilities of legislation evidently was to require that the revolted States should be re-admitted to participation in the government against which they had warred, only on such a basis as to increase and fortify, not to weaken and endanger, the strength and power of the nation. Certainly no one ought to have claimed that they should be re-admitted under such a rule that · their organization as a State could ever again be used, as at the opening of the war, to defy the national authority or to destroy the national unity. This principle has been the pole-star of those who have inflexibly insisted upon the Congressional policy which your Convention so cordially indorsed. Baffled by executive opposition, and by persistent refusals to accept any plan of reconstruction proffered by Congress, justice and public safety at last combined to teach us, that only by an enlargement of suffrage in those States could the desired end be attained ; and that it was even more safe to give the ballot to those who loved the Union than to those who had sought ineffectually to destroy it. The assured success of this legislation is being written in the adamant of history, and will be our triumphant vindication. More clearly, too, than ever before, does the nation now recognize that the greatest glory of the Republic is, that it throws the shield of its protection over the humblest and weakest of its people, and vindicates the rights of the poor and powerless as faithfully as those of the rich and powerful. I rejoice, too, in this connection, to find in your platform the frank and fearless avowal that naturalized citizens must be protected abroad at every hazard as though they were native born. Our whole people are foreigners, or descendants of foreigners. Our fathers established by arms their right to be called a nation. It remains for us to establish the right to welcome to our shores all who are willing, by oaths of allegiance, to become American citizens. Perpetual allegiance, as claimed abroad, is only another name for perpetual bondage, and would make all slaves to the soil where first they saw the light. Our national cemeteries prove how faithfully their oaths of fidelity to their adopted land have been sealed in the life-blood of thousands upon thousands. Should we not, then, be faithless to the dead, if we did not protect their living brethren in the enjoyment of that nationality for which, side by side with the native born, our soldiers of foreign birth laid down their lives?

It was fitting, too, that the representatives of a party which had proved so true to national duty in time of war should speak so clearly in time of peace for the maintenance, untarnished, of the national honor, national credit, and good faith as regards its debt, the cost of our national existence.

I do not need to extend this reply by further comment on a platform which has elicited such hearty approval throughout the land. The debt of gratitude it acknowledges to the brave men who saved the Union from destruction; the frank approval of amnesty, based on repentance and loyalty; the demand for the most thorough economy and honesty in government; the sympathy of the party of liberty with all throughout the world who long for the liberty we here enjoy; and the recognition of the sublime principle of the Declaration of Independence, — are worthy of the organization on whose banners they are to be written in the coming contest. Its past record cannot be blotted out or forgotten. If there had been no Republican party, slavery would to-day cast its baleful shadow over the Republic; if there had been no Republican party, a free press and free speech would be as unknown from the Potomac to the Rio Grande as they were ten years ago. If the Republican party could

22

have been stricken from existence when the banner of rebellion was unfurled, and when the response of "No coercion" was heard at the North, we would have had no nation to-day. But for the Republican party, — daring to risk the odium of tax and draft laws, — our flag could not have been kept flying in the field until the long-hoped-for victory came. Without a Republican party, the Civil-rights Bill — the guaranty of equality under the law to the humble and the defenceless as well as to the strong — would not be to-day upon our national statute-book. With such inspiration from the past, and following the example of the founders of the Republic, who called the victorious general of the Revolution to preside over the land his triumphs had saved from its enemies, I cannot doubt but that our labors will be crowned with success, and it will be a success that shall bring restored hope, confidence, prosperity, and progress, South as well as North, West as well as East, and, above all, the blessings, under Providence, of national concord and peace.

Very truly yours,

(Signed)   SCHUYLER COLFAX.

The author of " Across the Continent," who accompanied Mr. Colfax in his trip to the Pacific, thus sketches the portrait of the Speaker: —

" As a public man, everybody knows about Mr. Colfax, — how prominent and useful he has been through six terms in Congress; and how, by virtue of his experience, ability, and popularity, he has come to be Speaker, and stands before the country one of its best and most promising statesmen. But this is not all, nor the best of the man. He is not one of those to whom distance lends enchantment. He grows near to you as you get near to him; and it is, indeed, by his personal qualities of character, by his simplicity, frankness, genuine good nature, and entire devotedness to what he considers right, that he has principally gained and holds so large a place on the public arena. Mr. Colfax is short, say five feet six; weighs one hundred and forty; is young, say forty-two; has brownish hair and blue eyes; is a childless widower; drinks no intoxicating liquors; smokes *à la* Gen. Grant; is tough as a knot; was bred a printer and editor, but gave up the business for public life; and is the idol of South Bend and all adjacencies. There are no rough points about him.   Kindliness is the law of his nature.   While he is never backward in differing from others, nor in sustaining his views by arguments and by votes, he never is personally harsh in utterance, nor unkind in feeling; and he can have no enemies but those of politics, and most of these find it impossible to cherish any personal animosity to him.   In tact he is unbounded, and with him it is a gift of nature, not a studied art; and this is perhaps one of the chief secrets of his success in life.   His industry is equally exhaustless.   He is always at work, — reading, writing, talking, seeing, studying.   I can't conceive of a single unprogressive, unimproved hour in all his life.   He is not of brilliant or commanding intellect; not a genius, as we ordinarily apply these words : but the absence of this is more than compensated by these other qualities I have mentioned, — his great good sense, his quick, intuitive perception of truth, and his inflexible adherence to it, his high personal integrity, and his long and valuable training in the service of the people and the government.   Without being, in the ordinary sense, one of the greatest of our public men, he is certainly one of the most useful, reliable, and valuable; and in any capacity, even the highest, he is sure to serve the country faithfully and well. He is one of the men to be tenaciously kept in public life; and I have no doubt he will be.   Some people talk of him for President. Mr. Lincoln used to tell him he would be his successor; but his own ambition is wisely tempered by the purpose to perform present duties well.   He certainly makes friends more rapidly, and holds them more closely, than any public man I ever knew. Wherever he goes, the women love him, and the men cordially respect him; and he is sure to be always a personal favorite, even a pet, with the people." *

Mr. Colfax is by nature warm-hearted; his manners frank and cordial; and he has great personal popularity. He has always run ahead of his ticket whenever a candidate for office.   Even those of his constituents opposed to him politically are proud of him as their representative and personal friend.   When Gen. Grant was informed by telegraph of the nomination of the Speaker for Vice-

------

* Samuel Bowles, Editor of " The Springfield Republican."

President, he said to the gentlemen present, "Well, Colfax is the most popular man in the country ; and all the Democrats can say against him is that he is a Republican."

In public life, Mr. Colfax has shown wonderful wisdom in adapting means to ends. He has never attempted an impossible statesmanship. He has rightly interpreted the prevailing exigencies of the day, and endeavored to shape legislation to meet them. To be useful, the legislator and the statesman must be practical, and possess the homely virtue of common sense.

Both on the floor and in the Speaker's chair, he has won the entire confidence and respect of his associates, who have had opportunities to observe him for years. A recent writer says of him, —

"He is pure in his personal and moral habits; has a broad, outspoken, and catholic sympathy with every good work of reform, whether political, moral, intellectual, or religious; and has the warm and enthusiastic confidence of Christians and temperance reformers throughout the country. He attends, and, we believe, is a member of, the Reformed Dutch Church, and is a thorough teetotalist. Without being educated as a scholar, industrious reading has given him much of what is valuable in scholarship, unalloyed by its pedantry, its clannishness, or its egotism. Without being bred a lawyer, practical familiarity with legislation has taught him all that is most valuable in law, freed from the conservatism and inaptitude for change and reform which rest like an incubus on so many of those minds which are bred by the habits of the legal profession to look for precedents which show what the law has been, rather than to broad principles which settle what the law ought to be. Yet Mr. Colfax has frequently shown the happiest familiarity with precedents, especially in questions of parliamentary practice."

In dealing with men personally, he exhibits a tact equal to his wisdom in dealing with measures. If he complies with a request, the favor is enhanced in value by the kindness and courtesy with which it is conferred ; if he declines, the refusal is softened by his urbanity, and evident regret at the disappointment which he causes.

He is now forty-five years of age, and in the full vigor of his manhood. The breath of slander, which spares so little, has never touched his character; and his ability, integrity, and uprightness in all the relations of life, give promise of a long and brilliant career of eminence and usefulness.

APPENDIX.

REPUBLICAN PLATFORM.

The National Republican Party of the United States, assembled in National Convention in the city of Chicago on the twenty-first day of May, 1868, make the following Declaration of Principles : —

I. We congratulate the country on the assured success of the reconstruction policy of Congress, as evinced by the adoption, in the majority of the States lately in rebellion, of constitutions securing equal civil and political rights to all; and it is the duty of the Government to sustain those institutions, and to prevent the people of such States from being remitted to a state of anarchy.

II. The guaranty by Congress of equal suffrage to all loyal men at the South was demanded by every consideration of public safety, of gratitude, and of justice, and must be maintained ; while the question of suffrage in all the loyal States properly belongs to the people of those States.

III. We denounce all forms of repudiation as a national crime; and the national honor requires the payment of the public indebtedness in the uttermost good faith to all creditors at home and abroad, not only according to the letter, but the spirit, of the laws under which it was contracted.

IV. It is due to the labor of the nation that taxation should be equalized, and reduced as rapidly as the national faith will permit.

V. The national debt, contracted, as it has been, for the preservation of the Union for all time to come, should be extended over a fair period for redemption ; and it is the duty of Congress to reduce the rate of interest thereon whenever it can .e honestly done.

VI. That the best policy to diminish our burden of debt is to so improve our credit, that capitalists will seek to loan us money at lower rates of interest than we now pay, and must continue to pay so long as repudiation, partial or total, open or covert, is threatened or suspected.

VII. The Government of the United States should be administered with the strictest economy; and the corruptions which have been so shamefully nursed and fostered by Andrew Johnson call loudly for radical reform.

VIII. We profoundly deplore the untimely and tragic death of Abraham Lincoln, and regret the accession to the Presidency of Andrew Johnson, who has acted treacherously to the people who elected him and the cause he was pledged to support; who has usurped high legislative and judicial functions; who has refused to execute the laws; who has used his high office to induce other officers to ignore and violate the laws; who has employed his executive powers to render insecure the property, the peace, liberty, and life of the citizen; who has abused the pardoning power; who has denounced the National Legislature as unconstitutional; who has persistently and corruptly resisted, by every means in his power, every proper attempt at the reconstruction of the States lately in rebellion; who has perverted the public patronage into an engine of wholesale corruption; and who has been justly impeached for high crimes and misdemeanors, and properly pronounced guilty thereof by the vote of thirty-five senators.

IX. The doctrine of Great Britain and other European powers, that, because a man is once a subject he is always so, must be resisted at every hazard by the United States, as a relic of feudal times not authorized by the laws of nations, and at war with our national honor and independence. Naturalized citizens are entitled to protection in all their rights of citizenship as though they were native-born: and no citizen of the United States, native or naturalized, must be liable to arrest and imprisonment by any foreign power for acts done or words spoken in this country; and, if so arrested and imprisoned, it is the duty of the Government to interfere in his behalf.

X. Of all who were faithful in the trials of the late war, there were none entitled to more especial honor than the brave soldiers and seamen who endured the hardships of campaign and cruise, and imperilled their lives in the service of the country. The bounties and pensions provided by the laws for these brave defenders of the nation are obligations never to be forgotten. The widows and orphans of the gallant dead are the wards of the people, — a sacred legacy bequeathed to the nation's protecting care.

XI. Foreign immigration, which, in the past, has added so much to the wealth, development, and resources and increase of power to this republic, the asylum of the oppressed of all nations, should be fostered and encouraged by a liberal and just policy.

XII. This Convention declares itself in sympathy with all oppressed peoples struggling for their rights.

Resolved, That we highly commend the spirit of magnanimity and forbearance with which men who have served in the Rebellion, but who now frankly and honestly co-operate with us in restoring the peace of the country, and reconstructing the Southern State governments upon the basis of impartial justice and equal rights, are received back into the communion of the loyal people ; and we favor the removal of the disqualifications and restrictions imposed upon the late rebels in the same measure as their spirit of loyalty will direct, and as may be consistent with the safety of the loyal people.

Resolved, That we recognize the great principles laid down in the immortal Declaration of Independence as the true foundation of democratic government; and we hail with gladness every effort toward making these principles a living reality on every inch of American soil.

www.ingramcontent.com/pod-product-compliance
Lightning Source LLC
Chambersburg PA
CBHW051221120726
47905CB00004B/1217